Common Sons

He hugged himself tightly now to stop the shakes. Yeah…you were supposed to feel ashamed. But in the soft, familiar light of his room, Joel realized he didn't. In the crazy play of feelings that crawled over him, he knew nothing would ever feel as wonderful.

He tossed his underwear onto the rug and pulled his Levi's over his aching, mindless erection.

He brushed his teeth, rinsed his hair with cold water from the sink and, as he walked through the house to the kitchen, pulling on his shirt, he tried to dispel the feelings of dread. He would wait; when he saw Tom at the church where he worked on Saturdays, Tom would know what to say. He would be able to explain how things had happened; why, after all this time, they had stepped over that invisible line between friendship and…. He laughed without humor at a thought so alien; he stopped in mid-stride. There was a name for what they had done, but Tom would explain it, so fuck it.

Common Sons

by

Ronald L. Donaghe

Commonwealth
Publications

A Commonwealth Publications Paperback
COMMON SONS

This edition published 1997
by Commonwealth Publications
9764 - 45th Avenue,
Edmonton, AB, CANADA T6E 5C5
All rights reserved
Copyright © 1995 by Ronald L. Donaghe

ISBN: 1-55197-329-4

Printed in Canada

To my wonderful parents, whose unconditional love has always nurtured me and made me strong in the face of adversity

—Part One—

He that is unjust, let him be unjust still:
and he which is filthy, let him be filthy still:
and he that is righteous,
let him be righteous still:
and he that is holy, let him be holy still....

Revelation 22:11

Chapter 1

Joel woke up disturbed.

The breeze coming through the window made him shiver and he hugged himself, not so much feeling cold, but exposed. He was nude, as usual, but felt naked under the sheet. He threw it off and the smell of his own sex from the night before, along with the familiar smell of cologne and sweat, filled the air. The faintest, unfamiliar scent teased his nostrils. The more he concentrated, the fainter it got—just a ghostly whiff of someone else on his body. He sat up, looked around and picked up his Levi's from the end of the bed where he'd peeled them off in the dark. His shorts were curled inside a pants leg; they were cold and faintly damp with the same odor. And he knew.

You were supposed to feel ashamed.

He looked around his room as if something in it could help. But he lay back drained; an unpleasant tickling sensation nibbled at his legs behind his calves. He had to think, had to relax, but he couldn't forget Jeannie Lynn's cruel laughter and

the curious faces of the others who closed in to
see what she was laughing at. He felt embarrassed
again, like last night. It had probably only lasted a
minute, but it seemed to go on forever.

*Of course, everybody was drunk and probably
as confused as I was,* he thought, *but, sure as hell,
somebody will remember—like Jeannie Lynn. If we
hadn't gone to that dance, just hadn't drunk so
fuckin' much. I should've seen what Tom's mood
would lead to.* But it was no use regretting it now.
It was done.

Somewhere across the road a bird chattered
and whistled, a cacophony of musical shrieks that
mocked him as he lay staring at the ceiling. He
recalled with a cold shiver that something even
worse had happened later, after they left the
dance...something about Tom.

Every feature of Joel's handsome face was troubled—his pale, gray eyes with a strident slash of
blue, his dark, reddish lips with a bruised look,
even his jaw, which some would say was almost
too large for his face—all reflected a rare anxiety.
He stared at the ceiling, seeing nothing, entranced
by the scene that played across his mind. In the
pale sunlight he breathed heavily, his strong, hairless chest rising and falling in a quickening rhythm.
Last night had happened as if everything that went
before had been only a rehearsal. He saw that now.
But it was the jittery moment of the act, really
going through the long-unmentioned fantasy, that
had suddenly made things go crazy. The way Tom
acted disturbed him, gave it the scent of a night-
mare.

Tom just squeezed into himself. And it was that
silent shock, the way Tom drew in, that bothered
him the most.

* * * *

Tom was in a reckless mood when Joel picked him up at home, and when he got into the pickup truck, Joel sensed that something was different about the way he was acting. Maybe it was his grin, which wasn't exactly familiar, and then Tom said he wanted to go to the dance...and drink!

He was too surprised to laugh, even though it was the last thing he expected Tom to say. "But won't your father get mad? I thought people in your church don't dance."

"They don't drink, either," Tom said. He closed the door and slid into the seat close to Joel. He was freshly shaved and Joel caught a whiff of him. Always the same smell. Aftershave, or cologne, or something that reminded Joel of a fresh shower. It could be a hundred degrees out and Tom could be sweating, but he smelled the same. "But I want to! Don't you think it would be fun?"

"Believe me, it's a brawl," Joel warned. "Beer is rotten. And man, if your father *ever* found out!"

But Tom persisted. He didn't get angry, he just talked Joel's ear off as they drove around town in Joel's pickup trying to make a mutual decision. "I don't care what we do, you know..." Joel said, "but a western dance? Whyn't we catch a movie?"

Tom moved a little closer, grinning weirdly. "I like you, so why shouldn't I like your friends?" They were turning west for another cruise up Main Street. Joel glanced at Tom, who was squinting at him through the sudden burst of light from the setting sun. For a second, his face was cast in stark gold against it, and his eyes took on an imp-ish twinkle that made Joel shiver suddenly in the warm afternoon. "Besides," Tom grinned, "you're the best friend I've ever had. Your friends can't be too bad if they're anything like you!"

"They're not bad, man, just a bunch of country kids who never grew up." He wanted to tell him that they weren't his friends, as if Tom's question was an insult.

"C'mon, Joel. Let's do something different tonight! It's our only summer, and I don't want to miss a minute of it before I go away to college!"

"But a cowboy dance?"

"Well, sure! What difference does it make? My father keeps preaching against stuff like that. Don't you think I should see why?"

Joel began to think that Tom was joking. He'd never done anything against his religion. Then Tom moved to the middle of the seat and slowly slid his arm around Joel's neck, staring frankly into his face. His breath was cool, clean and pepperminty.

"But if you don't like it, we'll leave, okay?" Joel said. "It gets pretty damned rowdy."

* * * *

Dusk hung on a long time. It was his favorite time of the day; the hour before darkness fell across the desert and, as usual, it seemed full of delicious possibilities. Sitting around with all the guys watching people dance wouldn't be any big thrill. But Tom was making him laugh. They had the windows down, and a cool breeze blew through the pickup as they drove through town. At Main and Spruce, he turned south onto Spruce Street, and then as it curved southeast by the Jehovah's Witness church, he cut over onto the Columbus Highway, where it forked at Wheeler's Mortuary. The Mimbres County Courthouse on the west side of the street cast a long shadow that fell across the road and climbed halfway up the sunny wall of the mortuary. Beyond that, small, adobe houses marked the beginning of Mexican town, and there, in the narrow, shadowed street, children were play-ing in the long, dying afternoon.

They came to the railroad tracks that divided the town from the Country Club and the fair grounds on the east side. "This reminds me of go-ing to the circus or something," Joel said as he slowed for the tracks. Trains hadn't come up or down them since he could remember, and the rag-ged disrepair threatened to knock even the tough-est vehicle out of alignment. "See all those old airplane hangars?" He pointed off to his right.

Tom looked where Joel indicated and nodded.

"During World War II, we had the Army Air Corps out here. Dad says that after a few years, when the county started the Fair and Livestock Show, they rebuilt some of the hangars." From where they were, they could see the new, white-metal roofs turning pink against the setting sun.

Tom nodded again and smiled, but didn't say anything. "You've never been to a dance?" Joel asked.

"No. Really. I learned the Virginia Reel or some-thing in first grade, I think, but you don't do that, do you?"

Joel laughed. "I don't think you'll recognize anything these cowboys do. They're supposed to waltz and two-step and bop, but mainly it's just an excuse to bump and grind and show off their T's and A's, if you know what I mean."

Tom didn't. His face was a blank except for the excitement in his eyes and the little, sly smile that turned up the corners of his mouth. "Any-way," Joel said, "it isn't going to be what you're expecting."

"How do you know what I'm expecting?"

"Oh, I don't, but something sane, I bet."

Tom laughed weirdly again. For some reason,

it deepened Joel's surprise. It wasn't exactly a bad feeling. But it was strange.

A high, chain-link fence ran along the road beside the county fair grounds. Tonight, the big, steel gates stood open. The ticket booth on the left was boarded up and Joel drove through, thinking of what he'd just told Tom.

There was a time not long ago, Joel recalled, that he had come out here with a date every chance he could, looking for the same sort of excitement that Tom seemed to be hoping for. At other times, he went with the guys and just stood around all night drinking and cussing and halfheartedly playing horny like they did, dancing with whatever girls came along. Nothing special ever happened on a date. They always ended with Joel debating the big question—whether he should kiss her good night.

It was always painful, making him feel embarrassed when he walked her to the door. Sometimes the girl would stand there, purse clutched in front of her, as nervous as he, and Joel would reach up with a hand and maybe touch her on the elbow and mutter something stupid like, "Are you still sweating?" and she would turn quickly and go inside; he would practically run to the pickup and cuss himself out on the way home. *You stupid shit, shoulda kissed her and kept your fucking mouth shut. Now she probably thinks you didn't enjoy yourself.* Usually he hadn't. But that wasn't the point, was it? Guys swore up and down how hot it was to "make out," cop a feel, maybe even get laid. Then sometimes the girl wouldn't give him a chance to kiss her. She would bound out of the car, slam her door and bounce cheerily away, blowing him an imaginary kiss, and he would wonder what was wrong with him. When he did kiss them, it was usually a dry, closed-lip affair on his part. It would feel strange leaning over, expecting to be drowned in passion, and coming away feeling as if he'd just kissed the back of her hand. Nothing magical ever happened. By the time he and Tom were good friends, these dances were long forgotten.

He pulled into the gravel lot and parked on the north side, away from the few cars that were already there, and killed the engine. "Well, here we are, buddy." Tom started to open his door. "We may as well stay for a while," Joel said. "I'll go see if old Slim is set up out back yet."

"The beer?"

"Yeah. Be right back."

When he returned, Joel said, "It's not so bad cold," pulling two beers out of the cardboard package. He flicked open the glove box and pulled out the can opener he used to open oil cans. He cleaned it off on the cuff of his Levi's and punched holes in Tom's can. "Here." He watched as Tom took a big gulp, then laughed a little as he held his own can up to his lips and took a bitter sip.

Tom shivered, and Joel laughed at his face, screwed up like he'd bitten into a rotten egg. But Tom squeezed his nose shut and took another gulp.

"You don't have to torture yourself," Joel said, trying to take the beer can away from Tom. "You don't have to prove anything."

But Tom held the can out of Joel's reach and took a deep breath. He grinned sickly, threw back his head, and gulped, swallowed and gagged until he had killed the beer. He laid the empty can on the floorboard of the pickup and got another one. He handed it to Joel. "Open it."

Joel couldn't keep from laughing, and held the beer Tom gave him against his chest. "Wait, man! I've gotta catch up!" He chugged his own and imagined that his face was almost as tortured as Tom's. They drank the rest of the six pack like two kids sucking on soda pop, and watched the parking lot fill up with cars and pickups. By the time they slid out and walked toward the hangar, Tom was drunk and acting silly. Joel wasn't drunk, exactly. His face felt numb and hot, but he was too bothered to feel slap-happy. It especially bothered him that Tom could get into trouble with his father, the preacher, the hard-ass who always made Joel feel like his ass was hanging out, or something was hanging from his nose, the way the preacher studied him with a stern expression whenever he had to talk to the guy. The last thing Tom could be when he took him home was shitfaced; and he could have kicked himself for giving in.

The dance was held in the arts and crafts building, where school children displayed their handiwork every October during the Fair and Livestock Show. Around the inside walls of the old hangar, between the partitions that usually divided the fair exhibits, tables were beginning to fill up. The place was alive and noisy, echoing laughter and talk high up in the open rafters; the only light came from the stage where the band was tuning up. The drummer's erratic rhythms cut through the noisy crowd like gunshots and echoed in the wide space.

When they passed by a table in a dark corner across from the band, Joel heard his name being called. He peered through the darkness and recognized Jeannie Lynn, Betsy Weller and some guys he had graduated from the eighth grade with at the county school near his farm. As usual, Jeannie Lynn was collecting partners for the dance. She already had the Crawford boys, Cliff and Bill, fetching her beer and showing off. No doubt by the end

of the evening she'd have more in tow. Cliff and
Bill clapped Joel on the shoulders from either side
of the table. Their parents owned another farm
near the school. Bill was the oldest, a senior come
fall, like Joel. Cliff, his younger brother, was only
a sophomore, but went everywhere Bill did. Nicky
Coleman shook Joel's hand and introduced a girl
named Cindy, whom Joel recognized from high
school. Joel introduced Tom to the guys. They
shook the hand that Tom offered, but they weren't
all that friendly. Maybe even a little unfriendly. He
thought maybe it was because Tom's father was a
preacher, or maybe because Tom wasn't a rowdy
sort, or maybe because he didn't stand around
grabbing at his crotch like they did, trying to keep
hard-ons for Jeannie Lynn. He felt uncomfortable
with them these days anyway because they had
already let him know they thought Tom was a weird
friend for him to take up with. More than once,
Nicky or one of the other guys had asked him why
he was getting so standoffish. Joel had never been
able to think of an answer that wouldn't piss them
off, so he just let it ride.

Tom took Jeannie Lynn's politeness at face
value, but knowing Jeannie Lynn, Joel figured she
wasn't being polite to be nice. Maybe she was waiting to see if Tom would come on to her. If a guy
didn't slobber over her—and Tom didn't—she
wouldn't have much use for him.

But Betsy was practically climbing over the
table to get at Tom, and Joel laughed to himself
when she giggled and shook Tom's hand as though
she'd met Elvis Presley or somebody. Joel sympa-
thized with her. He knew just how she felt because
he'd reacted the same way about a year before. He
was glad that at least somebody was being nice to
Tom. They sat on the opposite side of the table

from the two girls, and Betsy leaned across the table to talk to Tom. Drunk and silly herself, she and Tom were soon rattling like old friends. Joel tried to watch Tom out of the corner of his eye and still keep up the prattle with the other guys.

Cliff, Jeannie Lynn and Bill talked about their old school days at Mimbres County School like it was yesterday and not almost three years ago. Jeannie still enjoyed telling mean stories about Leo Johnson, another of their old classmates. She laughed wickedly and let her wrists flap loosely, imitating Leo. Nicky had changed some, or maybe he was just a little quieter than he used to be. He was leaning back against the wall with Cindy, one arm around her and one arm resting on the table, tapping his fingers and looking coolly around at the others. Their eyes never met, but Joel got the feeling that Nicky was watching him. At least he was dating other people besides the same old county school crowd, and seemed proud of Cindy. He didn't have much to say about the good old days, either. Joel felt indifferent to the reminiscing; like Nicky, he had drifted away from this old crowd. The others never grew tired of these dances and drinking and endlessly dating one another, as if the town and all the other students at the high school didn't even exist.

He was struck especially with their crudeness, of Bill's *goddamns* and *shits* between every word, *like I used to talk*, Joel thought. Cliff was still chewing tobacco and kept an empty beer can on the table next to him to spit in. Every once in a while he bent over and squirted a black, lumpy stream into the can. When he laughed, his teeth showed a crust of black around the edges. Several times, Joel almost gagged when Cliff caught him by surprise and, in the middle of a sentence, leaned over and squirted a good one, then wiped the spit away from his mouth with the back of his hand.

When the band began playing, Betsy dragged Tom out to the dance floor, crushing her plump body against his. Tom had tried to tell her he didn't know how to dance, but Betsy wouldn't listen. Joel watched them struggle on the dance floor; Tom was having trouble standing up, and Betsy was trying to climb onto him. People danced by them, laughing at the way Betsy manhandled Tom into a semblance of romance, and Joel laughed at them, too.

"He sure dances like a pansy!" Bill said.

Joel looked around. He'd been leaning away from the table, watching Tom across the room. Bill was leaning back in a chair he'd stolen from the table next to them, arms crossed, laughing and shaking his head like he couldn't believe it. Joel hooked a boot under Bill's chair and jerked it out from under him, then laughed loudly as Bill fell ungracefully to the floor. "Lay off him, man, he's just drunk!" Joel said at Bill's shocked face.

"Shit, Joel! You're runnin' around with a strange one," Bill said, picking himself up and laughing back, but there was the slightest edge that warned. "You ain't that dumb, my old friend." Joel turned away to hide his anger. He felt sorry for Tom just then, insulted by the laughter, and he wished again they hadn't come.

In Tom's strange mood, though, he actually seemed to enjoy their laughter. But he did get weary of Betsy and, when he struggled back into his place at the table after about five dances, he slumped against the wall and grabbed Joel around the neck. He pulled Joel's face down to his mouth and whispered in a loud drunk's voice, "Keep her away, Joel!" His breath gave Joel cold chills, and the heat

of his chest against him was almost sexual. But
Tom was grinning helplessly; his eyes were glassy
and he looked as though he might pass out. Without thinking, Joel put his arm around Tom's shoulders and brushed Tom's hair back from his forehead. Tom leaned back against him.

"He get like this all the time?" Nicky said. Joel
looked across the table and met Nicky's frown.
"Naw—" realizing that the others had begun to look
strangely, too, he pulled his arm away from Tom's
shoulders. "He's never been drunk before."

Nicky shook his head. He pulled Cindy up beside him and looked straight at Joel. "Well, it's
gettin' a little too weird around here for us. Catch
you later, guys." He began to move off.

Tom pulled himself up, using Joel's neck for
support. He called out "Nice meeting you!" But
Nicky ignored him and walked away with Cindy.
Jeannie Lynn laughed and nudged Betsy. Tom
looked around, confused.

"Take it easy, Tom," Joel said, quietly, feeling
the undercurrents of his old friends' attitudes.
"Nicky can't hear you." He caught Jeannie's eyes;
they were teasing and mischievous. "Anything
wrong?" he asked.

"Your little boy*fwend upthet* Nicky," she
laughed.

"Oh, shut up!" Betsy said, surprising everybody. Then she mooned over at Tom. "You wanna
dance, hon?"

"I don't think he does," Joel said. "I think he
just needs to sober up."

"You his nursemaid, or what?" Jeannie said
and laughed, again. Her eyes glittered and she
looked around, sharing the humor.

Bill caught her eye and laughed too, showing
Joel he still thought it was funny. Then he put his

arm around Betsy and gave her a squeeze. "Come on, Betsy, let's show him how it's done," Bill said, and danced her off, easily maneuvering Betsy around the slick floor. Then Cliff took Jeannie out to the dance floor and, for a moment, he and Tom were left alone.

Tom didn't sense their hostility, but Joel felt it like a solid presence. "You ready to go?" he asked.

Tom looked genuinely surprised. "We just got here!"

Joel sighed. Tom leaned against the wall, his expression almost a caricature of seriousness, and Joel grinned. "What?"

Tom leaned against him. "Aren't you havin' a good time? Huh?" He spoke quietly, slurring his words a little; his eyes were still glassy. But he smiled more like his old self in the dim light.

Joel leaned against the table, resting his left forearm on it, his back to the dance floor. In this light he noticed how soft Tom's features looked and it made his chest feel tight. He sighed again and smiled a little stiffly at his friend. "I am if you are."

"Betsy's nice," Tom laughed. "But I sure am glad you told her I didn't have to dance anymore."

Joel settled back against the partition. In the smoky half-light he watched the dancers. The band was playing a waltz or two-step—something with a steady, paced rhythm—and the dancers shuffled in unison in a circle around the dance floor like a human wheel.

Tom sighed. "Well, I know what it's like to dance, now."

Joel had to laugh. "Sort of, you do."

"Whadya mean?"

"With you and Betsy? It was more like a wrestling match."

He looked at Joel, searching his face. "Then do you wanna dance and show me how?"

Joel started to laugh. "We can't do that! People would think—"

"Why not? Look over there."

A couple of women were dancing together near the ticket taker. "Oh, women do that all the time, Tom. My sisters used to do that, too. Two guys couldn't—"

"But it wouldn't be any different," Tom said, looking around as if his logic was sound.

Joel laughed. "No. It wouldn't raise an eyebrow!"

As he studied Tom's face, he suddenly realized that Tom wasn't kidding. Tom was looking at him as if he expected an answer. A thrill shot through Joel again, and he realized he was getting an erection, wondering how it would feel to dance with his friend. Tom's eyes glittered like crystals against the spotlight from the stage, and he smiled steadily at Joel as if he knew the feelings he was arousing in him.

Then Jeannie Lynn and the others came back to the table laughing and talking loudly; someone made a trip out back for beer and, soon, the cigarette smoke and noise, the smell of sweat, and the pumping rhythm of the band pressed in again. Tom helped himself to a beer, making a mess of it with the can opener. It was warm and spewed foam all over him and the wall. When he tried to put his mouth over it, it spilled out of the corners, wetting his chin and running down his neck into the open collar of his shirt. He wiped his face and rubbed his hands on his pants. He began acting silly again, and whatever he had been getting at when they were alone was lost in the noise and the swirling faces.

Joel continued to drink, as well, and soon felt himself slipping into a silly stupor. It was difficult to focus on the faces after a while. The night seemed to go on in waves of laughter and commotion, comings and goings. Several times he had to lead Tom to the rest rooms behind the stage where the band was playing. And each time it was becoming more difficult to get in and out of their place at the table.

Another old schoolmate, Kenneth Stroud, wandered by, causing a sudden stillness to settle over the table. Jeannie Lynn stiffened. Her eyes lost their coquettish gleam, became wary. The other guys got up from the table like Dobermans on guard. Bill leaned against the partition, arms folded, blocking Kenneth's approach. But Kenneth had already spotted Joel. He stood his ground at a wary distance, staring into the dark corner. Joel hadn't gotten up like the others. Their eyes locked long before the others had even seen him.

Kenneth's old animosity toward Joel covered him like an odor. Joel felt sorry for him but, at the same time, he dreaded every encounter with him. Kenneth leered at him as he passed. "I know that kid you're with, Reece," he snarled. "The preacher's kid, yeah!" Then he disappeared into the crowd. Joel shrugged to himself, confused as always by Kenneth. Why who he ran around with should bother Kenneth was a mystery, and Joel wondered for the thousandth time in the last few years if Kenneth wasn't just plain crazy. *Of course he hates me*, Joel thought. No big mystery there at all, after all those fights at school, which Kenneth always started and Joel reluctantly finished, beating the shit out of him and miserably wishing Kenneth would just give it up. Kenneth was both a real loser and too dumb to realize that he would be better off if he'd just try to make friends. But, of course, he wouldn't.

More people joined them at the table and, soon, Joel was pressed on both sides. On his left, Cliff had found a girl from somewhere and was trying to make room for her. On his right, Tom was being squeezed between him and the wall. Joel put his arm around Tom's back. It was so crowded no one seemed to notice, which suited Joel just fine. He was beginning to enjoy the feelings rushing through him, and when he felt Tom snuggle against him, he hugged him closer. Tom was hot and sweaty and very quiet. Joel spoke into Tom's ear, brushing it with his lips. "You all ri—" He felt Tom's hand on his leg, working its way up to his crotch. Tom was looking at him with his mouth partway open, and Joel felt the insistent throb in his pants. His heart pounded hard. Drunk and fascinated, he didn't think to push Tom away until it was too late. Even as he felt Tom's mouth on his it didn't register—

Then Jeannie screamed a long, shrill laugh. "Oooh, how queer! They're kissing!" Laughter exploded around the table, and the guys standing nearby suddenly became a wall, falling in on him and Tom. In the slow-motion getaway that followed, Joel pushed Tom away and tried to stand. For what seemed like a minute or more, he couldn't make Tom stand up, and finally hooked his forearms under Tom's armpits. *Gotta get out. Gotta leave*, he kept thinking, unable to say anything to any of them. He stomped his way blindly over feet and thighs, felt beer soak his calf, a thumbnail break to the quick against the table; they fell free onto the dance floor and Joel managed to get Tom to his feet. Over his shoulder, Joel heard the laughter and confusion they had caused. But the music from the band pounded into his head, and he couldn't hear what was being said. Jeannie's high-pitched laughter was like a siren over the rest of the noise. The last sound Joel heard when they passed the ticket taker on the way out into the sluggish night air was a general pulsing laughter, as if everyone in the hangar had seen him and Tom kissing and heard Jeannie's accusation.

The parking lot was a battleground. A fist fight was drawing a crowd and some girl was screaming and crying because her boyfriend was getting beat up, sounding to Joel more like cries of pleasure; a wiry bunch of girls were having a cat fight of some sort, crying and shrieking. A pickup and a Cadillac had wrecked in the bumper-car madhouse, and both drivers were fighting it out with their doors open and the engines snarling, locked together at the bumpers. Joel and Tom stumbled through it all. It was just another Friday night, but Tom clung to his neck. Two guys falling all over each other in the parking lot was not an unusual sight, except Tom wouldn't quit trying to kiss him.

When they got to the pickup, Joel fumbled for the keys in his pocket. Tom was leaning against the hood of the pickup, bleary eyed and holding onto Joel's shoulder, grinning and making funny faces. "Wha's a matter? Wha'happened?"

"Man, we coulda been beat up in there!" Joel said as he opened the door on his side and shoved Tom in far enough to squeeze in beside him. He got the pickup turned around and headed down the gravel road. Tom was in no condition to be taken home, for sure, so, instead of turning left at the gate, Joel turned right and drove through the edge of the old air base and pulled up against the dark shadow of a building that was sagging and abandoned. When he killed the engine, the clatter of crickets rose up from the tumbleweeds growing wildly against the walls. In the dark, in the steamy heat, Joel's embarrassment faded, and he just laughed when Tom took his hand off the steering wheel and pulled his arm around him. Joel pulled him close. "Why are you acting so.... Don't you know what we just did?" But is was no use trying to explain what had happened. Tom didn't seem to care.

He felt Tom's hand on his thigh in the dark, felt it moving slowly toward his crotch again and, this time, he let the feelings build. He spread his legs just a little, jerkily, against Tom. Tom moved closer and started doing something to his ear, making it wet and warm. "I love you," Tom breathed. Then he cried out, his voice edged with frustration. "Pleeese! Do—oo it!"

"What?" Joel said, feeling nervous. His legs began to shake. "What?"

Tom moved against him and sat up with his face close to Joel's. In the darkness, Joel couldn't make out his features. His clean-shaven skin reflected light from somewhere, but it was so faint, his skin had a ghost-like sheen, an indistinct glow. "This!" Tom whispered. He kissed Joel then, a real kiss, warm and deep. And Joel kissed back hard, amazed that they were mouth to mouth; Tom's lips were full and warm against his, and he recalled how stiff and dead it had felt to kiss girls. They kissed until it felt familiar, and the only sounds were their excited breathing and the soft sucking of their lips. Tom's clean, sweet smell drove Joel crazy.

They pulled at each other's clothes and Tom ran his hands under Joel's shirt and down into the back of his Levi's. Joel pulled at Tom's belt, unbuttoned his pants, and slid his own hands down into the warmth of Tom's crotch, fumbling gently with the underwear he had exposed. With the tips of his fingers, he felt the elastic against the soft skin of Tom's abdomen, then the pubic hairs. It was hard to get at him with Tom crushed up against his chest. Joel lay down in the seat and pulled Tom onto him, slid both hands back into Tom's shorts, and pushed them off Tom's unbelievably smooth butt. Tom helped Joel shed his own clothing and, in a few, quick strokes, they were naked and lay crushed against each other. The heat of Tom's naked skin against him, the throbbing of the hard, slick flesh pressing against his own made Joel cry out. He tried to move away, realizing even then that it would get messy, but, at the same time, Tom began gasping and shaking, coming in hot spurts. Joel let go then and felt himself coming. In their frenzy, Tom bit down on Joel's lip, and he tasted blood. In a few seconds, their stomachs had become slick.

Afterwards, lying together, smeared and sticky like kids at a birthday party, Joel tried to kiss Tom again, but Tom began to draw away. His strange quiet was more disturbing to Joel than the dance, or their sex. Tom shook his head wordlessly when Joel tried to talk to him, and fought him off irritably when he tried to clean them up. He pushed roughly away and clawed into his clothes. Joel dressed as quickly as he could, thinking insanely that they would go someplace for hamburgers and he would find out what the matter was. He kept stealing glances in the dark at Tom against the other door. But when he tried to speak, the words wouldn't come out.

As they pulled into town in the late night, oddly light and beginning to grow cold, he cut west and

Chapter 2

The house was quiet except for his father, Douglas Reece, in the kitchen, rattling around at the sink. He figured his mother was already in her garden, taking advantage of the last coolness of the morning. Douglas didn't look at him when he walked in. "Up already, Son?"

Joel yawned.

Douglas poured a cup of coffee and handed it to him, smiling very slightly with one of his jokes, no doubt.

Joel braced himself for it, knowing that particular smile. "What time is it?"

"'Bout eight."

"Oh."

"Yep, it is. But I didn't expect you up 'fore noon." He chuckled. "Here. Drink up. You've got a few hours before the tailwater reaches the other end. I got the irrigation early, today."

Joel took his cup of coffee to the breakfast table by the window. He yawned again.

"Got in kinda late, huh?"

Joel squinted at him. "Around five, I guess. I fell asleep in the pickup."

"Figured that. Coffee's good for a hangover if you got one."

Joel shook his head.

Douglas looked out the window toward the fields for a moment, then looked back at Joel, again, his expression serious. "You left a damn mess in the pickup. Smelled like a brewery this morning. I threw your beer cans out for you."

Joel caught his father's eyes and looked quickly away, wondering what other kind of mess he'd left. "Sorry, Dad."

"Just clean up your messes, Joel," he said, then grinned across the table. "Yes, ma'am, looks to me like you slept real hard. Found me a perfectly good pair of undershorts on the floor board, too. Been needin' me a grease rag, if you can spare 'em."

Joel felt his face go crimson, knowing that the underwear was Tom's. He ducked his head and laughed. His father had made his point and had his fun and, after he'd let Joel suffer under his gaze for a minute, he slapped his knees. "Well," he said, and pushed himself out of the chair and strode to the door leading into the garage.

Joel followed at a safe distance, feeling like an asshole, but in the driveway, Douglas laid out the work as if nothing had happened. He patted him on the shoulder. "Build up those borders, Joel. Don't let the irrigation water break down at the end or it'll cause a washout. That patch slicks water through quick. Check the hoses and set up more tarps on down the ditch. Meantime, I'll set up the cultivator."

Joel ran to the pickup, glad to get away.

The air was already hot and dry at the south end of the field where he parked. In the dry, desert air, he could hear the irrigation pumps on neighboring farms, their old engines droning on like low-flying crop dusters. Nearby on the Hotchkiss farm he could hear their old "Poppin'

Johnnie" tractor running up and down the field. To the east, across the green patches of cotton and pecan orchards, the rocky, Florida mountains towered above the valley, still hazy blue in the early sunlight. From the north, he heard the highway traffic moving through town, and, nearby, all the ordinary sounds of the desert morning.

He went to work immediately, mechanically, shutting out all thought of the night before, and soon he was lost in the work. When sweat soaked his shirt, he peeled it off and tossed it into the shade near the pickup. He stopped long enough to drink from the canvas water bag that always hung from the tailgate of the pickup, letting the tepid water roll down his throat and neck. For several hours he worked tirelessly. As usual, the work made him happy. He liked feeling strong. He liked the musty smell of the earth as he dug, straining his muscles against the earth's weight, forming a border of dirt at the end of the plant beds almost knee-high and stretching over a hundred yards.

He liked the clean sweat to roll down his back. When a short breeze came up, he unbuttoned his Levi's to allow the air to dry the crack of his butt where the sweat ran in rivulets. He stretched occasionally to flex his stomach muscles. When he stopped working, he was satisfied that the border at the end of the furrows would hold the irrigation water. It would collect at this end by mid afternoon. Already, the silver strands of the water in the furrows between the beds of tender cotton plants were beginning to lengthen across the field.

The sun was almost above him, near eleven o'clock. He tossed his shirt into the pickup and slid into the seat, wincing when his back touched the hot vinyl. Dust boiled behind him as he drove around the field toward the other end; the pow-

dery brown fog settled into the creases of his neck
and mixed with the sweat.

At the north end of the field, the water flowed
smoothly through the irrigation hoses lined up row
by row in the ditch. He jumped across it and knelt
down to drink and wash in the cold water. He
splashed himself until the water ran off in streams,
then went back to work feeling cool as the air dried
his skin. After setting tarps to dam the water farther down the ditch, he tossed more siphon hoses
along the ditch bank for the next patch of irrigation. This set would be started in the late afternoon and would run all night.

He found his father still working on the cultivator. Joel dusted his pants and scraped his boots
on the tractor wheel. Douglas found a loose nut
and tightened it. "There!" He looked up, squinting
at the sun. "You done already?"

"Yeah."

"Tarps're set?"

"Every ninety rows, like you said. And I did
the borders for the next three sets."

Douglas stood up and slapped him on the
shoulder. "Guess you have your chores to do this
evening, but there's not much else. I need some
diesel fuel for the tractor, if you don't mind goin'
to town." He brought out his wallet, fingered a few
bills, and gave Joel a ten. "Put in maybe twenty
gallons. Truck stop's got it for sixteen-nine. Gotta
girlfriend you wanna see?"

"Naw. Just Tom." Joel felt a tingle of excitement remembering, and felt his face turn pink.
He looked away, pocketing the bill quickly, and
waited for his father to show him how well the
cultivator would work.

* * * *

The blacktop stretched in front of him, heat-spiked with the noon sun. Hot air blew into the window, dry as a blast furnace, but his forehead still ran with sweat and his eyes watered in the heat. He passed cotton fields, corn fields, cotton gins and trailer parks, and everything was on fire in the blinding light; it formed heat waves on the highway like puddles of mercury. As he pulled into town, the heat seemed to grow worse, rising off the concrete and the whitewashed buildings. He passed the old air base and remembered crossing the railroad tracks right here at this intersection last night with Tom in the pickup, ominously silent.

In the broad, clear daylight with the relentless desert beyond, all was stark and naked. Everything was familiar and ordinary, but strange, too, like something he experienced once on a trip to Arizona to visit his aunt and uncle. They lived in a trailer park by the edge of the highway to Phoenix, in the middle of nowhere.

Joel remembered the boy he had met there, a few years older than he was. One evening they met by chance in the community bathhouse at the trailer park. They had played shuffle board earlier that day after the adults had gone indoors. Joel had liked the guy immediately, so when they met in the shower, they had begun talking and horsing around. The guy, Mark, was friendly, but began trying to treat Joel like a girl, telling Joel he sure was pretty. At first, Joel felt funny, then let Mark play with his genitals. His first orgasm was a surprise, especially since the guy had it in his mouth. Joel was frightened and excited then. And just like now, the next morning he felt strange. He hugged his aunt and uncle when he was getting ready to leave, the whole time feeling like he would explode, wanting to talk about what had happened between him and Mark, but realizing he couldn't. When they drove past the bath house on the way out of the trailer park, he felt a wash of anxiety that was strangely mixed with a kind of pleasure. *I'm different now* was all he'd been able to think.

Saturday shoppers milled slowly about on the sidewalks. The heat hugged everything like syrup. Some guys were shirtless, and he wondered now if other guys really did it, too, if the jokes about queers were true; but it made him feel uneasy.

Tom would be able to sort things out. He would be getting off work soon and they could talk about it. He remembered how quiet Tom had been afterwards, and that bothered him. But considering that Tom had started things, he was sure that he was only shocked, or maybe a little embarrassed by what they had done. To Joel, it had been a little like the guilt rush he used to get after jacking off.

The truck stop was busy; semis huffed off the highway, belching black smoke as they idled around the gas pumps. Drivers camped out in the cafe. Joel leaned against the wall, waiting until one of the trucks left, then he moved the pickup to a pump, climbed in the back of the pickup, and started filling the oil drum. He was careful to put exactly the amount his father wanted, because the rest of the money was his. And he wanted to treat Tom to lunch. Exhaust stung his nose. Heat rose off the hoods of the big semis, and he felt the gaseous fumes seeping into the pores of his skin and making him feel gritty.

In the men's room at the truck stop, above the urinal, someone had scrawled in a quick, firm hand with a lead pencil: "I'll suck any cock as long as it's fat, hard and juicy." Below that was the message, "Call Lucy!" He snickered grimly to himself,

struck by the idea that only a man could have
written that in here. He'd seen this message in
other public toilets around town, all the work of
"Lucy;" but he'd never felt more than mild curiosity about it. Today, he felt a begrudging kinship
with him. Again, the idea struck him that he was
supposed to feel ashamed, but that wasn't quite
it; the novelty of it was interesting, secretly pleasurable, not really disgusting or anything. *Unless
all other guys like that Lucy are weirdoes*, he
thought. That would make it pretty unbearable.

At Tom's church, Joel parked under a shade
tree. He hurried inside and tucked his shirttail in
on impulse, and like a man who has just removed
a hat, he smoothed down his hair, thinking of Tom.
In the vestibule, his boots sounded solid on the
tile. A vacuum cleaner roared inside the chapel,
which meant Tom was almost done. Good. He
would tell him he'd wait in the pickup. He smiled
as he pushed open the heavy, polished doors and
walked down the center aisle, sinking into the thick
carpet. Tom was running the vacuum behind the
pulpit with his head down, and Joel waited for
him to look up.

When he did, Joel caught his breath. Tom's
eyes were swollen and red. He looked awful. He
jerked his head and frowned.

Joel leaped over the wooden railing in front of
the pulpit. "You been in a fight?"

Tom glared at him over the lectern and yelled,
"Wait!" He jerked the electric cord from the wall,
keeping his face down as he coiled it. He shoved
the vacuum into the room behind the pulpit. Joel
followed and stood in the doorway.

"Hey! What's the matter?"

Tom shoved the vacuum violently into some
boxes and fell recklessly into them. Joel thought

he was having a fit or something. But then Tom stopped and turned around. "You should know, Joel!" he said. His face was a blur of anger and shock. "What are YOU doing here, anyway? Aren't you the least bit ashamed?"

Joel looked around at the empty chapel and shrugged at Tom blankly. "C'mon man, don't I always come on Saturdays?"

"Never mind," Tom said, disgusted. "I knew you'd come. You always do, don't you, Joel? Always. You're as dependable as a dog." Tom stopped then and frowned, started to say something, then clacked his tongue. He looked around as though he were trying to find something to do. He pushed Joel and ran out into the church.

Joel followed, embarrassed and angry. "Hold on, damn it!"

"Okay, Joel. As soon as I lock up. Then we'll talk."

"Sure thing we will! Look. If it's about last night, man, I know what you're pissed at, but you shouldn't...." His voice trailed off and he stomped outside and slid into the pickup to wait.

When Tom came out he went up to the pickup on Joel's side. "Look Joel, I'm sorry. I'm acting like everything is your fault." He flicked his thumb at the church. "I'm supposed to know better, you know. I'm so ashamed I can't even face myself in the mirror. I'm sorry." He lowered his eyes. "Last night was a mistake, okay?"

Joel felt stung. Tom's face was ugly with disgust. "No, it wasn't! You're just embarrassed, man. And I promise, Tom, next time you won't be."

Tom looked horrified and backed away from the pickup. Huge tears welled up in his bloodshot, brown eyes. "There won't be a next time! There shouldn't have been a first time and you know it!"

"Just think about that. Who was the one wanting it in the first place?"

"Stop it, Joel."

"No, man. I won't! You loved it! And so did I, so just stop it yourself and think! Don't you remember how long we kissed?"

"Yes, I remember! Damn it! I just can't handle it right now. We'll talk later, okay?"

Joel saw how upset Tom was—even worse than last night. He felt angry but checked himself. "Shit. Okay. Later."

As he drove away from the church, Joel's anger faded, leaving him feeling hurt. Sometimes Tom could insult him and not realize it. But this time was different. His face still stung from the slap of those words, "dependable, like a dog." Like a dog? Is that how I am? Other people had said similar things one time or another, too. Like Coach Hoffins last year.

Joel's sisters had married in December, 1963, in a double wedding, and their absence from home left Joel with a bigger share of the farm work. He had to choose between that and staying on the high-school boxing team. It was a hard choice, because he was the coach's star boxer and his parents' only helper. He had won the District and All State boxing tournaments in late November and the coach never stopped praising him. He pushed Joel everywhere. Secretly, Joel cringed when he was asked to say a few words about his plans when he and other athletes were invited to Lion's Club luncheons, but he made a brave effort, not wanting to let Coach down. Except when he had to choose. And to the disappointment of his coach and now his friend and advisor, Joel went to him one day, right after the new semester started. He explained about his sisters and the workload and told the coach he just had to quit to take up the slack. "But boxing training doesn't even start till fall semester, Joel. Surely by then...." But Joel said harvest season was even worse. The coach exploded. "You're a quitter, Joel! You're letting down the team! You'll never be nothin' but a country hick! Is that what you want?" Joel had screamed back that his parents were depending on him. The coach had finally relented and patted Joel on the shoulder in a friendly manner, his disappointment evident. He smiled sadly and said, "Okay, Joel. I know. I understand. But one of these days you'll have to get over being so tied to that damned farm and have a little fun."

The coach's admonition hadn't hurt because Joel liked being dependable to his parents, and they appreciated it. But when Tom had said it, it hurt. *I only hung around so much because I like him*, Joel thought. *Is that all I am—a pet*? Hadn't he just let his other friends drift away so he could spend all his time with Tom?

He couldn't say why, but Tom was just a different sort of guy. And it was that difference that had appealed to him. Tom was like Troy Donahue or James Dean. At the small high school, on the first day when Tom was the new kid from Houston, Texas, he had caused quite a stir. Joel began hearing about the new dream boat as soon as he stepped off the bus that day. It was shortly after the fall semester of 1964 had begun. During the day, Joel caught glimpses of the new guy. He was a good-looking guy all right. But Joel was disappointed.

The guy was surrounded by students who didn't mix with farmers. The townies, *cats*, as all the ag boys called the students who lived in town. The new guy was just another one of them. Even worse, Joel heard he was a preacher's kid. By the end of the first week, Joel saw that the new guy was alone much of the time, and he felt sorry for him. To be a preacher's kid was a stigma. He didn't try to meet the guy.

But he did meet Tom somehow. After getting to know him, he began to see what the coach meant about being a hick. At first, Joel felt awkward around Tom, just like he had at school with his new athlete's image and suddenly crawling with cat friends. When he passed by students he hardly knew, they would wave. He'd often heard girls whispering and giggling when he went by and, once, he'd heard, "He's so—o cu—ute!" Guys would slap him on the back when he stood at his locker. He got invited out a lot by the town girls to attend Rainbow Girl banquets, to be a girl's escort to the spring carnival, the homecoming dance. But he felt awkward most of the time and refused shyly.

In contrast, Tom's approach was different, so gentle and still persistent. And Joel was left making the giant step of introducing himself. Eventually he began to relax around Tom and, after a time, Tom had become, for Joel, a welcome change. He wasn't the kind of guy you had to put up a front with. You didn't always have to say you were horny when you weren't and brag about fucking the girls when you didn't. He wasn't like a girl, but Tom gave Joel the kind of satisfaction he was supposed to get when he dated a girl. Eventually they had become best friends, as close as brothers, as familiar to Joel as his parents, and Tom was easy to talk to. He didn't feel as dumb as he did with girls when he tried to talk about other things besides junk. Hardly a day went by now that they didn't see each other or at least talk on the telephone.

The differences in their backgrounds became invisible. They went on hikes out in the desert. They went to movies Tom had already seen in Houston. They drove up and down Main Street in Joel's pickup night after night during the school week, instead of studying at the library as they told their parents. In every way they enjoyed each other's company and hardly noticed how exclusive their friendship had become. Although they both had friends besides each other, they were transitory. Joel no longer dated. What was the point of putting yourself through that kind of torture? He realized he hadn't been anywhere with anybody else since October of the last year. But some of the other guys dropped hints now and then that things weren't quite right. Joel had failed to register these things until now. He didn't mind that his old friends no longer called. He got along fine without the others. *Tom is my best friend, after all*, Joel told himself now. *And I love him, too*, he thought, like Tom had said the night before.

It had seemed natural when Tom had kissed him, but, of course, it wasn't too smart in front of all those people, drunk or not. Even when you were drunk there were just some things you didn't let loose. The others made the difference. Joel shuddered to think what could have happened.

As he recalled that, Joel was amazed they'd gotten away so easily. He kicked himself now for having gone to the dance in the first place and letting Tom kiss him in front of Jeannie Lynn and the guys. And what if they'd been caught at the abandoned hangar—like that old man had been, at one of those dances, with Becky McNutt? The boys had dragged him out of the car like a pack of wolves. The old man was naked as a Jaybird. All the chaperons treated Becky as if she'd been raped, but no one cared about the old man, even if Becky had been flirting with him. She was always "doing it" with guys, and all the students knew it; some of the same guys who bragged about laying her were the ones beating the hell out of the old man right there in front of the doors to the dance—yelling, smashing the guy's face in, getting blood and snot all over the place before the cops came and broke it up.

I need to talk to someone, he thought, driving aimlessly through the streets. He passed the public library. Maybe the librarian knew some books he could read. But how did you ask? He felt afraid, remembering Tom's craziness. Who could you talk to and survive their reaction? "Er...ah...yes ma'am, last night, um...my best friend and I got...you know...horny for each other....Um...could you tell me what causes that?" He laughed thinking of the mess they made all over themselves afterwards.

For months, Joel knew both of them had been leading up to something like this. There were times when they were wrestling that they would stare at each other in a quizzical way, both speechless. Times when Tom was spending the weekend when they would take walks in the field at dusk and Joel would almost take his hand—then, realizing you didn't do that, would stuff his hands in his pockets.

Today, he should have knocked some sense into him, getting so upset over everything. He decided that if Tom was going to go wild-eyed, he'd just wait it out, let Tom calm down, then show him it wasn't wrong. They just needed to figure out what to do. He decided to go back now and start over. He wouldn't get mad, he wouldn't get hurt, and he wouldn't mention last night.

He called from a pay phone.

"Allen residence," a woman's voice said. "Mrs. Allen speaking."

Joel identified himself. "May I speak to Tom, please?"

"Hello, Joel." Her voice was kind. "Tom said if you called to tell you he's sick."

"But I just saw him an hour ago, Mrs. Allen—"

"I know, dear, but there's something wrong with him anyway. I'm sure he'll call you later on. Okay?"

"Sure. Yes, ma'am." Joel dropped the receiver into its cradle, feeling lost.

* * * *

Tom heard the telephone ringing in the living room, then his mother talking to Joel. He watched from a crack in his bedroom door as she explained, "Sick or something," which was all she would say. It was, after all, the most his mother could probably figure out. Until he heard her say good-bye to Joel, he hoped she would motion to him to hurry across the carpet quietly and say just a few words before his father returned to his desk. But she dropped the receiver into the cradle and walked away. *Father's angry, all right, the way mother dropped the phone like a live snake*, Tom thought, and now he was sorry he hadn't gone with Joel. It was worse getting his father involved. At least with Joel, as ashamed as he felt, he could have been honest. *But with father?*

Oh, why am I crying? I lay with Joel. Knew him...in the biblical sense, Father.

He kicked the door shut and leaned against it. He bit down on the edge of a thumbnail and stared at the white stillness of his room, the almost bare walls, and the blinding glow of light from his window. His bed was rumpled from his fight with it earlier, but looking at it now, tired as he was, he knew it would be hot and dry. He was sick—to his stomach—and he didn't want a repeat performance like this morning when Joel had dropped him off.

When he got out of the pickup, he'd made it to his room quietly, and lay down without undressing. But immediately, the room had begun to spin. As soon as his head touched the pillow, he felt like he was whirling around and around, and he actually held onto the edge of the bed to keep from falling. But the roiling nausea forced him to hurry to the bathroom and vomit into the toilet, leaving him rung out like a rag, leaving his nostrils stinking and burning and the back of the throat choked with mucus.

He managed to wash off the sharp, cheesy smell of vomit and sweat in the shower, but as he slipped into the church, intending to pray as the sun was just beginning to pink the sky, he still felt filthy. He knelt down in the back of the church in the last row and tried to utter the Lord's Prayer, but he couldn't make himself say "Father." He felt like a cheat—a pretender. Instead, he cried out in a loud voice for help and, in the empty chapel, it sounded like a howl, which shamed him into silence. He couldn't pray. He felt empty and stayed in the church, eventually able to go about his work. Maybe if Joel hadn't come in looking for him and acting like everything was ordinary, he might have avoided getting his father all excited. Instead, when Joel came in, it had made him angry. He had meant to hurt Joel. But seeing its effect on his friend, then feeling lousy for it, had only made things worse.

After Joel drove off, gunning his pickup down the street and out of sight, Tom had tried to sneak back into his room, but his mother caught him.

She took one look at his face and called his father, who demanded an explanation for his condition—his swollen eyes, his distracted behavior. "I'm sick," was all Tom could think to say. It was true, but not the truth. And, of course, his father wasn't satisfied. He couldn't get one past his father. Not that he often tried. But this? Sitting on the couch in the living room with his mother on one side of him, seeming to hold onto its rich brocade design for support, and his father standing by the desk, behind the couch, drilling questions into the back of his head, all he could think was *Just don't get him started, just don't....* The trouble was, being a preacher, his father made a religious issue out of everything, and so when he sent him to his room until he explained himself, Tom went without a word.

He was still speechless. He came out of the stare and looked down at his bloody thumbnail, which he had bitten to the quick. He dropped his hand to his side and forced himself to walk across the room to the desk. He resented being shut in like a child. But if the truth were known, he would have stayed away from his parents anyway, ashamed. He hated himself for chasing Joel off, but he had only wanted to get away from everybody—even himself.

He wanted to see Joel now, but his father's rules were unshakable. It had been easier to commit sodomy than to even think now of disobeying his father. He thought of writing Joel a letter. To explain things. To apologize. To tell him he loved him, but not like that...but then, why lie? Why not just tell him that it was wrong and they would just have to stop? *Couldn't we just go on being friends?* Surely, Joel could understand.

But he made no move to write. Joel wouldn't

understand, considering Joel's solution had been to do it again! *"Next time, Tom, I promise you won't feel embarrassed...."* Tom laughed bitterly at the thought, at Joel's puppy-dog innocence.

He thought about praying, but didn't give voice to the words that were rattling him: *Please forgive me, Father, for I want to sin.* God wouldn't understand that, would He?

It was a lie to pretend that getting drunk broke down the barriers between them. The only barrier the beer had broken down was his fear. Drunk, he had found it easy to kiss Joel, to turn him on. But the beer was not to blame.

He had tried for three years to believe that he would eventually win, that, one day, the desire would be taken away. When had everything begun to feel so false? Was it last year in Houston, the summer before they left there and came to this place? He was glad to get away from there. The schools were large and full of reckless students, and just about any diversion a person could dream up, he could find, practically within walking distance of home. And, for a quarter, a person could ride into downtown, where the porn strip beckoned, where the sleazy buildings with the bright-yellow and red-plastic signs promised sex, where he'd often gone, where he'd never had the courage to give in, except once. He shut his eyes and saw with the vision of a clairvoyant that dark, stinking booth with the flickering movie, the sudden rush of cool air coming from somewhere to his left, a shaft of light from the booth next to him coming through a hole, then the rustling sound, then the light ending, then.... *No! I won't think about that!* he thought. But he did. He saw the penis where the light had been, sticking through the hole into his booth, felt its heat, remembered reaching out

in the privacy of that stinking booth to touch it,
oddly anonymous, it being the only part of the man
in the booth with him, remembered holding it with
the tips of his fingers, then its sudden withdrawal
and the cruel laughter. "Suck it, bud, I ain't got all
night!"

He was relieved to move away, not having to
fight the nightly temptation to sneak out of the house
in the dead of night, to return to one of those booths
with the holes, where he knew with a certainty he
would one day have the courage to do as the voice
had demanded. Unbelievably, having the temptation taken away added to his frustration. And although he couldn't be precise about the moment
when he felt the doubt beating in him like a quickening fetus, he thought he must have become infected with it out here in the desert.

For the longest time—months at least—he had
fought against his love-hate relationship with the
church. He loved the quiet of the church. But, secretly, he hated being the son of a preacher, always
feeling different from ninety-nine percent of the guys
he ever knew. He loved singing the hymns. He loved
the way he often felt in church, listening, awed at
the power that his father wrought over the congregation. But he hated that cloying doubt most of all,
that he was only deceiving himself, deceiving his
father, his church, the congregation, into believing
that he was just a nice, quiet boy who seldom dated,
who never wanted to experiment with alcohol, who
could be counted on to be wholesome and clean.
On the inside—in that part of his mind that he
couldn't look at—he doubted that he really *wanted*
to be saved from this sin. But he couldn't admit
that he was lying like a crook about wanting to give
up the feelings that drew him so strongly to Joel; so
very undeniably strong were his feelings. Joel,
though, had taken to everything like a duck to wat—

He couldn't allow himself to even recall last night, especially the intensity of the brief pleasure in it, because such feelings, once unleashed…. He wanted things to be the way they used to be. But last night he had led Joel into this hideous sin, whether Joel would call it a sin or not. He remembered saying to Joel, "I love you!"

But it was just lust, wasn't it? Just lust. Only that could have made him break his secret open to Joel like a ripe melon and invite him to gorge himself.

He hadn't slept for over twenty-four hours, and when his head hit the desk with a crack that sent a can of pencils clattering to the floor and brought a light tapping at the door from his mother, Tom stood up wearily. He looked toward the door. "I'm okay, Mother. I was just cleaning out my desk." He listened for the soft brush of her steps across the carpet, then moved toward the bed.

He undressed. Maybe a nap would help. He sat on the edge of the bed and pulled off his shoes and socks, carefully tucking the socks inside one shoe and placing them neatly at the foot of the bed. He pulled his pants off, folded them and placed them on the bottom shelf of his night stand. Pulling his pajama bottoms from under his pillow, he slid them on, folded back the sheets and slipped between them. He shut his eyes, but images in the pickup returned and he opened them again to the familiarity of his room. His gaze fell on a snapshot of Joel taken in his yard. They had been washing Joel's pickup and Joel was soaked. His T-shirt stuck to his muscular chest, and his cutoffs had a patch of wet across the crotch. Joel was grinning broadly at the camera. Tom closed his eyes to shut out his blinding beauty, and began to drift.

* * * *

The house was near the high school, but Joel couldn't remember exactly where. He'd only been there once and that was at night. There was a small porch that framed little more than the front door with a concrete demi-wall enclosing it. He remembered that much, since he and Coach had talked longer on the porch than they had inside. Coach had a baby—a pretty sick baby, he remembered— and after staying inside for about thirty minutes, Joel—politely ignoring the stench of sour milk and dirty diapers—was relieved when Coach had suggested they go outside. He couldn't remember exactly why he'd gone over that night. Coach wasn't real social with his athletes, but for a few, he made a little extra time—especially before a match. Whatever problems he had at home, Coach was always willing to listen. And even off the boxing team, Joel had continued to visit him at school.

Joel drove slowly down the street. The houses looked different in the daylight. And several houses were logical candidates for Coach's. Three were brick like Coach's with those small porches—214, 216, 218—any of those addresses could be his. Each house had a free-standing garage, but only 218 had a basketball hoop over the garage door.

He'd take this blind, wouldn't think about being nervous, just like he'd done in boxing matches. *At the sound of the bell, Joel, just go in there slugging*…. Before his feet could twist him around, he pressed the door bell and jumped back as it clanged like a fire alarm above his head. It had been added as an afterthought. The wire for it, tacked to the outside wall, ran from the push-button to a bell above the door. *Got to talk to someone*, he thought again as he waited. Blood drummed in his throat, choking his vocal cords. *Just slug through it, just slug—*

"Hey, Joel!" Without hesitating, Coach stepped back and opened the door wide. "Come in, kiddo!"

The tiny living room was dark and Joel squinted at Coach's silhouette. Across the room, light burst from their kitchen and Joel saw Mrs. Hoffins at the table. "Did I interrupt your lunch?"

"Don't sweat it," Bill Hoffins laughed. He patted his barrel chest. "I'm supposed to trim down this summer. I'm entering a boxing contest at State in September. Coaches' meet." He sat down in a big, square chair and indicated the couch.

Joel sat down on the end closest to Coach's chair. "I got a problem, man." He dropped his head between his shoulders but looked earnestly into Coach's smile.

Bill leaned back, appraising Joel. "It ain't physical, is it, kiddo? Looks like you've gained about ten, fifteen pounds since the team. You kickin' a load of cow shit on your farm, I bet."

Joel laughed. "Ranchers are shit kickers, Coach. Farmers like me shovel shit. It ain't physical. I feel great."

"Can't be school. I know you passed all your courses. I keep a file on you. Did you know that? Just in case you decide to come back to the team. Joel, you could train this summer—we could bend the rules—and take up next September on the team. Best I've been able to get since you left is District."

"I know, Coach. I keep up. Marty Anderson took the district title for us. And did real well in Albuquerque. Second, wasn't it?"

Coach waved a hand almost irritably. "We're doing for shit and you know it, Joel. You took State when you were just a sophomore; just think what you could've done last fall. You'd have a scholarship, I guarantee!"

Joel leaned toward Bill, resting his arms on his thighs. "You wouldn't want me now."

"You have a big problem, don't you?"

"It feels like it. Yeah. I'm…afraid to tell my parents."

Bill's face went serious. "Well, Joel, I'm not sure you ought to be talking to me about something you don't want your parents knowing."

"Okay. Thanks." Joel got up to leave. "I'll just think about it for a while, then."

"Sit down, kiddo. Why can't you tell them?"

Joel was relieved and fell back onto the couch. "It's just something you don't lay on your parents, man. Not yet. I don't feel so good. Something happened. Then my friend…today, he'd been crying about what we did. He was freaked. He looked beat up."

"You look like shit yourself, Joel. You look like you just committed murder."

"I feel like shit. I had sex with my best friend…I.…"

Coach sat up, ran his hand over his receding hair. "Whew! Hit me with that again?"

"A guy. We had sex." Joel felt the shakes beginning and he took a deep breath, held it, then let it out slowly. Coach looked stunned, but hadn't lost his reasonable expression. Joel crossed his arms over his chest. "So what do you think?"

"What do you want me to say, Joel?"

"I dunno, Coach. See, I liked it. It… I loved it. But it freaked the other guy."

"I understand. And now, Joel, you think you're.…" He waved his hand.

"Well, yeah."

"It wouldn't help for me to say it's a phase a lot of boys go through?"

"I don't think so," Joel said. "All I know is, it

was like it was supposed to be. I've tried liking girls. I couldn't function with them. Not only sex, but even little things like talking to them. Holding hands. Kissing them was just nothing. We don't connect. But I don't care, because me and this guy...."

"And that made you think...that since you enjoyed it with...your friend...."

"A lot of things. You know how neat it feels to have a friend? I mean a really good friend? That's how I feel with this guy. Only he's freaked out. He's a preacher's kid."

"I know who you're talking about, Joel. It strikes me, now, that maybe I should have seen this coming."

"You mean I act queer?"

"No! Joel, I can tell you don't know a damn thing about what you're involved with."

"You mean something bad, don't you? Something that should make me sick."

Bill sighed. "This is a ticklish subject. I mean real ticklish! I've always tried to get you boys to trust me. Hell, I ask you to get in the ring and get your bodies slammed, your noses bloodied. Okay. You know how people feel about this. They hate it. Most guys your age would react like your friend did. I'm sure about that, Joel. But knowing you, I can see how you wouldn't see a problem with it. It's none of my business, but you didn't come here for me to tell you it was all right, did you?"

"No. But I don't know what to do."

"I'm afraid I don't either, kiddo."

"But aren't there books, or something?"

"Yeah. There are books. Psychology books. But you wouldn't understand them—I don't understand them."

"Except they say it's wrong. Right?"

"They say it's a mental illness. They say it's arrested development. They say you hate girls. They say...oh hell, kiddo, they say of lot of shit."

"Is it?"

"Is it what?"

"Is it like being crazy?"

"Insane?"

"Yeah."

"No."

"But you just said it was a mental illness."

"It's not crazy...." Coach bobbled his finger against his lips, making a blubbering sound. Joel laughed in spite of himself. "Not like that, Joel. Maybe an emotional problem, psychologists would say."

Joel started to get up to leave again. "Jeez! Coach. I feel good! And they say—"

But Bill stood up and pushed him back down on the couch. "Don't run away. That's what the books say. That's all you'll find, I think. But I've never looked into it much. Like I say, it's up to you. One of these days, maybe you should read up on the subject. But I don't think you'd agree with anything they have to say. You take the advice I give you on boxing because it feels right to you. But if you didn't believe it with your body, you wouldn't take my advice. Let the shrinks handle the mind. I think you have to feel your way along on this problem by yourself, Joel. Here's some advice, though, and it's against your nature, but like I say, this is ticklish. Work on your feelings, but don't go spreading them around. You know what I mean. You came to me without any idea how I would react. I could've slugged you. Some guys would have. Most guys would. So keep these feeling of yours...well, work them out privately."

"It's too late, Coach."

"Oh shit."

"Yeah. See, we were at a dance, and we started making out in front of a bunch—"

"Holy shit, Joel! What in the hell were you thinking?"

"But nothing happened. It just happened too fast."

Coach began laughing. "Remember all your boxing pointers, then. Jesus!" He got up and walked Joel outside. In the front yard, Coach put a hand on Joel's shoulder. "Give this kid a chance to calm down. If he's your friend, he'll be your friend when this is over. But Jesus, Joel, maybe you should think about this. You're a virgin, aren't you?"

"Am I still a virgin? We had sex. I mean we—"

"Don't." Bill put up a restraining hand. "We're not supposed to be having this conversation. To answer your question, I guess you're not a virgin in the technical sense, okay? But that's none of my business. All I meant, kiddo, was if you were a virgin with girls, you'll feel different maybe...when you have something to compare to these...homosexual...feelings." He shook his head. "Jesus, kiddo. In front of people? That was stupid. I mean that as your friend."

"Thanks, Coach." They shook hands. Joel ran to the pickup feeling stunned. It was a relief to know that Coach was the kind of guy Joel thought he was. Coach didn't say what to do, he realized. Except keep it quiet. Give Tom a chance. But Coach did give him a name for his feelings. He called them homosexual. He would have to think about that.

* * * *

At supper Saturday night, Joel was quiet. His

parents wanted to know what was wrong, but he didn't want to talk about it. Like Coach Hoffins suggested, he decided to stay quiet for a while, at least until he could get a chance to talk with Tom. How could he tell them anything? Wouldn't they get upset thinking he may be crazy? A homosexual? Maybe even worse? He imagined, like Coach said, that his father might actually slug him, or want to, and that picture was painful. *But surely Dad would be like Coach*, he thought, looking at him puzzled, until he realized what he was doing and excused himself from the table.

Later, he sat on the porch, gazing mindlessly at the glow of light over the mountains to the west, where the gray-pink color sometimes remained long after sunset. His father came out and sat down by him. He picked up a piece of wood and turned it thoughtfully in his hands, looking at it for peculiar shapes he could whittle out of it at some future time.

"You've been acting strange all day."

"I know, Dad. I'm sorry. It's nothing."

"Anything your old man can help with?"

"No. Uh...no. Thanks."

"You and your girlfriend have a falling out?" He smiled sympathetically.

Girlfriend? Oh yeah. He knew what his father was talking about, thanks to Tom's underwear in the pickup. He managed a grin. "Yeah. Sort of, I guess. But it doesn't matter."

"Maybe." His father tossed the piece of wood across the lawn and it landed in the dark shadows of the rosebushes. "I don't know where the time goes, but I can see now you're almost a man. You'll be eighteen in July, am I right?"

"Huh?"

"Getting to like women?"

Joel lay back on his elbows, blocking his face from the porch light so his father couldn't see it.

"You trying to push your girlfriend into something she's not ready for? That what's got you pissed?"

Joel touched his father's shoulder. Oddly, it comforted him. What if he told him, now, just at this moment? "No. Me and Tom. We got into a fight. It's okay."

His father nodded, distracted, then frowned. "There's only one thing'd make me disappointed in you, Joel."

He felt a surge of guilt. "What?"

"If I'm wrong, well, that's good. But if I'm right, then I'd expect you better hold your temper. Never show disrespect to people, Son, and you won't do anything to be ashamed of. If you want something from somebody, and they aren't willing to part with it, that's their decision and your tough luck."

Joel looked at his father in the porch light. He was smiling, the wrinkles around his eyes permanently fixed from it. Joel sighed. "I do respect Tom, Dad. It's just an argument...you know? A fight about something. Wish I could tell you, but I'm not even sure what it is."

Douglas chuckled. He patted Joel on the head. "You'll work it out, I'm sure. You need me, I'll be here."

Douglas got up then and looked down at his son. Joel had sat up and resumed his crazy stare into the yard. He doubted that Joel was even still aware of him. He shook his head. *Always a surprise, that boy.*

Chapter 3

*For this cause God gave them up unto vile affections:
for even their women did change the natural use into that which is against nature:
And likewise also the men,
leaving the natural use of the woman,
burned in their lust one toward another;
men with men working that which is unseemly....*

Romans 1:26—27

Sunday, May 30

5:35 a.m.

Tom slept for fifteen hours and came awake in the predawn, feeling the wet slime of semen on his skin. It was drying like flour-and-water paste under the waistband of his pajamas and smelled doughy, too. He just shook his head, realizing it was no use. *Just one thing*, he thought. *I didn't ask for this. And damn it—I've tried to get over it.*

But that was a lie. *Joel. God forgive me, I love you! Why did you have to be so DAMNED willing?*

Even the wet dream was sexy. Maybe it was a

sin to harbor sexual thoughts, but was it a sin to have wet dreams? Could you stop one? Wasn't it like being a bed wetter, or did it have something to do with what you thought about all the time? Would his father say wet dreams were just nocturnal emissions, to be cleaned up and ignored—or what?

Come to think of it, wet dreams were never discussed in church. Masturbating had been. Sex between boys and girls, sodomy, even lustful thoughts had been. But never wet dreams.

Funny. He didn't remember ever having one when he spent the night with Joel sleeping innocently on his side of their bed.

6:30 a.m.

The telephone wouldn't ring.

As usual on a Sunday morning, Joel was in the living room waiting, pulling on his socks and boots. He had been there since a little after six, but this morning the telephone stayed silent. He stared at it. *Tom said we'd talk, didn't he?* Joel thought. Besides, Tom always called on Sundays to let him know if he would be busy with church stuff or not. Except today. And he wondered if it was because of what they had done. He laughed soundlessly, bitterly, the knot of doubt and hurt in his stomach like a live thing, lying on its back and kicking. *Fuckin' right it was. Tom was really upset.* He'd never seen him like that. He felt sorry for him, and hurt by him, and embarrassed. Then, Mrs. Allen said he was sick. He finished dressing and drank a cup of coffee, but still nothing. By seven o'clock, his parents were ready to go, and he got up reluctantly. He decided that he would go sightseeing with them today, although he was jumpy and nervous about leaving the house. By now Tom would be in church.

His mother had fixed a large basket of sandwiches and cold drinks, which Joel carried out to the pickup as he walked beside her. They were able to talk eye-to-eye, since he had inherited her shortness. She was only five-foot-five and he was five-seven. She stopped him when they were out on the porch. Standing with her back to the sun, she studied his face. He had to squint at her against the sun. "What, Mom?"

"You're sick, aren't you?" she said. Her eyes crinkled. Her mouth formed a little "O", and he had to smile at her, secretly thinking she looked like a cross between *I Love Lucy* and Miss Kitty, from *Gunsmoke*.

"No, I'm not sick," he said. "But Tom is, I think."

"Oh. That's too bad," she said. But she was satisfied. "Oh, my goodness! I forgot Mrs. —" She hurried off the porch, looking about her. "Douglas! Did you call Mrs. Tucker to let her know we'd be by for gas?"

He stuck the oil stick back into the engine and closed the hood. "Yes, ma'am, I did."

"Well, that's good. I just hate honking her out of bed."

Joel brought the basket to the pickup and handed it his father.

"Foothills okay?" Douglas asked.

"Floridas or Tres Hermanas?" Joel smiled weakly.

Douglas clapped him on the back. "Floridas. I thought we'd get a better view of the valley, and I like it this time of year. That okay?"

"Sounds great." But he was relieved, since the Florida mountains were the closest. Maybe he could get hold of Tom early in the afternoon.

They headed south past their property along

the west fence; his father was sitting on the passenger's side of the pickup, leaning out the window like a curious little kid. He preferred letting
Joel drive so he could get a good look at the country they passed. On this stretch of road, the Reece
farm was on the left, and the desert began directly
across it on the right-hand side. It was still cold
out and the open windows let in the early morning air. But none of them were cold, since they
were all used to the iciness of the desert. Even in
late May, the hour after sunup was even colder
than predawn.

Eva sat between the two men. She kept a good
eye on the road, since both Joel and Douglas were
busy looking out at the scenery. She and his father kept up a running dialogue about the families of whichever farm they happened to be passing at the time. Her work with the County Exten-
sion Service kept her in touch with many of the
other farmers' wives. During the summer, she and
her friends spent several days a month at the university in the next county taking courses on gar-
dening and agribusiness—what she called "my
careers." Joel listened, but this morning he kept
his thoughts to himself. He didn't need to look to
see if they were talking to him. If they said something funny, he laughed when they did, but he felt
like crying or cussing—anything to relieve the tension.

Along the edges of the road, the weeds and
sand blurred by, creating green and brown stripes
that ran along beside them, but the farther he
looked away from the moving pickup, the slower
the fields passed. Toward the east, dominating the
land, the Floridas didn't move at all. They followed
the pickup across the miles the way the sun did.
A moving vehicle could eventually outdistance

them, but always, in this massive desert, as soon as the traveler passed one range of mountains, another would appear on the horizon. Joel slowed at the intersection and turned east toward the Columbus Highway. This was the same route that he had traveled every day for eight years on the way to the county school. Across the road, they stopped at the Pay and Save Store for gas. The sun was well above the horizon now, beginning to turn white against the bleached-out blue of the sky. Everything was cast in stark detail.

Douglas got out of the pickup and began pumping gas. Mrs. Tucker, the owner, came out of the store, shading her eyes.

"Mornin', Eva! It's been a long time!" she greeted Eva happily.

Eva got out of the pickup and hugged her. Then Mrs. Tucker peered into the pickup at Joel. Her old wrinkled face smiled at him. "Eva, this ain't your son!"

Joel grinned. "It's me, ma'am."

She came around to his side and Joel politely got out. She stood with her back to the sun and peered up into his face. "My! My! You're a pretty one now, aren't you?" she cooed. She turned her cheek up to him and stood on tiptoe. Embarrassed, Joel leaned down and kissed her. Her cheek was so soft against his lips that he could barely feel it. When he straightened up, he saw that her eyes had filled with bright tears. She was smiling. "You know my boy was killed last year, Joel?" She continued to smile. "I miss him so bad, sometimes. I hope you make your parents happy, Son."

Douglas finished filling the tank and paid Mrs. Tucker. "He's a good boy, Ina. Thanks for opening up for us. I hope it wasn't any trouble."

She waved an old hand stiffly through the cold

air, clutched her sweater about her, and smiled. "No! Proud to. I was up already." She pecked Douglas on the cheek and turned around. Joel watched her move slowly back to her store. These days, she didn't sell much food—just bread and canned goods—and when school was in session, candy bars and soda pop to the kids. Even when Joel was in first grade, Mrs. Tucker was an old woman. Her son was at least in his fifties when he died, but Joel thought that to her, he would always be her boy. She was a fine old lady, though, and he had always liked her. As Joel watched her small frame disappear through the darkened door of her store, he saw how much more stooped and thin she was, and he remembered the spry, laughing woman she had been, remembered the time she'd had the upper grades over in the back of her store, where her son had a pool table set up. She had filled it with snacks and brought the big, color television from her house so the kids could watch the astronauts fly around in space. She'd gone down in the last few years, Joel saw, but, like most people in this part of the county, she hung on to her old ways, her old property, not understanding the changes going on all about her.

They turned onto the Columbus Highway and headed south again. But now the terrain was rougher. The Floridas were east of them about ten miles, and the land on the east side of the highway was rockier—too rocky for farming, but still good for cattle. The grass in the foothills was more lush than anywhere else in the county because of the way the mountains collected the rain clouds as they moved toward them. Some of the biggest ranches in the county belonged to the ranchers who owned the Florida foothills. Out here, it was easy to see thirty or forty miles down the highway

toward Columbus, New Mexico, and its sister vil-
lage, Palomas, Mexico, just across the border. The
highway went straight for a while like the railroad
tracks that ran beside it and seemed to disappear
into the Tres Hermanas Mountains due south of
them. Douglas pointed out some of the farms and
ranches along the way. They didn't often get out
in this part of the county, and Joel thought it
looked a little more dismal than the desert near
their farm. The fields were larger, planted with only
one crop, and not rotated very often. "That'll ruin
the land for sure," Douglas often said.

They turned east toward the Floridas, finally,
onto a gravel road that led high up into the foothills. This close, the mountains were craggy and
ancient looking. Juniper bushes hung onto a pre-
carious life in the cracks of rocks high up, where
it was impossible to climb. The rocks were so
cracked from the dry sun and cold nights that rock
slides were common from hikers. Very few people
ventured into these barren mountains, since they
offered sparse deer hunting. But Joel remembered
the field trip the upper grades at school made up
here one year.

They had borrowed a tractor and a flatbed
trailer, making an all-day trip for the twenty or so
students, and he had thought how close it felt on
the back of the trailer, to be sitting shoulder to
shoulder with Nicky and the guys, joking around
and singing the silly songs they had learned from
Miss Bussay in chorus. When the school principal
had said "a field trip," he had imagined that they
would be free to roam all over, collecting plant sam-
ples, then taking them back to the school and using the microscope to study them and learning how
they survived in the desert without irrigation. His
favorite book at home was a book on cacti his

mother gave him from one of her college classes. The desert by his own house was lush with mesquites and yucca, some round, flat cacti, creosote bushes and sparse, wicked grasses. He had been excited to be going so far into the foothills that day. But the principal and the eighth-grade teacher made them stay around the flat rocks and bare desert within a few hundred yards of the trailer.

He couldn't remember much else about that day—except for the incident that left him troubled for several days afterwards. He'd been so damned embarrassed. He laughed at himself, thinking of it. It didn't take much to excite a bunch of guys going through puberty, eagerly comparing the growth of hairs on their crotches every few weeks. Earlier that year, sitting out underneath the trees that ran along the school's football field, Joel and a few of the guys had learned to jerk off. They had been introduced to the technique by Kenneth Stroud, who was by far the most sexual guy Joel had ever seen. The circle jerking was a pitiful affair, most of the guys not yet matured enough to "come," and only a few of them had stayed with Kenneth, when he got them to shuck their pants and form a circle. One or two guys watched and giggled. Bill Crawford, Nicky Coleman, Leo Johnson even, and Joel stayed in the circle. Kenneth showed them his cum, which he caught in the palm of his hand and called "jizzum." Joel managed to get off a few drops, then got up quickly and dressed. Then the day of the field trip, Kenneth got Cliff and Bill and Joel and a few other guys to watch Aileen Parker and Betsy Weller undress in the shadow of a large boulder and rub each other. Their nakedness captivated Joel. Their tits were firm like muscles on a guy's chest and although

not yet very big, were kind of nice. He liked that.
But then Aileen opened her legs wide and parted
herself, revealing a bright-pink area, turning the
bright-eyed boys into giggling, excited monkeys.
She let Kenneth rub it in front of the other guys,
and Joel had turned away, embarrassed for her.

He had left the rest of them and happened on
Leo Johnson, who had been watching the whole
thing from a place he'd been hiding in. Leo said it
was kind of sad that the girls would let the guys
see them naked. Joel agreed, and found that Leo
was the only guy who seemed to feel the same way.

He shivered suddenly, remembering Leo. He
hadn't thought about that particular shared feeling with him in a long time. Everybody at school
laughed at Leo. Then, in high school, the teasing
grew worse. If you wanted to see a real queer, the
guys said, just find Leo Johnson. Poor Leo. Joel
had always felt sorry for him, had tried to be his
friend, but Joel thought that Leo caused most of
his own problems, preferring to play with the girls
instead of joining the guys out by the football field.
The teachers who made the boys in the three upper grades play football and baseball wouldn't allow anything bad to happen, but Leo was afraid or
something, and he was constantly screwing up
when they played. He was always chosen last on
any team, and when the school played sports
against the other country schools, the teachers let
him work the concession stand with the girls. Joel
had always been confused by how Leo could be
such a sissy, considering that his four brothers
were real toughs. And, of course, the other students could be cruel if a guy didn't fit in.

I wonder what they think of me now? He
thought about Jeannie Lynn again, remembering
that she had always hated Leo. She was the one

who started calling him Leota, a name that had stuck like glue from the day Jeannie dreamed it up. And she was a hard one to figure, too. She was damn near as tough as any guy at school, but you wouldn't know it looking at her long, thick, blond hair and her tight, prim little waist.

Then he wondered, *Is that why Tom is so upset? He thinks we're like Leo Johnson?* This question disturbed Joel, because that is precisely what they were like, if it were true about Leo being queer—*homosexual*, Joel corrected himself, trying out the new word.

* * * *

They found a shady spot by an old barn and Joel brought the pickup to a stop. This area had been long abandoned and the barn was leaning wearily toward the mountains. They were high enough in the foothills now that he could see the great depression of land that formed the Mimbres Valley. Toward the northwest, the town was a glittering splash of silvers and browns, surrounded by green fields. He could definitely tell where the farms began and the desert ended this time of year; the crops lent a green haze to the usual browns, blues and violets of the terrain. Douglas stood on the flat surface of a rock in the shade of the old barn, one hand resting against the wall, the other shading his eyes. "Hey, Son, look over there." He pointed west; his arm made an arc along an invisible line toward the mountains north of town. "See that faint, black line running along there?"

Joel followed the movement of his father's hand with his eyes. "That jagged line or the straight one?"

"The straight one's just the highway to Silver City. The jagged one. When your mother and I first came here back in '45, that was a flowing river."

Eva laid out the lunch on the back of the pickup in the shade, and Douglas went on explaining that the farmers who settled the lower valley drilled wells until the river dried out. "Of course, nobody depends on it," he said, "and I guess they never did. Back then the town was an eyesore, a coal stop for the railroads. Just a bunch of storefronts, most of them saloons or cat houses."

Eva was sitting next to Douglas. She nodded. "My goodness, Joel, when your father brought me out here and showed me the place, I thought he'd lost his mind. We had Kathy and Tricia, and I was pregnant with Daniel Dean. I almost up and ran back to Texas. But we stuck it out." She looked wistful for a moment and patted Douglas on the knee. Joel wondered if she was thinking about little Daniel and the other brother he'd never seen, both born dead in 1946, Daniel in January and the other one in June, so premature that they hadn't even given it a name. Even though he was born in 1947, that time was ancient history to him. He had never thought much about what his parents were like when they were young. He had always felt so settled in their home and their farm, he'd never thought it hadn't always been there.

"It was hard back then?" He squinted at his mother.

"Joel, you just wouldn't believe it. We came out here with everything we owned. The land was nothing but mesquite and yucca. The year before you were born, your father helped me get started on my garden, after your Grandmother Reece died and I lost the first baby. Then we met a lot of other families who'd moved out here: the Hotchkisses, the Strouds, the Paulks, the Crawfords."

"We got together, it seems like, for dances every Saturday night," Douglas continued for her. "Not

your kind, Joel, just get-togethers where the wives
brought all kinds of food and some of the people
brought their guitars and fiddles. Men pitched in
with harvesting and crews would go around thresh-
ing beans and sacking 'em up in the fields. There
were a few house-raisings, too. A crew of men could
put up the shell of a house in a day. You know, it
was people like us, the farmers, who tamed this
valley. Pretty soon, people were moving in by the
droves. The merchants, the churches," he chuckled, "just sprang up like weeds."

Joel ate his sandwich, listening to them remi-
nisce. Families. Wives and children. He'd never
thought of the passage of time for his parents, them
in their younger days starting out, Kathy and
Tricia, and himself—children they hoped to pass
on a heritage to. And even though his sisters had
children now, they all said Joel would be the one
to pass on the family name. But now he wasn't so
sure. The Reeces were silent for a while. Joel had
been told many times about his parents' desire for
a large family, like the Strouds and the Johnsons
had, and his father had often shaken his head
sadly when he and Joel worked together in the
field, telling him a farm like theirs needed a family. "You know we could handle a dozen children
on this place, Son...." He felt weird out here with
them suddenly, hearing in the wind through these
unchangeable, old mountains, the ghosts of all the
homesteaders who came, planning and building,
from one generation to the next, and he realized
he was changing right before their eyes: if not visibly, then under the skin, already able to think
that maybe he had something in common with Leo
Johnson.

* * * *

After waking from the wet dream, Tom got up wearily and showered and dressed for church. He wanted to call Joel, as he usually did, and apologize for the shabby way he had treated him, especially since he had come to a conclusion. *I wanted it to happen—with him. It was my fault.* No big secret, and probably, to Joel, no big deal. And then he remembered with regret the hurt look Joel got on his face. It was quick, like the snap of a flashcube, bright and blinding, then gone in a split second, leaving the image of Joel's face on his retina.

Now, sitting in church, staring blankly ahead instead of paying attention to his father's sermon (which wasn't making much sense, anyway), he could only think of Joel's hurt.

When his father shouted suddenly, he snapped awake, feeling disoriented. He began to listen.

"...and think on this! Imagine that you have no church, and yet you still have all the problems that come from living. Without your spiritual home here on Earth, how would you know if you are lost? HOW!" His father stepped away from the microphone and spread his arms heavenward, then waved his arms like a conductor. "My friends, rise. Let us pray for our lives...."

In the silence that followed his prayer, the preacher disappeared through a doorway. The congregation began moving slowly through the vestibule. Tom had stayed seated, unable to believe that he had missed the entire sermon, amazed at his own confusion. He kept his head bowed, faintly aware of the people slipping passed. When he looked up, the chapel was empty, and Joel and he were standing by the lectern. Tom could see himself, angry and confused: Joel, confused and hurt. He saw Joel reach out, saw himself pull away.

Then footsteps echoed in the vestibule. Tom

was startled, hoping and afraid it was Joel. He faced the doors, saw them open. In the splash of white, noon daylight stood a figure, a slim sliver of black against the blinding sun.

"Tom?"

"Yeah?"

"We're waiting. Boy you look funny." Tom sighed and went toward the figure whose ugly, clipped voice he recognized as Paul Romaine's.

"Waiting?"

"Yes, Brother. The whole bus."

"Right," Tom said, resigned. "A wonderful trip to the City of Rocks State Park. Our Full Gospel Fellowship cookout."

His sarcasm was lost on Paul, who pushed him eagerly. "Yeah. Fellowship under the lesser lights," he sang happily.

Joel had once joked with Tom, calling it the Full Gospel Fullashit something or other, and Tom laughed at Paul's enthusiasm, surprised at himself for thinking that, right now, full of shit seemed appropriate.

Sitting next to him, uninvited, on the bus, Paul jabbered in Tom's ear while the rest of the teenagers filled the other ear alternately with church songs and camping songs as they bumped out of town. Tom pasted himself against the window, watching the people on the street turn to look as the bus passed. With the window shut, the town was silent and, in the heat, shimmered brightly and disappeared, quickly giving way to the desert north of town.

Paul jabbed Tom hard in the ribs. "Hey! What's wrong with you? Aren't you excited?"

Tom dragged his eyes away from the window, disgusted, but managed a weak smile. He shrugged. "It's hot's all."

"Just think! We've got all summer for things like this!" Paul said, excitedly.

Tom looked closely at Paul for the first time in weeks. Paul was, ostensibly, his best friend at the church. His face was skinny, his mouth was sharp and beak-like, his teeth barely covered by thin, tight lips that seemed to stretch and dry out. His tongue constantly darted out to lick them, and he had a nasty habit of grimacing, too, curling his lips and baring his tiny rodent's teeth. His mousy, brown hair was clipped short and he used hair oil to excess, giving his head a tortured, ascetic look.

Paul was so eager he was practically sitting in Tom's lap, leaning forward, talking right into his face, filling the air around them with an oniony, sour-milk smell. His right arm lay over the metal bar behind the bus seat. Tom felt crowded. He groaned inwardly but kept smiling weakly. "Yeah. Great. Could you scoot over a little, Paul? It's kinda hot, okay?"

Paul moved an inch. "Did you know your father was going to do that today?"

"What?" Tom was intrigued. He turned away from the window and shoved Paul farther away, then forced himself to fill up the space. Immediately he felt less put upon.

"His sermon. Daddy says your father can get away with anything. And today he proved it, you know. The church members should have been insulted, but they weren't. Not by your father. He's got a real command of that church."

Tom was confused. "Why? What happened?"

"You were there. Don't you know?"

"I wouldn't ask if I knew, would I?" Tom said, irritated.

Paul only looked at him and shook his head. "What's wrong with you, Brother? Your father deliberately...." Paul stopped. "Never mind. It was a great sermon and you slept through it, I guess."

"Okay. So I was daydreaming."

"Yes, Tom." Paul seemed angry. "You know, you've got to live up to people's expectations. You should hear the women cackle about you. They think you're so beautiful, it's almost irreverent. You're a prince to them. You've got to keep their trust. It's your duty...and you fall asleep in church!"

Tom turned away, again, looked out the window at the beginning traces of greenery as the bus began climbing into the foothills. The mountains north of town had grown closer and now, instead of pale, featureless, violet blue, they were taking on rugged faces. He pulled the window open and traces of coolness spread over him, instantly drying his sweaty scalp, sweetening and cleansing the stuffy air of the bus. He shivered involuntarily. He looked around the bus and caught the eyes of some of the others, surprised that he didn't know very many names. He turned back to Paul.

"I've been here almost a year, you know? You'd think I would know everybody, but I don't. Not really. There are people on this bus I don't think I've even seen."

Paul leaned forward and spoke in a low voice. "Yeah, well, it's no wonder. You're so distant. You keep yourself aloof. You only hang around with the men's fellowship on Sundays and hardly ever take the lead like you should. You know we've got all kinds of activities. All the elders' sons, me included, more or less have to fill in the gaps you leave. We need you, Tom, but you're just never available."

"Well, you know I hang around with Joel all the time. We're pretty close." He regretted saying that, and immediately felt like he had insulted Joel. *After the way I treated him yesterday*, he thought.

"Yes...your friend. Joel Reece, the heathen."

Anger rose in Tom's chest and he glared at Paul. "Heathen? How the hell do you know what he's like?"

Paul looked shocked, then grinned slyly. "Your foul mouth is a good example, Brother. He's a bad influence on you. Face it, Tom. He's not a member of our church, or any other, for that matter. And so he's a heathen."

"That's stupid!" Tom said hotly. "Joel is my best friend. We've got a lot in common, and he's taught me a lot about things."

Paul snickered. "He's all brawn, Tom." He tapped his forehead. "Too much sunshine on that farm of his."

"Joel and his father run more than a section of farmland, Paul. They do it by themselves, and they make a lot of money. He's brawny because he has to be, but he knows business well enough to make it on his own right now. He would surprise you how smart he is."

Paul looked skeptical. "So he makes passing grades in ag. Big deal! Can he cite Bible verse from memory? Can he make A's in English? Does he know anything outside of this little, hick town?"

"Do you?" Tom asked.

"I've read about lots of places," he sniffed. "Just because I haven't been to Europe doesn't mean I don't know about it." He grimaced and turned away, licking his lips.

Tom settled back in the seat, suddenly with enough room to breathe. He closed his eyes and let the rhythm of the bus rock him into a short nap.

* * * *

Tom was laughing along with the rest of the Full Gospel Fellowship that emerged from the bus when it parked beside a mammoth rock at the park. He imagined how Joel would react to the way the group was dressed—*most of us in our Sunday best and getting ready for a picnic!*

He looked around, smiling. The City of Rocks State Park dominated the top of a large rise of ground. From where he stood he could see down into the Mimbres Valley where the town of Common lay, utterly invisible in the haze of distance. It was almost forty miles away, and yet, bright glints of sunlight cracked off moving vehicles down there, themselves invisible. To the west, the desert dominated and rolled into eternity. To the east and north, the mountains rose over them with small, shadow-lit valleys between.

It was early afternoon and seemed much cooler. The laughter and the singing blew thinly away in the wide spaces. Tom pulled off his jacket and stuffed it through a window of the bus. He remembered his tie and threw it in after the jacket, then looked around for Paul, thought better of it, and struck out by himself away from the crowd.

He missed Joel; he would see so much more if Joel were to point it out. Then he felt lost and confused. It wouldn't be the same now, anyway, would it? Not after....

He moved naturally to the "city," composed of monstrous, free-standing boulders, wind-sculpted giants that rose over him like buildings. The caretakers of the park had even put up street signs with names like Mesquite Avenue, Rattlesnake Drive, and Piñon Trail, and in small, open areas were all sorts of picnic tables, portable toilets and, here and there, a drinking fountain. The city was large enough that he soon lost sight of the others and found himself alone. The wind sang though the rocks, changing tones over and over, like indistinct voices in other rooms. He came upon a small cave formed by two walls of rock that had fallen together. Inside, an adult could stand upright.

He went inside and brushed off a place to sit down. "I wish you were here, Joel," he said aloud. "I'm sorry." Tears began forming under his lashes, and he forced himself to stop thinking.

The cave had been visited by others who had scratched or painted their names and dates and messages on the walls. "Tina loves Louis," he read. "Killer was here 10/29/59," claimed one. "I fucked Billy here," said another. The floor was littered with plastic cups and broken glass; there was a sock and a wadded pair of Fruit of the Loom underwear; a piece of paper that once held writing was no longer readable; even the blue lines were mere ghosts.

From inside, he had a view of other hills with smaller rock formations. Suburbs, he supposed, then laughed. This was a good place to explore sometime with Joel. *Yeah. Tom…. Listen to yourself! With Joel, with Joel, with Joel!*

He left the cave and walked aimlessly through the streets. Other campers occupied some of the remoter parts of the city; occasionally, the high, strained voices of children wafted to him on the air. Sometimes he rounded a rock and came upon other explorers, some of them able to climb to the tops of rocks, giving them clear views of the area. After about an hour he felt better than he had since waking up in the pickup with Joel. The knot in his stomach had loosened its grip. He began to feel hungry and decided to rejoin his group. But he had no idea which direction to walk.

Ahead of him was a large stand of rocks; the tallest of them would provide a clear view of most of the city. He walked toward it, looking for a way to get on top. On one side the face was a sheer cliff. He made his way around it slowly because of the fissures and rocks in his path. The back side of the rock was curved and pocked with large holes and shelves. He began climbing and raising himself from foothold to foothold. Then, near the top, he pulled himself up and found himself staring at the bare buttocks of a boy and the legs entwining them; the couple was oblivious to him at first, panting and sighing in rapid motions. But, when Tom tried to let himself down without being heard, the two sat up. Tom sank below the edge of the rock, hoping they hadn't seen, but they crawled to the edge and peered over at him. Tom hung onto his footholds and stared up into the faces of two guys; he felt like a small, desert creature clinging to the side and wished he could just skitter away.

"Sorry," he croaked.

The two looked at each other and laughed. One of them licked his lips and grinned impishly. "Hey, man, it's okay. Join us if you want!"

Tom's ears burned with embarrassment; his head rang, barely allowing him to think. He sagged on the side of the rock, feeling weak and nauseated. "Sorry," he said again. Tearing his face away from the two guys, he allowed himself to drop the rest of the way to the ground.

He found the road running along the edge of the City of Rocks and followed it until he came upon the bus and the others. They had hardly moved from the spot where the bus parked. He joined them silently. His heart was pounding. He was unable to erase the vision of the two guys staring at him over the edge of the rock. Young guys, maybe 15, Tom thought. Inviting him for sex as easily as they would offer him a drink of water, their faces clear and innocent; but it was their nakedness in the stark sunlight shimmering against a crystal-blue sky that Tom could not dispel. His breath was short, and he wondered frantically if his face could reveal what he'd seen, the shock of it, the dreadful thirst—but the group had a fire going and were enjoying themselves. They seemed completely unaware that he'd even been gone. He helped himself to a hot-dog and a warm Coke in a paper cup and sat on one of the rocks that ringed the campfire.

* * * *

The afternoon faded into twilight, and the air grew cold. Tom retrieved his jacket from the bus and joined in the singing and praying that followed the meal. Afterwards, as night came on and the fire died down to glowing embers and the wind whipped orange sparks into the black sky around them, he and Paul and the others began packing up the supplies. In the darkness, he carried an ice chest full of sloshing water and ice cubes to the rear of the bus. He dumped the water from the chest, watching it soak rapidly into the sand. The rocks at his feet reflected silver light from somewhere and he looked up to see if the moon was out.

Overhead, the sky blazed with the silver brilliance of the stars, billions of them, it seemed, radiating enough light to form a white froth across the black velvet of space. "That's the Milky Way!" he whispered in wonder, seeing it so brilliant for the first time in his life. He followed it across the sky until it faded into blackness where individual stars burned brighter than the rest, much closer, or so huge, the unfathomable distance could not extinguish them.

"Lesser lights," observed Paul in a flat, unemotional voice as he passed by, breaking the spell.

Tom looked down at the ice chest forgotten in his hands and slid it into the storage area. He climbed aboard and took the same seat as before, accepting with the same resignation Paul's company, and prepared for his endless prattle. How much more interesting Joel was. How much richer the feelings that he evoked than the thin, worn-out phrases from Genesis. *Lesser Lights my hind foot*, Tom thought. On the trip back he tried to recapture the awe that had filled him as he gazed at the sky, but his imagination had shrunk to the limits of the inside of the bus. He thought of the two guys on the rock, wondering how they felt, doing that. Where they lived. Did they live together? Were there more of them? Had he really seen any of it? *I know what Joel would say*, he thought, then dismissed it, feeling lonely. He listened to the soft, tired discussions going on, the occasional, airy beginnings of a song. He felt smothered by Paul's contentment with all this rigmarole, Paul's reduction of everything to biblical clichés, his comment about lesser lights. He felt trapped, being a preacher's son. He'd no more wanted to waste a Sunday evening with these people than Joel would, but until his father gave the word, he could look forward to more of the same.

The bus stopped at the church and Tom walked home. Although it wasn't late, the lights were off in the house and only a pale, blue glow from his parents' bedroom shone in the dark. He sat on the front porch and tried to see the Milky Way again, but the street lights blocked its fragile light. The sky was a black void where only a few stars twinkled dimly. Cars passing back and forth along Main Street sounded like faint rushes of wind; occasionally, the cracking growl of a motorcycle broke the night.

Paul's reminder of his duty to the church eventually settled in his thoughts like a bad smell. He tried to consider the idea without distaste, but Paul's eager face, full of tiny rodent's teeth, kept intruding. He let himself into the house and stood in the darkened living room, hearing the loud clicking of the grandfather clock. Standing by his father's desk, he let his hand touch the dial face of the telephone, feeling the cold metal of the dial. He wanted to call Joel, but knew that his voice would disrupt the silence, would wake his father.

He went to bed reluctantly. Joel would still be up. It would be easy to talk things out now. The guilt had shrunk to the size of a small fist in his stomach, and he allowed himself to recall him and Joel together in the pickup after the dance, thinking also of the two guys at the park.

Chapter 4

Tom woke up with an erection. He often did, but he never let himself acknowledge it or touch himself down there when his penis was in that state. He usually got up and showered immediately, from a habit developed over years of practice at ignoring his private flesh. Wet dreams were one thing, but to handle himself in the genitals other than to wash and urinate was definitely a sin. The Catholics called it self-abuse.

Joel called it whacking off, jacking off, beating your meat, pounding your pole—anything but its real name. Tom called it masturbation this morning when he touched his erect penis. It jerked, and a thrill of intense feeling washed through his thighs. His hand shook with the excitement he felt, and just this once, he threw back the covers and pulled his pajama bottoms off.

He ran his hands over his nakedness. His nipples were hard. In the pale, purple-gray light of dawn, his flesh looked smooth and hairless, like Joel's, except for his legs, which were lightly covered with black hairs. He looked at his erection and he remembered Joel holding it, his hands on

him in the dark, slow absorbing touches full of
warmth and just the slightest scratchy feeling from
the calluses on his palm and fingertips. He remembered Joel's hands the most. During these past
few months in the maddening, unconscious way
he had of allowing his hands to touch, Joel had
made him feel weak. But this morning, he didn't
care. He lay back then, allowing himself the freedom to feel the delicious rushes through the shaft
and his thighs and stomach, and seeing the
splashes of semen, he dipped one finger into the
mass of it on his abdomen and tasted it, surprised
that it was merely a little salty, a little sweet.

Shame and fear hit him then like the after-
shock of a bomb. Now the cold, unwelcome liquid
began running off his stomach, threatening to stain
the sheets. He looked around for something to
clean himself with. He wiped one hand across his
stomach, getting his fingers slick; they smelled
faintly like yeast. He grabbed a box of tissue on
his desk, jerked several tissues from it and cleaned
himself.

He showered a long time, allowing the hot water to wash him, allowing it also to wash the shame
away. Scrubbing briskly, he soaped and washed
his genitals; and for the first time, he explored his
private flesh with clean, soapy hands, listening to
his fingers...and for the second time in his life, he
masturbated.

Twice as much shame didn't feel any worse,
he discovered as he dressed. He gathered up the
wet tissues, made his bed. As usual, he had wak-
ened early. The sun broke through his window,
casting a yellow-pink glow over the room. He put
on his socks and shoes and went to breakfast.

His father and mother were sitting at the breakfast table. His father had finished eating and was

sipping coffee from a china cup and, when Tom
sat down, his father set his cup down on the sau-
cer. It clinked precisely.

His mother got up and prepared a plate of eggs,
toast and bacon. She set it in front of Tom. "Good
morning, dear." She sat back down and poured
her husband another cup, then folded her hands
primly into her lap. She always sat straight with
her shoulders barely resting on the back of her
chair. She was wearing an ordinary house dress,
but her prim manner, her flawless hairdo, her
clean, sparse makeup suggested that she and her
husband were going out, no doubt visiting members of the church.

"Good morning, Mother...Father."

His father looked directly at him, his face stern,
as usual, and allowed only the faintest smile to
play about his mouth. It disappeared when he
spoke. "Thomas, you enjoyed the outing?" It was
not a question.

"Yes, Father," Tom said. He quickly bowed his
head and mouthed the words of a quick prayer.
He began eating as if he were at a formal banquet,
with one hand resting in his lap.

"And you're no longer sick?"

Tom swallowed a bite of egg, felt it crawl down
his throat and stick somewhere in his chest. He
drank orange juice, trying to force the lump down.
He felt it slide reluctantly into place. He wiped his
mouth with his napkin. "I'm fine, thank you, Sir."

"I'm still waiting to hear about it. Saturday
morning you were hysterical. Yesterday you
seemed to be in a daze, yet you haven't said anything, you haven't asked me to counsel you, Son."

"I'm sorry." Tom tried to relax, but his knees
began shaking under the table. His hands shook
very slightly under his father's powerful gaze. He

wanted to sit up and frankly tell him to mind his own business. "I'm okay." He glanced toward his mother, but she deliberately concentrated on her husband's face.

"I'm waiting for a reasonable explanation."

"I don't know what to say. Joel took me to a dance Friday night, but I'm the one who suggested it."

"A dance?"

"We didn't stay very long, because...."

"What? Something happened. You got upset. Over what?"

"Just the dance."

"Nonsense, sonny boy." His father looked at his wife as if to say *Listen to that, will you!* Tom hated the way his father's profile looked. Like a slab of meat with just the bead of one eye showing. But the look was gone in a second as he swiveled his head around to face Tom fully again.

Tom jerked.

"I know that was wrong, and what happened, I mean, what I saw...you know, drinking, fighting." His voice sounded lame, like a child telling tales, and he shut up.

His father's face remained unchanged. "God only knows what kind of wickedness took place. You could have been upset, Thomas, but you were hysterical. And I happen to think your behavior needs a rational explanation."

He watched his father across the table, but kept his head down while he toyed with his egg. He attempted another bite, but as he brought it to his mouth, its bland smell made him almost gag. He put down his fork and folded his hands in his lap like his mother's. His father was composing some sort of statement, rule, something that would further demonstrate his power as the head of the household.

"Is the Reece boy the sort you should be hanging around with, then?"

"Oh, sure, Father! It was my fault." Relief flooded through him. "Joel is a great guy."

"I'm not so sure about that. If he doesn't respect your—"

"I said it was my fault, Father!" Tom felt his stomach lurch, realizing he'd just snapped at his father. He saw his father's face become angry. His lips were quivering as though a nerve was jerking involuntarily, and his dark eyes held Tom's like a clenched fist holds the seat of an errant child when the parent is angry enough to hit.

"You have just bought yourself home detention, young man!" his father shouted. "Grounded until I say otherwise!"

Tom sighed. "May I call Joel, so he won't wonder what's wrong? We were supposed to—"

"No, you may not, Thomas!"

"Yes, sir."

* * * *

After breakfast his parents left the house, leaving it quiet. He did the breakfast dishes, looking out the window over the sink, looking at the dark, brick walls of the church across the way. When they had moved to Common nine months before, the Allen family quickly demonstrated to the congregation their active interest in the church, and for all their strictness at home, Tom respected his parents. They really did work hard to make a decent home. In several cases, their visits had brought whole families into the fold, where before, only the wife or a child had been attending.

They had lived in Common only since the end of the previous August, and until this summer, Tom's weekdays had been spent in school in his senior year. Rarely did he have so much free time during the week, and until last Friday, he had intended to spend most of the summer on Joel's farm, but now things were upset. *Because of me...because of Father, too!* he thought, feeling resentment rise in his chest, feeling like an idiot for losing his temper at the breakfast table.

He felt a relentless stirring of sexuality, too (Joel would say "horny"), which was directed back to Joel, the masturbation in the shower and his bed, the boys at the park; but drumming in his head were passages from the Bible he knew by heart: "Sins of the flesh," "reprobate mind," "unnatural lusts." And on top of that he had committed the sin of omission, talking to his father under his oppressive gaze, wanting only to get him off his back.

He cleaned his room and shined his scuffed wingtips, placing them neatly back in his closet. He rearranged his clothes, dividing his dress clothes from his few casual ones. He was wearing a T-shirt and a pair of Levi's. And in spite of the nagging tugs of shame about masturbating, he was nowhere near as crazy as Saturday. He felt clean, even. It was strange, finally yielding to sex, bursting through some membrane of self-discovery; it forever alters you, he thought. He stood in front of the mirror, staring at his reflection to see if it showed.

He looked into his own eyes. The dark irises reflected miniatures of his face. He looked frankly at himself. What would Joel see? He felt his looks couldn't compare with Joel's. He was the most beautiful guy he'd ever seen, who had so captured his secret feelings that he had forced their friendship. Even in this small town of a couple thousand people, he and Joel had nothing in common, and Tom had no pretext for even meeting him at school. But then Joel had responded, *and what did he see in me, if it wasn't the same longing*? He shivered with pleasure, remembering.

For days after first seeing Joel, Tom had followed him around school, keeping a safe distance to avoid arousing his attention. When he saw Joel coming down the hallway, he would arrange his position in the crowd to be pushed near him. He'd excuse himself, or make some trite comment. In a few more days, he was talking to him.

Joel began showing recognition and occasionally smiled. At first, he had looked surprised to be called by name, and then one day he passed by Tom at the drinking fountain next to the gym. Tom felt a *whump* on his back and turned around to Joel's wide, toothy grin; Joel had hit him with a rolled-up towel with gym clothes in it, and the air was slightly tinged with the smell of sweat and Zest from the damp towel. "Hey, man, what's your name? I keep seeing you around and you already know mine."

Tom allowed himself to look frankly into Joel Reece's eyes which, in the dull, shadowed hallway, were soft and smiling. It was the boldest, frankest stare he had allowed himself. He told him his name. "I met you in September at the Junior-Senior slave banquet."

Joel's eyes brightened and he threw his arm around Tom's shoulder. "I remember, now! Yeah. How are you, man?" and Joel had walked him down the hall as freely and innocently as if Tom had been a girl. Nobody paid the least attention to them, Tom realized. Joel walked with an easy, assured grace and seemed to dominate the space around them, so no one would think it was odd. Nope, nothing wrong here, except Tom was quietly dying from love and embarrassment. This was exactly what he'd often seen in the section of the school near the vocational shops and the agriculture classrooms—Joel animated and joking, cussing and aggressive with the other guys from the country, so much different than the timid friends that Tom had always made. Joel became an obsession. Joel would throw his arm easily over a guy's shoulders and sort of hug him, completely unconscious of the sexual arousal it might cause. And it was this very unconscious, physical closeness that Tom craved and got, that October afternoon.

Joel kept his arm around him and walked him to the east end of the hallway, which led out to the bus parking lot. They burst through the double glass doors and Joel finally took his arm off. "You wanna go somewhere later, man? I have chores, but I can get back into town for supper. We can grab burgers or something."

"Yeah! Hey, that's great. Sure!" And Tom gave him the address. His fingers were trembling as he pulled out a pen and tore a page from his notebook. His mind was racing. Telephone number... address. *Should I mention Father being a preacher?* "I'll be on the porch waiting. What time?"

Joel grinned and began walking away. Tom watched the sashay of his hips and nearly died of excitement. "Give me a couple hours?" Joel called over his shoulder.

"Okay!" Tom called, and turned back toward the school. He bumped into Paul Romaine.

"Why were you talking to Joel Reece? He's a clodhopper!"

"Just because I was," Tom said curtly, feeling annoyed with Paul, as usual.

Tom began to walk away, but Paul followed close behind. "I saw you walk out with him like he was your best...like you were his date or something."

"We do have a date, Paul," he said with satisfaction.

Tom stood in the middle of his room and realized he'd been staring at Joel's picture. He went over to it and picked it up. "I messed things up this time, Joel. But I promise we're still friends."

* * * *

In the afternoon, the Elder and Mrs. Romaine were invited over, which also meant that Paul would be there, but Tom didn't mind. When Paul came, he would suggest that they invite the usual guys to study for the Bible class on Wednesday. *That should satisfy Father, too*, he thought. *If I can stand it.*

But killing the afternoon took time. Several times after the guys got there, Tom secretly read the clock on the nightstand by his bed. Paul mopped up on Tom's attention, as usual, and ignored the others. Kevin Todd, an elder's son, Mike St. Germaine, a deacon's son, and little Pete Thompson, the shiest kid Tom had ever met, spent the afternoon in his room. They studied a little, Paul dominating and nauseating Tom. And time passed like eons. The bright spot was Pete. The little guy sat next to him, and Tom could feel the kid's adoring eyes on him. Secretly, Tom imagined the kid was like himself, discovering a nameless emotion that he was not yet aware of. Tom envied Pete's frank, open stare, his innocence, his own gone now—if innocence were virginity or the desire to lose it.

Pete's face shined up at him. "Are you going to college, Tom?" They had been talking about school, summer plans, jobs. Tom looked down at Pete. His face was small like his body—a teenager in a kid's body. He doubted that he even shaved. He was red-haired, and a small splash of freckles ran across the bridge of his nose. He looked into Pete's pale, blue eyes and smiled.

"Yeah. But I haven't decided where. It'll probably be Baylor, but I've also been accepted by UCLA."

"Where's that?" Pete wrinkled his nose. "UCLA?"

"You stupid," Paul interrupted. "It's in California. Los Angeles. Tom'll go to Baylor."

Tom glanced at Paul, then ignored him. He spoke to Pete. "UCLA is a good school. They also have branches of the university in other cities in California. If I go there, I'll have to decide on just the right kind of study. They offer better engineering courses than Baylor."

"Oh," Pete said. "I thought you'd be a preacher, too."

"'Fraid not, Pete."

"You'll be breaking a long history of preachers in your family," Paul interrupted again. "I don't think your father will agree."

"I have a scholarship for UCLA," Tom said. "If I go there, it won't matter if Father agrees or not."

Mike St. Germaine whistled softly at Tom's remark. Paul laughed derisively. "Sure, Tom."

Tom looked directly at Paul, then let his eyes slide away and back to Pete. "We've talked about it. Of course he wants me to go to Baylor. We have relatives on the Board, but it's my decision." He put his arm on the back of Pete's chair. "What about you, kid?"

Pete brightened, delighted to be kept in the conversation. "I have another year of high school." He looked embarrassed but determined to continue. "I was hoping you'd be close by so we could keep in touch."

Paul snorted. "With you, why?"

Pete's pale face turned bright red. He frowned at Paul, but didn't respond.

Tom said, "Don't mind him, Pete. It doesn't matter where I go. If you want to write, or even visit, that would be great."

Tom tried to salvage Pete's feelings, but he drifted out of the discussion. "Thanks," he mumbled.

Angry at Paul, Tom got up. "Looks like we've got Wednesday's lesson straight. How about meeting at six Wednesday before class?"

The others got up. Tom said good-bye to them. "Would you stay a minute, Pete?" Then Tom caught Paul's arm and pulled him out in the hall. He whispered so his parents couldn't hear. "Why were you digging at Pete?"

Paul looked surprised. "Oh, him. He's a nobody, Tom. He's not one of us disciples, you know, even though he's always there. I don't know why he hangs around. But you can't shake him. He was at Kevin's when I called over there."

It was just like Paul to take seriously the name of "disciples" that Kevin or somebody had called their group one day. "Well, you were mean. Why don't you see if your parents are leaving?"

"Sure thing," Paul said. He barely registered Tom's insult, which he accepted as a normal response to him. "Don't waste your time on Pete, though. His father will never become a deacon. He's been trying for years. He—"

"Bye, Paul." Tom turned and went back to his room. Pete looked nervous when Tom opened the door. "What's the matter, Pete?"

"Kevin was my ride, and he left before I could tell him to wait."

"Oh, that's okay. How far away do you live?"

"Next door to Kevin on Zinc Street." Tom tried to remember where Zinc was. "We can walk, if you want. I wanted to talk to you anyway."

"Sure. That'd be great!"

"I need to get out anyway. I was going crazy just sitting around, weren't you?"

They were by the front door. The Romaines had left. "Is it all right if I walk home with Pete?"

"Fine, Thomas." His father looked up from the desk. "Dinner is promptly at six, so be back in time, and no detours."

They left the front yard and turned north as Pete indicated. "What'd he mean, no detours?"

Tom looked down at Pete. He was almost a head taller. Pete must have been barely over five feet tall. Even compared with Joel, whose forehead was at Tom's eye level, Pete was short. "I'm under house arrest." He tried to make a joke of it, but saw that Pete was startled. He smiled sadly. "Come on. Let's get out of here."

The pavement in this part of town was kept in good condition, and all the sidewalks were wide and curbed. The trees in the yards were well established and in some places hung over the fences, shading the sidewalk. Tom was in no hurry to get to Pete's house, and Pete seemed happy to be walking with him. Tom suspected he was right about Pete's feelings and wanted to come right out and ask. But Pete was also very shy, and he could mistake Pete's real feelings. He tried to make his questions sound offhand.

"Do you hang around with Kevin much outside the fellowship?" Tom asked.

"Sometimes, I guess. I like Kevin, you know. We've been neighbors for, well, all our lives."

"Oh, I see. And Paul?"

Pete frowned. "I don't like him, and I wish Kevin

wouldn't hang around him, but don't tell Kevin I said that."

"I won't. Truth is, I suppose, being elders' sons, they get thrown together a lot."

"True," Pete said. "Their fathers are pretty active in the church."

"They run the church," Tom said. "Them and the deacons. Preachers come and go, but they hold the church together."

"I guess so. I don't know much about it. I'm not very religious. Just Kevin's friend. You know, where he goes, I go. Like that."

"But you've been with the disciples, right? You'd have to be pretty dedicated to the church for that."

"Of course," Pete said. "I'm part of the group, but mainly because of Kevin. I've been baptized. But religion's not a strong thing with me, really."

Tom considered this. "It's not important?"

"It's not a way of life, if that's what you mean."

"Then why do you come to church?"

Pete looked up at Tom as they walked. His face was troubled. He got nervous easily, Tom saw, and regretted his question. But he waited for an answer because Pete was struggling to compose one.

"Well, the easiest answer is to say that my parents make me," Pete laughed, and Tom laughed, too, thinking it was pretty funny. "But really, it's because of Kevin. He's always been nice to me, at least nicer than a lot of other guys. I don't make friends too easily."

Tom saw that this was hard for Pete to admit. They walked along in silence for a few minutes. Although it was hot out, Tom was enjoying the walk. The pace was a lot slower than with Joel. Joel was always in a rush to get where he was going, even if it was across the room. The slower pace allowed him the perfect rhythm for thinking, and getting out of the house was like waking up from a disturbing dream.

Tom told Pete about the dance. "That's why Father grounded me. For going. Joel said I was too drunk to realize it, but we were about to get beat up Friday."

Pete's face dropped in horror. "Why?"

It was Tom's turn to be reluctant. "Oh…people were just drunk and looking for excuses. Maybe because…they…they don't like preachers' kids."

Pete shook his head. "I've heard about those dances out at the air base. I heard about their fights and stuff. I can't imagine going to one."

Tom had to laugh a little. "It wasn't so bad. Mainly just a bunch of kids from high school. Everybody was drunk, though. I've never seen that before. Or a fist fight, for that matter."

"Well, that's about what everybody in this town does best," Pete said. "Drink their guts out, but I guess it's just an ordinary town; like any place, it appeals to some people and some people hate it because it's ordinary. Maybe a little too ordinary, like maybe the original mold, like its name, *Common*." Pete burst into a peal of laughter, then smiled up at Tom. "But underneath, if you want my opinion," Pete continued, shifting to a frown, "most people here aren't very happy."

"Not much to do here," Tom said. "Do you think that's why?"

"The schools offer a lot of programs, like the plays and sports, and then there's the bowling alley and the theater," Pete said. "But you're right. It's pretty dead otherwise. I guess that could be why people seem unhappy. But that's not really what I think causes it. There's just something missing." He shrugged. "That's all."

"You ever been anywhere else?"

"No. But we shop out of town, you know, clothes and Christmas shopping. And we go to Texas and Arizona some Christmases to visit my grandparents. But I haven't really been anywhere. You?"

"I've lived in little towns in the south, and some cities like Baton Rouge, New Orleans, Houston, a few small towns in Georgia, even West Virginia when I was a baby. We've traveled a lot; that's just the way it is when your father's a preacher."

"How did you wind up here? I'd think you'd be going crazy."

"No. I like it here. I was glad to be out of Houston. Too busy. We came for the drier climate. Mother's got asthma—at least a touch of it."

They crossed into an area of town where the houses were newer and the sun beat down on bare sidewalks. Tom had always liked Pete but had never gotten to know him very well. He was as wide-eyed and naive as Joel was when they'd first met, and vulnerable and shy like Joel was, too. He'd meant only to undo the cruel way Paul had treated him, but Pete was open and talkative now, and Tom was enjoying himself.

"Paul told me yesterday that I was aloof," Tom observed.

"Oh, him again," Pete said. "You're not. I know you and Joel Reece are best friends, so I think Paul is just jealous."

"Yeah?"

"Yeah. He doesn't really have any friends. He's hard to take. And he's snotty."

Tom chuckled. "Snotty. That pretty much describes him."

"But you better watch out for him, too."

"Why?"

Pete slowed his walk. He'd been walking fast to keep up with Tom.

Tom slowed down. He looked at Pete and saw that he was nervous again. "What's wrong?"

"He tries to put wedges between people. Last summer, he decided to get Kevin to ditch me. One day Kevin told me Paul said I was a weakling and, you know, things about my size, things he thought would hurt my feelings. Then Kevin said Paul told him I was queer! You know, hanging around with him because I love him, or something."

Tom felt embarrassed. "That made you mad?"

"Well, yeah!" Pete said. "I mean, Kevin is a neat guy. He's tall and strong, he's on the A team in basketball. He's not the star or anything, but really solid. He got nervous about what Paul said. For a few weeks there, I thought he was going to brush me off. That hurt. And to think a snot like Paul could influence him."

"Isn't Kevin still your friend?"

"So-so," Pete said, betraying the hurt in his voice. "Truth is, I'm not in his league at all. He dates a lot. We're friends, I think, mainly because we live next door to each other."

It was obvious from what Pete said that he wanted to be Kevin's friend, but Kevin was apparently not quite as enthusiastic. He felt sorry for the short kid beside him. He'd been hurt badly, probably over and over by Kevin, then by Paul. No wonder he was so shy and nervous.

"I'm glad we got better acquainted, Pete. Before today, I didn't realize you liked me."

Pete's eyes widened. His face lit up. He grinned. "I've wanted to talk to you outside the fellowship for a long time. You're really nice. I've seen you and Joel together, and I can tell, man. You two really are the best of friends. It's ideal. You go everywhere together. And I bet you never run off without letting the other one know, do you?"

"No. We don't," Tom said. "Except last Friday, we...well Saturday, we had a fight—an argument."

"Serious?"

"Real serious."

"That's too bad. Anything I can do?"

"Thanks, Pete, no...." Tom stopped, feeling a strange apprehension, but decided to go on. "Joel isn't religious, at least not like being a churchgoer or anything. He's really smack-dab solid, totally earthbound. Know what I mean?"

"He's not interested in what's a sin and what's not, right?"

"Right! Exactly."

"And so?"

"So, something we did, I felt was wrong, and he didn't. And I can't sort it out."

"Something bad, really?"

"He doesn't think so. I do."

"You do? Or you think you should think it's wrong because your church tells you?"

"Because the Bible says so, flat out, no excuses."

Pete looked thoughtful. He chewed on his lip. "And you can't decide...because of Joel?"

"Man, you hit the nail on the head."

"You know what, Tom?"

"What?"

"If Joel doesn't think it's wrong, I'm not so sure you should allow your church's Bible to control you."

"What do you mean," Tom said, "my church's Bible? It's just a King James Version."

"C'mon, Tom, you should know. Our church takes everything in the Bible at face value."

"They do?"

Pete laughed. "You're playing dumb. For example, that Jonah was literally swallowed by a big fish, or that there really was an Adam and Eve."

"You don't believe that?" Tom was dumb-founded.

"No way, man. You get a whole new slant on religion if you allow that the writers of the Bible were just ordinary men who wrote as best they could a couple thousand years ago."

"But God made them see perfectly," Tom said.

"Then why is the Genesis description of the universe so screwy? It doesn't jive with modern science."

"Like what?"

"The writer of Genesis," Pete said, "thinks the moon gives off its own light, for one thing, and you know it's just reflecting sunlight."

Tom considered this. "That's true."

"And that idea about making the sun stand still?"

"Yeah?"

"Obviously that writer thought the sun revolved around the Earth and not the other way around."

Tom grinned. "That's true, too! But it doesn't change my particular problem...." He trailed off.

"Who's to say that everything the Bible claims is a sin, really is?"

"I don't know," Tom said.

"You are. You're to say."

Tom looked at Pete. They had stopped walking. Pete's eyes had a playful gleam that Tom found unsettling. "You do a lot of thinking, don't you? Are you a genius or something?"

Pete laughed. "Thanks for the compliment. No. But I know more than Paul thinks I do."

Tom laughed, too. "No, I mean it."

"It's simple. You've been smothered with one kind of religion. The world is made up of thousands. What makes your religion any truer than the others? Just because you believe yours is right, just because you believe that the writers of the Bible had a corner on truth, doesn't prove that they did. You ever look into other religions?"

"No," Tom said. "I've never even thought to do that."

"Well, you should, man. I mean, if you're miserable, wouldn't it be a good idea, considering how Joel feels, to take a look around? Like I said, you're like, nailed down to one tiny religion, one of hundreds of the one-and-only truths. I only go to your church because my parents do and because Kevin does, but people in the church, they're like reborn Puritans. If it ever causes me pain, man, you better believe I'll try something else."

"I bet you know what my problem is, don't you?"

Pete looked embarrassed. "I honestly don't. I've got an idea, but I wouldn't dream of bringing it up. If I'm wrong, it would destroy me to say it to you."

"Scared?"

Pete pointed across the street. "That's my house. I can get my parents to run you home if you want."

"No. That's okay. But listen, Pete, can't you tell me what you think?"

Pete sighed. "No. Not right now, okay?"

Tom gave up, realizing that Pete knew. He knew, but was afraid. "Well, nice talking to you, Pete."

"See you later, Tom. I hope we can get to know each other even better."

* * * *

In the evening, Joel paced through the house, waiting. Long after his parents had gone to bed and the television had signed off with "The Star Spangled Banner," he hoped the telephone would ring. But finally he gave up and, in his bedroom, pulled off his clothes and put on a bathrobe and his boots.

He left the house by the front door. There was already a chill in the air, and by dawn, when he would go out to set the irrigation, he would have to keep the heater in the pickup running as he did his chores. But now, the chill felt good against his legs. He let the robe flap open as he strode across the familiar farmyard in the moonless night, but even in the darkness, he could see a sheen of ghostly light on his stomach and legs. The air breathed across his naked skin and tickled deliciously against his groin. He climbed the banks of the irrigation pond out by the cowshed and walked along the top of the bank until he came to the pier. He walked to the end of it where the pipe from the well pumped water into the pond. At night, the water looked black, but he knew how clean and deep the pond was and, without hesitating, he shed his robe, pulled off his boots, and stood naked in the starlight. He stretched his arms heavenward and let the soft, chill breeze play across his skin. Always it was a sensual feeling that made him feel happy.

He dived into the black pool and swam under water until he reached the middle. Then he burst to the surface and floated on his back. The water was warm against his skin. He let himself relax, feeling less anxious in the warmth. As always, when he felt good, he thought of Tom. It was only Monday, after all. *He'll call*, Joel thought. *He did look miserable Saturday, poor guy. Maybe he just needs to be alone for a while*.

He swam vigorously, back and forth across the

pond; then, wonderfully tired, he climbed onto the
pier and let the water bead and dry in the cold air.
He listened to the silent desert and closed his eyes.
He listened to his own smooth breath and thought
of Tom listening to this same silence beside him
when he spent the night.

In the beginning, during those first wonderful
nights when they were in bed with the lights off,
before the drag of sleep had begun to pull Joel
into unconsciousness, he had tried to fill up the
silence by talking endlessly until Tom dropped off
to sleep. Tom had said the silence of the country
was a lot louder than city noise, a particular con-
tradiction Joel appreciated. Then later, he tried to
get Tom to value it as he did, making him listen to
the least sound, helping to train his ears for the
desert's messages. And in that silence he often listened to Tom's soft breath as the rhythm slowed,
sometimes watching his face in the moonlight, often getting an erection as they lay side by side. He
would roll away from Tom, then, saying softly,
"Goodnight, buddy."

Chapter 5

Wednesday, June 2

William Dean Hoffins wound his way through the stacks at the university library. He let the fingers of one hand trail along the spines of the books, the other held a sparse list of quickly jotted Library of Congress numbers. *Three goddamn books!* The card catalog had listed at least ten (still a pitiful number), but on the upper right-hand corner on most of the cards was typed "closed stacks." He had argued with the clerk at the reference desk about getting into the closed stacks, but the clerk had smiled nervously, taking his assault on the chin. "Sorry, sir. Policy. These books are closed to review until the summer semester begins, and then only by permission of the professor."

"I'm only after a little information. I'm a teacher. I'll just review them at the table."

But the clerk prevailed. "Sorry, no. The university doesn't consider most of those fit...ah...for public consumption."

Maybe it was the topic that closed the clerk to further cajoling, and he had felt like pointing out the university's contradictory policy. *For Christ's sake, you've got a banned books display in the lobby!* But instead he had walked away grumbling. The other three books were written by psychiatrists.

He stopped to consult the numbers and looked carefully along a shelf, narrowing the search. Nope. Missing. He scratched the first number. Both of the other books were there. He picked up the first one, a forlorn hardback with frayed edges. He opened the cover. Christ! Published in 1948! He laid the book down and pulled the other one off the shelf. It was newer by eight years. The title glared at him, and he recalled from a brief encounter with some required psychology course the old nature/nurture questions, but this was a new twist: the writer wanted to know if homosexuality was a disease or way of life, caused or chosen.

He'd imagined taking home a carload of books, inviting Joel over, and helping the kid sort through the crap. Reading the title made him feel uneasy. He shouldn't be involved in this at all. He couldn't trot these damn books out. *Here kid. Read it and weep.* He spent only an hour flipping pages in both books, taking a few notes. His most lucid impression was that these psychiatrists had this topic nailed shut. The books began with Freud (naturally) and launched their own theories with the worst kind of data—personal testimony and interviews. In the newer book, he carefully read the author's conclusion and copied a few paragraphs word for word. Meticulously, he put quotation marks around the writer's words, wondering for one second if Joel would know that quotation marks meant the writer's exact words and not his opinions. He had been careful not to let Joel know what his opinion was. Oh, shit, what the hell. Let the pieces fall where they may.

If someone had asked, Coach Hoffins wouldn't

have been able to explain why he took any notes at all from these books. They held no answers for a kid like Joel, storming through his first sexual experiences. The writers' conclusions struck him as vindictive, as though they had a score to settle with their patients. Maybe he would show these notes to Joel, after talking up to it, with fair warning, poor kid. If nothing else, it would give him a good idea of what he was up against.

He thought of Joel. Just a regular kid. A little crude around the edges, a little shy with girls, always friendly and well liked by the other boys, and, come to think of it, always touching his friends, but nobody had ever suggested that he was queer, never the slightest hint or objection to his physicalness.

But against the writers' conclusions, he rejected the idea that all homosexuals were neurotic. Wasn't there something wrong with the use of words like "all," "always," "never"? It struck him that real scientists never said "never."

He slammed the book shut in disgust, stood up and stretched. Libraries always made him feel sleepy. The air was musty on this floor in this little wing under the third-floor stairs. He yawned and looked around at the dimly-lit interior. The concrete walls weren't even painted in this begrudged space. But the area was frequently used, he bet, considering that the edges of the cards listing these books were heavily smudged from repeated handling, the body oils secreted through nervous hands as they flipped the edges of the cards. The books were heavily marked in, too. He flipped to the back of one book and pulled the narrow checkout card from its little envelope. The names of the borrowers were scrawled in a list down the card, then crossed over with a pencil or pen. He didn't doubt that many of those who used this wing and read this garbage were trying to understand themselves. He had never felt sympathy for homosexuals—or revulsion. And except for Joel, to his knowledge, he had never met one. But he was not so sure Joel was one. Kids his age couldn't possibly have any idea, could they?

He made a point of stopping by the reference desk. "Sir?"

The same clerk looked up with dismay, prepared for further battle. "Yes, Sir?"

Sliding the list of book numbers across the counter, he tapped the sheet of paper. "You would be doing a lot of young men and women a real favor if you took these books off the shelves, too."

"Sir?"

"The books in the closed stacks? How could they be worse? The two I looked in are garbage."

"I'm sure you're entitled to your opinion. Will there by anything else?"

As he walked away from the bewildered clerk, he kicked himself for venting his anger on him. At the turnstile, he opened his briefcase for inspection and walked out into the blistering afternoon sunlight. Some perverse sense of protocol had made him dress in slacks and sports jacket and, as he slipped into the MG, sweat popped out on his back in the heat. He struggled out of his jacket, feeling no cooler for the effort, and he didn't look forward to the long haul across sixty miles of desert for home.

He considered Joel Reece one of his failures. Joel had been a great success for him while it lasted. He remembered the first time he appraised Joel's body, when he accepted the kid's class ticket. Most boys were already surpassing the coach in height, who was wide and burly, and had reached his mid-thirties in perfect, stocky health. But comically short, he thought. He usually had to look up, even to freshmen. But Joel was even shorter; the only difference, however, was that his body was perfectly proportioned for his height, and he thought Joel could become a gymnast, maybe. The first few weeks of PE seemed to prove him right. Joel was quick and aggressive, graceful, and completely trusting, always ready to hurl his body through the air without the slightest indication that he was afraid. Gymnastics looked good. He always saw his students in terms of the sport they would be best at, and tried to marry them to one pursuit or another through the two years of required PE in hopes that he could discover a winner. But when it came to gymnastic competition, even informally among the other boys, Joel fell apart. He was much too nervous, and at first, the coach dropped the idea that Joel could become a winner at any sport.

It was Joel, though, who asked about boxing, and the coach agreed to train him. Boxing proved to be the best release of Joel's tension. He always came out slugging, aggressive, tireless. Joel's "style" electrified the crowds. And he knew from the first time Joel stepped into the ring that he had a winner. The next year, when Joel was a sophomore, he took even the state championship effortlessly. He wanted to take Joel all the way, had already contacted friends in several colleges, hinting that one of his boys coming up through the ranks would at least smash collegiate records.

Sports were important to the coach, not so much because of their healthy effect on young bodies as because of their being an avenue to channel a youngster's fuming energy, as a direct line to opportunity into adulthood. The discipline that any sport demanded spilled over into every facet of a person's life. He believed that. The study of sports was much more than boxing or swimming or football, more than the study of the body, of brawn. It directed the will to achieve, endure. Oddly, Joel had all these drives. But they seemed so casually achieved. Most students he coached—those who became competitors, anyway—had to work damned hard to achieve any success, had to give up much of their free time, and work hard to win, one painful niche at a time. Training boys and girls to make their bodies hurt, to sweat and grunt for one more ounce of stamina, took all the respect and trust his kids could muster. And he had always tried to return to them the reward of that work. But Joel was different.

In the end, he had failed to infuse in Joel the drive to pull away from Common. Most teens were ready to get on with their lives, to go out into the big, wide world and see other things. Joel had quit, suddenly, without warning, not because he was a quitter, but because his loyalties lay in a few hundred acres of desert in the middle of nowhere. *Not at all the kind of place for a kid to live from birth to adulthood without ever going out into the world*, Bill thought. But try as he might, he couldn't shake Joel's decision.

For Bill Hoffins, the choice to live in Common was made because the coaching job offered a substantial income and latitude in his coaching program. He had studied as many sports as he could, and this position offered him the chance to open a wide range of options for the boys and girls. He did not believe in funneling all boys through football or basketball. Why make an excellent swimmer into a lousy left end? Or strive to produce aggressive basketball players out of graceful, streamlined runners? JoAnna had been hired, too, in a less-rewarding position, maybe, but the school paid for further education, so she could continue school at the university. She had often told him that her boss, David Wier, had the tightest sphincter at the school and characterized him from then on as anal retentive. She also didn't like her boss's attitudes when it came to closing opportunities for girls so that boys could advance. She walked on eggshells at work and was often frustrated in her attempts to work around him without endangering her job.

The desert wind scraped his face raw. In his briefcase were the few meager pages of notes. He hadn't decided yet to let Joel read them. Gnawing at his conscience was the school board policy of staying out of sexual discussions with students. *And especially this sexual discussion*, he told himself. But he wanted to do something for Joel because, aside from his disappointment in him, Joel was still a wonderful kid; he would have loved to have had a son exactly like him.

JoAnna met him at the door wearing a light, breezy, summer shift with narrow straps tied into bows on either shoulder. She had combed down her hair and brushed out the kinks that always formed under the tight, pinned-up style she wore at her job within the high-school counselor's office.

"That was a quick trip," she said as he climbed out of the MG. "I thought you were going to research that stuff for the Reece kid."

"At least I made it back in time to go to the hospital with you. It was a lost cause, Jo. You can read my notes on the way. I don't know what to do about Joel."

"I told you, you wouldn't find much. We had that Johnson case, remember? The kid came in crying and nervous, said all the guys in shop were pushing him around, calling him queer. He wanted help. But David wouldn't touch it, of course. I did all the research I could find and even talked to a psychiatrist. But then David told me to file it. He called in the kid's parents, but I don't think anything was ever settled."

Some enterprising fundraiser had managed to get a special wing built onto the county hospital, complete with its own special staff. It was the newest wing of the small hospital that served the southern county residents. But the special wing received patients from all over the state. Children. Townspeople referred to it as the children's nut ward, completely misunderstanding the difference between emotional and physical disturbances of the mind.

The interior of the hospital was one of the few cool places in Common. It was equipped with refrigerated air conditioners, rather than the evaporative coolers that sat atop most houses and businesses in town. Bill had not changed from the clothes he wore to the university and, as they walked down the long, shiny, waxed corridor to the west wing, he began to feel cool and comfortable. He put his arm around JoAnna's waist and they walked in like that to their son's bedside.

Linton William Hoffins was severely autistic, and Bill and JoAnna were glad that they were able to live so close. The few hours a week they visited did nothing to benefit Linton; he was too withdrawn to even focus on their faces or to react to their hugs, except to screech and pull away. He could barely stand to be touched or held, and they eventually came only to sit and watch him smile to himself with that strange, inner calm he had developed in his third year of life. They sat beside each other now on two metal-backed chairs next to his bed, holding each other's hands, silent and contemplative as always. For a time, both were lost in their own thoughts. Occasionally, JoAnna softly brushed Linton's hair from his eyes or gently extracted his tangled limbs from the bedclothes.

Linton was four, now, and had lived in his hospital room for almost two years. At first, the Hoffinses didn't realize that their son was autistic. Realization that something was terribly wrong with him came painfully over a year's time, when his development fell off drastically; after learning to crawl, he stopped. Physiologically, Linton was a perfect, beautiful child. But when he was two, one could get lost looking into his blank, inward stare. He fluctuated between unaccountable bouts of screaming and absolute serenity when he would stare blankly at them, then lie back and smile or laugh. They had been prepared to take care of him at home. But his temper tantrums were always directed at himself. He could become agitated without warning, and with the little strength he had developed in two years he could inflict bloody wounds to his body. Bill and JoAnna had realized his need for constant supervision.

Having Linton at home had been a strain on them both. As married people in a family-oriented town, it was a natural activity to visit with other teachers and their families, with other couples from their church. But because they both worked, it was hard for them to keep a clean house, or to keep a constant babysitter, especially because of Linton's strange behavior. It was impossible to keep a maid because of Linton. Bill also wanted to make it a practice to invite his athletes over, wanting to round out his training in sports with a little of the human side. He felt he could be a positive model for many of the teens, and the school board smiled on teachers who took an active interest in the community. As the principal, Robert Whitman, was fond of saying during staff meetings, "The town needs its schools to provide Common with family activities." And the Hoffinses agreed. Except for the emptiness of a childless house, they were happier now that Linton was receiving good care.

As he sat at Linton's bedside, Bill squeezed his wife's hand. "I'm going to help Joel if I can, Jo. I miss having a kid to talk to."

JoAnna stood up and leaned over Linton, who was lying flat on his back and smiling. It was hard to tell he was conscious, except for the little shrieks that gurgled in his throat and the quick snatches his fists made at his clothes. She sighed. "It isn't fair, is it? We'd make good parents, and we can't even talk to him."

She turned around and pulled Bill up. She was taller than him by an inch. She kissed his forehead and tasted the salt of the dry sweat. It bothered her that Bill might get caught helping with Joel's problem. But at the same time, she agreed that kids needed help sometimes when even their parents were not aware of their problems. She had looked forward to the summer, with a real chance to get their house in order, cleaned from top to bottom, and to begin inviting people over for small dinners and bridge. But Joel was the first one to show up, bearing more problems. Not that she resented it. Like her husband, she missed having a kid to talk to, but Joel Reece's problem was as difficult in its own way as Linton's autism. It was considered an illness, too, and, like autism, as confusing and vague. "But at least you can talk to him."

Bill followed her out of Linton's room and into the quiet corridor. He wasn't sure that he was doing the right thing. "What do you think, Jo? Should I?"

She looked at him strangely. "Didn't I just say that?"

"But even against policy?"

"When did that stop you before? Yes, honey, talk to him. We both will if he comes back. If I can't do real counseling at work, I can do it on the side."

* * * *

Wednesday was another church night. Joel hadn't heard from Tom all week so, after church was surely over, he called Tom's house, breaking his promise to wait. Tom's father answered this time, and he also said that Tom was sick. "But what kind of sick—" Joel managed to get out before the buzz of a dead line came back. *Fucker!* Okay, so it was nine o'clock at night. Who would be in bed? Surely Tom wasn't bedridden. Maybe he wasn't being allowed to talk, Joel thought, with a pang of fear.

Maybe he told his father what we did. That idea made him look at the black telephone with apprehension, and he turned away, as confused as ever.

* * * *

On the other end, when the telephone rang once, it was snatched up instantly, its ring choked off by Tom's father. On a chance that it might be Joel, Tom slipped out of his room and passed by his father on the way to the kitchen for a glass of water. From his father's abrupt monologue into the receiver, Tom knew it was Joel. "Still sick. Goodnight."

That's a lie! Tom whispered under his breath. Then he caught a glimpse of his reflection in the

kitchen window over the sink. His fragmented
frown and wild eyes met. He was surprised at the
anger on his face, and a little frightened that it
showed. His anger made him restless, but there
was no place to go to get away. He gulped down
the cool tap water and set his glass on the counter. It was the only dirty dish in the house.

His mother was in her bedroom reading, probably, but he didn't know for sure what she did in
her room all the time, either. For both of them,
shutting themselves away most of the time was
habitual. This realization was new, but he could
see it was true: practically every evening at some
point, he would go to his room and would only
come out if his father called him out for some duty
around the house or if Joel came to pick him up
and take him somewhere. His mother would go to
her room like that, as well. And his father would
work at the desk. Like other things tonight, that
realization added to his anger. He turned away from
the window and marched right past his father and
into his room without a word.

He lay on his bed feeling angry, discovering
that his anger was many-headed. He was angry at
himself for playing the fool at the dance, for initi-
ating the sex with Joel in such a drunken way. He
was angry at himself for getting into trouble with
his father most of all, and angry that his father's
response was to make the snap judgment to
ground him. *Father would be surprised, wouldn't
he, to know that this time his rule-making was irrelevant, that he failed to "first define the problem,"
as he's so fond of saying?* That thought made Tom
angrier still. His father's decision to ground him
was like many of his overreactions. Now it hung
on like the odor in an alley. *It's his power,* Tom
thought suddenly, "this power to make rules," he

said aloud, "That, Father enjoys!" He was stunned at the clarity, the simplicity of this realization. It was true. His father pounced on a crisis, and generally had it quickly under control. But like a pit bull, once his mind had locked onto a problem, once his jaws were clamped at the throat of the argument, there was no pulling him off of it.

He looked at the black rectangle of window and felt a jolt of temper at the passing of another summer evening. He had geared himself for the long wait until he could call Joel, until his father lifted his stupid rule, but seeing how abruptly, disrespectfully, his father had treated Joel, Tom felt as if he was going to explode with anger, or stamp his foot through the floor in frustration.

You're a crybaby, Tom. If you were as mad as you think, you'd call Joel, sneak out of the house, maybe, something, anyway, to let Joel know what's going on! But the fact of his cowardice hit him. Even the thought of defying his father made him nauseous. Breaking one of his father's rules...if he did that, things would get out of hand. A small infraction would be open rebellion.

He clicked off the desk lamp and the room turned a shiny gray. The blackness of the night outside was obliterated by the darker darkness of his room. He sighed.

Pete said you do. You decide. Joel said you loved it, Tom. "And I started it," he said aloud. There was something he had missed. Pete had touched on his private conflict so quickly the other day that he began to wonder what blind spot there was. It was something Pete had said about who decides what a sin is that had gotten Tom to thinking less hysterically about having sex. And now, he realized that he wasn't ashamed anymore. It didn't hurt. It didn't hurt at all.

Joel never said if it was wrong or right. *But I didn't give him a chance*. Joel wasn't concerned with the idea of sin, anyway. He seemed not at all concerned with spiritual comfort. Joel never asked God for anything—even his cussing never called on God to damn anybody. And when Tom had asked him once, a long time ago, "Don't you worry about your soul?" Joel had said, "My soul? If you bust my lip, my soul will bleed down my chin." And that had settled the religion subject forever.

Tom wanted to be more like Joel, sometimes wished Douglas and Eva Reece were his parents. Even Pete was closer to Joel's thinking, not quite so caught up with religion.

He sighed as he lay down for bed. He had analyzed his anger to death. His father, as usual, had been central. *Soon, Joel*, he thought, *I'll figure out how to get past Father, past the rule-maker, past my own cowardice*. He hoped Joel would be waiting for him when he did.

Friday, June 4

Wilting. That was her word for it. "He's wilting, Douglas. That's the only way I can describe it." Eva Reece was resting against Douglas on the couch in the living room. The same old news was playing. Johnson had just announced more troop deployment in South Vietnam. Douglas patted her shoulder and squeezed her to him a little. She was warm and comfortable. Over the years, her slim figure had disappeared and she had become plump like many of the other farmers' wives. But Douglas preferred her now to the frail thing he had married the year before he was drafted into the army.

"There's something bothering him, all right, hon. I thought a girl might be giving him fits, you know?" He laughed softly, thinking about the underwear he'd found, but he didn't share that with her. "But he's not one to talk about a problem, 'less it's more'n he can handle."

Eva sighed. "You know how bad that would be, don't you?"

Douglas detected her old amazement. Joel had always been so independent, he'd caused them several years of fright, practically from the time they'd brought him home from the hospital. Eva was a little overprotective at first, he recalled, after the two miscarriages before him, but Joel soon proved that she wasn't wrong in keeping an eye on him. "Do you remember that year—guess he was five or six—when he dug up that plum tree?"

"It was the summer he turned seven, honey. I think it was, anyway, because you said you wished you'd never told him he had to get rid of it. I still don't know how he kept from chopping a foot off, as mangled as the tree was! Remember, he worked on it for days? You said at least he would be good in school. You said if the teachers just gave him something to do, he'd do it."

Douglas nodded. "Yes, ma'am, I remember." He watched the weatherman drawing on a map of the United States.

Joel was looking at him from the hole he'd dug. The hole was at least a yard deep. Joel's face was streaked with mud. His blond hair was wet and glistened from the top of the hole like something metallic. Douglas chuckled. "He said he wanted to see how many roots it had! Can you imagine that, Eva? He goes and digs for days just to find out?"

For Joel's size, the tree was enormous, but something Douglas could have worked loose in a couple of hours. Luckily, too, the tree was one he'd been thinking of cutting down anyway to build a garage. And the loss of the scrubby thing wasn't serious, but to punish him, he'd told Joel he had to straighten out the yard, fill the hole, and get rid of the tree. He didn't care how—but he fully intended to hook it to the tractor, when Joel saw he couldn't handle it, and drag if off. A little frustration, Douglas hoped, would teach him to ask before he did something like that again.

But Joel worked steadily on it for several days. Douglas would see him from the dining room. When he glanced up from his work at the shop where he parked the tractor, Joel would be busy. Dirt would be flying, and he would wonder what kind of further mess he was making. But he had given Joel a job, and he decided to wait and see how it turned out. At night, Joel came in for supper tired and happy, his sleeves rolled up like his father's, his hands blistered, so that Eva would have to put iodine on them. He washed at the sink, standing on a chair that he dragged from the breakfast table. At supper, he shoveled food down hungrily, quietly, completely content with himself. Then one day, he met Douglas as he came in from the field. "I'm done," he said simply.

"With what? The tree?"

Joel had beamed proudly. "Yeah! Wanna see?"

Douglas followed his son to the site where the tree had met its end. The ground was clear, the hole filled in and level with the rest of the yard. "But where'd you put it? He expected to see a small stack of mangled branches lying nearby. Joel had carted the entire tree, branch by branch, twig by twig, to the north side of his mother's garden, away from the house. Although the branches were cut badly, Joel had managed a fairly respectable stack.

Douglas laughed softly as he related the story. "Yessiree. I thought he could handle anything."

Eva sighed again. "But he's too quiet, Douglas. He's been moping around here all week. He says his friend, Tom, is sick, but I think it's something else."

"I've tried talking to him, hon, but I guess it's not bad enough, or he would say something, surely."

"But did he say where he was going?"

"Well, it's Friday night. I imagine he's got a date."

"Joel? Douglas, he hasn't had a date in almost a year. He just doesn't seem to be interested."

He patted her on the shoulder. "He's interested, all right, Eva, believe me. I think he's probably mooning over some girl."

"I hope so," Eva said. "It's unnatural for him to be unhappy."

"You're right. Yes, ma'am. He is a happy boy, most of the time. But he's always been quiet, too."

"And sometimes he just disappears," she added. "That used to scare me, and him just a baby, barely able to walk. I couldn't keep up with him and I never could get through to the girls to watch him."

Douglas chuckled. "I would come in from work for lunch and you'd be frantic because he was lost again. But we'd find him out in the yard playing or asleep under a tree. Remember that time—he was just out of diapers—we found him running down the road between the alfalfa and the cotton, naked as a Jaybird?"

Eva shook with laughter until she had to wipe away the tears. "He was happy as a lark," she laughed, "and so filthy! That was when you built that little seat with the steering wheel and put him up on the tractor with you while you worked."

"I remember that. I couldn't believe how content he'd be, either, with that loony smile just pasted on his face the whole time. You know I thought back then he was a little simple-minded?"

"Douglas! Whatever made you think that!"

"Well, he just never said anything unless I pulled it out of him. 'Tinkin','' he'd say. 'I as just tinkin', Daddy.' I'd pull him down from the tractor and we'd sit on the ditch bank for a drink, and I'd ask him if the cat got his tongue. 'No, Daddy,' he'd say. 'I as just tinkin' about a sky ana cowds!'" He never cried or fussed, no matter how hot or tired he got; he just wouldn't give it up. 'Me wuk. Me wuk. Me not tired.' I swear, Eva, that's why I thought that boy was simple."

"But he turned out to be a big help. As young as he was, when he started school, you decided you needed to hire someone to take his place."

Douglas found himself blinking back tears, remembering the day Joel boarded the bus with his sisters. He hugged Eva. "I really missed him when he went off to school. Even as young as he was, he could work like a kid twice his age. He was hard to replace. It was lucky for us he wasn't a blue baby like the two before," he said gently.

Eva smiled at him. "Those were rough times," she agreed. "Joel was a miracle, I guess. I just wish I knew what was hurting him now."

* * * *

He had tried staying home, but his parents were getting too insistent. His mother fussed over him too much at supper, making him feel embarrassed. He didn't like her to be constantly jumping up from the table to pour more tea for him, or to keep pushing the peach cobbler she'd made;

and he was sorry, too, that after working all day outdoors, she'd come in and baked it. He'd tried to cover up by smiling, but he couldn't get over the lump in his stomach well enough to eagerly accept seconds. "Naw. Thanks, Mom. I'm full."

He felt empty when he left. They were watching television, as usual, when he came in freshly bathed, wearing a new shirt and fresh Levi's, his hair combed. "You like nice, honey," his mother said. "You going dancing?"

"Just out."

He drove slowly by the Allens' on 9th. Plenty of times, he'd come in on this street to pick Tom up after finishing his chores. Tom would usually be on the front porch waiting. The few times that Joel had been in Tom's house were uncomfortable. The preacher was always right there waiting, giving him the once-over, his face as mean as a bulldog, his big, square jaw and stern mouth barely cracking a smile. Joel had often imagined it suddenly splitting open, fractures running from the chin to those fierce-looking eyes, pieces of granite falling away to reveal something worse. Mrs. Allen was almost the exact opposite, fragile as bone china, thin and neat, but her smile was strained, too. Outside, he would suck in fresh air, realizing he'd practically been holding his breath the whole time, as if something were about to happen.

Driving by now, seeing the lights on, he realized he'd wasted his time hoping to catch Tom outside. He knew his bedroom was toward the back, but as he passed where he could see the side of the house, the light was out, which meant Tom was either in the front part or out somewhere. But who would he be out with?

A prick of jealousy coursed through him, hurt that he had no real friends now but Tom, and yet

Tom probably had plenty more from church, maybe friends he had more in common with now.

He drove up and down Main Street, joining the procession of other teenagers out on a Friday night with nowhere particular to go. He made the complete tour a couple of times from the east end of town to the west end, feeling bored and lonely, seeing only the crowds at the hangouts, the line at the Mimbres Valley Theater, the teenage couples at the A&W. He envied the others out on the street, doing the same boring thing, but at least having someone to be bored with. But going back out to the farm was unthinkable.

Some of the guys, other ag boys, would be out at the old riverbed north of town with a keg and campfire. He shrugged to himself and turned north onto the highway to Silver City. Ten miles north of Common, he turned west. His lights bounced up and down on the bumpy, dirt road, catching the mesquite bushes and drifts of sand along the edges. In the distance he saw the glow of the campfire behind a large sand dune. As he came closer, his lights reflected off the other pickups and caught the flutter of crickets and moths swarming around the edge of the light. Laughter and loud voices sounded through the open window of his pickup as he bounced to a stop.

In the bottom of a gash in the earth where the river had run, the campfire was blazing brightly, swirling with hot, red ashes. Ten or fifteen guys and a few girls stood around its edges. One or two noticed him as he came up onto the bank, but they didn't say anything. Their faces were indistinct, half in dark and half reflecting bright orange against the fire's glow. He jumped down into the sandy bed and saw Bill Crawford. Joel moved up next to him and nodded. Bill got a funny look on his face, as if he'd been caught and didn't want to be seen. "Hey," he said, and started to move away.

"Hey," Joel caught his arm. "You gotta beer?" Bill led the way, staying ahead of him. The keg was buried in ice in the split half of an old oil drum. Most of the beer he got in a plastic cup was foam, but it was cold. Joel flicked the head off with his finger and drank. "What's goin' on?"

Bill shrugged, still eyeing him uneasily. Joel felt the hostility, barely concealed below Bill's expression. He squinted at Joel, studying his face. "You alone?"

Joel nodded and quickly sipped on the beer. "Nice night," he observed, looking around at the blackness.

"Yeah. Not much doin' in town?"

"Not much. Never is, though," Joel said.

Bill began walking back to the fire. "You want somethin' else, man?" Bill asked coolly.

Joel looked at the beer in his hand. "Well, no." He followed, feeling embarrassed. "Just seein' what's goin' on, you know?"

Bill shrugged. "Haven't seen you around much, 'cept the other night."

"Well, you know, me and Dad have the farm work all to ourselves these days."

"Yeah. I heard your sisters got hitched. Where they livin'?"

He told him. "We don't see 'em much, except around Christmas."

"I'm gettin' married myself. Fuckin' truth," Bill said. He looked around as Joel did. "She's not here, man. She's pregnant."

"Oh. Well…congratulations, huh? Who is she?"

Bill was staring into his cup. He glanced at Joel and kicked a hill of sand into the fire. "Jeannie

Lynn's cousin. You don't know her. Her mom and her're stayin' with the Lynns. She was a fuck machine, man. I thought she'd take precautions."

"Oh." The fire's heat burned Joel's face. In its light, he saw some of the guys from the ag class at school. But nobody made a move toward him, even though one of the guys nudged the one next to him and jerked his thumb in Joel's direction. Bill moved off, and Joel found himself wondering why he'd come. He drank his beer and went back to the keg. Nicky Coleman was helping Cindy get a refill. "Hey, Nicky."

Nicky twisted around, met Joel's face, then turned back to the keg. He pushed the pump again and a clear stream of beer flowed into Cindy's plastic cup.

Joel held his under the spout and felt the cold move up his hand, the cup getting heavier as it filled up. "Thanks."

Cindy regarded Joel as she sipped daintily on her beer. "That guy you were with the other night?" She giggled. "He was really shit-faced."

Nicky grinned in a funny way, showing his teeth. "He queer or what, man?"

"Huh? Tom?" Joel felt the heat of embarrassment in his face and felt himself choking up. It would be easy to admit it, then laugh it up. *Yeah, that queer bastard, man, I thought he was one of us, you know?* But a moment too long had passed. "I don't know," he finally said, which was the truth.

"Yeah?" Nicky said, with an edge in his voice. "I wouldn't want to find out. I'as you, man, I'd get me a girl, quick."

Joel couldn't think of anything to say. Nicky's face was stone cold. Cindy was grinning like an idiot.

"Jeannie Lynn says he *kissed* you, man. Then

you two left," Nicky said. He pushed Joel on the shoulder. "Here's advice to an old friend; you make it in this town, you get yourself a girl like normal guys. We been tellin' you for a long time that kid's different. And people are talkin'. I can't believe you had the balls to show up out here." Nicky indicated the guys around the fire. "Not more'n five minutes before you showed up, man, they were laughing their asses off about you. Now, excuse us." Nicky and Cindy left him standing by the keg.

Joel moved off to the side into the darkness and sat down on the edge of a rock. His knees were shaking badly. From where he sat, he watched the group around the fire, and now it seemed they were all looking in his direction, their laughter derisive. He fought against the paranoia, but couldn't shake it. One guy walked away from the fire and stood just inside the glow of light. He unbuttoned his Levi's and peed shamelessly into the sand between his feet. Somebody laughed loudly. "Hey, pervert! There's ladies present!" Then someone else shouted, "Don't let Reece catch you. I hear he's queer now!" More laughter. The guy shook his cock and wobbled back, obviously drunk. He buttoned his fly and wiped his fingers on his thigh. "Shit. Ain't afraid of no fuckin' queers," he said.

Joel threw the cup away and jumped down from the ledge. He moved back into the light, angry, breathing rapidly, feeling the adrenaline flowing through him. Fifteen yards or so away from the fire, he stood with his feet planted defiantly, arms folded across his chest, staring across the flickering light at his old friends huddled around the campfire, daring anyone to say something. A few of them looked in his direction, their faces like little imps grinning at him, but, of course, nobody made a move to challenge him. He knew as well as they did who'd win a fair fight. He itched to smash somebody's face, but nobody moved. *Fuck it. Not tonight. Not worth the effort,* he thought.

He turned his back on them and walked back to the pickup. Their laughter now sounded sharp and piercing against the night, more like the distinct yelp of coyotes that lived in the desert and ran in packs in the darkness, their marauding often leaving damage farmers would discover in the light of day. He didn't hear Bill Crawford's low laughter. "Anybody hear him deny it?"

Saturday, June 5

Joel called again.

"Mrs. Allen?" Joel identified himself.

"Hello, Joel. Yes?"

"Is Tom okay?"

"Well, yes. It's just that—"

"What? Isn't he or not?"

He heard, very faintly, a sigh. "You can see Tom at church tomorrow if you come."

Mrs. Allen seemed nervous suggesting that. Then, the telephone went dead.

* * * *

Tom had almost run down the hallway and grabbed the telephone from his mother when he heard her say, "Hello, Joel...." But he was held back by his old dread as effectively as if his spinal chord had been severed. His feet turned to mud. And his mother carried out her husband's wishes. This time when she got off the telephone, she tapped on his door and came in. He saw that she was angry—well, as angry as she could be. She stood in his doorway looking at him with her arms folded protectively across her chest. "Thomas, Joel is getting a little persistent, and I think you ought to tell him that he's not to call here again, unless you make arrangements for proper times."

"And how am I supposed to tell him that, Mother?"

She came into his room and shut the door. "Don't snap, Thomas." She smiled, begging for a little understanding. "I know you've been sick."

"I'm sick of staying home, Mother. I'm sick of Father's unreasonable demands. Joel and I had plans for this summer. Then Father comes along and ruins it!"

She shook her head. "Your father knows what's best, Thomas. You know that."

"No, I don't! Not any more. He makes mountains out of mole—"

"That is quite enough!" she said in a louder voice, but its undertone was still one of pleading. "Your father has been quite lenient, considering you still haven't offered any good explanation for your behavior."

"I've gone all week without giving Joel an explanation, and that doesn't bother anybody! You know he's my best friend, and now he probably thinks I don't even like him!"

She laughed softly. "Oh, for goodness' sakes, dear, Joel is just a kid. He doesn't need to have your father's actions explained." She smiled as though the understanding was simple.

"Then please, Mother, be reasonable. If I can't call him, how's he supposed to know not to call me?" It was an effort, but he softened his tone, knowing that she was not to blame at all. He sighed. "I'll make amends to Father. You're right. We're just kids, Joel and I. What respect do we need?"

Unbelievably, she smiled, looking pleased. "Besides, I invited him to church tomorrow. Won't that be okay?"

When she shut the door, Tom lay on his bed and stared at the ceiling. If Joel did come to church, it would at least be a chance to see him, and if they could talk, he might be able to explain. But he wasn't sure if Joel would want to; every time that he had called, his parents had hung up without telling him anything. *He probably thinks I don't care any more.* And then he thought, *If only there was some way to satisfy Father….* More than ever, he resented his father's unshakable rules.

Chapter 6

Sunday, June 6

6 a.m.

His father would be praying. His mother would be preparing a light breakfast before church and, by now, Tom would be in the living room, sitting back in his father's leather-backed office chair at the desk talking with Joel for a few minutes before he unlocked the church.

His father was praying. His mother was in the kitchen, but Tom was already back in his room. After unlocking the church, he had tried to call Joel, his heart pounding, knowing that if his father caught him, it would be over. He had waited anxiously at his father's desk, ready to drop the receiver and duck if one of his parents appeared. He had expected Joel to answer on the first ring. Waiting for the muted clatter of the ring on his end, Tom had gone through a bad case of the jitters. Then he had sagged as the telephone rang. And rang. A little, faraway sound. But nobody answered. Nobody was there.

He put his tie on without checking it in the mirror. He changed out of his house slippers and took his wingtips out of the closet. As usual, dust from the dry, desert air had found its way into the closet, and the black shoes were lightly powdered. He rubbed them on the bedspread as he sat on the edge of the bed to put them on. His face was a blank. He went through the process of being busy. But he saw nothing he touched; he crammed Sunday school papers into his leather Bible, pulled his window closed over his bed, locked it.

Come on. Be there, Joel! I tried to call, but you weren't home. Did you finally give up?

At breakfast, he ate his toast without buttering it, and wasn't even conscious enough to make small talk. Nor did he see his father look at him a little suspiciously, then shrug, and continue working over the index cards he studied in final preparations for the sermon.

I never thought he wouldn't be home! But maybe he will come.

"...lock the church?" Father was saying. "Well, Thomas?"

He looked up, catching only a few words. He took a blind shot. "Yes, Sir."

"Good. We're going over then. Wash up these dishes, Thomas, before you come."

"Okay, Father." He started on the dishes then and listened to them leave. The sun would have broken through the kitchen window facing east, except for the tall church steeple slicing through the sun perfectly and, as he carried the dishes to the sink and began running water, his face was cast in its long shadow. The job took him longer than he expected and, as the clock in the living room began to clong, he realized he would be late. Even if Joel had come before church, it was too late now. They would both have to endure it. And there wouldn't be a chance to tell Joel what he had decided to do.

6:20 a.m.

Joel parked at the church but sat in the pickup with the engine running and the heater on. The night had sucked all the heat from the earth and, until the sun was fully up above the Florida Mountains, it would be cold. He was still not sure that he should try to force Tom to talk to him, and wondered uneasily if Tom really didn't care anymore.

Now he waited for God and His congregation to arrive. Late in the night he had bathed, then walked out into the dark predawn. Overhead, the stars were a blaze of cold light, but nothing stirred in him at the familiar sight. He had walked over the farmyard without feeling his usual pride; he sat on the tractor staring north toward town where Tom lay sleeping. Common was a necklace of lights shining through the dark like jewels on the velvety blackness of the desert. He had stayed out in the chilly night until the string of lights had turned gray, growing pale against the coming sun, blinking out one by one.

Joel felt obsessed, which is why it made perfect sense to be polishing his shoes at five o'clock in the morning. He had put on his only suit, stared at himself as he combed his hair, wondering why he couldn't just forget the whole thing for a while— forget Tom, too.

Later, he left the warmth of the pickup and walked up to the church. The dark-red bricks were cool to his touch. His hands were cold, the skin across the knuckles taut.

He tried the door. It was unlocked, which meant that Tom had been here. He looked in the chapel, hoping to find him before church. But the chapel was empty. Then, by God, he would sit through

the whole damn thing, even though it was repulsive. He'd gone once with Tom, but the preacher
strutted and preened, stretched ordinary words
like rubber into strange sounds. He stuttered and
spit, he whispered and screamed, and seeing that,
Joel had felt embarrassed for Tom. But to see Tom,
he would just have to sit through it.

He walked slowly up the aisle. The pews
gleamed in the dark and the stained glass windows on the south wall were beginning to glow
from the sunlight outside. Light broke through a
skylight, casting a cone of brilliance across the
pulpit. The microphone was a blinding sphere of
silver where Tom's father would deliver the sermon.

His deeply suntanned face was blank. It had
been hopeful, then confused. Now it held a blank
stare waiting for Tom, knowing he would have to
sit through the damned sermon so they could talk.
"You fucking coward!" His voice jolted him in the
hushed chapel.

He closed his eyes and listened to the hush. It
echoed with an emptiness greater than the desert.
He couldn't hear himself breathing, but he could
feel the steady flowing in and out of his breath.
The church was odorless, but he smelled the clean
smell of his own flesh.

Nothing came to mind when he thought of
church. He didn't pray, because he knew what he
wanted. *Obsessed*, he thought, again. *I've never
acted so silly before now, unless it was over Melissa
Benson when I was a freshman. Yes. That was
exactly like this.* Except that where she had been
practically like a goddess, with big eyes like eggs,
a steady flow of lacy, gauzy, swirling rainbow-
colored dresses and a high-pitched laugh, Tom was
just a guy. Another male like himself. That was

different for sure. But from the first time Tom had spoken to him, something in his eyes overwhelmed Joel. He was struck dumb by Tom's black, girlish lashes, struck by the way he looked in ordinary sport shirts and Levi's. Melissa had a way of making Joel feel uncomfortable, and eventually he'd seen that she was losing interest in him because he never tried anything with her. He'd actually been relieved when she had dropped him. He'd often thought of her when he tried dating other girls, and he had to admit that the others had been downhill from her striking beauty. But then, along came Tom Allen.

At first, he'd been hesitant to introduce himself to Tom, because he was a townie. *And maybe I never should have*, he thought now, a little sadly. *Maybe I should forget about him.* But he knew he couldn't. The sex, which was only a hint of what making love with Tom could be, was a thousand times more powerful than anything he'd ever felt. Kissing Tom, holding him, just the thought of it made Joel feel frustrated. *I'll fuckin' make him listen*...was his only thought, his only plan.

Cars began to pull up outside. He heard the front door opening, people walking across the vestibule. He stayed where he was until he felt a light touch on his back. He jumped, hoping it was Tom. But he turned around to a stranger's face, the kind, wrinkled face of an adult.

"We're about to start Sunday School if you would like to join us."

He shook his head. He didn't want to. He heard more people behind him in starchy dresses, talking in low, churchy murmurs. The chapel was getting full, so he decided to wait outside.

The sun was above the trees now and a hot wind gusted over the sidewalk, making men reach for their hats and women hold their skirts as they hurried into the classrooms. The street was crawling with cars looking for last-minute parking places. Whole families emerged squeaky clean from their cars and scattered toward classes.

Soon he was alone on the sidewalk. He sat in the pickup; he was beginning to sweat. For a time, he dozed, spiraling downwards into a spinning sleep. He awoke suddenly. He looked anxiously about at the crowd coming out of Sunday school. Little kids pranced around like lambs in their little dresses and miniature suits, with their little Bibles, around the legs of the adults. He got out of the pickup feeling like a yokel among them. His suit, which he hardly ever wore, felt too tight; his shirtsleeves were too long and stuck out too far under the jacket sleeves. His clip necktie bothered him; he kept feeling to make sure it was still hooked. The shirt collar choked him, and he kept swallowing. He joined the crowd on the sidewalk.

He recognized some guys from school—but they were ones he didn't have much to do with. In another group, a couple of girls recognized him and waved pretty, white-gloved hands. Joel walked away feeling seedy.

Finally he saw Tom with a flock of young guys— all of them carrying Bibles and walking about the rest of the crowd, talking seriously, puffed up with their seriousness. Tom saw him and waved stiffly; he tried to break away, but a guy next to him grabbed his arm and followed. They walked up to Joel. It was Paul, of all people, whom Joel knew from school.

"Hi, Joel," Tom said. He tried a smile, but it barely lifted the corners of his mouth. Tom said, "Paul, meet Joel."

"Oh, we've met," Paul said, with a hint of a

sneer. Then he stuck out his hand.

Joel was shocked by the limp thing he took hold of, like a dead fish. He dropped it; it made the palm of his hand tickle. He shook hands with Tom, who got a searching look on his face when he met Joel's eyes. Joel squeezed hard, feeling Tom releasing his grip, and he pulled Tom a little closer, almost off balance. "I'm here to talk, Tom. You're not sick anymore, are you?" He forced himself to smile as widely as he could. Tom's face brightened a little; his eyes were appreciative. Joel let go of his hand.

"I'm glad you're here," Tom said. "I tried to call this morning, but…." Then a little guy walked up to Tom and he pushed him up to Joel. "This is Pete Thompson. Pete, this is Joel, my very best friend." Both the little redhead and Tom seemed pleased.

Joel shook hands, noticing at least the kid's wide-open smile and firm grip. He looked at Tom again. "So, when do we talk?"

"Come on," Tom said with a helpless look. "It's time to go in."

They followed the crowd into the church and sat near the back, for which Joel was relieved. Next to him in the pew on his right, an old couple smiled warmly at him. Tom sat on Joel's left, then Paul filed in next to the aisle, on Tom's left. Pete Thompson was left standing in the aisle, looking nervous. Joel poked Tom and whispered, "Tell him there's room next to me." Tom reached over Paul and pulled Pete into the pew. There wasn't as much room as Joel thought, but Pete squeezed between him and the old couple, leaving the four of them squashed together. In situations like this, Joel usually curved his shoulders forward to alleviate the crunch. But this time he spread both arms around the kid's and Tom's shoulders. Pete's body felt like that of a child, but Tom's felt familiar next to him, and Joel closed his eyes and breathed deeply of Tom's cologne.

As the church filled up, the crowd's whispers filled the room with a soft, sibilant hissing. But when a man walked up from the first pew and stood in the aisle in front of the pulpit, the whispering faded; someone coughed loudly. Directly in front of Joel, a young woman bounced a small baby on her shoulder; the little kid's face bobbed up and down facing him, its little, blue eyes unfocused.

"A few announcements first," the man said. His voice was small and thin, and Joel wondered why he didn't use the microphone behind him. "At two o'clock in the courthouse park, weather permitting...." Joel squeezed Tom's shoulder, and when Tom turned and smiled, Joel wanted to ask him to explain why he hadn't called. He was about to whisper when the announcer walked back over to the pew and sat down. Then immediately the piano player rolled her fingers over the keys to the opening of a song. The crowd rose noisily to its feet, and the room was loud with the turning of pages. Joel stood up next to Tom; he shared a hymnal with him.

When the piano player paused, Joel sucked in his breath. As the crowd began to sing, he felt his own throat vibrate. He could not hear himself, lost among all the voices. Tom's voice rang sweetly, flat against the melody, and then toward the end blended smoothly with the rest.

When the song ended, Joel started to sit, but everyone else remained standing; he felt embarrassed. Another man stood up below the pulpit facing the crowd. "Let us pray." He turned and knelt toward the pulpit and bowed his head.

"Our most kind and gracious, heavenly Father: Bless this congregation this morning. Go with it, Father. Help us to prosper, to strengthen our ties, and go with our brethren in that strife-torn battle in Vietnam. Help our boys, and bring them all home safely. Bless Sister and Brother Hutchins, Father, whose son has suffered the ultimate tragedy of battle, and who now awaits Your blessed call. And bless all the mothers and fathers of that other country, who likewise suffer the loss of loved ones. But especially be merciful, Father, in their ignorance of Your Grace. Go with us, today. Help those who are poor in spirit to be revived again, in Jesus' great and good name, we pray: Amen."

He rose from his knees and turned back to the congregation. "Please remain standing for hymn number 48, number 4...8."

When the hymn was over, the congregation seemed to fall to their seats like a great wave. Joel looked across the tops of their heads.

On the stage behind the podium sat the choir. Behind them, with the curtains open, was the baptismal font, with an oil painting of a forest behind it. A river ran through the forest. He couldn't see the real water below, but the skylight was reflecting off it, causing a beautiful glow to shine on the water in the painting.

On one wall a bulletin board gave the church's attendance record. Then on the next line the amount of money collected, and on the last line, the church's expenses. On the opposite wall was another bulletin board with the hymn numbers. Below that was the SERMON FOR TODAY: The natural Sin of the Flesh. Below that was the SCRIPTURE FOR TODAY: Gal. 5:1, 15, 21; Gal. 6:1-8.

Tom's father went immediately to the pulpit. He flipped the switch on the microphone; a high-pitched screech burst from the speakers in the ceiling. He held his hand over the mike until one of the men behind the pulpit adjusted it for him.

"Thank you, Brother Temple!" he boomed out of all proportion, Joel thought, to the man's simple deed. "And thank you, brothers and sisters, for once again filling God's church! Oh, bless this day that God has made!" He spread his hands out widely on the pulpit as Joel had seen other preachers do. He paused majestically, surveying his flock, and leaned toward the microphone. "Our topic for today is one that has long vexed me. How will I talk of this? How will I tell you about the wonderful gift of Jesus' love, when He asks us for so much in return?"

He stepped away from the podium, snatching the microphone by the throat and pulling it from its holder. He paced back and forth across the stage, whipping the cord on the floor and chewing off the end of the mike as he spoke. "'You must lose your life in order to save it, Saith the Lord.' But do you know what this means? That we must LOSE our lives? Please turn to Galatians, the fifth chapter, and read along with me! First verse:

"'*Stand fast, therefore, in the liberty wherewith Christ has made us free, and be not entangled again with the yoke of bondage.*'

"'He's telling us to be free, Brother Allen!' you might say. But brothers and sisters, He does not mean free to bite and devour one another. Verse 15:

"'*Take heed that ye be not consumed one of another!*'

"All that is of this world is rotting, brothers and sisters, and every day you must live this truth! You might say, 'Brother Allen, I work hard, I help my fallen brethren.' But if you clothe them, if you bear them up with food, and yet do not minister to their ailing spirits, you have NOT done what the Lord on High has commanded. Verse 16:

"*This I say then, Walk in the Spirit, and ye shall not fulfill the lust of the flesh.*

"Verse 17:

'*For the flesh lusteth against the Spirit, and the Spirit against the flesh; and these are contrary the one to the other; so that ye cannot do the things that ye would.*'

"Are you thinking, therefore, that you are not free?" The preacher paused in mid-stride. He turned and replaced the microphone in its stand. He stood behind the lectern and spread his arms and smiled benignly. "Jesus loves each of us the same, and lives in us when we give up the flesh. Your body may cease to breathe. That is NOT death! That IS freedom, friends. Your flesh is the bondage! Verse 18:

"'*But if ye be led of the spirit, ye are not under the law.*'

"You are free of the laws of the Jews. I am not telling you to quit your work. All of us must labor: the farmer with the plow; the soldier with the sword; the housewife, to provide us food to nourish our bodies. But the work that we are all called to is the saving of our souls!

"Read now in Chapter 5, Verse 6 and onward:

"'*For every man shall bear his own burden.*

"'*Let him that is taught in the Word communicate unto him that teacheth in all good things.*'

"But it is in the spirit that we must work, or else our other good works in the flesh are corrupted. Verse 8:

"'*For he that soweth to his flesh shall of the flesh reap corruption; but he that soweth to the Spirit shall of the Spirit reap life everlasting.*'

"But:

"*let us not be weary in well doing: for in due season we shall reap, if we faint not.*'"

With every word the preacher spat into the microphone, Joel felt the vibration of the loudspeaker in his chest. His breath was shallow and, occasionally, he glanced at Tom, whose face was riveted to his father's. *What is the use of living,* Joel wondered, *if my body is no good?*

"I will tell you a story," the preacher continued, but Joel didn't listen. He made faces at the little baby and was rewarded with a gurgly laugh. The baby's little head bobbed spastically and, after awhile, the baby's mother tried to rock it to sleep. Pete, too, seemed restless and busied himself with a hymnal. Joel watched him out of the corner of his eye, wondering if Pete was Tom's best church friend. The idea hurt him. He looked around the chapel at the heads inclined in various positions as the preacher droned on and on. Most people were listening, it seemed, by the way they nodded or held their heads high; but some of them may only have been pretending to listen, Joel thought.

The preacher was telling the story about Goliath, the famous giant, and David, the famous giant killer, killing the life of the story, Joel thought, by his frequent preaching about symbols and how one thing was likened to another, until Joel thought he would go crazy. But the preacher finally said, "And that day, David killed the giant. So you may be strong in body, or you may be weak, but you will lose your life if that is where you place your reward. The sins of the flesh, the temptation of them, even the luxuries that our nation loves—all this is like to Goliath. And it is frail against God and, for Christians, it is frail in the Spirit of Christ who gave up His body!

"The works of the flesh are manifest, my friends. Who amongst you have not beheld the silver jets of the air, or the mighty buildings in our cities and not marveled at the works of man?"

He paused to let the crowd think about what he had said.

"And yet!" the preacher boomed through the electronic microphone, his voice magnified, so that his words stabbed Joel's ears. "And yet! In our cities, and yet...even here! There is great EVIL among us."

The baby began to cry.

"Adultery...fornication...envy...drunkenness...all manner of abomination...."

Joel's head felt as if it would crack with the booming words, his heart pounding, caged in his chest, beating itself against his ribs, and he could feel the blood pumping under his collar. The congregation was quiet as the preacher named the sins, and the words dropped into the silence like stones into water. Tom began to sniffle.

"...reveling, and on and on," Tom's father said, his voice growing deeper, sadder. "...the likes of which I tell you, friends, are the ways of the flesh, and they that live for these things, as Paul tells us, shall not inherit the kingdom of God!"

Once more, the crowd stood up at the waving hands of the song leader. Once more, the piano player rolled a few keys of introduction and paused. Tom's father regained possession of the podium and Joel cringed, afraid that he was going to keep preaching. But he held out his hands in supplication. "If you are among those who have fallen to the sins of the flesh, come forward today, in Jesus' name. Do not let your sins fester and rot the divine spirit within you. Come home, today, as we sing...." The pianist pounded again.

"COME HOME!" They sang loudly. "YE THAT ARE WEARY, COME HO-O-ME."

Tom suddenly broke away from the pew that he had been holding onto. He swayed. Joel reached for him, but Tom pulled free, his face blank, his eyes riveted to the pulpit. Joel felt the color drain out of his face, then pulse back out of embarrassment for Tom. A sinking cold washed down his back; his knees began to shake.

As Tom walked up the aisle, people craned their heads. Some of the faces that turned to look at one another registered mutual, shocked approval. "Why! It's the preacher's OWN SON!" their faces said, as smiles shadowed their eyes. The singing almost died, but the pianist began to pound louder until the voices rose again. Paul Romaine's face was rapt and held high, but he turned and grinned at Joel—a sly, triumphant gleam in his eyes that Joel found unsettling. Between them was an emptiness where Tom had been.

At the front, the preacher came out from behind the pulpit and took his son's hands, and they knelt on the floor. When the music stopped, Tom got up and faced the crowd. His shoulders were shaking; his face looked tiny and sharp-featured, like a Kewpie doll won at a sideshow. The preacher stood next to him and put his arm about his son's neck. "Be seated, please, brothers and sisters," he said. His voice was husky with repressed emotion. "One of us has come forward this morning. Let us rejoice! Rejoice in the power of the Holy Ghost! Oh, flesh! You have been vanquished. Let us pray!"

And that was it. Joel walked outside. The little kid, Pete, followed. Joel turned to look down at him. "You want something, kid?"

The kid looked grim, head down. To Joel he seemed jumpy as hell. "Yeah."

"Well?"

"I...ah...that is...Tom and you...He...told me...."

Joel was losing patience. He could see that the kid was really nervous. He tried to be nice. "Look, kid, I won't bite. Just spit it out."

"You and Tom. You're best friends, like Tom says. He said you had a fight, right? He says serious. So, I know that. I can tell, and this morning, well, he gets, you know, the Call. But don't worry, man. His head is screwed on right, okay?"

"Sure, man. Nice meeting you," Joel said. Pete smiled and, in spite of himself, Joel grinned. The kid disappeared quickly into the crowd.

The men and women of the congregation ran to their cars in the dust storm that had begun. The wind had grown violent, and it gusted through the trees, blasting the new leaves with flecks of sand.

Joel sat in the pickup and waited for Tom. He was revolted. He looked over the hurrying crowd, suddenly afraid of them. Under their fluffy dresses and white gloves, beneath the suits of dignity and fine brotherhood, they seemed to Joel to be hungry, appetites merely whetted by Tom's repentance. Through the thickening sandstorm, Joel waited, hearing the wind roaring over his pickup like gigantic waves over a dam. He waited an hour, but Tom never came out of the church. Joel cried as he drove through the storm.

* * * *

The wind blew furiously, bending the trees along the street. There wasn't so much sand blowing in this neighborhood and, as Joel pulled up to Coach's house, he killed the engine and rolled his window down, letting the hot wind dry his sweat and tears.

The MG came roaring down the street and Coach made a neat, quick turn into the driveway. Joel jumped out of the pickup and ran to open the garage door. Coach drove in, waving.

Mrs. Hoffins got out, smoothing her dress and fiddling with her hair. She rearranged hairpins as she passed him. "Hi, Joel," she said, and hurried across the space between the garage and the kitchen door on the side of the house.

"You look like you're about to puke, kiddo," the coach said.

Joel shook his head. "Naw. Just got outta church."

Bill Hoffins laughed at that. He followed Joel out of the garage and shut it behind him. The wind blew his blazer out and whipped his necktie into his face. "Didn't know you went."

"I don't, Coach, only that was the only way to see my friend."

Bill's eyes still smiled. He put a hand on Joel's head and gave it a hard, affectionate shove as they entered the house by way of the living room. Once inside, the sound of the wind dropped. "JoAnna and I are going to have lunch right now—"

"Oh, sure! Sorry, Coach, I'll take off—"

But the coach gripped his neck. "Settle down, kiddo, I was trying to invite you to stay."

"Oh. Thanks. Mind if I call my parents?" Bill showed him the phone and left Joel in the living room.

JoAnna was automatically making a place for Joel at their small, kitchen table. She looked up at her husband when he came in shaking his head. "What happened?" she whispered so Joel couldn't hear.

Bill opened the refrigerator and pulled out two beers. He opened one and handed it to her. "I'm not sure, Jo. He seems worse off, for some reason. Maybe it's beginning to sink in."

They heard Joel put the receiver down. "Coach?" he called from the living room. "Can I use your bathroom?"

Bill showed Joel down the short hall and went back to his wife. They were seated when Joel came in. He had washed his face, but it was obvious he'd been crying. His eyes were bright and glassy. He tried a wide smile, but it sagged, and Bill eyed JoAnna quickly. She was doing her best not to look embarrassed for Joel.

Bill waved at a chair across from him. "Sit! Sit, Joel. JoAnna's got some stew. Hope you like cabbage."

"Yeah, sure, Coach." He pulled out a chair and sat down, bumping the table, getting the chair too close, doing a bad job of functioning. He crossed and uncrossed his arms. He stared mutely as JoAnna dipped the stew into his bowl.

Bill studied Joel's troubled young face. Kids kept getting younger-looking all the time. The freshmen last semester were like babies. Joel was an adult compared to most of them, except in one area. He hadn't been surprised last Saturday when Joel told him about himself and his friend. Locker-room talk always told him more than he wanted to know about his boys. Occasional banter included Joel, who was usually mute on the subject of sex, except when it came to the games in the shower with their own sexual undertones. Joel played around more than the others, although he was sure Joel wasn't aware that these games were any kind of sexual experimentation. It was all innocent, Bill thought, and then he realized this was all hindsight. Even he hadn't noticed the locker-room gamboling as anything unusual.

Joel picked up his spoon and ate politely. "This is good, Mrs. Hoffins," he said between bites, then looked around. "Hey, don't y'all have a little kid?"

JoAnna smiled a little sadly at Joel and patted his hand. "Linton's in the hospital, Joel. He's autistic."

Bill watched Joel's smile fade and something like embarrassment pass over his face. "Autism is a sort of mental illness," Bill said. "Nobody knows what causes it, or what to do about it. Linton lives in his own little world. He doesn't know us, maybe doesn't even have a way to communicate with us or anyone else."

"Oh." Joel looked up. "I didn't know. I'm sorry."

"We're always hoping a psychologist or medical doctor will one day find a way to reach him. But...." Bill stopped. "Anyway...he's well taken care of."

In the silence that followed, the three of them ate quickly. In the tightness of the house, the sandstorm was quiet, a steady moan interrupted by the occasional banging of the front gate. "What will this storm do to your crops, kiddo?"

Joel shrugged. "I dunno, Coach. Depends on how long it lasts."

"We've been here three years, and the weather constantly surprises us."

"They say wait five minutes...." Joel's voice trailed off. He dropped his spoon and squeezed his eyes shut. "I'm sorry, man...." He pushed his chair back and folded his arms across his chest.

Bill pushed his bowl away. "Tell us what happened, Joel."

Joel's eyes pleaded. "I thought things would work out."

"With your friend?"

"I was supposed to meet him at church,

because...well, he's been freaked all week. His parents always answered the phone when I called. They never would let me talk to him. And then at church we couldn't talk, and then he confessed in front of everybody! And I waited, Coach, but he didn't come out!"

"So your friend..." JoAnna smiled. She didn't seem embarrassed now. "You think maybe he thought he had to ask forgiveness?"

Joel shook his head. Then he looked up only with his eyes. "But why? For what, Mrs. Hoffins?"

JoAnna looked at her husband. "You know it's considered wrong by religious people, and your friend is religious, isn't he?"

"Yes, ma'am. But I'm his friend! Why wouldn't he talk to me?"

Bill sat back and let JoAnna piece together Joel's confused feelings. She never ceased to surprise him. Younger than him by seven years, at twenty-eight she barely looked older than Joel. Yet Joel became a kid with her, somehow meek. She brought out a side Bill had never seen in the Joel he knew—his super slugger. He saw something like a tender side, a vulnerable spot, emerge in his character. Joel was not so simple. The side of Joel that made him a boxer, the fighting side, was not Joel's essence at all. That was a physical response; no matter how intelligently Joel behaved in the ring, no matter how perfectly timed were the rhythms of his body, his athletics were mechanical. Joel laid out a complex field of responses to his friendship with Tom. "We teach each other things," Joel told JoAnna. "He's real. Do you know what I mean? He doesn't bullshi— He isn't the kind of guy you put on a show for, I mean. Like with the other guys, I'm kinda nervous about some things. They don't know me. I can't get to know them. I never would be able to tell them things like I do Tom. Because he's real. He's familiar...."

"But now you think you two might have gone too far, and he's feeling guilty?" Bill asked.

"He probably does. Yeah, man. He's scared stiff."

"And you don't feel guilty?"

"No! He started it, man! I just went along, until I...no. I don't see why it's wrong, do you?"

This, of course, was the danger Bill and JoAnna had been aware of—that question that now hung in the room. And Bill recalled JoAnna's warning: *"You certainly can't tell him to engage in sex of any sort! If the school board found out...."*

"Let's just say that's something you'll have to work out yourself, kiddo," Bill said.

"I need him, Coach. We were happy all the time. Do you think that's stupid?"

Bill breathed easier. It wasn't the sex Joel was concerned with, he saw, but these feelings of closeness that he was afraid of losing. There was no question that his needs were decent. Under his rattled exterior, Joel was still holding onto a basic need that outweighed the physical act of sex, although to Joel, of course, there was no way he could separate them. It was emotional satisfaction. That it just happened to be another boy was unfortunate. That made things tough. But he had to lay the facts out, which came close to saying they thought it was wrong. "No, Joel. It's not stupid to feel affection for another guy. What you've got to understand, though, is you can't be reckless."

Joel's biggest flaw was a sort of reckless honesty. In that, Joel was naive. That had been amply and painfully illustrated by the fact that Joel had jeopardized himself by even coming to him, a teacher, for help. If Joel had gone, say, to his ag teacher, Russell Thorpe, all hell would have broken loose. He had learned unsavory things about some of his fellow teachers, in control of children's minds. Bill Hoffins often said, "*You have a grave responsibility to bring out the best in children.*" The biggest challenge a teacher faced, he believed, was to challenge the students' minds and bodies to reach...

JoAnna apologized, but said she had work to do, and Bill took Joel into the living room. "Sit down, Joel. I want you to know that JoAnna and I are your friends." He straddled the arm of the big chair and tapped Joel on the knee. "But I'll be straight with you...." He held up four fingers. "Look here, kiddo." He held the little finger. "This is Tom's church, his religion. Hell, Joel, all religions probably hate homosexuality. Okay?"

Joel nodded. "I figured that, Coach. The way Tom reacted."

Bill curled that finger under his thumb. He touched the second finger. "This is the law. I looked it up, Joel. It's a felony in most states to commit homosexual acts." He folded that finger down and touched the third. "This is medical science. In the field of psychology, homosexuality is considered a mental illness, but you've got to understand that the research is...vague." He folded that finger under his thumb, and there was one finger left. "And this is each person you'll meet in your life. It's me. It's JoAnna. It's your friends at school." He shook the finger at Joel. "It's your parents and the rest of your family. You'll have to decide for each person you meet if you're going to tell them who you are. Sometimes, Joel, you have to keep some things private. It's society I'm trying to tell you about. There are good people, like your parents, but there are also unfriendly people. You'll meet some people who are just plain mean. And these people make up society, and they don't like homosexuality because it's against their religion, against their law; they've been told it's a mental illness, as well, and most people get shivers at the thought of two men having sex. You understand?"

Joel looked up. His face was opaque, his eyes full of questions, but he didn't respond immediately. He nodded so slightly that Bill wondered if he'd even been listening. He realized he was still pointing his finger and dropped his hand.

"Coach?" Joel's voice was quiet and flat.

"Yeah?"

"Most guys...I know they hate it. It scares them. It doesn't bother me, except that it bothers Tom. I'm not religious, and I don't feel sick in the head. And if it's against the law, the cops can put me in jail. But it can't change how I *feel*." He touched his chest with the fingers of both hands. "Right now, I just want to see Tom."

The coach found himself breaking into a soft chuckle. He looked at Joel's confused face. "I'm sorry, Joel. I've been making a mistake. I went to the university and did a little reading—the psychiatric stuff. I copied down some notes if you want to read them. But I can see you wouldn't be concerned, would you?"

"What?"

"About what the psychiatrists say.... Shit, I'll give you the notes," he said, and retrieved the spiral notebook. He ripped the pages out and tossed them onto the couch beside Joel. "Then later, you tell me what you think. About your friend, though, I can't give you much advice. I certainly can't tell you to experiment with him. But I don't see anything wrong with his being your friend." He put up both hands. "And that's it, kiddo." He stood up.

Joel didn't. He folded the paper and stuffed it into the back pocket of his pants. "But how do I get him back?"

"He'll come around, I bet. Just don't push him. JoAnna's right about the religious angle. We're Unitarians, Joel. That's quite a bit different from his church, but even our religion is uncomfortable with homosexuality."

* * * *

When Joel left, Bill joined his wife. "Thanks, Jo."

She turned around to meet him. She was at the sink. She smiled, confused. She shrugged. "I wonder what his friend is like, Bill. Do you suppose one of them...pretends to be a girl?" She shook her head. "It's so bizarre to hear that kid talk about being a homosexual. He's so masculine!"

"No. Neither of them is effeminate, as far as I've seen. Not like the Johnson kid. Now he does seem to fit the stereotype. It confuses me, too. At Joel's age, though, sex is like drug addiction, I imagine. If he doesn't at least get to see his friend, pretty soon...."

"What? You don't think he's going to be okay?"

"I'm afraid," Bill said, "it all depends on that friend of his."

"Which reminds me, Bill. I was thinking, why don't we talk to the Reverend Suskine?"

"Why him?"

"Since Joel's friend is religious, wouldn't it be a good idea to find out from Mr. Suskine what kind of problem that presents?"

"Our Unitarian approach may be too alien for the Allen boy's belief."

"We haven't stuck to one specialist for Linton. But I was thinking of help for Joel. He needs to understand the religious angle, I think, before he can understand the Allen boy's fears. If anyone can reach him, it'll be Mr. Suskine."

Bill smiled at his wife. "Maybe you're right. Mr. Suskine can at least give us a little perspective. But you don't have to get involved if you don't want to. The way I see it, Joel and Tom are at extremes right now. Over the summer, they'll probably work things out. They're definitely close. At school, if you saw one, you saw the other. I'm just surprised, now, that they waited so long to have sex."

JoAnna sighed. "It constantly surprises me how many problems kids have, even in a small town like this. I just wish my boss was more aggressive about it. I'm sure Joel and his friend aren't the only kids getting messed up around here."

Chapter 7

Joel sat alone in his room.

Sunday afternoon was terrible. After he left Coach's house, the wind had gone wild. It blew topsoil away from the fields and dried the acreage he had irrigated just the week before; and everywhere, the mountains were hazy ghosts behind the dust choking the wide desert. In town, the signs rattled above the buildings. Travelers ate in cafes, staring out across the billowing dust, listening to the incessant bumping of loose window panes. Birds foundered against the wind; feathers ruffling, they dived in sudden vacuums. Highline wires hummed and whipped in the wind along the highway.

He couldn't get the radio station because of the static. The television antenna on the roof of the house swayed violently in the wind and the television picture was a blizzard; without television, his parents sat at the dining room table drinking coffee, poring over the farm's ledgers.

It was the kind of day when doing chores would mean getting stung in the eyes and mouth with sharp flecks of hay when he broke open a bale to throw over the fence into the cow shed. His eyes would get red, tears would be slashed across his face, and the sand would get gritty in his ears.

From his bedroom, he heard the sand soughing against the walls of the house. He hated being
shut indoors. He avoided his parents, who tried to
cheer him up but were really too worried with the
sand storm to be bothered with his problems. But,
of course, he couldn't tell them anyway—not this
problem, not just yet, not until he thought more
about what Coach said. He'd been over this a hundred times. "It was just an argument," he told them.
"He's been sick all week," he said. "He's busy with
church...." He'd told them everything he could
think of. What did it matter, anyway? If he could
walk in the desert he could think and learn from
its vastness; from its indestructibility he could
rediscover how to make the best of things. But the
desert was also an inferno of boiling sand against
an infinity of space. If he could be with Tom, he
could at least enjoy companionship. But Tom had
become a stranger. By now, Tom should have come
to his senses, but he seemed to be growing worse
and worse. What if he never came back to earth?
Him and that fucking religion!

Worst of all, their friendship seemed a lie; it
had been ruined by one little night. Tom made that
clear with his tearful display in church, his joyful
return to the arms of the congregation. *All week
he kept me wondering; then, just when I thought....*
But remembering church was painful. Tom had
chosen, had stayed away from him with no explanation, had not bothered to explain a damned
thing.

He lay back on his bed and closed his eyes.
What was it Nicky had said? He wouldn't want to
find out that Tom was queer? *He meant me.* It was
clear now, especially seeing Tom again, exactly
what it was. *I don't need Tom's opinion. I know.*

"I am a queer, a homosexual," Joel said aloud. His words hung in the stillness of the bedroom. Already the sting of those words were weak. What would Mom and Dad do if I went into the dining room and said it to them? What would they do? *"You know what's been bothering me? I'm a queer, like Leo, like the man who calls himself Lucy and writes on bathroom walls, like the kid in Arizona."*

How funny, all those other guys thinking Tom was the queer. *Tom isn't any different than they are*, Joel concluded. *Tom hates what we did as much as everybody else.*

The sermon was pretty interesting—how the preacher zeroed in on things—but he rejected the preacher's ideas. Hating the flesh? *What else is there to life as certain as my body*, he thought, waking up every day, working, trying to make the crops grow better this year than last? You could drive yourself crazy ignoring the world, just waiting to die so you could go to heaven!

The Bible world, now that was strange. Things just didn't happen like that anymore, if they ever did. Giants like Goliath belonged in fairy tales like *Jack and the Beanstalk*. When he walked outside and looked at the millions of stars over the dry desert, Joel couldn't see where heaven could be, or even why it was necessary, when he had such a beautiful place to live in. He could see forever into the blackness, could see the constellations and know that they were so far away, that they were other suns, with other planets revolving around them, with other worlds of beings. In school he learned about Galileo, about the people who were afraid to look in his telescope because they would see planets that might have life on them. The idea about God riding in a chariot, coming down to Earth out of the clouds to appear to people seemed as much a child's tale as *Jack and the Beanstalk*. God would command people to do something impossible. If they refused, He would send a plague down; if they said, "Sure, God, okay," He would perform miracles for them.

He had learned that a long time ago people had gods like Zeus and Thor on their sides, and to gain these gods' allegiance and powers, the people were required to bow and worship them, to sacrifice innocent people and animals. Joel could not understand the value to these gods of such rituals and sacrifices, unless it was for the mere pleasure of seeing the people of Earth bow and scrape. And then when people grew up a little more, they didn't find those gods, and somebody said there was only one God, with a big G—a lot higher up, past the realm of the fixed stars. And in the Bible, that one God did things just like Zeus did, for some of the same petty reasons. God was said to play favorites, choosing one people over another. But what could people think nowadays?

He and his father used to get up early to watch the launches of the astronauts who would fly around the Earth at thousands of miles an hour, and he would wonder how science worked. But if he asked, somebody could explain it, and if he didn't believe it, he could experiment for himself. And science worked, better than things in the Bible, when applied to the real world. Joel suspected that a lot of people who went to church believed that, too, and that some of them were wearing masks, pretending to believe—but he couldn't think what special advantage that gave them.

In the Bible, people were always getting warnings and talking with God, but nowadays they just went to church because, apparently, God had stopped appearing out of the clouds, had knocked

off the frequent performance of miracles. Attending church, where people sat down and listened
to the story of David and Goliath, where the
preacher shared his knowledge of sin and accused
the congregation of harboring sinners, seemed to
be the important activities nowadays; the point of
the sermon seemed to be for sinners to confess
their sins, to repent and cry in public, so that people, not God, could approve. Then he wondered: if
you never confessed and somebody noticed, would
you get picked on or stiff-armed into saying, "Yes,
I'm a bad guy, help me save me?"

* * * *

Tom took advantage of his father's generous
mood after lunch. What had been meant as a comfort on his shoulder, his father's heavy hand op-
pressed him as they walked back from church. It
was as close as his father ever allowed them to
get—that hand, heavy and meaty like the paw of a
bear, as powerful as a bear. Then, during lunch,
his father announced that he was no longer
grounded. So Tom had asked if he could spend
the night at the Reeces' house. "That would be fine,
I think, Thomas." But Tom didn't know if Joel
would want him to and didn't call him. Instead,
he changed into a pair of Levi's and the shirt he'd
worn at the dance. It was a western cut with long
sleeves, a sort of dark gray, almost black. He liked
the way it looked, the way it made him feel. It lifted
his mood a little, gave him a chance to go back to
the place where things went wrong and start over.
Truth was, Tom was emotionally drained, again
on the verge of tears. Seeing Joel at the church
had almost made him cry. Then having to endure
the prayers afterwards, knowing that Joel was
waiting and wondering...but the praying seemed

to last forever and kept him from going with Joel right then. Everything had added to his frustration and his anxiety, and he regretted his little show in front of the church—except that it had worked to get his father off his back, as he hoped it would.

He slipped out the front door and had to hold it with both hands to keep it from cracking against the hinges. The wind slashed across his face, stinging it with sand. His shirt billowed out as he bent into the east wind, heading toward 8th Street. The wind changed directions continually. When he headed south on 8th Street, it came at him from the south. In the country, the sand was thicker, searing his face, making his eyes water. When he closed his mouth, his teeth ground flecks of sand between them. His need to get things straight, to talk with Joel—now to ask him for help—carried him steadily through the storm. His legs didn't grow tired and the wind offered the advantage of continually drying his sweat, making him feel cool. By car, the trip took a few minutes. Walking against the relentless sandstorm, pushed back without letup, his progress was slow. At this rate, it might be several hours before he saw him.

* * * *

Joel wished he *could* find the scripture that made Tom say it was wrong. If it was there, Joel felt sure what it said was probably not really clear at all. But even if it said in plain black and white, "homosexuality is a sin," it wouldn't necessarily be so, especially in a book that also thought stuff like slavery was okay. He looked through the Concordance, but didn't find the word "homosexuality". Earlier, he had found that word in the dictionary, but it wasn't any help. And the word abomination meant "anything abominable, anything detested or abhorred." He took out the notebook paper with the psychology notes Coach had given him. It was damp with sweat from riding around in his hip pocket. He unfolded the three limp sheets of paper and lay back on his bed. Coach's handwriting was small and neat, the sentences crowded and dense, covering the paper from margin to margin. He'd never seen so many big words crowded together on one sheet of paper.

It is granted that heterosexuality per se does not guarantee emotional health; there are innumerable neurotics among heterosexuals, too. But there also exist healthy heterosexuals, and there are no healthy homosexuals....

He counted eight syllables for the word meaning the opposite of queer. He got stuck on the idea of "emotional health." Coach had mentioned that, too. And here it was, in black and white, a real psychiatrist's words. The psychiatrist called him neurotic.... *No healthy queers,* Joel thought, *Yeah, if you went to a shrink, you probably did feel shook up—neurotic.* But if you didn't go to one, how would they know you existed, whether you were healthy or not? Tom would probably go, Joel thought, wouldn't he, if he thought he was sick? He was shook, all right—except Tom hadn't said he was sick. He said it was wrong, a sin. And JoAnna brought up the idea that Tom thought he needed to be forgiven. But if it was sick, why would he ask forgiveness? Could he help being sick? He read down the page and stopped. He mouthed the words silently:

Long ago I learned to use this rule of thumb: homosexuality is to be suspected in people whose methods of achieving their aims combine daring with unscrupulous behavior and a certain amount of cruelty (pseudoaggression). The hidden masochis-

*tic aim, plus the psychopathic technique, is indica-
tive....*

Great.

*Homosexuality is not the way of life these sick
people gratuitously assume it to be, but a neurotic
distortion of the total personality....*

Man, such ugly words. Joel smiled to himself.
Like Coach said, this was a ticklish subject, all
right, if it was a sin and a sickness at the same
time. He dropped the paper on the floor beside the
bed and stared vacantly out the window at the
brown, swirling world.

The minutes dragged by. He'd been home since
one o'clock or so, and it was only two. The wind
had grown worse. It was too hot to have the windows closed and too dusty to have them open. The
air cooler in his parents' room left a musty smell
in the house but didn't cool things down.

He was lying on the bed with his shirt off. Absently, he began running his hand over his stomach. The little, blond hairs tickled under the gentle pressure of his fingers. He stared at the whiteness of the ceiling and watched a fly crawling up
the wall. The ridges of his abdominal muscles were
relaxed, and below his hands the skin was smooth.
He felt the slow rise and fall of his breath. There
was a tiredness within him that made his legs feel
dead. He closed his eyes. The last sound he heard
was the quiet soughing....

* * * *

They were lying naked against each other
again. This time, Joel was more aware of the feelings against his skin as echoes of something in
his head. He felt love flowing from him. But Tom
was sweating, and his back felt clammy. His breath
was hot against Joel's neck, and he could feel Tom's

tears on his face. He was rubbing Tom's back. "Don't cry. Don't cry, please! I love you!"

But Tom raised up. He grinned, pointing at him like the man in *The Body Snatchers:* "*Abomination!*"

* * * *

He woke up shaking. He had been hugging himself. It was his own skin that was clammy with sweat. The wind had stopped, and the room had begun to darken. He looked out the window to the west; the setting sun was lost in a haze of dust that still flew around higher up. He heard the television in the living room and recognized the "Bonanza" theme song. After he had washed his face, he intended to tell his father that he would still do the chores, but the living room was empty; his mother was in the kitchen.

"I hope Dad hasn't done my work," he said.

She dried her hands on a dish towel. "Don't worry about that, honey."

"Why not? He has enough to do without me messing up." But she smiled sympathetically.

"Your friend came out a while ago. He and Douglas did the chores."

"Tom did?" Joel could hardly control the tears that felt like breaking out in relief. "Is he still here?"

She laughed. "Of course, Joel. My goodness. He came out here to see you! You and Tom did have a bad fight, didn't you?"

Joel shrugged. "It wasn't much."

"Is that why you've been moping around here all week?" She patted him on the shoulder. "Over nothing? Honey, you should have said how bad you felt. Tom looked awful! And you said he was sick. Did you know he walked out here, five miles, in the storm?"

"What?"

"That's right, in the storm."

"Where are they?"

"I don't know, Joel." She went back to the dishes. "Douglas came in a little while ago and said he was taking Tom out for a drive."

She kept her back to him, bent over her work.

"Mom!" He touched her shoulder. "Did Tom say why he walked? That was stupid!"

"Oh, I don't know, Joel! My goodness! He acted like he was afraid you'd be angry." She said this with her back to him. Then she turned around and looked him in the eye. "Did you do something to him?"

He stepped back, surprised at her question and her accusing look. "No! Come on, Mom, you know me better than that! I...." He almost said *love him*. "Why didn't you wake me up?"

"Because you needed to sleep. I know how little you've been getting." She studied his face with a hard look, then it softened. "Besides, they'll be back for supper."

He didn't know what else to say. He went outdoors.

The evening was cooler than the night before, but the air still held the taste of dust. He sat on the porch and watched the sun sink behind the mountains to the west. All he could do was wait.

When dusk had given way to the night sky and the stars were beginning to come out beyond the dust, when the breeze from the yard carried smells of blowing earth, when he was about to go crazy waiting and his mother was checking the supper in the oven again, trying to keep it hot, he finally heard the rumble of the pickup coming from behind the house, from the north end of the field. His first thought was to jump up and run to meet them, but he sat on the edge of the porch. He heard one pickup door slam, then the other.

Then he heard his father's low voice, muffled at the side of the house. It was the same tone he'd heard him use with sick animals. And then he heard Tom laughing, so loud it overpowered the thickened voice he'd had at the church. He wanted to go meet him. But he was also afraid. What a pile of shit it had all been. He stayed where he was. He couldn't even stand up. After all, what do you say to someone who has been driving you crazy, turning you on, then turning you off like a faucet?

Tom passed behind him and mumbled, "'Lo, Joel."

Joel looked at his hands; calluses on his palms suddenly became fascinating. "Hi, Tom. Glad you're here."

He turned around, but Tom disappeared through the front door. Then his father met his eyes. He shook his head as if to say, *go easy*.

Eva hurried around the kitchen, cleaning as she went, so that the air was fresh. She worked even faster when Tom and Douglas came to the sink to wash. Hand soap and towels appeared on the counter next to them.

"Would you like something to drink, Tommy?" she said, and gave him an affectionate pat on the head—a gesture Joel found embarrassing when she did it in public to him, but which he now appreciated. Tom smiled widely at Joel for the first time as he sat down across the table from him.

"Anything is fine, Mrs. Reece," Tom said.

She went back to the kitchen, rattling dishes and dropping ice into glasses. She returned with them on a silver tray and fussed over Tom as she set the glasses down. "Now, let's see, do you take sugar in your tea, honey?"

She was standing directly over him so that he was sort of slumped over his tea glass, and he smiled sideways over his shoulder. "Without."

"Good for you," she said. Then she took the tray back into the kitchen.

Joel watched the exchange, feeling shy. It seemed that she and his father were treating Tom delicately, and he wondered if his mother could sense the embarrassment between them. Most times when Tom stayed over, his parents treated him like one of the family. But tonight, she acted as though she were meeting him for the first time, and Joel felt shy in a way, seeing more than just his old friend's face.

Tom was beautiful, even if his face was battered looking from the sand and the wind. His dark lashes were slightly wet, his cheeks were stained with tear marks that didn't go away with washing. But the work in the sandstorm had left more than tear marks. Tom needed a shower just to get the sand from his hair. Joel's scalp itched from the sand, and he could imagine how much Tom had gotten walking in the middle of it. Tom's arms were blistered and, under his shirt collar, his neck had a little crease of dirt mixed with sweat. Joel noticed the faint traces of hickeys on his neck and closed his eyes for a quick second, recalling how he'd given them to Tom.

"Tired, Tom?" Douglas asked.

Tom grinned at that. "Just a little, Mr. Reece."

"You ought to get him out here more often, Joel," Douglas said. "He's a real worker."

"That'd be great, Mr. Reece," Tom said. Then he looked at his hands and showed the blisters on his palms to Joel. "These wouldn't be so soft, either."

Tom was happy, Joel realized, and he began

to feel a little better himself. "Hurt?" he asked.

Tom looked at him directly for the first time. "Hurts so much it feels good."

Douglas laughed loudly. "That's what it takes, isn't it? Sore muscles. I've given Joel his share, haven't I, Son?" He reached across the table and squeezed Joel's forearm. "Tough now, though."

Eva brought a large dish to the table. "Goulash," she pronounced when she set it down. She left and came back with a pan of cornbread and a bowl of Pinto beans. "I hope you like this, Tom. Joel loves it."

As the Reeces and Tom ate supper, Joel began to feel that things might look up. When he sorted it all out, it was pretty simple. They were still friends. They still had the rest of the summer, and it looked as though it would still be pretty good.

When Eva began clearing the supper dishes, Tom pushed back his chair and surprised Joel by jumping up and taking the dishes from her. "No, Mrs. Reece, Joel and I will do these. It was a great meal! You and Mr. Reece go relax."

She smiled. "Why, thanks, honey!" She squeezed Joel's shoulders. "Well, don't just sit there, Joel! You heard the man! Scoot!"

* * * *

Later, when they were in his room, Joel said, "You know, your father's sermon sounded like it was directed at us."

But Tom laughed. "That's what you're supposed to think. That's why Father is such a powerful preacher. He gets me every time."

"Gets you?"

Tom was leaning against the wall near the door. He picked up a magazine off Joel's desk, flipped a few pages, and set it down. He looked hesitant.

Joel watched him. He was sitting on the edge of his bed with his shirt off, barefooted and hugging the knee of one leg, swinging the other leg over the edge of the bed. "What, Tom? C'mon. No more stalling, okay?"

Tom sighed. "All right." He came over and sat down by Joel and put his hand on Joel's leg. Joel was surprised at his old gesture, but didn't dare comment on it. Then, just as casually, without noticing that he had done it, Tom took his hand away. "It's just that Father always manages to get to me. I should be used to his sermons. He practices at home, for God's sake! He goes over some phrases again and again, but up there in his pulpit his sermons take on power. Today, I'd already decided to do what I did...in church. I'm ashamed to admit it, but I did it so he would leave me alone." He smiled sadly at Joel. "He pestered me all week about everything. His sermon got to me, and I think I went up to the front of the church in part because of him. At the last minute, I went blank. I didn't know what I was doing until I wound up at the front! Joel, that scared me."

Joel shrugged. "Well, sometimes when I look back on things, I see I did 'em without thinking."

"No, Joel...."

Tom looked funny, his eyes almost as glazed now as they had been on alcohol. Joel shuddered, feeling that Tom was going weird again. But he couldn't think of anything to say.

"I was a wreck when you showed up at the church last weekend, so soon after.... I wasn't angry at you, but at what we did. I acted stupid and mean. But couldn't help it. I wanted to call you, Joel, but Father made me wait. It's a game of his, but this time I couldn't explain what it was and so I had to just.... I couldn't stand knowing you were thinking I didn't care. But I do. I had to act like nothing was wrong all week, that every day I was feeling better and better. So I decided to go through that ritual of repentance." He smiled weakly. "I'm really sorry. I'm a coward."

"Pete said you 'got the Call' or something. Mrs. Hoffins, Coach's wife, said you were asking for-giveness when you did that."

"You talked about this? With JoAnna Hoffins, the counselor?"

"Mainly the Coach, Tom. I couldn't tell Mom and Dad."

"You trust him, don't you? What did he say?"

"Trust him? Yeah. Why not? He didn't say much, and he didn't tell me it was wrong or right. He said everybody hates queers."

After an awkward silence, Tom said, "Joel, I wasn't as drunk as you thought the other night. I knew what I was doing."

"Then you remember kissing me in front of everybody?"

"No! I don't! I'm sorry, Joel." He got up and began pacing the room. "They all saw us? Oh, man...all I remember is sitting next to you think-ing how good it felt. You had your arm around me and...." He stopped and stared at Joel. "But how did we get out?"

"It wasn't easy. I had to drag you. Everybody was crowding around like you wouldn't believe. I guess it was quite a show. We just bulldozed our way out. Everybody was laughing at us, but they were too shocked to do anything." He laughed. "It wasn't very funny, really. I'll be surprised if we ever live it down."

Tom shoved his hands deep into his Levi's and squeezed his arms into his chest, a gesture he usually got as a defense against the jitters. Joel had seen him do it a lot in school before big tests. His eyes were shadowed under the bright, overhead light. His face was a blank. He paced back and forth, and Joel waited. Finally he stopped. "Look Joel, I want to tell you something."

The way he said it without a hint of humor made Joel more afraid, apprehensive. "Okay," he said.

Tom squeezed his arms tighter against himself. He sat down and put his hands between his knees. He took a deep breath and looked at Joel. "I am a homosexual. I admit it. Even before we met, I knew I was."

"The whole time?"

Tom held up his hand. "Yes, but I thought I could beat it. You don't know how hard I've tried. You can't imagine. When I went up to the pulpit, I faced it, Joel. Of course, God knew. But I finally faced it myself. And when we were praying. I didn't ask forgiveness. I just said 'Okay, God, I give up. Now what?'" His voice cracked. "And after church, I was swarmed with elders and deacons wanting to pray with me. But the whole time, I just kept repeating it over and over. I guess I wanted God to tell me what His will is. I just can't choose by myself. And I came out here for you to tell me what you want. You understand?"

Joel was stunned. He looked down at his feet, felt Tom's eyes on him. "You're saying it's between God and me? Forget it! I don't believe in your God."

"I know. You've got a real blind spot when it comes to that."

"And you're blind when it comes to reality, if you ask me."

"That isn't fair! Who's to say what's real?"

Joel sat up next to Tom and wrapped his arms around him. "Do you feel me?" He took Tom's hand

and forced his palm open and held it under the left nipple on his chest. Tom's hand was warm and moist. "Feel my heart?"

"It's beating fast, like mine."

"It's pumping blood all through my body to my muscles, my head. I'm just flesh and blood, man. That's real." He let go of Tom's hand. He leaned back and looked at him. Their eyes met. "But there's no choice for me. I want you, because I love you. I don't ask anybody's permission. I just do. And *that's* real. You know, when we started kissing I was surprised, but that's all. I liked it, and I realized that it was what we should be doing. I didn't know I was queer, like you say you knew. Maybe I did, in the back of my mind. But I do now. I'm a homosexual, too. I don't give a shit what you or anybody thinks, either." Joel took a deep breath. He had to say how it was to Tom, had to let him know what conclusion he had reached. "But if your church and God are more important than I am, man, we can't even be friends."

"What?" Tom sat up, looking stricken. His face was unbearably pained. "Don't say that, Joel!"

This time Joel got up and began pacing back and forth out of his need to get Tom to understand. "Night before last, I went out to a keg party...." He shuddered with anger at the thought, and told Tom what had happened. "I wanted to fight them, but it would've been stupid to, because they weren't worth it. Nobody said anything to my *face*, see, but they're convinced we're queers. They were talking it up before I got there. Don't you think everybody will if we hang around together, whether we do anything queer or not?"

"It won't matter," Tom said, still looking distressed. "We can go on just as before."

"No we can't, Tom! Because in this town, if people see us together...it automatically ruins our reputations. I don't give a fuck, but if you want to stay on God's side, you have to ditch me. If you don't, man, your father will find out, and even he will think the same thing."

Tom squeezed his arms between his legs nervously. "God...."

Joel sat down and put his arm across Tom's shoulders, fighting the urge to kiss him. "I'm sorry, Tom. It's the kind of problem we have. I just remember this guy who went to the same school I did. He was a sissy and got teased all the time. He couldn't get away from all their teasing, and then in high school, people started calling him a queer, just because he was a sissy. He never could live it down. And any guy that's stupid enough to hang around with him is going to be called a queer, too. I'm not kidding. So, if your church is as important as you say, man, you have to ditch me, or suffer the consequences."

"Is that what you want now, Joel?"

"Are you crazy?"

Tom looked at him seriously for a moment. Then he sighed, slumped forward, and let his head hang. "I think I am, Joel."

Joel thought about the psychology notes. "Look, if you want, we can just be friends. But we won't get away with it because of what people will say." He laughed. "It's hilarious! You say it's a sin." He picked up the sheets of notebook paper and laid them in Tom's lap. "And this guy says we're sick. You don't have to choose. Somebody else will."

* * * *

For hours, Tom lay awake in Joel's bed. Neither of them had considered changing their old routine, and the Reeces never thought anything of them sleeping together. Joel had once told him that when they visited relatives, the bed space decided where everybody would sleep. He told him that the boys always slept together. "I woke up one morning," he said, "and there were three cousins in bed with me. During the night, when I was asleep, my aunt and uncle brought their three boys, and instead of fixing them a pallet on the floor in the living room, Dad bet Uncle Sean he could sneak 'em all in my bed before I woke up. I slept right through it." Tom had laughed about that, telling Joel that his relatives always rented motel rooms. He had never even slept in the same room with another guy.

Tonight, when Joel slipped into bed next to him, Tom said, "I'm nervous," and laughed.

Joel looked genuinely puzzled. "But why? I'm not gonna do anything to you."

Tom didn't answer. He didn't want to admit that tonight was like the first time he had spent the night with Joel all over again. Then as now, the light in the room seemed unnaturally glaring. Just as they had the first time, Joel's shoulders, his naked back and chest, his thighs—even his shorts, which were supposed to cover his nakedness—aroused Tom almost more than he could stand. The very pain of lying next to Joel was pleasure beyond relief.

It was impossible to sleep. Long after Joel had gone to sleep, Tom lay awake, thinking. "It's the end of our old friendship," he whispered to himself, finally. What Joel said about choosing, that was right. Oh, maybe he could go to church and carry on as if nothing had changed, but if Joel was right about what people would think, he knew he would eventually have to choose. But how could

he choose anything that would put a barrier between them?

As if in answer, Joel rolled against him. Tom
felt his body's heat, the inviting warmth, but
couldn't reach out. He couldn't move away, either,
so he lay still, his heart beating rapidly. In his sleep,
Joel rolled back to his side of the bed just as suddenly. Not until near dawn was Tom able to fall
asleep.

Chapter 8

Monday, June 7

"Sandstorm didn't do it much good. Look here," Douglas said. Joel knelt down where his father had dug out a small cotton plant. The dirt on the row bed was crusty, but just below the surface it was still moist and dark. The plant looked scorched, blasted. The edges of the leaves were ragged, but its stem and roots were healthy. In the heat of the morning sun, the plants were wilting a little. They moved down the rows, stopping every two hundred feet or so, sampling the plants. When they had stopped for the third time, Joel knew what to look for.

Now he dug up a handful of the little plants and felt the stalks for firmness. Most of them were moist and firm between his thumb and forefinger; only a few felt dead. "Looks pretty good, Dad." Joel said. He squinted down where his father was pushing soil back into place.

"I guess it'll do. Maybe a little thin." He dusted his hands. "Unseasonal weather. Can't tell how it'll turn crops. If we don't have no more, we might do all right."

They drove around the field to the ditch line and stopped to check the irrigation. The rows were soaking up the water, taking a little more than usual because of the sandstorm. But doing fine, Douglas said. They stood on the ditch bank gazing out across the field. "See those weeds, Joel?"

Joel looked where his father indicated. The weeds gave the field an uneven look, growing a few inches above the tops of the cotton plants. They were easy to spot, attracting attention to themselves in their riotous, chaotic growth among the more uniform, organized rows of cotton.

"Cultivation'll get 'em this time. We can start that maybe Wednesday. We'll give the land a little while to dry out after this round of irrigation so we can get the tractor in the field."

When they finished checking the crop for damage, they went to the cow shed. They tied the tarp back over the haystack where the wind had whipped up the corners. Joel handed Douglas bailing wire and watched him put the neat, wire twists in the tarp holes. Then they drove more cedar posts into the ground around the haystack and wired the tarp down securely. The cows came up to the fence where they were working, and Joel scratched them on the head. His father chuckled at the cows and climbed the fence into the pig pen. The pigs grunted and lay down under the roof in the shade, watching him refill their water trough.

"Not much damage anywhere," Douglas said as they left the livestock area. "Guess we're just going to have an unpredictable summer." He looked heavenward and Joel followed his gaze.

The sky was piercing blue, not a cloud. Toward the mountains in the east, it was almost white from the heat of the rocks. Joel turned a full circle, looking at the sky. Beautiful. He let his eyes wander down the stark face of the Florida Mountains, traveling along the crevices where the shadows played. He was happy looking at the serene faces of the unshakable, massive giants. He turned back to his father. "So now what?"

"Not much for a few days, Son. We'll just keep on irrigating like before, put the cultivator to 'er, and go from there."

"Son?"

They were walking back now to the house. Douglas threw his arm over Joel's shoulder.

Joel tried to match his father's stride. He watched his feet, then skipped to get the same step. "What?"

"Oh, nothing much. I was just wondering how Tom is; after last night, I mean."

Joel looked at his father, appreciated his concern. He felt lucky, even if he couldn't confide everything. "He's okay, Dad. You helped him."

Douglas laughed quietly, then squeezed Joel's shoulder, almost till it hurt. "Damnedest thing, Son. I never could get it straight exactly what he was talking about. He mentioned church, and said he was sorry he missed you. He asked me if I thought you'd be mad at him." His arm left Joel's shoulder and he squinted. "And you were."

"Yeah." Joel dropped his eyes. "I was mad. But it's okay now, really. I'm still mad about a few things, but I think I see what Tom's problems are like."

"Good."

They walked on, then Joel said, "Dad?"

"Uh huh?"

"It's his religion. Why do people rake themselves over the coals when they haven't done anything? It seems like, you know, it takes away their chance to make natural mistakes. People aren't so bad they can't tell right from wrong, are they?"

Douglas shook his head. "Some people are, Joel. But then, of course, religion wouldn't do 'em much good." He chuckled. "One thing, though...."

"What?"

"That father of his, the preacher."

"What? Did he do something to him?"

"Wouldn't let him call you! That don't make sense, does it? How you going to fight with a guy if you can't get close enough to hit him? The gist of it is he couldn't see you until he told his old man what was eatin' him."

"I know. That's why I can't understand how he could take religion like that. The thing that bothers Tom is he thinks he needs it."

"Aw, he's not a bad sort, that Tommy. But if he was raised with a strict father, it would take a powerful will to figure out he's not a rotten kid."

Joel told him Tom had made a spectacle of himself, going up in front of the church. "And those old biddies enjoyed seeing the preacher's son, of all people, repent. Least that's what it looked like to me."

Douglas nodded with understanding. "Well, that won't do him no harm, maybe, if he feels like he needs to get approval for feeling lousy. I guess that's partly what his religion's all about. Your mother and I have gone around to a few churches, but seems like the basic decency gets lost squabbling over who's gonna be head honcho, more than everybody settling down to worship."

"Amen to that," Joel said.

"Another thing.... I don't think Tom likes his father too much, especially right now."

"But he loves his father, Dad."

"I don't doubt it. That's only natural, you know. At least at his age. But he doesn't much like him.

He didn't have to say so. I could tell. I think he's even a little afraid of him."

"Is that what he said?"

Douglas laughed loudly. They stopped by the front porch. He turned Joel around to face him, putting both hands on his son's shoulders. "If you were talking about me to somebody, would you call me 'Mr. Reece' or 'Dad?'"

"Dad, of course."

"That's what struck me funny, Son. Tom can't seem to decide what his father is to him. I'd never call my father by his last name. I'd say 'Dad' or 'Father' and sometimes maybe 'my old man.'" He winked at Joel. "Huh? But Tom kept saying 'Mr. Allen,' like he was afraid to call him his dad. I think that's too much respect and not enough like."

Joel thought about that. "Well, he says 'Father' to me. So maybe he was just trying to be polite."

"Maybe, Joel. Maybe so. But that was my impression."

Joel stayed on the porch. Having Tom spend the night like old times was good. For a time, they'd even managed to forget everything. And it sure had felt good to have him back. He had slept fitfully, drifting off, then coming bolt awake, assuring himself that Tom's warmth next to him was real and not a dream; that was enough. He felt ashamed for ever doubting that their love, the friendship part, went both ways.

It was almost noon. He had been up for hours, back to his summer morning routine. And as much as he had wanted to wake Tom this morning to go with him, he let him sleep. Probably, Joel thought, it was the first good sleep he'd had in a while. In the pale dawn, Joel had watched Tom sleep. His face was at peace. His long lashes lay on his cheeks like a sleeping baby's. His pale, full lips were turned up in the slightest smile. Joel leaned over and kissed him gently, not wanting even Tom to know. "I love you, man," he said, then left the room.

He wondered if Tom was awake now. A kind of nervous tension that wasn't exactly uncomfortable, not exactly good, came over him. It was time to see how Tom was getting on. Joel hoped his mother hadn't smothered him with kindness.

He opened the front door intending to go to his bedroom, but as he shut it, he heard Tom's laughter coming from the dining room.

Tom and his parents were already at the table when Joel sat down. Tom nodded his way, then turned back to Joel's mother, grinning.

Eva looked at him. "Oh, Joel, guess what?"

Joel shrugged. "What?"

Tom joined Eva. "Go ahead and guess, Joel."

Joel looked at his father. "Do you know what they're talking about?"

"Work," Douglas said with a straight face.

"Well?" Tom persisted.

Joel laughed at their faces. His father's was so deadpan that he suspected something was up. His mother's face was a dead giveaway, and Tom was just grinning. Joel shrugged again. "What?"

"We're taking a week off and going to the mountains to James and Mildred's!" Eva said.

"We are?"

"No." Douglas said. "Just us. Eva and me."

Tom said, "We're going to work the farm!"

"Who?"

"Us. Your father said he thought we could run it."

"Tom is going to keep my grass watered and mowed," Eva added, "and tend my garden."

"Have you asked your parents, yet?" Joel said to Tom, hoping it was really all set.

"Yes, Joel. Father said okay. We have to go back and get my things."

* * * *

Later that afternoon at the Allen house, Joel parked by the gate. Tom hurried inside by himself.

A moment later, Mr. Allen came out to the pickup. Joel got out reluctantly, slicking his hair down, wishing he had put on cleaner Levi's, but the preacher didn't notice. "Hello, Son."

"Hello, Sir," Joel said.

Mr. Allen cocked his chin. "While Thomas is packing and saying good-bye to his mother, I wanted to have a few words with you."

"Sir?" Joel's heart thumped with anticipation.

"You know what you're doing? Out there by yourselves?"

"Yes, Sir."

"Good. Don't let Thomas around any of that machinery. He's never had a chance with something like this, and I don't want him to be hurt. Not that he can't work. I understand there's going to be plenty for the both of you. That's good. Hard work never hurt. So make sure he does his share. He's been acting rather funny lately; maybe this will take his mind off himself."

Damn sure, Joel thought. He glanced shyly at the preacher's stern face and swallowed hard. "We'll come to church on Wednesday and Sunday, like we said."

Mr. Allen snorted. "Thomas had better, Son, or he won't get another chance like this."

"Yes, Sir." Joel was embarrassed.

"Okay, Joel. I hope you boys can handle this

responsibility." He turned on his heels and walked into the house.

Joel leaned against the pickup and waited. In a few minutes, Tom came out with his mother on his arm, shaking a finger at him. Tom smiled at Joel when they stopped at the pickup, then he let his mother finish chiding him with last-minute warnings that Joel didn't listen to. She pecked Tom on the cheek and retreated quickly.

Tom waved to her. He threw his suitcase into the back of the pickup and slid in. Joel smiled to himself more than at Tom.

Tuesday, June 8

They left at dawn the next day, giving Joel final instructions. His father gave him grocery money and spending money; his mother gave him a kiss from her side of the car. "Now you be sure to call if you need anything. I've set out a roast you ought to be able to cook and some hamburger to grill. Just open some green beans; use the jars on the top shelf in the pantry. They're the oldest. And use plenty of potatoes. I've got to get rid of them or plant them."

Joel waved them off. He watched his parents disappear down the road, then went back into the house to wake Tom.

They set the irrigation for the day. There wasn't so much to do except start the siphon hoses, which Joel made look easy. With one dip of the entire hose into the water, one hand cupped over an end, he pulled it into the furrow and dropped it. The suction pulled the water from the ditch in a steady stream. "See how easy?" He smiled at Tom.

Tom stood on the ditch bank holding the six-foot length of rubber. It was curved in a permanent bend, like an inverted "V," rounded out at the middle. He bent over the ditch, submerged the hose, and pulled one end out with his hand cupped over it. Water gurgled for a second, forming a dark-brown patch of wetness in the furrow, then stopped. They both laughed.

"Or, you can do it this way." This time Joel dipped only one end of the hose into the ditch and cupped his hand loosely over the other end. He popped his palm off the end as he pulled the hose up in a graceful movement, and laid the hose into the furrow. Water gushed out again in a steady stream into the row. "Try it."

The water that Tom managed to pull into the hose spurted through the end with his palm over it and wet his Levi's; then the suction was gone. He dipped and spurted three or four times, until his pants were soaked. But he was rewarded with a stream of water that ran smoothly into the fur-row. "Hey!"

"Only eighty-eight more!" Joel teased, and slapped Tom on the back.

When all the hoses were flowing they drove around the field to the other end and, as Joel had been doing all week, built up the borders. Joel gave Tom the lightest shovel and occasionally stopped to watch him bent over the work. Tom sweated and shoveled, but he seemed to enjoy the work and he did it well. Close to noon, they drove back to the other end to check the irrigation's progress. Beside him, Tom was acting lively. "The alfalfa's so green!"

Joel laughed. "There? That's cotton." They were in the north field, the newest land the Reeces had put under cultivation. "Last year we had alfalfa planted here," Joel explained, "and there's a lot of regrowth, but it's going to be real good cotton, since the kind of minerals and things the alfalfa takes from the soil the cotton doesn't need. And we let the cows graze and shit here. They break down the alfalfa into rich fertilizer for the cotton."

"So your father rotates the crops like they teach in school?"

"Of course, man. Dad experiments with a lot of stuff. He's been written up in *The Farm Journal*."

Cooler weather had set in. A few heavy clouds built up in the west and meandered across the fields, their shadows forming dark patches of green in the cotton. Around the edges of the shadow, sharp sunlight glittered off the leaves, turning them pale green. In the background, the Floridas were brown and purple, looking closer than usual.

"I never noticed how the mountains change shapes," Tom said.

Joel looked across the field at them. "They do, don't they? My cousin from Texas came out here one summer. He asked me if I'd like to walk over there before lunch!"

Tom laughed. On the many hikes they had gone on, Tom had been amazed at how puny they were in the desert, how long it took to get from Joel's yard to his favorite spot. A couple of hours of walking toward the mountains made so little difference in them that he knew they must be far away.

By noon, the work in the field was done except for checking the irrigation to make sure no hoses had clogged and no water had broken the beds. For lunch they ate the leftovers Eva had set out. Now they were sitting on the front porch with the day stretching before them. Ordinarily they would have found something to do, as they did when school was in session. Weekends had hardly seemed long enough. But now the whole week

stretched before them and they were enjoying laz-
ing around in the front yard. Joel watched Tom
out of the corner of his eye. Neither of them had
spoken for a few minutes and the sounds around
them intruded on Joel's thinking.

That motor sound that kept waving in and out
south was the Hotchkiss's well pump. The wind
gusting across the pond hampered the clear sound
from getting through. To the east, the Mulligans'
pump milled on, never missing a beat; just like
everything else there, it was in great condition.
Birds were screaming and singing in the trees
across the yard from them. And the fat, family cat
stalked below them, hidden by the rosebushes,
waiting for a bird to land for seeds and bread
crumbs.

Joel watched the cat. It circled around the tree
at the base, beneath the rosebush branches, casing the scene of the crime from all angles. Patient
and sly, it lay down in the shadows and waited,
flicking what to it must have been a dangerous,
prehensile tail, the only movement it permitted itself. Joel laughed aloud.

Tom sat up beside him. "What's so funny?"

"Just watching that cat," Joel said, pointing to
the rosebushes.

Tom squinted, then shook his head. "I don't
see it."

"Ah, but you're not supposed to," Joel teased.
"See those birds?"

Tom looked. "How could I miss them?"

"Right. Neither could the cat. She's about to
go for a kill. She's ready to pounce. I can barely
see her myself, but I can because I know where
she is. I saw her move across the lawn like a jun-
gle cat." Joel pounced as he said it and dug both
hands into Tom's ribs. Tom jerked back startled,
then laughed helplessly, lying back with his fore-

arm over his eyes, shielding them from the sun.
Joel straddled him, tickling. Tom struggled and
grabbed Joel around the neck. They wrestled off
the porch into the grass, and Joel landed on top
again.

Tom's strength surprised Joel. Joel began ap-
plying holds and twisting rapidly, but Tom trapped
him between his thighs. Tom couldn't get away
from the shoulder lock, but Joel couldn't spread
his knees for balance. Each struggled for domi-
nance, rolling over and over in the grass. They
stopped wrestling suddenly. Joel was on his back
holding Tom by the neck. Tom was on top pushing with both hands against Joel's shoulders, trying to pin him against the ground.

Neither of them noticed the ancient, red pickup
that slowed on the road beyond the fence. Kenneth
Stroud and Paul Romaine looked at each other as
they drove slowly by. "You see that?" Kenneth said.
I told you somethin' was funny about those two.
They're kissin'! And I told you I saw 'em leave that
dance the other night and head off into the old
part of the air base."

Paul grinned at his companion. "So you think
it's true, what you heard?"

* * * *

Tom gave in first, when they hadn't moved for
several minutes. He had an erection, and released
Joel's legs. Joel let his arm fall away from Tom's
shoulder, but Tom didn't get up; he rolled off Joel
and lay next to him with his neck in the crook of
Joel's arm.

"It seems funny, huh?" Tom said.

"What does?"

"This." He waved a hand around him. "We're
here, and there's nobody else."

"And?"

Tom sat up, resting his chin on a knee and looked down at Joel. Joel's eyes were closed against the sun and he was smiling slyly. His jaws had a slight growth of whiskers, giving his face a tougher look than usual. Tom felt a slight shiver of pleasure watching Joel's chest rise and fall in an easy rhythm; his shirt was open and his long, lean stomach glistened. Tom looked away, feeling too drawn to his body.

"Joel?"

"Yeah?"

"I was just thinking."

"About what?"

Tom got up and paced. "I can't shut it out."

"What?" Joel got up and sat down on the edge of the porch. "I wish you wouldn't do so much thinking, if it's what I think it is."

"It is, Joel."

"And?"

"And I'm confused. That's all. You're the first guy I ever did it with. At first, I felt so guilty I thought I was going to die."

"So? Feeling guilty...that's understandable," Joel said. "It's your church that did it to you. And even if you weren't a religious sort, there's that psychiatric stuff. There's the law against it, too. If you believed half what they tell you, man, you'd feel guilty all the time. So knock it off. Relax. You can't let everybody else tell you what feels good. I mean, take religion. Can you really imagine God getting so involved in our puny little lives that He cares who's sleeping with who?"

Tom laughed nervously. "Sometimes you scare me, Joel."

Joel looked at him puzzled. "Why?"

"No offense, but my father would explode if he

heard you talking about God like that. He'd say you're doing the devil's work. Do you know that?"

Joel's jaw dropped in disbelief. "Oh, come on! You think there's a devil, too, giving me ideas? I was pretty sure I came up with my own."

Tom wanted to explain, but Joel teased too much to listen.

"Do you jerk off, Tom?"

Joel's question made Tom feel giddy. "I did a few days ago. It was the first time in my life. And sometimes, I have wet dreams. Why?"

"Everybody does," Joel said. "When I first started, I would feel so guilty afterwards I didn't see how I'd ever get over it. But when I needed to, I'd jerk off again. And pretty soon, I barely noticed the guilty feelings; after that, I whacked off every day. I got careless where I did it, and one day Dad was picking cotton with the cotton picker and I was tromping down the cotton in the trailer he dumped in. While he was going for another load, I felt like whacking off. I didn't know Dad had trouble with the picker and left it idling in the field. I had my pants down around my knees, beating off, about the come, when I heard, 'Mess up more'n a pound of that cotton, Son, and you'll pay for it.'"

Tom's heart pounded. "He caught you, actually?"

"Yeah. I cried and Dad laughed so hard I thought I'd die. He said when he was a kid his parents told him if he did that he'd get diseased and end up in an insane asylum. But it didn't stop him or his friends."

"So did you...masturbate after that?"

"Sure. But I didn't exactly feel comfortable around Dad for a while. He loves a good laugh, and I didn't want to give him any reason to laugh at my expense."

Tom sighed. "I wish my father was like yours, Joel. If he caught me masturbating he'd cut my...balls off." He saw Joel laugh, felt himself turn red. "You call them balls, don't you? He still believes you'll go crazy. He says it's a sin to spill your seed."

"Do you think it's a sin?"

"Sort of. Anything sexual is a sin in my church, unless you're married...and there's things even then that are sins, like anal intercourse. In Sunday School, they drill it into your head, and it drives me up the wall. I can't decide anymore."

"Guilt is a bitch," Joel said. "I only told you that because it kind of describes how I feel about what we did. I didn't feel guilty, except seeing how you reacted. That got to me. But you'll get over it, eventually, you know?"

Tom frowned again. Then he snorted. "Hey! I'm still hungry." He was also nervous about the talk and wanted to stop.

—Part Two—

Against an elder receive not
an accusation,
but before two or three witnesses.
Them that sin rebuke before all,
that others also may fear.
                                        1 Timothy 5:19—20

Chapter 9

Tuesday, June 8

8 p.m.

Edna Stroud scrubbed out the cracked, stained porcelain sink. She was sweating in her long dress, with the sleeves catching her just below the elbows. A strand of gray-streaked blonde hair fell limply across her nose. She blew ineffectively at it as she ran water through the sink to wash the scraps of the supper dishes down the drain. This water would end up in the back yard, forming a mud puddle the kids would get into.

As usual, Henry was dog-drunk on the couch in the next room. He was drunk at supper again, too, which usually made her stomach queasy with dread; he was so spiteful when he was drunk. But tonight, Henry and Kenneth, the oldest boy, acted like old war buddies, talking about shooting and hunting, talking about the Reece kid again, just like in the old days when Kenny was at school. Kenny hated that boy, and Joel Reece so nice! No telling what it was this time. It doesn't matter, she concluded. Henry enjoyed hearing it repeated; he kept saying over and over, "Naw! You saw 'em?

Kissin'?" She tuned them out as usual and managed to sit through supper seeing them laugh and point imaginary guns at one another without hearing; she never could quite figure what they were going on about.

She wiped down the table and emptied the ashtrays into the trash bag between the sink and the water heater, looking hopelessly around at the grimy shambles of her kitchen, clean as she could get it considering that the roof leaked over in one corner, making the linoleum buckle. Underneath the table, the chairs had scraped all the pattern off the floor, leaving the black showing. And those dreadful cabinets she hated would never be more than grimy areas where roaches crawled over greasy cans, chipped dishes, dusty boxes of dry rice and stale tea. She had tried to make them look better by hanging curtains she had made from flour sacks on straightened clothes hangers. But over the years they had become smoke and grease stained, and although she washed them constantly, they faded and added to the grimy effect. She sighed as she poured a cup of coffee from the pot on the stove.

Wisht Eva Reece would call on me sometimes, she said to herself. She thought fondly of her. *Used ta send Joel over with jars of canned vegetables from her garden back when Joel was little.* Always a shy kid, he would knock timidly on her kitchen door, holding the box of food he'd carried over on the back of his bike. His pale, blond hair and beautiful, little-boy's smile had always tugged at her heart. He would hand it to her with the same little speech: "Mama said to give you these. Hope you like 'em!" Then he would smile and pedal off. Back in those days, Eva had often come to visit, bringing her curtains that looked practically brand new for the living room, bringing her clothes for the children—mainly boys' clothes for the twins who were younger than Joel by almost four years. And for a time, Eva had taken her to PTA meetings, 4-H Club affairs, trying to get her involved. For a few years, she had been involved, hoping to make a better life for the children, at least until Kenneth and Henry brought that to a stop.

Joel and Kenneth had been friends, almost up to the sixth grade, but then Kenneth started getting in fights at school. One day, he came home with torn clothes, a black eye, loose teeth. He was madder than she'd ever seen him. All he could say was that Joel and his friends had ganged up on him, beat him up. She didn't believe a word of it, but Henry did. He screamed at her "What'd I tell you, woman? That Reece lot're not yore class! You think they got rich bein' decent and hard workin'?" When she protested, he got mad enough to hit and screamed, "She shows herself round here to gloat and you know it! Kenny knowed it and got near kilt on account of it!"

He raved for days. Months went by and Kenneth's hatred of Joel became as strong as Henry's. It was misplaced, Edna felt, but for Kenneth, like his pa, there was no letting go of that anger. The last time Eva had come by smiling, bringing over more things, Henry took them from Edna and threw them against the Reeces' car. "We take care of our own. Now you git!"

Like the house, like the kitchen full of grime and rot, Kenneth got worse. And in his eighth and final year of school, a few months from graduation from Mimbres County, he got thrown out. The principal himself brought him home one day and took Henry aside. Henry's face was ashen, and he hung his head and talked low, cowed at the principal's indignation. That night he beat Kenneth and kicked him around until she had to drag Kenneth to bed and doctor his face with Monkey Blood. Henry hovered over her, "Let him be! Oughta cut your balls off, exposin' yerself, you goddamn bum." The crime was such that Edna could only guess, since even Henry wouldn't tell her exactly what he had done. He turned on her suddenly with the back of his hand and slapped her across the room. "I said let him be!"

She sat at the bare table in her usual place, able to see into the next room where Henry was snoring and where she could watch for car lights out the window by the front door. She was worried about Kenneth. He was mean, just like his pa. And tonight, what horrible talk, cussing like sailors all during supper, then Kenny taking off in the pickup. Going rabbit hunting, he'd said, but more than likely out shooting up highway signs again. The stretch of highway in front of the house was all shot up. And he'd done it. Henry wouldn't do anything about it, though, except buy more shotgun shells.

Outside, the sun was gone, but there was still the faintest pink in the sky. The air from the irrigation reservoir across the highway was cool and moist and brought with it muggy, earthy smells. The breeze came through the back door into the kitchen and lightly brushed her sweaty forehead. She recalled times when she would have been happy sitting like this in a quiet kitchen, her work done for the night, the little ones asleep, enjoying a cup of coffee. But she couldn't shake the depression that the evening brought on.

* * * *

Kenneth and Paul hid the pickup near the

gravel pit on the road that led to the Reeces' farm. Kenneth cut the lights. They parked behind a hill that had been made from the gravel pit. The stars were out and the slice of moon had just begun to rise over the mountains. In the light they managed to make good time walking in the ditch across the road from the Reeces' house. Inside, the lights were on and the living room window curtains were open. From their vantage point they could see into the living room and even through the wide doors to the dining room and the kitchen beyond.

"What time you got, Kenneth?" Paul said.

"I ain't got no damn watch, shitforbrains. We been gone bout'n hour. It's about eight."

"Well, I don't see Joel's parents. Isn't it too early for them to be in bed?"

Kenneth squinted through the darkness. "Maybe they have a TV-room. Rich folks like them."

"Yeah. Or maybe it's just the two of them. Maybe they have the place to themselves."

They shifted position in the ditch, squinting through the darkness.

The kitchen light went out, and two shadows walked toward the living room. From where they watched, neither could tell which was Tom and which was Joel. The two figures seemed to walk aimlessly around the living room, picking up things, setting them down. One of them turned on the TV, which was nothing more than a display of blue and white flashes. They sat down, one on the couch with his profile to the window and the other in a chair with his back to them. From time to time they appeared to talk, then turn back to the TV. "I say we move in a little closer while they's sittin' still," Kenneth whispered into Paul's neck. Paul felt an unpleasant thrill shiver down his back.

His nervousness increased as Kenneth led the

way, running across the road in a crouch, then sliding into the ditch on the other side. Paul made a lot of noise sliding in beside him. "You idiot! Keep it quiet," Kenneth whispered. His breath stank of beer and Paul almost gagged. "What if they got a dog? You want it to set up yapping?"

Paul suppressed a shiver. "Hope we see something worthwhile; my parents are going to be worried if I don't get back soon."

"You sure are a nervous Nelly! You wanted evidence, you little shit!"

Paul slumped against the ditch, feeling the rough gravel through his slacks. His stomach felt queasy; he had broken out into a cold sweat. In the daylight, Kenneth wasn't quite so scary, but sitting next to him in the darkness, his animal presence and stink bore down on Paul. He glanced nervously at the shotgun Kenneth rested against his cheek; Kenneth kept moving his face back and forth against the black, shiny barrels, idly caressing it with his hand. Only the thought that he might see for himself what Kenneth claimed about Tom and Joel kept him from running.

They were close enough now to distinguish the two figures. Tom was sitting with his back to them. Joel was sitting on the couch. They were looking at each other, and Paul guessed that Tom was talking, because Joel smiled, then nodded. He faintly heard the TV coming through a raised window near them and could make out shapes on the screen.

Kenneth motioned to Paul to follow him through the barbed-wire fence into the tree line that ran parallel with the road. This movement brought them within ten yards of the living room. As they had moved closer and closer to the house, Kenneth's excitement seemed to grow; his breathing had become shallow and quick and when Paul squatted next to him, Kenneth grabbed his shoulder so suddenly Paul almost screamed.

Kenneth pulled Paul against him in the dark and, in a low, quiet voice, he said, "Now we watch."

"It better be worth it!" Paul whispered back.

* * * *

The night was cooling off a little, and with the windows open, a breeze flowed through the living room. Out of habit, Joel turned on the TV. Tom seemed content to be doing nothing. Joel looked over at him, where he was sitting in the chair. "Tomorrow," he said, "I'm going to work your ass off, so don't worry. By tomorrow night you'll be begging your father to let you come home."

Tom laughed. "I doubt that."

"Good."

"Good."

They stared at each other across the space between them. Joel looked at Tom's familiar face, what one girl had called *kissy-faced*, meaning his lips were soft and full. *Incredibly soft*, Joel thought. He had never suspected how soft a guy's lips could be, but he knew now and wished he could stop thinking about it. He wanted to kiss him, but knew it would probably make Tom run, faster than all the farm work put together. It was difficult to get past that—that Tom would run, that he was afraid. On so many other nights he'd looked at Tom and felt the weird, little tugs in his chest. He had often tried to express his feelings but, lacking the right words, he'd stumbled across trite little expressions: "You're like a brother to me, you know that?" or "We'll always be buddies, won't we?" Now that he had the words for what he felt, he had to keep his mouth shut.

Although it felt late, it was only eight, going on

an eternity until they would go to bed. Just the two of them here, Joel could imagine how wonderful it would be to go to bed and make love again. But Tom was afraid.

Joel's hand shook a little as he reached over and touched Tom's fingers. Tom didn't respond, but allowed Joel to hold them. He looked helplessly at Joel, but allowed himself the slightest smile; his eyes still betrayed unease and fear.

"Does this bother you?" Joel asked, whispering, although he didn't know why.

Tom sighed. He pushed his hand palm-to-palm with Joel's and entwined their fingers. "I want to do this, Joel, but I'm just plain scared."

"I know," Joel said. Tom's hand was warm and dry under his palm, lean and smooth. Definitely a guy's, and part of the wonder of all this was that very fact—two guys! He looked at their hands clasped together. "But we're not hurting anybody. Are we?"

Tom laughed suddenly. "It sure doesn't hurt me, but it would disgust people if they saw it. You can't even imagine."

"I can, too, but I don't want to. And if you weren't afraid, I'd dare every creep in town to make something of it!"

"Joel! What about God?"

"Who?"

Tom shook his head sadly. "Never mind."

"Okay. I'm sorry."

He felt Tom's hand tighten on his own. "No you're not. But that's okay. Okay?"

"No. I am. I don't mean to push. But we've got so little time left. I don't know what I'm going to do when you go away to college."

Tom smiled across at him. "Me neither. But if we're friends, we'll stay in touch. But let's not talk about that."

Joel watched their hands and his feelings continued to rise.

Tom felt the strength in Joel's hand, felt it pulling from within him a familiar and frightening stirring. If Joel insisted that they make love, he thought, he knew he wouldn't be able to stop. He wouldn't want to. He waited, full of anticipation.

* * * *

"Sure as hell! Look at that, Paul!" Kenneth whispered in the dark.

Their faces appeared through the trees, ghost-like ovals that would be barely perceptible to someone looking directly at them from inside the house. But they could see clearly into the living room. Paul watched, fascinated. Now that he knew for sure, he felt sickened. It was worse knowing, and he wondered just how long it had been going on. Part of him gloated, knowing he held the cards now. Something bothered Tom about it, also, else why repent? He shivered, feeling Kenneth moving closer to him in the darkness, and wished—

Kenneth began to giggle. It was nervous and high-pitched, an elongated "Hee, heeee!" that pierced the night air and made the hairs on Paul's neck prickle. They saw the faces in the living room turn quickly in their direction, peering through the slightly-raised window. Paul panicked and crashed noisily through the trees. His shoes thudded on the side of the road then crunched rhythmically on the gravel as he ran heedlessly back toward the gravel pit.

Kenneth watched him with disgust. He wasn't frightened, just angry that Paul, shitforbrains, had interrupted the two queers. He merely pulled his head back into the shadows of the trees and continued to watch. A smile crept across his face that he was not aware of. It was a smile full of teeth. Joel got up to investigate the sound. He peered directly at Kenneth though the living-room window, and spoke into the darkness. "Kitty Cat, is that you?"

Kenneth allowed the darkness to conceal him and didn't move a muscle. Joel shrugged and said something to Tom. They got up suddenly and shut off the lights in the living room; a moment later, a light broke the darkness in a hallway, but Kenneth couldn't see either of them. He waited until the house was dark, then walked boldly through the trees and back toward the pickup where he imagined Paul was hiding, trembling in fright, the little, nervous Nelly. He screamed from deep in his chest and, holding the shotgun pointed toward the sky, fired both barrels. The explosions cracked loudly in the night and reverberated over the desert like the rumbling thunder of an imminent storm. Hundreds of steel beads pelted Kenneth a moment later, like metal rain from the exploded shells.

Wednesday, June 9

Joel opened the refrigerator. "Now let's see…" He was wearing Levi's but hadn't yet put on a shirt or his boots. Tom, similarly dressed, stood next to Joel with a hand on his shoulder. Both of them peered into the refrigerator. Joel looked backward at him. "You want some eggs?"

"I feel like I could eat a horse."

Joel moved some containers around. "Horse…horse. Sorry, Tom. We're fresh out."

Tom laughed delighted. "Eggs."

Joel pulled out a bowl of eggs, unwrapped the bacon and handed it to Tom. He pointed to the sink cabinet. "There's a frying pan over there. Juice?"

Tom nodded.

"Comin' up!"

Joel got out juice and coffee while Tom fried the bacon. "Listen, Joel, I cook a lot, so why don't you let me? You just sit there and plan my torture."

Joel got out plates, plugged in the coffee, showed Tom the salt and pepper. He stood behind Tom at the stove and held his hips. Tom moved around beneath his hands. "That feels good, Joel, but you shouldn't."

Joel let his hands drift away, saw where they had been just above the edge of Tom's Levi's. It didn't matter. Right now, looking was as good. He felt happy. Soon the kitchen smelled of bacon and coffee and, as they ate by the dining room window, the sun washed the grass in the front yard with flecks of gold in the dark, moist green.

Joel dug into his breakfast. "Hey, these eggs are delicious. What did you do?"

Tom shrugged. "I found some stuff in the spice shelf and threw it in."

Joel gazed out the window but could see Tom sitting to his left out of the corner of his eye, and it struck him that Tom was in the place where his father usually sat. Joel recalled a morning similar to this, and the most exciting conversation he ever had with his father. It must have been a year ago, but it could have been yesterday. "If you want it, Son, you and I can become partners. You finish school, go to college if you want. And this will belong to you." At certain times, his father simply presented adult, man-to-man proposals to Joel as though he were a business partner, and it left Joel feeling proud, loving him completely. He and his father had looked out the window at their land in the dawn. "Your mother and I discussed it. Fifty percent when you graduate. You pay yourself a salary, like your mother and I do. The rest stays in the business. Or, you can light out on your own, if you've got an itch to. Make your own way in the world. There's a lot going on out there, Joel. Places you could see."

He looked beyond the fence line of the farm toward the south. Patches of desert still dominated. Yucca plants, some of them ten, twelve feet high, stood around in the dawn in groups like bizarre creatures, discoursing on matters of state. They cast purple shadows over the light-flooded sand, and beyond that were more patches of green and yellow, and then a sweeping away of ground toward the distant southern mountains that closed the Mimbres Valley. Beyond them lay Mexico and the curve of the earth into South America.

It wasn't a hard choice for Joel, back then, to agree eagerly to his father's proposal. It had been put seriously. Joel had accepted, and his father had thanked him. "I have to plan for the future, Son. I couldn't handle this place without you, and if you decide to take over, inherit this place, you need to think about your own family in a few years. You sure don't need to marry any time soon, but you'll need to think how you'd run this place when I retire." And back then, just a few weeks before Tom came along, Joel had assumed that getting married would be his next big step. He dropped his gaze and looked at Tom. You could talk to Tom that way, too, man to man, adult to adult.

He thought of asking, *"Will you marry me, Tom?"* and shivered, delighted at the way it sounded. "You were hungry," he said, instead.

Tom mopped up the egg yellow on his plate with the last bite of toast and stuck it in his mouth. He chewed rapidly, his jaws working overtime. He drained his orange juice. "I'm hungrier out here. I don't work like this very often. My muscles are sore!" He grinned and rubbed his arms. "But I like it!"

Remembering that, Joel set a leisurely pace for them. They washed the dishes and finished dressing. It was seven or so by the time they left for work. At first they made a poor team; they were late getting the chores done, but Tom worked eagerly and happily. And all morning Joel wanted to talk about them. Somehow…this couldn't end. Not this summer. Not ever.

* * * *

They were west of the garden outside the equipment shed, stacking the metal tarps from the irrigation ditch. Tom was looking at one of them as he washed the dry mud cakes from it with a hose. Their trapezoid shapes made them fit cozily into the concrete ditch and Joel told Tom about irrigating with the dirt ditches when he was a kid, the way the real tarpaulins rotted eventually from constantly being hung across the ditch and covered with mud.

When it was free of mud, he handed it to Joel, who tossed it easily onto the neat stack against the outside wall of the shed.

"You work like this all the time?" Tom asked.

"Yeah. But once you get it done, it feels good. Dad always insists on taking time to clean and store things. That makes the job easier next time."

Joel was shirtless, but Tom still wore his. His neck was runneled with sweat and his pants were muddy up to the knees. Joel smiled to himself, thinking how even now, trying to be neat, he kept his shirttails tucked in. "Aren't you getting hot? Whyn't you take your shirt off?"

Tom handed him the last of the tarps. "Good idea. I'm tired, and I'm going to be starved by lunch. But I like it. I don't see how you and your father handle the whole farm!" He took off his shirt and hung it over a hook on the outside wall of the shed.

"Everything is done in large chunks, I guess. We'll be finished with the irrigation by Friday, and by the time we get to the northeast field with the water, I'll be able to get the tractor in the south field and cultivate the weeds. But we'll hire crews for the real work, like harvesting."

"I'd like to see that!" Tom said. He followed Joel as they walked toward the pickup. "But I guess I'll be in college before that."

The thought of that brought Joel up short. He stopped and looked at Tom. "I keep trying to forget that, you know?"

Tom looked grim. But he brightened. "Well, maybe Father will let me stay out here the rest of the summer. When I asked him the other day, he said he'd think about it. This week is supposed to be a test." He laughed. "You know, more games. I think he'll be pleased to see how my muscles are developing."

Joel looked appreciatively at Tom. "You look great like you are."

Tom felt of his arms, then Joel's. "Mine are like toothpicks beside yours!"

"They're just longer than mine." Joel stood beside him and touched their shoulders together. His fingertips came to the back of Tom's hand. "See? Your muscles are more stretched out." Tom pulled his arm away and slipped it around Joel's waist. If felt awkward to, but Joel moved closer to Tom and let himself be held. It was a switch, and a surprise. Neither of them spoke for a moment, then Tom pulled away.

"Sorry," Tom said.

"Just one of your moods," Joel said. "It's okay with me, you know?"

Tom sighed. "I know."

* * * *

By the afternoon, everything was done, and they walked back to the house from the livestock pens. "Don't you milk the cows?" Tom asked. Joel told him they were letting them dry up, getting them ready for calves. Tom looked tired. He had been quiet all afternoon, except for asking short questions about the work they were doing, but even though they didn't talk much, Joel had been constantly aware of him. Painfully aware, too, that come September, he would be gone. He had counted out the weeks left until then like a death-row inmate.

"You like what we're doing?" he asked.

"Yeah. It would get old after awhile maybe, but I love this place, Joel! If I had to pick a place to live, it would be in the country. I get so tired of moving. You know I've never lived any place for more than two years?"

"I thought you'd prefer living in a city."

Tom laughed softly and shook his head. "If I could, Joel, I wouldn't go to college for a while. If Father wasn't pushing me, you know? All I want to do is take a little time to think about what I really want to do. I don't even like living in town, small as it is... I don't know...maybe it's because I feel so happy out here. If Father just wasn't pushing. Except without a degree, I'd probably never get a very good job."

The same idea tugged at Joel's mind again. *Live with me then, Tom. I need a mate.* It made his heart pound, and he was bursting to share it with

Tom, but he was afraid of being laughed at. "I don't know if I could stand the same job year 'round," he said.

"You oughta try being a preacher," Tom said. "I think that'd really get boring."

"But you said you don't want to be one."

"I don't. I won't! And besides, being...you know...like I am, I don't think I'd make a very good one."

"Come on, Tom. Knock it off! You can be whatever you want, with your brains. Yeah, you probably would make a lousy preacher. But your personal life is your business."

"Well, of course," Tom said, "you're right."

But Joel got the feeling that Tom didn't really believe that. And he remembered how easily his father had kept him at home, how Tom had worried about his willpower. Joel bounced onto the porch and looked back over his shoulder at Tom, who was a little more weary. "But don't go thinking it's a sin. It isn't wrong."

Tom followed Joel into the house and into the kitchen. They washed up at the sink and Joel got busy preparing for their supper. "I guess it'll take a couple of hours for the roast. What time do we have to be at church?"

"Six-thirty."

"Yeah, that's right." He peeled all the potatoes. If his mother wanted them eaten, they would eat them. He cut some of the potatoes into quarters and washed them at the sink. He nudged Tom out of the way with his hip and dropped them around the edges of the roast pan. He cut the rest of the potatoes into long strips. Later, they could eat fries for a snack. Joel imagined them sitting together with his arm over Tom's shoulder, feeding him potatoes, and he got chills. He laughed at himself, looking somewhere between the potato peels scattered over the table and bright, afternoon sunshine outside in the yard and across the road. The sun was still high in the sky but was already casting a yellow glow over everything as late afternoon approached.

The road was busy at this time of day, especially during the week. It was still the season for buying supplies as the farmers set up for the maturing crops. The farmer's market in town, the equipment supply stores and the feed stores were doing brisk business and stayed open until long after sunset. Joel recognized the Hotchkiss's old, dilapidated pickup rattle by on its way home from town, heading south. He saw it and the Strouds' '48 Ford pickup almost collide right outside the gate, and sat up to watch. The Hotchkiss truck lurched into the ditch, feeble horn coughing, then back onto the road. The Stroud truck slowed down and drove by the gate. As if he knew he was being watched, Kenneth flashed his hand over the top of his truck, middle finger waving; a moment later, the bright glint of metal caught the afternoon sun. Joel continued to stare, feeling uneasy; last night, he thought he'd heard laughter, then the unmistakable sound of a shotgun. As the truck passed out of sight, Joel realized he'd been holding his breath. His scalp tingled, the hairs on his neck bristled. What was Kenneth doing on this road, anyway?

Kenneth Stroud and his father were a bad pair, Joel thought. But Mrs. Stroud and her younger kids seemed all right. It was said that Kenneth had raped one of the Hotchkiss girls. He had been kicked out of school his eighth year, as well, for taking his dick out in class and playing with it in front of everybody. Sue Mulligan was the only girl who didn't burst into tears and scream; she was said to have watched Kenneth calmly for about a minute while he played with himself, then she got up quietly and walked out of the classroom to the principal's office to report it. The teacher had left them alone that afternoon, as usual, to attend to another class. Joel was in the seventh grade when it happened. All the boys in the three upper grades were herded into the auditorium and lectured by the principal, asked questions about any other incidents like the one that had occurred. None of the boys mentioned the sex games everyone played under the trees near the football field. After this incident, there was a heightened interest in sex at the school. As usual, the teachers and the principal all thought they'd nipped the problem in the bud.

The events of that day stayed with Joel. He recalled precise details every time he saw Kenneth Stroud. If Joel feared anybody, it was someone like Kenneth. He was the kind of guy who didn't fight fair. He didn't understand anything but brute strength. He enjoyed making girls scream and cry. Back then, he was the biggest bully in the whole school. And now he was playing with real guns, getting more dangerous by the day, and Joel thought one of these days he'd end up killing somebody.

Chapter 10

Crickets plopped on the sidewalk under the street lamps in front of the church. People were standing around again, but not nearly as many as on Sunday. Joel supposed these were the devout ones. Then he laughed, thinking of what his father had once said about James and Mildred, that Baptists like them had a lurking suspicion that someone, somewhere, was having fun. He laughed self-consciously, wondering if he was supposed to seem so happy, afraid he might lose control. He wanted to throw his arm over Tom's shoulder or something as they walked up to the rest of people. Tom laughed.

"What's so funny, Joel?"

Joel whispered, "I'll tell you later," and he tried to put on a serious expression. The adults looked so constipated when they smiled at Tom, Joel thought. A few of them gripped Tom's hands. "We were so happy having you back in the fold," they said, implications left unstated.

But Tom didn't seem to mind. "Thank you, Brother Leon. Thank you, Sister Thomason." Thank you, so-and-so.

"It's truly comforting to know your father was there for you in your time of need, Brother Thomas," a round, plump woman said breathlessly.

"Why, thank you, Mrs...."

"Smith, dear! It's such an easy name to remember." She glittered and fluffed off.

Inside, the church was blinding in fluorescent light and the stained glass windows were opaque against the growing darkness outside. Joel followed Tom to one of the classrooms where teenagers were forming a circle of folding chairs. "We don't have a sermon on Wednesday," Tom explained.

Joel felt uncomfortable in the brightly painted classroom. Paul Romaine came in and took an empty chair next to Joel, then immediately leaned over him to talk to Tom. "Where have you been?" he whined. "I wanted to study tonight's lesson with you!" Joel thought he sounded like the fat lady outside. He stretched his legs, then threw a foot over his thigh. Paul had to sit back.

Immediately, he felt Paul's hand on the back of his chair while he talked to Tom over his shoulder. In his left ear, Paul yammered like a whiny cat. Joel leaned back, deliberately squeezing Paul's fingers against the chair; then, seeing Paul's shocked expression, he said, "If you want to talk to Tom, why not sit next to him?"

Paul's eyes rolled heavenward, as if Joel's comment was stupid. He leaned forward again. "Well?"

Tom grinned slightly. "Didn't my father tell you?"

"I couldn't ask him," Paul whined. "No one was home when I came over last night."

Tom told him about spending the week at Joel's while his parents were on vacation.

Paul sneered. "Oh? You two are *alone* out there?"

"We're big boys," Joel said.

"Yeah. Kenneth Stroud and I saw you were at

Joel's, yesterday," Paul said to Tom. "In the front yard—"

"Then you knew where I was," Tom said. "Why did you act like you didn't?"

Paul's face went through a series of rapid changes that finally resolved itself into a sneer. "Your repentance surprised me." He grinned slyly. "Kenneth said he saw you and Joel at that cowbarn dance. You were drunk, weren't you?"

Tom released his breath through clenched teeth. "If Kenneth said so, then I musta been, huh?"

Paul's face sharpened. "No wonder you repented!"

Joel noticed the little redhead from Sunday watching them from across the room. Unaware that he was being watched, his face was pinched with hatred. And no doubt he could understand Paul easily, since Paul meant for the whole room to hear. Then Pete saw Joel looking at him and moved across the room. He stood in front of them shyly. "Hi, Joel. Glad to see you made it."

Joel nodded; then, remembering the kid's attempt to help him Sunday, said, "Could you show me where the rest room is?"

They walked out into the hallway and Joel whispered, "What's this Paul up to?"

Pete shrugged. "I was trying to figure that out myself, man. He's spreading rumors about you two."

"You mean the dance?"

"Yeah."

"What's he saying?"

"That you and Tom were dancing together out at the old air base a couple a weeks ago, that you two got kicked out...when you started kissing."

Joel couldn't believe his ears. "When did all this start?"

"Oh, just tonight, man."

"Thanks, Pete. We better go back."

A young man, who Joel guessed was in his twenties, had taken control of the class. He was apparently chewing Paul out. "We can talk about this some other time. We're supposed to be discussing our lesson. Brother Allen's spiritual motivation for going forward Sunday is his business, Brother Romaine, not yours." The teacher gazed around the class. "The act of repentance is not to display yourself, but to draw on the indwelling of the Holy Ghost that Christ tells us is present when we are gathered in His name, so...class, may we get started on our lesson?"

Joel felt out of place here, as he had in church a few days before. He shared a borrowed Bible with Tom. Their hands met beneath it. His discomfort continued, and his armpits were soaked by the time the class ended.

In the chapel, they sang hymns and closed with a prayer.

Afterwards, like a fly continually buzzing around spoiled meat, Paul followed them out and tried to pull Tom aside. But Tom kept moving toward Joel's pickup and got in, finally having to push Paul away with the door. Paul leaned into the open window. "Well, what about the Young Men's Fellowship tomorrow?"

"Forget me this time. I told you, Paul. I'm working at the Reeces'. I'd be too tired to come back in tomorrow."

"But we were going to group pray! I'm going to lead the prayers!"

As he pulled into the street, Joel glanced over at Tom, who was smiling and looking relaxed. Joel knew that he had to let him know what was going on. He felt apprehensive, afraid that the last two days were the last of the old friendship. He had warned Tom, and here it was happening a lot sooner than he thought. "That little kid, Pete, says Paul is saying we got kicked out of that dance, says we were dancing together and kissing on the dance floor. I told you, man...." He trailed off, unsure, seeing Tom's quick frown.

"He was?"

"Yeah. Kenneth Stroud was at the dance, too, so I bet that's where Paul is getting that."

"I guess I didn't see Kenneth the other night," Tom said. He slipped his arm around the back of the seat. His palm was warm and comfortable against Joel's shirt. "You were right, Joel." Tom squeezed Joel's shoulder but seemed to be unaware that he was doing it. "Paul. That figures. Pete warned me about him the other day." He shrugged, then laughed nervously. "Screw it! I'm sick of being such a...a wimp. As long as Father doesn't find out, man, I don't care. Let's drag Main."

Joel laughed, wanted to feel good about Tom's new sense of determination, but it was too soon after seeing how hysterical he had been for Joel to feel as relaxed as he acted.

* * * *

Tom was sitting on the far side of the pickup, with his arm out the window. His hair blew in the warm, night air. On the east end of town, Joel pulled off the road in the darkness and cut the engine.

Tom looked around. "Why're you stopping here?"

"The graveyard? You know, see who's in town, tonight." They watched the steady stream of cars pass them on the highway and make U-turns in the road by the Luna Drive-in Theater.

"There go the Crawfords," Joel said. He remembered Bill's cold behavior and Nicky's warning to get a girlfriend. Tom pointed out Mike St. Germaine's new Corvair as it followed close behind, followed by several Oldsmobiles, Pontiacs, and the Bensons's Cadillac. For just a second, Joel's heart pounded a little faster when the Cadillac U-turned and headed back their way. Melissa Benson's silver-blonde hair billowed out of the driver's-side window; one dainty wrist was draped over the top of the steering wheel, guiding the car over the smooth roadway. She was staring straight ahead and, as though she had seen Joel's pickup parked under the evergreen trees in the dark, she gunned the engine and the Cadillac almost skidded, leaving only the glow of its taillights. He sighed with relief. "There went my old girl-friend."

"Melissa Benson—I know," Tom said flatly. "When I first moved here, I went out with her sister. She pointed you out to me one time. That's how I knew your name. Did you know she had a crush on you—Debbie, that is?"

"Melissa's older sister had a crush on me?" Joel asked, laughing. It felt funny even talking about it.

"Yeah. She didn't know I was just as anxious around you as she was!" Tom ducked his head, embarrassed that he'd been so blunt.

"C'mon, Tom. Don't. We're doing okay. Let's just enjoy ourselves. We won't talk about anything that gets you down."

But Tom laughed. "No. I'm fine. I just surprise myself sometimes. I told you I know what I want. And I did have a crush on you!"

From the west, another flock of cars was coming up the street, their headlights playing through the cab of the pickup. In the flickering light, Tom's face was streaked in shadows that moved from his chest and up his neck, across his dark eyes. They blinked in the sudden flashes. Joel saw that he was still bothered despite what he had said. "I want you too, Tom," he said, softly.

"Joel!"

Tom jerked up in the seat and looked past him. "Who said that?"

"I don't know," Joel said. He watched the cars that had just passed. "I think it came from that Mercury. The one turning around."

They watched as the white Mercury swayed in a large loop left and off the far side of the road, where it parked. Sure enough, the driver kept glancing across the road. His face would be clearly lit in the glow of car lights, then flicker out like a candle in the darkness. Joel recognized the car. "Think that's one of the Johnson boys," he said to Tom, "But I don't know which one."

They drove across the road and Joel pulled up behind the car. The driver didn't get out or wave, but waited for them to walk up to the window.

Leo Johnson was hunched down in the seat. He glanced shyly up at Joel. "Thanks for coming over, Joel. I can't believe I yelled at you out the window." He giggled nervously.

Joel introduced Tom. "Gee, man, I haven't seen you for a while!" Joel said. "I was just thinking about you the other day. What's up?"

Leo looked surprised for a moment. "Me? What were you thinking about?"

"That time we went on the field trip up in the Florida foothills."

"Oh. Yeah."

"What'd you want?"

Leo looked around nervously. "Get in."

Joel looked at Tom. Tom shrugged. "Okay with me."

They got in the passenger's side in the front seat. Joel waited for Tom to get in the middle. Leo drove the car as awkwardly and hunched up as he carried himself when he walked. They lurched down the street. At a dark corner, Leo suddenly made a sharp right and pulled up against the six-teen-foot, red wall of the Mimbres County Lumber Company. He leaned forward and his shy, nervous face stared at Joel.

He told them both in a halting and apologetic voice about the stories that Jeannie Lynn was spreading "...to the customers at the Farmer's Association. I was there coupla days ago and she goes...'Leota!'" He stopped and blinked. "She does that all the time. 'Leota...I hear you got competition.' And I asked her what she meant. I just wanted to get out of there 'cause she had that mean look in her eyes, but I had all these groceries, see? And, so, anyway, she goes, 'Yeah...Joel Reece is working your corner, hon!' And I still didn't know what she meant."

"I do," Joel said. "You figured it out, didn't you?"

"Yeah," Leo said. "She told me and just about every person in the checkout line about you guys at the Fair Grounds."

"Shit. I figured she would, man," Joel said. "It'll probably blow over."

Leo shivered. "It may not, Joel. I know. You won't be able to live that down. I couldn't."

Joel thought about saying, *"Well, just look why!"* then realized that, sissy or not, he couldn't assume anything about Leo. He was, after all, just another guy, with bigger problems than most people, maybe, and poorly equipped to deal with them, but there was no real way to know that he was like him and Tom. Joel wanted to ask him if he really was, but all he said was, "Thanks for telling me. I figured she would be doing something like that. Thanks."

"Sure. Well." He started the engine and drove them back to the pickup. "Guess there's not much you can do, but I guess knowing will help."

Joel and Tom were getting out. "Tell you, Leo, I don't give a shit what people say. Me and Tom don't care because we're friends and we're going to stay that way."

Leo was leaning toward their side. "Hey, Joel. Keep in touch, okay?"

Joel tapped the top of the car. "Sure, man. Maybe we should. Come on out and see us. Me and Tom. We're taking care of things while my parents are away."

Leo grinned. "Well, hey! Thanks. I will...but only if you don't mind!"

Tom looked thoughtful when they got back into the pickup and resumed the trip into town. "He's the guy you were telling me about the other night, isn't he?"

"Yeah."

"Poor guy. He sticks out like a sore thumb," Tom said.

"See what I mean?"

"I saw a lot of guys like him in Houston in the area of town I used to hang around in sometimes."

"What kind of area? You mean for sissies or something?"

Tom laughed so hard and slapped Joel on the shoulder so many times that Joel thought Tom was going to choke. "Oh, Joel!" He could hardly talk and went off into another peal of laughter. Finally he wiped away the tears. "You really should get out of this town!"

Joel felt embarrassed. "Don't make me mad, man, just tell me!"

He did his best to stop but his shoulders still shook. "I'm sorry! Yeah. It was kinda like that. I mean, Leo would fit in there. But it's not because he's what you call a sissy." He told Joel about the area where he was sure homosexuals met. "They have stores that sell these magazines and have movie arcades and, at night, guys roam up and down in all kinds of clothes, and some of them are pretty weird. I used to go down there, when I was—"

"What?"

"Trying to figure out things."

"You never told me that!"

"I'm telling you now, aren't I?" Tom patted him on the shoulder. "I didn't mean to laugh. You just have such a—"

"Dumb idea about stuff?"

"No. Clean way about you."

"Dumb."

"Okay. Dumb. Anyway, Leo is probably a homosexual. I wonder if he knows."

Joel laughed. "I guess you never can tell by the way people look. I sure didn't know I was. I was so stupid. Maybe we should tell him."

"That's awful. You're right. He can't help how effeminate he is."

"But he needs a friend, I bet."

Tom patted Joel on the shoulder again. "That was nice, inviting him out to see us. You really aren't afraid of getting a bad reputation, are you?"

"It's too late to worry about it now, thanks to Jeannie Lynn. You heard him."

"And then there's Pete Thompson. The redhead. I think he's one of us."

Joel laughed at the thought. "Can you believe it? In a town like this?"

The idea gave the night a strange air. As they

drove back and forth through town, they watched the steady stream of cars and made up stories about the faces they saw in the flash of headlights.

Several times, as they passed the truck stop across the highway from the Triangle drive-in, Joel noticed the Stroud pickup.

"The Strouds go to your church, Tom?" Joel asked, finally.

"Yes. A real poor family."

"So, you know Kenneth?"

"He's been to church, but not very regular. Not like his mother. Kenneth has a bunch of brothers and sisters. Mrs. Stroud brings some of them every Sunday. And once in a while her husband comes. She's a pitiful woman. Sometimes she looks like she's going to cry. Sometimes she's bruised. Some people think they fight. The husband repents almost every time he comes. Then you don't see him for a while, but there she is, Sunday after Sunday."

"They live about two miles from us," Joel said. "How do you know so much about them?"

"Father tries to visit with the families in the congregation. He just loves to minister to families like the Strouds."

"And Paul?"

"What about him?" Tom's tone went flat.

"How does he know Kenneth of all people? Kenneth wouldn't like Paul. They haven't got a thing in common."

"Nobody likes Paul. I don't either. It just happens that our parents are good friends. I guess that's why Paul thinks we should be friends."

"Well, that explains a few things, anyway," Joel said. "But Kenneth?"

"Paul knows Kenneth because Paul's father does a lot of visiting. And you can bet Paul likes to get in on things like that."

Joel was planning to turn south for home when he got to the A&W. As they passed the truck stop again, the Stroud pickup pulled out of the parking lot and entered the highway behind them. Kenneth's face was a tiny, grinning apparition in Joel's rear view mirror as he came up fast behind them with his brights on. The lights flashed from the mirror, blinding Joel and making him swerve slightly to avoid the light. "He's doing that deliberately," Joel said. He adjusted the mirror until he saw the light flash in Kenneth's face. "Stupid ass! Thinks he can blind me!"

Tom watched out the back window. "That did it. He's falling back," he said. "But do you think that was such a good idea?"

Joel knew it wasn't. "He won't do anything. At least not in the middle of town. He's a coward by himself. Guys like him are pretty easy to fight when it's just you and him."

Tom grinned. "So how many times have you been in a fight with him?" he teased.

Joel grinned broadly and glanced over at Tom. "I've been in fights with him off and on all my life."

"You never told me that, Joel!"

"Since I've known you, I haven't been in a single fight. But I used to fight all the time."

Tom was surprised. "Why?"

Joel told him about the country school he had attended. "It used to be one of the roughest schools in this county. Besides the elementary and junior high schools here in town, out south and out east, there're these country schools. Mine had eight grades. Since we were south of town, most of the students came from the bigger farms and ranches. So there were all of us, about a hundred students, and the Mexican children—Braceros. Some of them were actually old enough to be in high school but they could barely speak English, so the county put them in grade school with us. There was always a lot of fighting. Even though we used the Braceros to work for us, the kids at school treated them pretty mean. Dad says they got it straight from their parents."

"So why did you fight so much, Joel?"

"Because I was always taking up for the Mexicans. And guys like Kenneth—but especially him—were always bullying the Mexican kids. I had a best friend from Mexico. His family moved to this country and bought a farm right next to ours. Tony was my age, but when he started at Mimbres, he was put back with the third graders. I was in the sixth. He didn't know a word of English at first, so he couldn't do very well on our tests. But he was smart. Anyway, he got teased a lot, so I took up for him. And that's how I fought Kenneth."

"What happened to Tony?" Tom asked. "He sounds like you'd still be friends. But you've never mentioned him."

Joel sighed. "He got struck by lightning in a cotton field one summer. He was working his field and I was working mine with Dad. When it started to get bad—you know those summer lightning storms—Dad and I went to the house. We stopped to tell Tony he should get in out of the weather, but he wouldn't stop. He said his father wouldn't let him. That night, we heard that his father found him dead."

From his rear view mirror, Joel saw Kenneth coming up behind them again, dangerously close, as if he intended to ram the pickup. Joel swerved and skidded off the pavement so suddenly that he stalled the engine. Kenneth shot past, horn blaring, then slammed on the brakes in front of them. In reverse, the tail end of the pickup swayed recklessly toward them, but pulled up on Joel's side.

Kenneth leered drunkenly at Joel from his pickup. "Hey, you fucking queers! I got somethin' for ya!"

Joel stared at Kenneth's flushed face. His eyes were red and full of hate. "Fuck off, Stroud!" Joel yelled. He felt Tom's hand on his shoulder and wished he would take it away.

"Oooh! Get her!" Kenneth said, and grunted with satisfaction. "Hey, preacher's girl!"

"Get out of here, Stroud!" Joel said. He tried the engine, but it wouldn't start.

Kenneth snorted. "C'mon girls, my dick's hard over here. Wanna see?"

A moment later, Joel was staring down the double barrels of Kenneth's shotgun. He ducked. "Shit!" he said under his breath. "Tom! Get down!" He tried the starter again and the engine kicked on. He threw the pickup into gear and peeled out, careening onto the highway. Kenneth followed, swaying recklessly, zigzagging over the white lines. He caught up with Joel, pulling alongside long enough to jab the shotgun wildly into Joel's window. It clanged against the door. He grinned, then pulled the shotgun out of sight. Joel stomped on the accelerator; behind him, the Stroud pickup raged, its engine screaming. Kenneth couldn't keep up, but hung on doggedly, receding by degrees, his hate-tortured face growing smaller and sharper. As they neared the A&W, Joel skidded around the corner and sped down the street. He turned right at the next corner and pulled into a dark parking lot next to the Five and Dime Store.

His breath was ragged when he let it out. "Damn it!"

Tom was huddled against the door, hugging his knees. His face was hidden in the shadows, but his eyes caught faint light, like two spheres. "Do you think—"

Joel held his finger up to his lips: Shhhh!" They listened. From the direction they had come, the sound of a racing engine drew nearer. "That's him. I bet he thinks we're going home."

The Stroud pickup ran through the intersection, heading south. Joel backed out of the parking lot and drove back onto the street. At the corner, he turned south as well, keeping Kenneth's taillights in view. Kenneth was weaving wildly ahead of them, and looked like he was losing control; the truck skidded dangerously and ran off the road. It smashed into a light pole.

Steam gushed out of the hood. Kenneth saw them and waved his shotgun. Joel drove by slowly, and saw that he wasn't hurt. He was obviously too drunk to hit a moving target.

"I don't think we have anything to worry about from him tonight," Joel said. He patted Tom's thigh and smiled weakly. "But we've got troubles, if I know that son of a bitch."

Tom was quiet and still huddled in the corner. "I'm scared, Joel." His voice was shaking and he drew in rapid, shallow breaths.

By the time they got home, Tom was more relaxed, but he stayed quiet. They walked to the house in silence. The night sounds were loud, all of them familiar to Joel—the rustling of the leaves in the breeze, the crickets, the banging tin-can sound from the cowshed, and, beneath it all, the silence of the country. In its welcome familiarity, Joel tried to relax.

It was around ten o'clock and the night air felt comfortable. Joel sat down. "Let's sit out here for a while, Tom."

But Tom leaned against the front door. "No. Let's go in. Lock up the house."

Joel wasn't angry, but he was frustrated by Tom's fear. "Nobody's gonna hurt us out here! And besides, if we stay outside, we can hear cars coming down the road, practically all the way to town. We'll have plenty of time to get in and lock up if Kenneth is stupid enough to show up."

But Tom shook his head. "I'm going in. You stay out here if you want."

Joel handed Tom the keys. "Don't lock me out, okay? I'll be in after a while."

He was much more frightened than he let on. He knew he could take Kenneth if he tried anything. He was confident of that. But Leo Johnson's story of Jeannie Lynn and the lies Paul Romaine was telling right there in Tom's church would do far more harm than anything Kenneth could do. He hoped Tom was ready for it and wouldn't freak out again, because things were going to get ugly.

* * * *

She listened to Henry's phlegmy snoring, smelled his sour breath on her neck. In the dark of their bedroom, she stared at the ceiling. Kenneth wrecked the truck. This fact was not so much a surprise as something she knew was coming and couldn't prevent. Now what? She doubted that he would learn his lesson.

She got up and dressed. It was almost four in the morning; she would have to be up soon anyway to get wood for the kitchen stove. Kenneth wouldn't do it anymore. And even though the twins could have, at fourteen years old, to her, Patrick and Detrick were still mere babies. She didn't want them to lose their precious sleep. Growing boys. So much different from Kenneth, him so much like his pa. Mean. She thought of Patrick and Detrick as her boys, Kenneth as Henry's.

Kenneth had come in drunk and belligerent again, but this time so angry that his eyes burned with hatred. "I had to fuckin' walk!" he growled at her gentle question. "The truck's fuckin' smashed! That rich bastard queer and that fuckin' preacher's queer kid chased me off the goddamn fuckin' road!" Then he had pushed her aside and made his way to bed. She shivered as she walked outside to the woodpile, wrapping her long arms about her shoulders. *Henry's gotta do something now. Kenneth is gettin' too crazy, and me with more children than I kin feed. Weren't for pa's pension we'd be in dutch. And now the truck wrecked, up to me to get it hauled up and dumped in the yard like the rest of the worthless junk around here. But he don't learn, neither.* "Kenny…" she cried in the darkness, "please! What's happened to you? Whyn't you stop? Just stop!"

* * * *

The noise came from the hallway. The creaking steps sounded loud to Joel. He had awakened suddenly, feeling that something was wrong. Now he froze. He felt the sweat pop out on his back. He reached over, and felt tentatively for Tom, not wanting to awaken him. But he wasn't there. He curled out of bed. Through his open window, the pale light in the yard shed light on the shiny surfaces in his room. He opened the door and turned. Tom was standing in his pajamas. His dark hair was tousled, his face troubled. "I didn't mean to wake you. I couldn't sleep."

Joel shut the door and sat on the bed next to Tom. Tom kept his head down. His breathing was rapid, quiet. Small gasps escaped as he tried to speak.

Joel pushed him back, holding him by the

shoulders to make Tom look at him. They stared at each other. "What's the matter? You letting Kenneth bother you?"

Tom shook his head. "No. It's what Paul's been saying."

"He doesn't know anything! He's just farting in the wind. Look, Tom, I told you people would talk. He's crazy, probably."

They lay down together on the bed, Tom against Joel. "Hug me."

Joel rubbed his back, remembering his dream of a few days before. Now he pulled him close, feeling Tom's breath coming stronger, and Joel felt him relax.

"I do...love you, Joel." Tom said into his neck.

Joel felt a rush of warmth spread through him. He spread his legs, encircling Tom's thighs, and pulled him hard against him, trying to enfold as much of Tom's body as he could. "I love you, too. No matter what happens." He was afraid to do more than hold him. In the early dawn that began to creep across the fields from the east, he drifted into sleep.

Thursday, June 10

They awoke to bright sunshine and warm air puffing through the window in the pre-noon heat. Tom stretched against him and Joel came awake slowly, felt Tom's heat like a warm bath. They kissed so suddenly, so deeply, that Joel panicked, afraid of how Tom would react. He tore himself away, ready to apologize. Tom merely looked startled, then smiled weakly. Joel relaxed, swore to himself that nothing would make him ruin the slow building of confidence Tom was showing. They were content to lie side by side, staring at each other.

* * * *

Mrs. Allen brought a silver pot of coffee in to their unexpected guests in the living room. She was wearing the same navy-blue suit she'd worn at the evening services the night before. She smiled as brightly as she could when she set the tray on the gleaming mahogany coffee table. She sat at her place next to Mr. Allen on the love seat and leaned back against his powerful arm, felt the tension in it as he clenched and unclenched his fist. She knew that sign, but kept smiling as their guests poured more coffee.

Elder Leon Romaine leaned forward from the edge of his chair. "So I thought it best we report this little incident. Our son has been so troubled."

Mr. Allen nodded gravely. "So Paul is now saying he…he *saw* my son and the Reece boy? In the yard out there, lying together? When was this? He said Tuesday? I see." In his mind came unbidden certain rough pages of scripture, which he could read as if the Bible were open in front of him. Leon Romaine and his wife Jessica seemed embarrassed to be relaying the story. Old Leon's face revealed how painful it was to embarrass the preacher. That alone made Mr. Allen appreciate this friend and made it possible to avoid losing control of his anger.

Brother Leon cleared his throat and seemed about to speak, but he sat back into the chair and sipped from his cup. In the void of conversation, now that the embarrassing story of their son hung in the air between them, Mr. Allen grasped for a polite response. He was seething with anger at Paul's audacity and his own son's fraudulent repentance a few days before. But, of course, he could not show his anger. He willed his voice to continue in the same modulated tone he always used.

"I believe…with the blessing of the Holy Ghost…that Thomas will come around. I'll have to take some stern measures, of course…."

"Well, we certainly hope we haven't alarmed you," Brother Leon said. "Paul says he just happened by. But I found it a little strange, considering that Edna Stroud's boy was the one Paul was with. I suspect that your son, a fine, fine young man, has a perfectly good explanation. Sometimes appearances can be misleading."

"He's so much like you!" Jessica Romaine put in.

"Why, thank you, Jessie," Mr. Allen said, thinking her remark irrelevant. "I think I would be very interested in Thomas' explanation."

* * * *

Kenneth Stroud sat in the Rexall Drug cafe. He had been watching the asses on the girls over by the greeting cards. He had undressed them, fucked their asses with his cock, then made them lick it clean so many times he was bored imagining it. *Rich bitches*, he sneered. He was dressed in his usual grease-fouled Levi's and a filthy T-shirt. He rolled a pack of Camel cigarettes out of a grimy sleeve and flicked out a smoke. He lit it and shook out the match, looking around for Paul. *Fuckin' wimp*. The wall clock said it was 12:26. *Fucker gonna buy me lunch or not?*

Paul hurried in from the sidewalk. Kenneth saw him and beckoned him with his middle finger. Paul came up and sat down, a Sears Roebuck sack clutched to his stomach. "Sorry I'm late. I had to get a new jacket for the Brotherhood."

"Cut the shit, Paul. I told you I don't give a fuck about that. So just shut up."

Paul winced. His mouth twisted into a pout.

"Okay. Just tell me about it. Go ahead and order. Steak."

Kenneth related the story of their chase through town after church; how Joel had admitted being a faggot and how Tom had hugged Joel the whole time, saying "Come on, dear, let's go home."

Paul listened to Kenneth's lies. Maybe Kenneth had chased them down the drag, then maybe yelled out something as he passed them on the road. But he doubted that he had run them off the road. And he sure didn't think Tom would act so conveniently out of character like an effeminate homosexual. But he played along with Kenneth's story, getting a sly pleasure out of his embellishments. Paul evaluated this story against the other incidents: that Kenneth did see them acting like queers at the dance, making out and dancing together, which is what got everyone talking in the first place, and the fact of what he'd seen with his own eyes through the window. That, at least, was a real fact.

Paul felt he had been clever, waiting until Wednesday night to talk with his father about Tom, although he regretted not being able to tell him about what he had seen through the Reeces' living room window. He thought that telling his father just before the evening services was a stroke of genius. That way, when Tom and Joel showed up looking so happy, it was all the more damning, easy for his father to see what he was saying. As he told his father afterwards, Tom was slack in his religious duties. He told him also how Tom said he wasn't interested in prayer meets right now. And that had done it. His father had said he would talk to the preacher about his son. Paul had capitalized on that by saying, "I've tried, Daddy, but

he's so distant lately. Seems like his mind is somewhere else."

He watched Kenneth with distaste, so filthy.

Kenneth finished eating and put down his fork.
He lit another Camel and blew smoke deliberately
into Paul's face. "You got what you wanted?" he
asked.

Paul tried to smile, but just said, "Yes. Believe
it or not, I mean Tom no harm. But it's my duty,
you know."

"Yeah, sure, Paul. Duty. Like I say, I don't
fuckin' care. Ma's glad to go to your church; I jes
thought you'd wanna know they's fuckin' queers,
like I said."

Paul winced at Kenneth's foul language. He was
insulted by his attitude, revolted by his meanness.
But, like Kenneth, where Joel was concerned he
didn't care. "And so what're you gonna do with
Joel?"

Kenneth was bored with Paul. He mashed out
his cigarette in his plate. "You got what you wanted.
Don't butt yerself in my business. I'm gonna get
him for making me wreck my truck." He looked at
Paul and wanted to smash his fruity little face. He
decided to get rid of him. He leaned forward like
he was going to whisper a secret, and Paul leaned
toward him, grinning slyly.

"What?" Paul whispered.

Kenneth snatched Paul's cheek, squeezing it,
watching with pleasure Paul's eyes shed water.
"You know what I think?"

Paul shook his head, pulling free of Kenneth's
grip. His eyes betrayed his sudden fright. "What?"

"I think you're a queer, too. And you're next,
you little shitass, if you ever come to my house
again. It's my fuckin' house. Ma can stand you. I
can't. You stay away, you hear?"

Paul got up and snatched the ticket for the steak. "I will." He tossed a quarter on the table, grabbed his Sears Roebuck sack and hurried to the counter. Kenneth took the tip that Paul had left and leaned back, patting his stomach. The unusual fullness made his stomach hurt, and he resented feeling like he might throw up. It was the first real good meal he'd had in a long time. Goddamn! He fought back tears, dreaded the walk home in the heat, and swore he'd get even. Through the blur of sunlight in the big, plate glass window of the pharmacy he caught a glimpse of himself, and he thought of Joel's strength. *I'll kill that fucker!* As he plodded down the sidewalk in the heat, his mind sang, *KILL. BLAM! KILL. BLAM!* That guy and all his rich farmer friends needed to be shook up a little, the sooner the better!

* * * *

Joel felt like he would burst with happiness as they ate lunch. In the few days Tom had been there, he felt proud that they had run the farm. He checked off their chores in his mind, to make sure they were taking care of everything. When they finished lunch, they took the tractor into the field and spent the rest of the afternoon making endless trips up and down the furrows, cultivating the cotton. Tom rode over the back wheel on the mud guard. They couldn't hear each other without yelling over the tractor's noise, so Tom kept his hand on Joel's shoulder, occasionally slapping it and pointing something out, occasionally squeezing it. In the evening they slopped the hogs and fed the cows, put away tools, refueled the tractor. They were tired.

They ate leftover roast and washed and dried the dishes as darkness fell. Outside, night owls swooped and dived around the roof of the cow-shed, crickets and moths gathered around the yard light. The cat curled up in the garage. On her cheeks, the blood of her latest victim dried.

* * * *

In the chapel, empty on a Thursday night, the preacher was praying on his knees.

When the Romaines had left, his first impulse was to call Tom back home. It was a nasty business all around. At all times, he admonished Thomas to act in the manner befitting his station, and except for that one indiscretion of going into the heart of drunken revelry, Thomas had never given him any reason to believe he would lie until now. The Reece boy was too masculine, too confident, to be one of those...he could not even permit himself to think the word. So the story, the horrible one implying some sort of sexual perversion in the yard, out in the open, had to have another expla-nation. He had quashed his first impulse. His wife, too, who rarely interceded, had this time said, "It just can't be true!"

And the preacher prayed now that it was not. As he prayed, it came to him that an unexpected visit would tell him if the rumors about the two boys were true. He would be able with his own eyes to judge the truth of Paul's accusations. He thought of Joel now, remembering, as his wife had said, that he was a polite, though undisciplined, child. The Reeces were well respected in this rural community, and their only flaw, the preacher con-sidered, was not at least attending a regular church. That too was strong reason for quiet, un-obtrusive action. One did not go about making hot-headed accusations in a community such as this, especially against people of the Reeces' caliber. The two boys were friends. Uncharacteristically for the preacher, he had been glad for his son to have found a friend at last with whom he could spend time pursuing outdoor activities. Thomas was getting a chance to work hard—honest work. So, overcoming his first impulse to vent his anger immediately, he was satisfied that whatever Thomas had done, he would be made to see. That he should push forward with some action to settle this thing before it spread was also called for, if not for Thomas' sake, then for the sake of his own reputation in the community and the congregation. He could not act in anger, unless it was controlled and focused to accomplish just the right job.

Chapter 11

Tom woke up curled against Joel's chest with his butt tucked into his crotch. They were naked and it felt strange. But, stranger still, he felt not the least shame. Joel's leg lay over his calf, and the feeling of the hair on his leg, more than any other sensation, brought the reality of the last night home to Tom. During the night, Tom had moved next to Joel as he lay sleeping. When he was asleep, Joel's movements were heavy, which surprised Tom. But he responded automatically when Tom touched his chest, and suddenly they were lying entwined. But Joel didn't wake up. Tom allowed himself to feel Joel's body around him, without considering its wrongness, allowed himself to just feel. Except for the day before, when Joel had held him close to give him comfort, they had never slept so close. The respectable space had always remained, and it surprised him that one tentative touch from him had made Joel unconsciously open his arms and enfold him. He had done it naturally, and yet, even with the erection that Tom felt, Joel had not responded sexually. Tom had lain there, feeling the physical weight of Joel's body, feeling enfolded with gentle strength and capability, but most of all feeling safe and warm, and where he belonged. It was he who broke the barriers, at last, that he had built between them. He had moved his hand tentatively between them and, without waking him, had held Joel's erect penis, had explored its shape, its silky texture. When Joel woke up, his hands moved to Tom's face in the dark; palms on both cheeks, Joel had whispered, "Are you sure?" Tom had felt himself melt against Joel, wanting nothing else.

Remembering that, Tom allowed himself to cry, now. From the beginning, he knew he would give in. He had always responded helplessly to Joel with that part of himself he had fought for years to kill off. Their bed was warm; lying together, their flesh was feverish, dry, smooth. This was good-bye forever to his former life. He knew it as surely as he felt Joel now around him, strong and healthy; certainly no match for God, but he knew Joel would probably fight with God Himself if He came to take him away. In his sleep, Joel was holding him lightly; his hands were curled into relaxed fists. They looked gentle but were strong hands, so young, but already hard, callused, capable of fight as well as love. Tom closed his eyes, remembered Joel's gentle hands all over him in the night. But he felt safe again. Joel had always looked up to him because he was the older one. But that division had faded in the last two weeks. For his seventeen years, Joel was by far the wiser when it came to feelings. He smiled. *We've come this far. There's no turning back.* And he relaxed again and slept.

Joel was the first to get out of bed. He stood nude by the window, looking out at the daylight, his back to Tom, one hand resting on his hip. One foot scratched the other absently. He spoke facing the window. "I know last night was hard for you...but I swear I love you." He turned around, arms out in a pleading way, his young face a shadow in the morning sun behind him. "I mean it. I couldn't love you more than I do right now." He laughed. "Mom was married when she was sixteen, and my two sisters married straight out of high school. I'm almost two years older than Mom was. It doesn't matter to me if I'm still in high school. I know it's right!" He crouched by the bed, took Tom's hand and kissed him. His gray eyes peered into Tom's. "Are you okay? I mean, I know you think it's a sin. Are you sure you can live with that?"

Tom took a deep breath, sobered by Joel's serious expression. He let it out slowly. "I'm okay. I'll handle it. I love you, too, Joel. It feels...good and right. I trust you. And if you say we'll be okay, we will."

Joel grinned suddenly. He tickled Tom. "My feelings say I'm hungry for some more of your eggs, if you can remember what you did to them last time. Otherwise, the deal's off. You'll have to pack your bags after breakfast."

Tom smiled. "I guess that's fair. It's a deal."

The eggs were burned.

Tom smiled slyly across the table, watching Joel's reaction. "Guess I get thrown out, huh?"

But Joel picked up the two hard, gelatinous lumps and shoved them both into his mouth. cheeks bulging, he grinned. "JuthlikeIlikem!"

They laughed till tears ran down their cheeks. Then Tom went to the stove and opened the oven door. He pulled out a pile of golden-brown eggs, toast, and thick sausage patties. "Or you can have these. I cooked 'em while you were out setting the irrigation."

Over breakfast, they divided the work. Tom would do the chores for the livestock and water and weed the garden, and Joel would work the field, since the cultivating would take all day.

They walked outdoors with their arms around each other's shoulders, *exactly the way Joel's father walked with me*, Tom reflected. Funny how the same gesture could mean two completely different things. With Joel it felt heady and wonderful. With Douglas Reece, comforting, like a refuge. They walked to the garden; Joel showed Tom where his mother kept the tools and the water hose.

Later, Joel sat on the tractor with the motor running. He spoke loudly against it. "I'LL COME BACK ABOUT ELEVEN! I'LL HELP YOU MAKE LUNCH! I LOVE YOU!" He waved and left.

Tom watched as Joel drove off. Then he went to the garden to work. He was aware of the energy and affection of Mrs. Reece everywhere in the garden, from the tool shed to the rows dug by hand, with a cornucopia of vegetables and greens growing in neat rows in an area that seemed much too large for one person to manage. But this was her work. All of it, Joel had said. Tom was astounded at its productivity, the work that it must have taken to make it so lush.

The garden was enclosed by a tall fence of corrugated tin. It was a sanctuary that Tom liked the feel of immediately. He went to work, and was startled a little later by the sound of a car pulling up in the driveway to the Reeces' house. He ran out of the garden and looked across the yard toward the driveway. He recognized his father's car. His heart began to pound. He wondered what he was doing here. He left the garden reluctantly. He was shirtless and the burning sun had begun to turn his skin pink.

He reached the car as his father was closing the door and peering under his hand toward the field where Joel was a tiny figure, riding a toy tractor. His father turned at the sound of Tom's footsteps. "Oh, there you are." He scrutinized the boy standing before him, flushed with sunburn, hair slick with sweat, smiling in a squint at him against the sun.

"Hi, Father."

"Hello, Thomas."

"Joel's out there." He pointed toward the field. It's an all-day job. I'm working in the garden. It's great! I think I'm going to start one in that empty area behind the church. Do you think that would be okay?"

Tom was surprised to see his father's quick smile, a change from its usual stern set. "I'll consider it."

"Well, gee, thanks!"

His father smiled, then his stern face snapped back like a rubber band. "You look happy. Healthy. Everything is fine?"

"Yes!" Tom said. But he felt apprehensive. "What brings you out here?"

He took Tom firmly by the arm, close to the shoulder. His grip hurt. He walked Tom to the porch and sat him down. Then he paced back and forth while Tom watched, resting his forearms on his thighs, squinting at the sun in his face, his father between him and it like a dark cloud. His father didn't say anything for a few moments, but the muscles in his jaw alternately bulged and relaxed. Thick veins in his neck began to swell, which Tom knew was his preparation for a bombshell. He couldn't imagine what his father could be concerned about, but it must be something serious.

Finally he said, "I'm going to give you the benefit of the doubt; I'm going to tell you exactly what has been told to me. Then I'm going to give you a fair chance to answer. If what you say strikes me as truthful, I will consider the other source and see what action needs to be taken. But I promise, if I feel that you are not telling me the truth, or if I find out later that you've lied to me, I will make certain you shall never forget this day."

Tom was glad he knew about the rumors Paul was spreading, but he assumed that his and Joel's real secret was safe from his father. He was genuinely confused and, therefore, appeared innocent as his father studied him now.

"Do you agree, Thomas?"

"Well, sure, Father." He couldn't imagine what would happen if he didn't.

"I will be blunt: it has been said that, as you told me, you went to that dance, but in addition you got drunk and danced with Joel Reece. It has also been said that you and he got kicked out of that place, your behavior upsetting even those people. And then, a few days ago, you were seen right here in this yard, lying with Joel. Is this true?"

Tom squinted at his father's silhouette. "Father, it's true only that I got drunk. I danced with a girl named 'Betsy'. I didn't get kicked out."

Mr. Allen waited for his son to begin explaining. But he was not prepared for Tom's simple admission of guilt. He took this to be a good sign, because he took into account his son's extraordinary show of faith in front of the congregation. Although the truth was repulsive to him, he felt pride that his son did not flinch from it.

"Good. I believe you, But this other thing with Joel—I am ashamed even to speak of it—fondling? Kissing? Is any of this true? Is it?"

Tom felt his chest caving in. He was unable to

draw a breath. *Yes. And worse. To deny it was a lie. To admit it would be*...Tom searched for a way to tell the truth, as he had been commanded to do. He faintly heard himself asking, "In the front yard?"

"Paul Romaine says he saw you one afternoon lying on top of Joel right here—*laying* with him—as it has been implied. Now you tell me why he should say that."

Tom remembered one day. He felt his father's eyes searching his face. Then it struck him. He managed to brighten. "Father, Paul must have seen us wrestling. We do it all the time."

His father visibly relaxed. "That is a logical explanation, after all." Then his face grew stern. "I believe you about this, Thomas, but just this time. If I hear just one more hint of something deeper, just one more...." He didn't finish. He looked back toward the field at the green, liquid shimmer from the crops. "You and Joel are taking care of all this?" He waved his hand across a wide arc from south, east, and north. "Why, this is truly magnificent!"

Tom still couldn't relax. His stomach fluttered nervously. He watched his father's whole body arch as he waved his hand in the direction of the fields. His father could appreciate such work. He had been generous, Tom realized, in holding back just now. His father walked toward the car and turned back to Tom, still sitting on the porch. "Better get back to work. See you in church!"

Tom returned to the garden. He could barely breathe and felt like he was about to faint. He sank to his knees in the soft earth, intending to pray. He intended to pray about deliberately lying to his father. *I've never done that before*, he thought. *No. That's a lie. I've been lying for years....* He bowed his head and tried to think of a way to begin. But he was unable to concentrate. He had sunk to his knees in the shadow of the fence, just inside the south entrance to the garden. At this hour, the sun bore down everywhere. But the earth was cool against his knees. He had fallen into a moist patch of ground. He dug into it with his fingers, and was surprised that the earth was crumbly, like old cornbread. It was dark and its aroma had a musty under-odor. It was different than the dirt he had been shoveling out in the field; it was richer. The mustiness came from the final stages of rot, he imagined, the rot of plants, the rot of insects that once ate the plants. But the things of which the earth was made, this *soil* was alive and only waiting to give life, from the rot of dead things. He let it fall through his fingers and stood up.

Praying was no use. The garden pulled his thoughts to it with too much force, denied him the choice of thinking of anything but the garden. He looked around feeling dimly anxious that he hadn't prayed, but everywhere he looked, plants in various stages of growth caught his eye. The garden was an organized conspiracy against his senses. In the play of sunlight and shadow, in the smells that ripened in the heat, in the gentle sounds, the garden was alive. A light breeze rushed through it and dried his sweat. The garden remained serene, but its indifference somehow soothed him. He began working again, stepping carefully among the plants, looking for weeds in the garden. Joel's mother was thorough.

Soon, he was absorbed in his work again. He felt relaxed and able to consider what had just happened. Lying. That was another step away from his old life. He had let his father assume his innocence mainly because his father hadn't wanted to believe Paul's accusations. At least there had been a good explanation for what Paul had seen. But he'd deliberately clouded over the kissing of which he was being accused. *Father believed me*, Tom thought, astounded. *He believed me, but I was lying*. As he worked, this realization became a litany in his head. *He believed me, but I was lying*; the fact echoed in his mind, but Tom felt much better. He thought of Joel.

From the day they met over nine months ago until now, Tom realized, he'd been progressing to this day. He would remember it, just as his father said. But not for anything his father could do to him. He would remember it because of what Joel had said to him earlier this morning, when they awoke from their night of lovemaking. It wasn't just sex between them. It wasn't just lust after all. How could it be? *Joel loves me*, he thought, and because Joel had promised that Tom could trust him, and because he accepted the truth of that promise without question, he felt, just then, as if a wall inside of him had been razed. *I am a homosexual, because my feelings say so. And*, he thought happily, *it isn't lust*. That was a dirty, little lie he had allowed other people to put in his head, he concluded. It was *love* between them. And that truth, Joel's declaration of it, made him feel stronger, made him determined not to flinch away. It was clear to Tom, as he left the garden near eleven o'clock to look for Joel, that he would soon have to test his own commitment.

He peered across the field. The tractor was coming up the road but was still far away and seemed to be traveling at a crawl. He returned to the garden and put away the tools, locked up the shed and walked to the house.

He washed his face in Joel's bathroom and looked at himself in the mirror. His face had a shocked expression, but there were no tears, and his dark-brown eyes had only a bruised, wet look. He was presentable. He didn't want Joel to make a big deal out of anything. This could have been serious, but it was over. He was sure he could keep Joel from getting excited.

He was wrong.

Joel wanted to confront Paul, and do it fast. Joel's anger would not be soothed. "Listen, Tom, Paul can't get away with this. If it wasn't for him, we could have worked everything out just fine, and taken our time to do it, but that fucker almost blew it. If you hadn't lied to your father you'd be gone right now, stuck at your house. And you think it was hard getting to see each other last time?"

The more he talked, the angrier he got. "That fucker, Paul, is bad news!"

* * * *

"Tom?" Paul said into the telephone. "I thought you'd be calling— What? No, I only told my father. I can't help it if he— What? Yes. About the dance. I know I wasn't at the dance, but everybody's talking about it."

On the other end of the line, Paul heard rustling, the phone being bumped, then Tom firing a rush of questions. Paul let the receiver fall to his chest. He was sitting at his desk with his feet on the desktop. On the wall behind the desk was a mirror. Paul watched himself smile with satisfaction. Then he put the receiver back to his ear and listened.

Finally, he said, "What am I trying to do? Simple. Your friendship with Joel should stop. You know it's a disgusting sin, my friend. What? Oh, I think it *is* my business. You see. I told my daddy about you two in Joel's yard, too…. Come on, Tom,

I saw you lying on top of him. He was holding you! Wrestling! Boy, that's a good one. Who's gonna believe that?"

Paul couldn't believe what Tom said next. He saw his face fall with disappointment and looked away from the mirror. "He believed you, huh? Spying? Kenneth Stroud and I were just driving by!" Paul looked at his hands, studied the perfect clip of his nails. He listened to the tirade on the other end.

"Sure, Tom. Look. What did you expect? I only told Daddy. I was concerned, and I still am. You should be, too.... Don't cuss. It's disgusting!" Tom's anger surprised and pleased him. Tom had a surprise coming, anyway. "Now listen, Tom, I haven't even told anyone that I saw you and Joel one night in his living—"

The telephone went dead.

He stared at the receiver, surprised. "How...dare...you...hang up on ME!" He slammed the receiver down hard. Catching a glimpse of his red face in the mirror, and turned away, again, his temples pounding. He took in small breaths to calm himself, his mind spinning. *Gotta think! Can't lose! Can't let him get away with that!*

When his own anger had subsided, a realization came to him. Tom's anger was completely out of proportion to what he had expected. So intense. But why? Paul thought about Kenneth's fantasy story, which he'd assumed was a lie. But then, "the guilty dog barks loudest," he mused. Could it really be true? Could they both be so out of control that they were reckless? A grin crept onto his lips. Even if Reverend Allen believed Tom this time, the seed could be tended, and soon be made to bring forth.... Even without real evidence to back him up, it would do for now. All he needed was proof that they were having sex. And he would watch for a time, with or without Kenneth.

* * * *

They took a walk before supper. The sun was turning yellow just above the distant mountains to the west. They crossed the road with the house behind them. On the west side of the road the desert began—an area of untilled soil, lying fallow until irrigation rights became available. It was here that Joel had always played as a boy. Here he went hiking, toting the .22 rifle his father gave him on his thirteenth birthday. And it was in this patch of desert, leading farther away from the farms, farther west toward the rough terrain of the Red Mountain district, where he and Tom had hiked on other days.

The air was still hot. As they got farther from the road, the silence became more complete. When they spoke, their voices sounded loud in the stillness. But they talked little. Joel was content to walk and feel Tom beside him.

They came to the clearing where they usually ate lunch. The mesquite bushes completely surrounded them, thick and tangled and tall enough that, even standing up, Joel doubted anyone could see them. He liked the privacy. The clearing was flat and nothing grew on the pale dirt. Nothing but the wind sounded in the clearing. The place brought back Joel's most pleasant memories of the times he and Tom had walked out here while getting to know each other, Tom telling him about all the places he had lived. Joel hadn't been any place much and doubted that he ever would, but he enjoyed hearing about New Orleans and Atlanta and the lush greenery of the South. Joel had listened, imagining all those places. His own knowledge of the world seemed so small by comparison and, at first, he felt he had nothing to share, nothing to make Tom's imagination soar as his did.

"Remember the first time you asked me to spend the night?" Tom said now as they sat Indian style in the clearing.

"Yeah. I had been working up to it for days. That was about a month after we met, wasn't it?"

"That's right. In all the places I've lived, I never felt as good as out here with you. And your mother and father were so nice. I was excited to spend the night. I didn't know that you really liked me all that much."

"I was just shy. I was only a junior. I couldn't believe a senior and someone so sophisticated could like me. I couldn't believe that night in early September last year at the junior class slave banquet when you called me by name. Remember?"

"Of course I do. You were one of the slaves serving us seniors. I was with Debbie Benson. She's the one who pointed you out. She thought you were the cutest guy in your gold toga and sandals with your blond hair and tan. I didn't want to seem too interested, but the rest of that night I couldn't take my eyes off you. I had a crush on you from then on."

"You did?" Joel laughed, delighted, feeling giddy.

"Yes. But I promised myself you'd never know."

"I thought you were nice. I'm sorry I acted so weird when you first started saying hello at school after that. I thought you were teasing or something. You know how the townies act about us farmers."

Tom nodded. "I haven't been happy at home since we moved here, since I met you. My father is a hard man to live with, Joel. Not like yours. I respect him, what he lives for. But sometimes he asks too much of me. I've never had a chance to question anything, or learn anything from him except religion. He's always right. Perfect. And there's no room for mistakes. But when he came out here today, he seemed really glad to see how I was doing. And then he just dug right in, throwing up all those accusations. That's his way. But it oppresses me. I could have told him it was true about how I acted at the dance and pleaded being drunk. But I didn't. I heard myself lying to him."

"So you could quit lying to yourself," Joel said. "Which is more important?"

"Telling him the truth. And facing the truth about myself, about us. Telling him the absolute truth, everything. And then living my own life and making my own mistakes."

"I've wondered how my parents would react, too," Joel said. "It feels strange to think of telling them. But I'm going to, and one of these days, we'll be able to live together without fear from either of our families. We'll be adults, too."

They stayed in the desert until night had fallen and the first slice of the coming full moon had risen to guide them back to the farm. In the moonlight, Joel took Tom's hand. It was warm, as always, and felt familiar, yet still held a mystery about it, partly the indefinable thrill of holding hands with another guy. At bottom, that was it. He couldn't explain why. But he knew that if Tom were a girl, something would have been lost in the transformation.

The ghostly cooing of night birds was magnified in the darkness. Wind whined soft and low all about them and, ahead, they could hear the pickups and cars on the road. Here and there they heard car doors slamming in someone's front yard.

As they drew closer, they could see the trees in the yard—tall, black shadows, and through them shined the outdoor yard light in the Reeces' yard. It was fixed onto a tall pole that stood beside the driveway. Then a shotgun blast cracked in the darkness and, simultaneously, the light exploded. They heard a faint tinkling of glass as the light fixture hit the ground. Then silence.

"What the hell?" Joel said. Tom was startled but he followed as Joel began running toward the house.

They followed the moonlit shine of the dirt and found an easy path through the bushes. They bent down and walked low to the edge of the road and looked across it in the darkness. The trees were hard to see through, but part of the house was visible. From where they were, they could see the edge of the porch and the driveway beyond.

They saw shadows but nothing else. Then, on the side of the house facing the road, they clearly saw a figure crouched below the living room window with his back to them. Some light in the house allowed them to see into it. The figure below the window rose up. Caught in the light from the house they saw his shotgun.

They hid behind a mesquite bush and listened. "I know you're in there, girls! Come out and suck my dick!" The familiar sound of Kenneth's voice echoed off the side of the house.

Then he moved from the living room window to the front yard, standing just off the porch.

"What're we going to do, Joel?"

Joel's face was set in anger, but it was controlled. "He's not going to touch a thing, or I'll cut his balls off."

"But you can't fight him! He's got a gun! Joel, he'll kill you!"

"That's my house, damn it, and I'm going to take care of it!"

"*We* are supposed to take care of it, remember?"

Joel sucked air through his teeth. "That bastard!"

They moved through the darkness and slipped quietly across the road. Joel led the way north, planning to slip around the house, to get a better view from the other side, but then Kenneth yelled, "I'm coming in!" Another shotgun blast echoed through the night, followed by a sickening crash of glass. "Holy shit!" Joel whispered. "He's destroying the house!"

They crouched by the tool shed near the garden, with a clear view of the house in the moonlight. It was about a hundred feet to the driveway. Joel motioned for Tom to stay, then ran to the east side of the house.

Forgetting his fear, Tom ran after him. He could make out Joel's figure at the corner, so close to the porch that if Kenneth appeared, he'd have a dead drop on him. In the pale light against the whiteness of the house, Joel looked small and vulnerable. Just as Tom drew closer, Joel jumped away from the corner and ran around to the front, out of sight.

Tom raced around the corner in time to see Joel crash against Kenneth. The shotgun clattered to the ground. He closed the distance and grabbed it. Kenneth and Joel were a tangle of arms and legs, but Joel was on top; his fists flying, making dull, thudding sounds on Kenneth's face.

"Now, get up, you fucker!" Joel jerked Kenneth up, bending his arm behind him. "You're gonna pay for this, you scumbag!"

Tom came up on the porch with the shotgun.

His heart was pounding, his breath coming painfully in his throat. "Joel, what're you gonna do?"

"This stupid fucker used up his ammo. Two shots, you asshole. Can't even count!"

Kenneth's breath was ragged. "I'll kill—"

Joel slammed him into the wall. Kenneth's head crunched sickeningly against it and he crumpled to the concrete, moaning.

"Take it easy, Joel!" Tom said.

But Joel put his boot in the small of Kenneth's back. "Look at that!" He pointed to the black hole where the window had been. Part of the window casing was splintered. "Throw his shotgun in the pickup. Let's take this asshole to his mama."

* * * *

Tom got out a broom and swept up the glass that lay splintered all over the dining room floor, then cleaned the glass off the table. Across the room, the flying glass had shattered the dishes in the china cabinet. Joel set the broken china aside, thinking he would show it to his mother. But even when every shard of glass was cleaned up, the broken things set neatly aside, a piece of plywood tacked across the window and the curtains closed on the carnage, the room somehow looked violated, raped. But Joel's rage was gone.

Kenneth was beaten. He had pissed in his pants like a child, and the smell of it in the pickup as they were taking him home had been overpowering. They had been crowded together in the pickup. The stink of sweat and blood and fear and hatred filled Joel's nostrils, even now. What had always been a casual, sometimes vivid, thought that Kenneth was crazy, now stayed in Joel's mind. Kenneth was probably humiliated, Joel thought, to have peed in his pants, to have had that pre-

cious shotgun taken away, but Joel refused to feel
sorry for his humiliation. Crazy or not, Kenneth
was a killer and he felt sorry for Mrs. Stroud, whose
hard life had gotten worse with every passing year.
She had wept shamelessly, slapping Kenneth over
and over, crying out, "God! God!" He and Tom had
left quietly.

Joel's anger was further deflated when he saw
that the damage to the window looked fairly easy
to repair. They could attach the plywood more securely tomorrow; it would have to wait for glass. If
Tom had not restrained him, though, he realized
he could have killed Kenneth. He still felt angry,
but with Tom there he could keep it under control. Tom made him relax in the living room while
he made coffee and sandwiches. He brought the
tray out and set it on the coffee table in front of
Joel. He laid his hand on Joel's shoulder. Joel
looked up at him, his face confused. "Things just
keep getting worse and worse for some reason. Why
can't we just be left alone? Are we hurting anybody? I feel like I'm going to explode!"

Tom sat beside Joel on the couch. Joel was
sitting rigidly, staring over the plate of sandwiches.
When Tom sat against him, Joel automatically put
his arm around his shoulder and smiled stiffly.
"*That's* how Kenneth and I have always fought.
You see why I didn't talk about it?"

Tom leaned over and retrieved a sandwich. He
broke off a piece and pushed it against Joel's lips.
Joel's breath tickled Tom's fingertips as he opened
his mouth and took the bite from him. His lips
closed softly over Tom's fingers. The wet warmth
made Tom shiver.

"I could get to like this!" Tom said. Joel laughed
with his mouth full and pulled Tom against him.
He hugged Tom so hard that his chest hurt. He

freed his arms and hugged Joel in return. "Will we always be like this?"

Joel pulled away. He took the ragged sandwich Tom held forgotten in his hand and began eating it. He looked seriously at Tom and without smiling said, "I hope so, but maybe not."

Tom felt himself sag. "But why?"

"Not why. If."

"If?"

"If we can really believe in each other, if being queers isn't someday going to be more than you can face. If, if, if. I think we can make it with each other, that we'll always be like this, loving each other, I mean, if we can beat people like Kenneth and Paul and your father, and a million other problems I can't even imagine. But if we allow things like happened tonight to make us afraid, if we let things like belief in sins about what we are get in the way, then no, we won't always be like this. I mean, you're religious. You think it's a sin. How do you know that you can really keep loving me, once your father gets involved? He will, you know."

"Yeah. I know he will," Tom said. "Paul will make sure Father finds out that I lied to him. But listen. If you help me through it, I can win. I don't want to fight against my feelings any more. I could go the rest of my life wrestling with the devil, wrestling with God. But I've got to be free, like you."

"Free?"

"Yes. I can see what it's like to let my feelings lead me, even when my head says 'no'. And one thing you can count on: I know I'm a homosexual—a queer, as you say. It just took me a long time to admit it. It took years. But when I met you, it only took a few times being with you to know I didn't stand a chance to kill it off. From here on, Joel, I think things will get better. Don't you think? I've gotten better. And with both of us, whatever happens, we can handle it, after tonight. Don't you think?"

"Sure we can," Joel said. "If we just stick up for each other."

Tom stood up. He looked around the living room. In the few days he'd been there, the Reeces' home had become familiar. Until tonight, he had unconsciously felt like a visitor, but so strong was the impression suddenly, looking about him, that this was his home, too, here with Joel, he felt confident they would always 'stick up' for each other. He smiled slyly down at Joel. "There's one more *if* we've got to take care of."

Joel looked puzzled, but seeing Tom's grin, he smiled in return. "What?"

"I want to go make love right now. I want to watch you take your clothes off. I want you to undress me and make love to me and let me make love to you."

"But what's the 'if'?"

"If we don't hurry," Tom grinned. "I might cream in my pants."

* * * *

They undressed silently in the bright light of Joel's room. Joel pulled off his shirt facing Tom, showing off his lean torso. His skin was shiny with pale, blond hairs that fairly glowed in the bright light. His tan, the product of a life in the desert, was solid down to the waist of his Levi's. He smiled and turned his back on Tom; he unbuttoned his Levi's and slid them off his butt. In contrast to his back, it was pale white, smooth and hairless, as delicate looking as porcelain.

Tom felt his groin begin to awaken. His stomach was fluttering. The beauty of Joel's flesh astounded him. The symmetry of his nude body, the fluid way he moved, stepping out of his clothes and standing naked, was a vision that had been celebrated since the time of ancient Greece. He could only stare in wonder. In every tone of his emotional response, he felt love. It overpowered his reason. And shutting out all thought he let his feelings rise and rise, knew what it was to feel, utterly without fear. From his full mouth and strong chin to his shoulders and torso, to the curve of his butt, to the way he moved, Joel was perfect. He came to Tom with his arms out, offered himself with a smile so clear and bright that Tom felt he would burst without a single touch from Joel.

Joel helped him undress. Four hands fought with the buttons on Tom's shirt. Joel stood behind him with his arms over Tom's shoulders, kissing his neck, burning deeply, taking root deep down inside. His breath was warm and smelled sweet, and Tom got cold chills. He shivered and laughed. They pulled his shirt off and Joel turned him around and kissed him. Tom cupped Joel's butt and pressed himself into his groin, feeling Joel's heat, feeling Joel's hardness against his own. Joel slid both his hands between them and unbuttoned Tom's pants. Tom stepped out of them and felt Joel place a hand on the bulge in his underwear. The warmth and gentleness of his fondling made him feel weak. Their lips were barely touching and they were looking into each other's eyes, seeing the visual translation of what each was feeling. Joel broke the gaze first, then dropped to his knees. Tom felt his underwear slide down his legs. He kicked his shorts away, holding onto Joel's broad back. The heat that engulfed his groin rushed through him. He held Joel's head, felt his mouth open against him, felt Joel's lips take him slowly, the pressure of his lips as they slid along the shaft enclosing him in warmth, then relaxing, then closing tighter. He exploded in a release so complete that his knees gave and he began to shake. He felt deep down within his groin, at the base of his maleness, his semen drain slowly and completely.

Joel picked him up and laid him on the bed. They curled together and, some time later, Tom reciprocated, felt again the excitement building within him, the fullness in his own throat, the hot, live flesh of Joel quickening, pulsing. Salty tastes and fullness mixed with his own saliva. He swallowed, feeling Joel writhing beneath him. Joel's hands rushed over him, then stopped and held tightly as his body shivered and released his own semen.

Afterward, they lay together, both filled, both surprised and shocked into silence. They hadn't turned the light off, and Tom allowed himself to look at Joel, to study his face, and he was struck by Joel's total serenity.

"Joel?"

"Um-hm?"

"Why are you so quiet?"

His eyes moved slowly to look at Tom. He smiled. "I was remembering what we just did. It didn't last long, huh?"

"No."

"But I'm total mush. I'm completely happy right now, and it lasted only a minute! I can't get over it! You?"

"I..." Tom said. He waved his hands. "I'm...." He sat up. "I've been so blind." He pushed Joel playfully, and Joel grabbed him. They wrestled lazily, in slow motion, naked, kissing then giggling. And finally, as they lay beside each other, silent

again, Tom said, "Your parents come back day after tomorrow."

"I know."

"That means we only have one more night together."

"I know. I've been thinking about that."

"Well, what are we gonna do?"

"You mean sleeping together after that?"

"Yes."

"I don't know."

"Well, we can't go back to the way we were."

Joel slid up on his elbow. "You're sure? It may
not be too late...."

Tom laughed at Joel's serious expression.
"Fuck you, Joel Reece. I mean, I don't want to go
back to Father and Mother."

"You don't?"

"No!"

Joel hugged Tom close. "You mean you want
to live together? Now?"

"Yes! Don't you?"

"Of course I do! But how?"

"I don't know."

"I don't either."

Chapter 12

The light was pale and the air blowing across them was cold. Joel shivered and pulled Tom closer. He ran his hand down Tom's back, still disbelieving it all, like he was dreaming—as if suddenly he would wake up and this beautiful guy next to him would become insubstantial and his hand would grasp the cold air. He explored the soft intensity of his own feelings; beneath the tips of his fingers, Tom's skin was a pattern of valleys and curves. His shoulders were sunburned, felt warm, his butt thickening a little from the developing leg muscles. Joel let his hand come to rest on Tom's butt. Inside, in his chest, he recognized another feeling not connected with the sensation of touch, not excited by the feel of Tom beneath his hands—a connection of feeling that arose from something nonphysical. It was the same sort of connection he felt for his family, and sometimes for the farm, the earth. But it was even more than that. With Tom, this connection allowed him to reveal his deepest self, if only he could communicate these feelings. Words weren't adequate to describe them. He looked out the window. The sky was black with early morning thunderclouds, and the breeze coming in through the open window felt damp. If it rained now, by noon it would be sweltering and humid. If the storm passed over, the rest of the day would be cool and pleasant.

Tom moved against him and woke up. Their faces were so close that Tom's eyes looked like an owl's. Tom grinned and the owl's eyes narrowed into a smile. Joel felt the warmth of Tom's lips on his own. Tom's body heat, Tom's stiffness against him. He couldn't distinguish, from the feeling, which cock was his own.

Reluctantly, he got up and dressed. "We're gonna have to fix the window a little better," he said. "There's a storm coming. But we'll have to wait till Dad and Mom get back to put a new glass in. That damned, stupid bastard!"

They prepared a quick breakfast of toast and bacon and ate at the dining room table, listening to the thunder. The smell of the rain was musty and immediate. Tom was quiet, but he seemed recovered from the fright of the night before. He was staring at the mangled window. "Joel?"

"What?"

Tom broke his gaze. He shrugged. "What we talked about. You know, living together. I just can't stand the thought of going back home. I'd rather we ran away and joined the army. They have the buddy system, you know."

"Yeah..." Joel paused, "but we wouldn't have to join the army."

Tom shrugged. "I hope not, but.... You don't sound very excited about it today."

Joel smiled. "Listen, man. I meant everything I said, every time we've talked—especially since the dance. I've tried getting information about us. I've talked to Coach. I haven't changed my story. Or my mind."

"But what about your parents? When I tell my father that I'm not coming home, he'll dig and dig; he'll pester me and you and your parents. They may not like knowing about us, either."

"When Mom and Dad come home, I'm going to tell them anyway, whether your father bugs them or not. I'll be as easy on them as I can, but it's time I leveled with them about things."

"And you don't think they'll be upset?"

"I don't know. Probably. Yeah. They're my parents, man."

"Then I hope you have a better suggestion than the army, because I'm not going back, Joel. I'd drown at home this time, especially after being together like we've been."

"Better than the army? You bet. There's something...I don't know...between us. It's always been there. I'm stupid about most things, but not about you. And one thing I see real clear...you've got it up here." Joel tapped his forehead. "You haven't once mentioned college. You could go to State University, or Western, like Mom does—with Mom—if we get to live here. But even if we can't, you've got to think about school. We can make it. We could go to college together. Dad would at least send me to school, even if he was upset about me and you. I'd bet my life on that. On Dad...."

"Okay, Joel. Not the army," Tom said. "We can stay here, if your parents let us."

"And college?"

Tom sat up straight in his chair. Joel had to laugh to himself at the precision with which Tom moved, at the conviction in his face. "Screw college for a while," he said. "Father has marched me up and down, back and forth over everything. Even college. To tell you the truth, Joel, I'm bored with thinking all the time. It's school all year; then, during the summer, I go to Bible school, Bible camp, prayer sessions, visitations, and all it's done is junk up my mind."

"You mean if my parents don't mind, you'd really prefer just being here, not go to college? How could you stand it?"

Tom laughed. "Look Joel, the whole reason we're even talking about this is so we can be together! It's not just wanting to get away from Father, you beautiful...dummy. So don't expect me to go away to school once we start living together."

"But you're too smart to waste your time on a farm. We could at least live here until next summer. And then move to the university."

Outside, the wind was getting up; it shook the plywood violently and threatened to blow it off the window. The dining room grew visibly darker and thunder rumbled from the west. Joel could almost feel the storm moving across the desert toward them, violent, coming on relentlessly. When he pried the plywood from the windowsill, the wind blew into the dining room with a violent gust. Together, he and Tom laid the wood across the table and Joel hurried into the garage for the electric saw.

He measured and cut the plywood to fit within the window frame and Tom held it while he nailed it into place. The rain came in earnest right after in a blinding fury that blew under the roof of the porch and attacked the plywood with the sound of millions of fingers tapping rapidly. They enjoyed rushing out into the downpour, slipping and sliding as they ran across the farmyard to take care of the livestock and to make sure nothing else was in danger of ruining.

They dried each other off in the kitchen and hung their pants in the garage to dry. For the rest of the morning they stayed indoors and made an early lunch.

Tom was standing at the stove, pushing the hamburger patties around with a spatula. "It's so complicated."

Joel pulled mustard and pickles out of the refrigerator and set them on the counter. "No, you just peek under the patty to see if it's turning brown."

Tom flicked his free hand at Joel's stomach. "I was thinking about our plans!"

Joel laughed. "Yeah?"

Tom slipped the patties onto plates and turned off the burner. "I know if I stay with you, my father will make trouble. But even if he doesn't, what if your parents don't like it? What if your father won't pay for your college?"

* * * *

Edna Stroud sat at her usual place at the kitchen table. Eddie and Henry Jr. were playing outside already; the twins, Patrick and Detrick, were off with Henry, helping him with the truck. He'd said it could be fixed if he could find a damned radiator at the junk yard. Kenneth was laid up in bed, but her little girl, Sally, wouldn't leave. As always, she plucked excitedly at her doll's soiled dress. She had already snatched the doll bald from her constant abuse. Now she was blubbering, close to tears. She was the little, talkative one, though only the other children could understand her. But this morning, Edna understood perfectly. She smiled wearily down at her. "No, no, honey, Kenny's not dead."

"But he bweed, Mama!"

Edna picked her up and held her. Sally began sucking her thumb.

"Kenny's hurt, honey. That's all."

Sally reached up with her small, grimy hand and touched her mother on the cheek where a red welt was slowly turning blue. "Dis huht?"

Edna felt the bruise where Kenneth had hit her after Joel and the Allen boy had left. Sally's touch hurt, but she smiled and kissed Sally's forehead. "No, Sally." She set her down. "Whyn't you go play with Henry Jr.?"

Sally snatched her doll and hurried off. Edna watched her go, then allowed herself to cry.

She got up and paced the room, collecting the dirty dishes from the table and piling them in the sink. She poured more coffee. Maybe Joel and the Allen boy would be all right, she thought, doubting Kenneth's wild-eyed threats. She wiped the table off with a dingy rag and rinsed it in the sink. She squeezed it out and dried her hands on a towel hanging on the refrigerator door.

She looked out the grimy windows over the sink. Eddie, the gentle one she loved because he was so frail, was sitting under a mesquite bush under a tarp with Henry Jr. Her heart hurt as she watched him scooping up mud and forming little people that he had standing in a circle about him. Henry Jr., only eight years old, was protective of Eddie who was ten, but skinnier, runtier and sickly. Henry Jr. had laid the old, rotting tarp over the scrawny branches of the mesquite bush for Eddie. Edna was afraid that the rain might be too cold on Eddie, and now she watched him, worrying about cold and the croup and pleurisy. Several times she had tapped against the window and called to him. But he wouldn't come in. She watched the storm diminish slightly and finally gave up.

She turned away from the window and tried to think what they could have for lunch. Three days without the truck, they were out of milk, out of meat. She pulled out the bare bones of the roasted chicken, smelled it. She got a large pot from the shelf below the sink and ran water into it. Soup with turnips and a few potatoes would have to do.

Eight mouths to feed and Henry drinkin' up half his pension on whisky. That mad dog, she cried in her mind, not realizing that her names for him were growing steadily worse. She looked down at the knife she was gripping; her knuckles were white, and pain shot through her wrist. She chopped at the carcass until the breast bones broke. She picked out the splintered pieces and cut up the last of the potatoes, leaving the skin on them, cutting out only the soft spots.

She looked down at her work, seeing only the scrawny bones. "You wanna go ta prison?" she asked aloud. "That what you want, Kenny?" *You will*, she thought. *Keep threatenin' to kill people, now shootin' up folks' homes!*

She set the pot on the stove and poked the wood to get it hot. *Cain't go on like this*, she thought, *leastwise, without goin' to church of a Sunday.*

"Ma?" Eddie shivered in the kitchen doorway. "Kenny shoot somebody? I heard Pa yellin'."

She put the lid on the soup and went over to him wrapping him affectionately in her thin arms. "Eddie, he done somethin' bad."

"Wull, what was it? Pa seems awful mad. An' ah seen Kenny, jes now, lit out afoot, totin' his shotgun."

She studied his troubled face, wiped the snot off his cheek with the hem of her dress where he'd smeared it with the back of his hand. Henry had been like a maniac since she told him about Kenneth shooting up the Reece home. His eyes had widened with shock that Kenneth, even Kenneth, would go so far. One thing about Henry that Edna could always count on, his brave, heated rage was always just barking. "You come in here and set with me for a spell, okay?"

"I'm okay, Ma. I jes wanted ta know."

Edna wiped her eyes and turned back to the stove. "Well, go on now. Whyn't you go play in the back bedroom?

* * * *

By the afternoon, as Joel had dreaded, the sun beat down on a hot, wet desert, and now it was sweltering. There was no other way to get cool but go swimming in the irrigation pond. They took old towels from his bathroom and walked past the garden, past the cowshed, and climbed up the banks of the pond. When they were standing on the wooden pier where Joel had taken his midnight swim, Joel grinned at Tom. "You ever go skinny dipping?"

"No," Tom laughed. "Father believes nudity is a sin. You should figure that."

"I did. But I just wondered. Guess you've always gone to public pools."

"And swimming in the gulf. But then, you don't want to go nude with hungry fish in the water."

Joel pulled off his shirt and flung it over the towels. His skin was a sheen of sweat that made the blond hair appear pale gold against his dark skin. He sat down on the edge of the pier and pulled off his boots and socks. He stood up and unbuttoned his Levi's. "You'll like skinny dipping. C'mon." He tugged playfully at Tom's pants.

Tom began undressing, folding and neatly piling his clothes. He grinned sheepishly at Joel, who stood naked in front of him, with his cock beginning to stiffen and stand out. Tom peeled off his own Levi's and stopped. He stood before Joel in his underwear, his pale skin a blinding vision, innocent of sun. He lifted both arms away from his body. "What do you think?"

Joel kneeled and pulled Tom's shorts down. Tom laughed and kicked them away. Joel touched him very lightly and laughed as Tom's cock jumped and began to lengthen. "How does it feel?"

Tom's lashes fluttered. He grinned and spread his arms to the sun. "Unbelievable."

"Yeah, I know. I love nude swimming." Joel rose, turned away from Tom, and dived into the water.

Tom followed and came up gasping and laughing. "It's cold!"

Joel laughed at him. "Feels great, huh?" He swam away on his back toward the cold, deep middle of the pond. His cock bobbed in the dark patch between his scissoring legs.

Tom swam quickly after him, face down, doing a simple breast stroke. When he reached Joel, he grabbed his legs and pulled him neatly under. Their two bodies twined and writhed, gaining energy from the cold, crisp water. Their laughing and splashing cut the air with happiness neither had expressed in a long time.

In their play they forgot everything but each other, forgot for a moment that this was their last day together, forgot the foreboding they had expressed in the darkness of the night before. They were two boys, playing across the clear water of the pond, swimming and splashing over and under like otters in the wild.

An hour later, they swam to the edge of the pond and lay down on the wooden pier, breathless and happy. They lay on their backs side by side, their bodies touching from their shoulders to their butts. Joel put his arm out and Tom nestled against him. They let the sun dry their wet skin, and the warmth felt good.

Tom finally sat up and looked down at Joel. He bent over and kissed him on the neck. "I love you," he said happily.

Joel felt Tom's words as breath on his neck, and in the heat he shivered. He spread his legs and pulled Tom down on top of him. He arched his back so that their cocks met. But Tom pulled away.

"Out here?"

"Sure!" Joel said laughing. "Who's gonna see?"

"But I feel so naked!"

"Gee! I hadn't noticed," Joel teased. "It's a fantasy of mine."

Tom shrugged and lay back down on Joel. His cock had stiffened and he pushed it between Joel's thighs at the base of his crotch. Joel's thighs were cold from the water, but still warm and wet between his legs. He felt the heat of Joel's cock hard against his cold stomach. Resting his forearms on Joel's chest, he raised his face to look at him and shuddered with feelings that raced like tiny feet all over his body. He wiggled his butt, pushing his cock deep inside Joel's thighs. He stared down at Joel's unbelievably beautiful face. Joel's mouth was open slightly and he had closed his eyes, enjoying the feel of Tom over him.

They were completely unaware of the figure that had been crouching behind a salt cedar bush not more than ten yards away on the bank; unaware as he rose up and now stood completely in view of them as he took aim and shot.

* * * *

Kenneth emptied both barrels; then, with trembling fingers, reloaded and fired again. He was sweating, watching the blood splatter, feeling the power course through him, and it satisfied him, even against the pain from the shotgun's recoil. He reloaded and emptied both barrels again, pleased with the carnage of the bodies. He had come upon the baby rabbits by accident and, even in his mind, it struck him as odd that they were neglected, lying together in a small hollow of ground beneath a mesquite bush. It didn't occur to him to carry the rabbits to the children. He imagined that these rabbits were Joel and his family, and that gave him a kind of satisfaction, but it wasn't enough. The ground was covered with chunks of rabbit and bloody bits of fur. He didn't reload again, but sank to his knees and cried.

* * * *

The camera's click was fainter than the crickets in the dry grass. Paul had been watching them cavort in the water for half an hour. He'd driven up and down the road wondering if he should stop, but he'd finally parked in the same spot near the gravel pit where he and Kenneth had parked a few nights before. Very carefully, he had circled around the house, peering into windows, but couldn't see them. It was possible they were off walking somewhere, because Joel's pickup was still in the driveway. He had been about to give up when, on the clear air, he heard loud laughter coming from the irrigation pond. To his delight, he found them swimming, almost shocking him into shouting at them for their nakedness. But he hid in the salt cedar, waiting and watching for a perfect picture.

Eventually, they came out of the water and began playing with each other's genitals. He'd seen them kissing and rubbing against each other like two animals. He began backing down the banks of the pond, now that had what he needed. Grimly, he was pleased that he'd been successful, but the cost was almost unendurable. In his own pants he had felt his penis grow and swell as he watched. He felt sticky and dirty, sickened at the feeling. Once out of sight, all he wanted was to get away. He stumbled like a drunk at the bottom of the bank in the thick bushes, fighting the disgusting images in his mind, seeing how...how physical it was, how disgusting, their horrible, swollen penises and their shameful grins of lust. He imagined them tasting the smelly white stuff....

He felt betrayed. Tom had apparently been having sex with Joel for a long time, only pretending to be his friend, only pretending to repent, and the whole time, behind his back.... He fell headlong into a fence running near the road and clawed his way through it, leaving a long, bloody gash in his back. He began running down the road, heedless of the noise he was making.

Joel heard the crashing in the undergrowth from the direction of the road. He climbed onto the bank of the pond and ran along it. Paul Romaine was disappearing, running north, toward the gravel pit.

He felt numb. Paul had seen them and freaked, probably, but that was enough. He walked back along the bank, careless of the fact that he could be seen clearly from any direction. He jumped down onto the pier and stood there looking at Tom's questioning face. "Paul saw us."

Tom looked oddly calm, and it scared Joel. But Tom only smiled weakly. "Well, he knows for sure now, doesn't he?" His voice was quiet, and even that frightened Joel.

"I guess he does, Tom. I am so sorry. I just never thought!"

Tom laughed then, nervously. "You know what?"

"No, " Joel said, with a voice as heavy as lead.

"I...don't...care! I hope he got his squirmy little eyes full!"

Joel was surprised at Tom's reaction. "But you know what he'll do, don't you?"

Tom jumped up from where he was sitting. He grabbed Joel and shook his shoulders. He laughed again. His eyes were glittering with determination. "Of course. He'll spill his spiteful little guts."

"But aren't you afraid?"

"Of course I am, Joel. I'm afraid that Paul will go to my father and tell him what he saw. And I am afraid of what Father will try to do. But I was more afraid of lying than telling the truth. And now I don't have to any more, thanks to Paul. Thanks to Paul...." Tom repeated thoughtfully. "But if you meant what you said. If you and I stick together, then it will be all right, won't it?"

"But what will you father do, Tom? Don't you think he'll keep you away from me, pick on you in church? Make your life miserable?"

"He'll try," Tom said. "The worse thing is wondering exactly what he'll do. Whatever it is, you can count on it being something we didn't think of." He stopped and looked earnestly at Joel. "Everything has changed. You know that, don't you?"

"You mean about our plans?"

"Yes." He shivered violently, and Joel laid his arm over Tom's shoulders. Tom was beginning to sweat, and his skin stuck to Joel.

"What's changed, Tom?"

"No more 'ifs'. So I hope you meant what you said about everything this morning. Remember last

Sunday, when you said if I didn't make a decision, somebody else would?"

Joel nodded. "Yeah."

"Well, Paul's the one who made it for me. Looks like he's been sneaking around a lot. And it won't matter if he really saw anything at all. Father told me, just one more accusation about us...."

Joel hugged him tightly, held onto his naked back, kissed his neck. They were both breathing nervously, clinging to each other, their two bodies puny under the expanse of endless sky above and the consuming desert all around them.

Joel felt exposed, as Tom had earlier. They were as vulnerable as the rabbits he had hunted, having only the choice to run or hide somewhere. Not even old enough to make their own decisions, unless they ran away and faced the world without families. The final remnants of the morning's storm clouds drifted eastward, casting shadows across the fields and patches of desert. His mind was as blank as the sky; shadows moved there, too, full of foreboding. The sun was warm against his skin but he suddenly felt a penetrating cold move within him.

Tom held Joel as tightly as Joel was holding him, trying to comfort Joel as much as to be comforted. "Remember when Father came out to visit me?"

"Yeah." He made a move to pull away to look at him, but Tom held him tighter.

"I was afraid, then. I went back to the garden and tried to pray. But I couldn't. I felt abandoned, tried to feel God, the Holy Spirit, tried to feel anything connected with all that. But when I looked around at the garden, it was exactly the same as it had been. And I realized that God wouldn't answer. I thought I had been forsaken because I had lied to Father."

Joel was confused. He managed to pull away this time. "Of course the garden would be the same, Tom, if you had committed murder, it wouldn't change. Only a storm, or a drought, or the weeds, or neglect would change it. I don't understand."

"Exactly!" Tom said. "But you see, all my life I've been told that God, or the Holy Spirit, reacts to every little thought or change in me. That I was somehow connected spiritually with them; so, naturally, when I tried to pray, I expected the garden to shimmer somehow, to cast the same aura over me I sometimes get in church. But that's not true, is it? In a way, you feel connected inside to God or Jesus; that's not really connected to everything around, like now."

Joel pulled Tom down beside him on the pier. He was no longer concerned with his nakedness. "I can't put things like you're asking into words exactly, but I'll try." He thought a minute. He put his arm across Tom's shoulders and sighed. "I don't believe in the same sort of God as you do. It seems to me that the God of religion is just made up. He's jealous. He gets pissed. He throws temper tantrums like a spoiled kid. He's even mean and spiteful. But if there were a God, Tom, God wouldn't have to be a 'He', or even an 'it'. God just is. God is being. So everything, the Earth, the moon, you name it, is just being, also. If a storm destroys a boat at sea, it's not because of some pissed-off god. If a whole country gets washed away in a flood, there's no god doing the punishing. There's no punishment or salvation, other than what people do. That's what I believe. Especially, I don't believe in the devil. Why leave it up to a god and a devil to tell us what's good and what's bad? Can't you tell, really, what's bad, just by thinking about it? I can. But I can also tell when something is good. And what's good makes putting up with the bad a lot easier. I don't think about spiritual things, either, like supernatural happenings. And I don't see how the garden has anything to do with you. It's a nice place to be, don't you think? It's soothing and quiet and peaceful. It's Mom's special spot, you know? She started that garden after her second baby was born dead.

"Mom and Dad decided not to have any more children after that, but after she started the garden, after all the work she did in it, I guess in its own way it worked a kind of healing on her. She loves that garden. You see how lush she can get it. Anyway, I think just working it, making it live, had a sort of what you'd call spiritual effect on her." Joel laughed. "And maybe the work healed her body, whatever it was that kept killing her children, because she had me! I never tell people, but you know what my middle name is?"

Tom blinked. "No! I never even thought to wonder, now that you mention it."

"It's Hale. I think it's a dumb name. But you know what it means?"

"Yeah. Robust, healthy."

"Exactly! Mom says when I was born I came out, sat up, and looked around and asked her how long we'd be stuck in the hospital!"

Tom laughed. "You shickle the tit out of me sometimes!"

Joel laughed, too, feeling better. He hugged Tom tightly. "Anyway. I guess my point is, without a god, what better way to be religious than to live and work and take care of our bodies and our world?"

"And each other," Tom said.

"You don't think it's corny?"

Tom smiled. "No, Joel. It's exactly what I would expect from you."

"Then, see? We are connected to things. It could be spiritual, if you want. But just because you prayed doesn't mean *it*, the garden, is going to re-act to what you pray about. I mean, plants respond to sunlight and water and mineral nourishment. That's their way of being connected—hey! What's wrong?"

Tom was crying. "Nothing. It is up to me, to decide things. It's crazy, isn't it, to be ashamed because I want to be with you? We aren't hurting anyone, are we? I guess I was ashamed out of habit. I'm not used to letting go of my feelings. In my father's home, feelings, especially ones that make you vulnerable, that show your emotions, these are signs of weakness or worse, signs that you're not right with God. You have to be real strict on yourself, keep things like affection and tenderness from coming out too carelessly, but with you, and even with your parents, Joel, these kinds of feelings are natural. The way you touch each other, you and your parents, the way you've always touched me...." Tom trailed off. He sighed. He wiped away his tears and smiled. "I have to learn to trust these feelings, to give in to them, and be happy because it feels right."

"But because of the others, your father, especially," Joel said, not forgetting the reality of their danger, "we're going to have to be strong. I'm still afraid of what your father will do."

* * * *

They were in the living room on the couch, holding each other close, trying to make plans for what threatened to come. They had drawn the curtains, remembering that Kenneth had crouched there before. But the threat was without substance, a hovering menace without a face, a dread they could not articulate. It was impossible to decide what to do until they could see what happened. Car lights played across the curtains. Joel was afraid that it might be Tom's father. He went to the front door, but the car was gone. He ran out to the driveway; then, hearing the garage door opening, realized that his parents were home a day early.

Joel turned the television off and they went to meet his parents. The came in through the kitchen door from the garage. Eva Reece set her suitcase down and hugged him and Tom. Douglas followed her in with the rest of the luggage and shook hands with the boys. "Welcome home," Joel said to both of them. "I've got some bad news."

Their smiles disappeared when Joel led them into the dining room and pulled back the curtains on the dining room window, revealing the plywood. "We had a prankster out here last night," he said. "Dad, you know Kenneth Stroud? He shot out the window."

Douglas Reece's face went from concern to distaste. "But why?"

Joel didn't know exactly how to respond. "It's a long story."

Eva saw the china cabinet and went over to it, giving off little gasps as she surveyed the damage. "My goodness!" she exclaimed. "Honestly, Douglas. Would you look at this!" She faced Joel. "When did this happen?"

"Kenneth Stroud has been harassing us. He ran us off the road after church on Wednesday night, and then last night he came out here and blew the window out with his shotgun. The glass just flew everywhere."

Douglas sat down at the table, speechless, waiting for an explanation.

In the kitchen, Eva took charge of her territory again. In no time, she had a pile of sandwiches and a pot of coffee set out on the table. Joel spoke mainly to his father, but occasionally turned to her, telling them how he and Tom, coming back from taking a walk, had seen the yard light explode from a shotgun blast, and then, when they were coming around the house, heard another shot that blew the dining room window out. He told them how he and Kenneth had fought after that. There wasn't much to tell after all, he discovered, dealing strictly with those facts. He wasn't able to hide his nervousness, and he left his parents more confused than ever.

"But why? Son, did you do something to piss him off?" Douglas asked.

"That's a lot harder to tell, Dad," Joel hedged. "Kenneth has always hated me—at least since school at Mimbres, you know. Then...a lot has happened. You won't like any of it."

Tom, who had been sitting quietly, said, "I was the one who started it, Mr. and Mrs. Reece."

For the first time in a half-hour, Eva laughed a small laugh. "Oh, honey, what could you have done?"

Tom blushed, his long, dark lashes fluttered nervously. He looked at Joel now, and some sense of determination passed between them.

Joel began with the argument with Tom two weeks before. "Remember how bad it was? I moped around for a solid week. It was a bad time for us." He looked at Tom, nodded, then looked at Douglas. "I know I told you it wasn't, but I couldn't tell you how bad it really was."

Douglas stood up and Joel felt his strong hands on his shoulders. "You're confusing the hell out of me, Son. Nothing can be so bad that you can't tell me."

Joel felt tears of frustration breaking at the corners of his eyes. He wiped them with the heel of his hand. "Yes, it is, Dad."

Eva looked from Joel to Tom, then back to her husband. But she said nothing.

"Okay," Douglas said, "it's bad. You murder someone?"

"No. Dad...."

"You kill the crops?" He attempted a laugh but, seeing his wife's face, he backed off.

"Me and Tom got drunk at that dance. Remember?"

He nodded, but looked confused. "I thought—"

Joel remembered his father's joke on him that morning about the underwear. "I know. But I was with Tom that night. At the dance, Tom got a few guys pissed. At least I saw they were, so I took him away. But we didn't go straight home. I wanted him to sober up."

"We went parking," Tom said.

"These guys..." Douglas cut in. "Kenneth was one of 'em?"

"No, but he was there," Joel said. "They didn't like the way Tom was acting. I didn't know Kenneth would be so persistent, but one thing led to another and every chance he got he tried to hassle us, like I said."

"That's kind of strange, Son. But no tellin' what's gonna make drunk cowboys mad, you know. So?"

Eva stood up. "Well! I know you two had an awful fight, but you seem to be friends again. I think I'll go unpack. I'll be back in a few minutes." She started to leave the room, but Joel touched her arm.

"Mom, you've gotta stay." He spoke as calmly as he could, but she was alarmed. She sat back down and nervously picked up one of the forgotten sandwiches.

He felt sorry for her; he had never intended to scare her. But he was resolute. "We are friends. That wasn't the problem. The night of the dance when we got drunk, Tom kissed me. In front of all those guys. I guess some of his self-control was let down. But I could tell that people didn't think it was funny. And I knew he would get slugged if we stuck around so we left the dance, like I said, but I couldn't take him home, as drunk as we were."

Neither of his parents moved or spoke. His mother's face had turned white. While Joel was telling them the story, her face had changed from sympathy, to surprise, to anger. But she had smiled bravely through it. Now her smile thinned. Her eyes opened, confused, as though Joel had suddenly begun speaking Greek. Then the words seemed to register. Just a hint of surprise had crossed his father's face. Joel took a ragged breath. "We went parking behind one of the old hangars out there. I just intended to get him sober but, well, we started kissing again. It surprised both of us, and pretty soon we were, you know, doing everything."

His mother's face sagged horribly. "Oh, Joel! Why? That's despicable!" She began to cry.

But Joel couldn't stop now. "Tom thought it was, too, Mom. We argued about it the next day. He tried to tell me it was wrong, what we did, but I just couldn't accept it. So he decided to take time by himself."

"And that's why Kenneth started hassling you, isn't it?" Douglas' face was still calm. He put his hand on his wife's shoulder. She was crying and shaking her head. "Eva, that's enough. Please. Stop it."

She dabbed at her eyes. She smiled weakly.

"I'm sorry. I never thought of anything like this."
Her voice was full of repressed sobs. Her face
showed her pain. "At least that explains why you
were so miserable all that week. I should think it
would bother you. It did, didn't it, honey?" She
was all prepared to pour out her sympathy, and
Joel regretted having to continue, to destroy what
sounded like a prayer from her, wanting to hear
him say how badly he felt about what they had
done."

His father was almost the exact opposite. He
was smiling mildly, looking amused—sort of, but
not quite. It had taken him a moment to fix on
Joel's words, but when he had understood what
the words meant, he had settled for amusement.
Joel looked back and forth between them, letting
his attention stay on his father's calm face.

"Mom, I did feel sort of bad," Joel said, attempt-
ing to soften the blow of his words, "but what really made things worse for us was Kenneth. His
mother is a member of Tom's church. He told the
son of one of the elders about the way Tom was
acting at the dance, and this guy tells his own
parents, and they tell Tom's father and, well, it
just kept snowballing. Then last night, Kenneth
came over for a showdown or something, and you
see what happened. He shot out the window, trying to get us to come out. Fighting him wasn't really hard because he'd already used up his shells.
Mrs. Stroud offered to pay for the window last night
when we dumped Kenneth off. But you know she
can't. If you press charges, they could put Kenneth
in jail, but I just don't know. Maybe he won't bother
us any more."

"Oh, that poor woman!" Eva said, in spite of
herself.

Joel wanted to let it rest, now, but he had to

press on. Any minute, he expected Tom's father to call. "I told Mrs. Stroud that we'd fix the window. Okay? They can't afford that. But you'll need to decide if you want him to go to court because of what he did."

Douglas waved his hand. "Depends on what that asshole father does." He looked thoughtful. "It took guts for you to tell us about everything, Joel."

"That isn't everything," Joel said. He hated what he had to do, but he would not stop.

"When Tom's father came out here, Tom denied everything...about us kissing. But Paul, the elder's son, caught us this afternoon messing around at the pond. And we know he's going back to the preacher with that. So now, Tom is in a real bad situation at home...and probably in church, too. Me and Tom.... See, after the dance, and after everything, me and Tom...love each other.... We've been *sleeping* together. You understand?"

This time, Douglas slammed his hand down on the table and, for the first time, his anger showed. "No, I don't understand! You're telling your mother and me that you two are homosexual?"

Joel was finished. "Yeah." He braced himself for a further explosion, but was met only with silence.

His mother left the room without a word.

He and Tom looked at each other sheepishly. After a moment, his father went into the living room, leaving him and Tom alone in the dining room. They heard him rummaging through a bookshelf. Joel watched through the wide doorway, afraid to say anything. He felt sick to his stomach, but also relieved. He felt better, having told them everything.

Tom touched his hand. "It'll be okay," he said.

Tom's touch made him turn to look, and he was shocked to see that he was crying large, silent tears. For a moment he was afraid that Tom was sorry for telling his parents; then he understood. They were tears of relief. He smiled then and whispered to Tom. "I do love you. I told you I meant everything I've said."

Tom wiped his tears with his sleeve. He sniffled, stood up, and went into the living room. Joel heard him saying, "I'm sorry, Mr. Reece."

He strained to hear what his father was saying, but he heard only the gentle tone of his voice. Then the telephone clanged like a fire bell.

Almost immediately, Joel heard his father's abrupt change of tone. "Reece here."

"Pete? They're both here.... It's up to them, Son. Okay. I'll have Tom call. Goodnight."

Joel couldn't stand it any more and went into the living room. Tom was standing by the telephone. His father turned to him. "That was a kid named Pete." Then he smiled again, both amusement and something else playing around his eyes. "You two sure have stirred up a hornet's nest. He says you've got to call back tonight. You can do that when I'm finished. Now, both of you, please sit down." His tone was firm, but there was no anger in his voice.

They sat close to each other on the couch like two children about to get a spanking. Their shoulders were touching and Joel felt how shaken Tom was. He was trembling slightly himself and having a hard time breathing regularly. They waited.

Douglas turned on the overhead lights. In the bright glare, Joel saw the hurt. But his voice was steady. "Here, Joel, take a look at this." He handed Joel a family album.

Joel took it. It was open to a page with old

pictures, taken sometime in the thirties, he guessed. Douglas pointed to a picture in one corner of the page. "See those two women?"

Joel looked at the picture. Two women, dressed in old-fashioned dresses with lace around the edges with long sleeves and tight waists, had been captured by the camera; their faces were without expression. They looked old, maybe in their sixties. The photograph was sepia tinted, trimmed around the edges in a white cloud. He looked up at his father. "Who are they?"

"One's a great-aunt of mine, on my mother's side. The other woman is her friend. Like you say between you and Tom. No one in the family knew until after they both died. When my mother went to pack their things, she found out. I don't remember how. Anyway, I remember them. Everybody else in my family, well, they burned everything that belonged to them or gave it to the Salvation Army. But I kept that picture. I used to go over there when I was a kid. They gave me sweets and things and, years later—I musta been about your age when they died—I was told what they had been. I didn't know what they meant, saying they were perverts. But eventually I figured it out. I was shocked, but it didn't mean much to me. They were dead. They were never anything but nice to me— too nice for me to let their personal lives bother me."

He looked down at them, paused a moment, then continued. "Things were different then, I s'pose. They had to be careful. If anyone had found out, they probably would have gone friendless from then on. But nowadays in other places, I hear, there are bars and clubs for people like that. Can't say I understand, even now, what causes it." He took the album from Joel and closed it, held it against his chest like a treasured book. He looked over their heads and took a deep breath.

"I had a buddy in the army during the war against Hitler. You two are lucky. You haven't been through a war like that. Times out there, you took what comfort you could get. I was just a little older than you are now, Joel, and there for a while, this buddy of mine and me shared a bed."

Joel felt his heart stop, and it was his turn to look odd, to suddenly feel very odd. He glanced quickly at Tom and saw surprise on his face.

"We were just kids, and some nights we took comfort from each other and had relations. But when I got back home, I went back to your mother. I had a family, Joel, and responsibilities. I knew the thing for what it was. I'm not like that, though, never really was, but I ain't never forgot him, either. I think he was that way, but I never got to find out. Anyway, I never thought I'd tell a soul about that…at least after I squared myself with your mother. I told her about everything. She understood, Son, eventually. But it took time. She reacted about the same way she did tonight, except…well, I wasn't telling her I wanted to be one of those, like you just did. And I never thought you'd be telling me you were…like that, either. So, in a way, I guess I understand what you say. But, Son, it's one thing when you go through a war, sleeping and living close together in the trenches, month after month, so frightened and on edge all the time, you think your next breath will be your last. It's different when you have a choice, it seems like to me."

"Dad?"

He was staring over their heads, and Joel thought he had forgotten them. He looked down. There were tears in his eyes. "Yes?"

"I didn't mean to hurt you."

He smiled down at Joel. "You haven't. You've made me proud tonight. Telling me something that you could have denied. Now I'm not saying I strictly believe you're what you think you are. That remains to be seen. But I know you. You deserve the same respect I would want. You, too, Tommy. But if it's true, I suspect you have a hard row to hoe. Now, please, call your friend back. Take care of whatever business he's got with you, then get to bed. If you've got trouble brewing with your father, Tom, I suspect it would be a good idea if we all went to church tomorrow."

Chapter 13

Sunday, June 13

2 a.m.

He lay awake.

His hand grasped the sheet and nothing else. In so short a time, it felt strange to be lying here alone; he had grown used to having Tom beside him. But Tom may as well have been a million miles away instead of down the hall in the guest room. It was Tom's idea, since they had told Joel's parents. But Joel agreed, seeing the decency of Tom's suggestion in the face of how his mother had reacted. But he figured it was just as hard for his father. Joel had been amazed, but not altogether convinced, when his father said he was proud of him tonight.

He shuddered at the power of words, how, once spoken, couldn't be taken back, how words themselves could hurt. Words made his mother run from the room in tears; the same words had made his father remember two old ladies he had liked as a child, a long-forgotten war buddy, and he was amazed that his father had found love, for a time, with another man. "We love each other," he had told his parents. And wasn't it funny, not a single one of those words were bad. The sentence, even, had all the genuine sound of goodness and affection, and yet…somehow it stabbed his mother to the heart. "But we do love each other!" he said, now, and he felt good about it.

It seemed so long ago that everything had changed. And he wondered what had gone wrong. What he could have done to change it. He thought again of that first time in the pickup, their lovemaking a fevered rush to get at each other, so hungry had they been, as if starved, and then Tom's shame, equally consuming. But it had all the qualities of a dream; nothing was distinct— just images that had become a memory, with a memory's selective quality. But that first time he cherished now. Without that, of course, they would still be friends. But just friends, and he thought with a little relief that Tom may well have gone away to school as his father had planned.

So what would he have changed? Maybe beating up those smirky faces at the dance. But he hadn't; and that might have made matters worse, anyway. Sure as hell they both would have been beat up. Maybe, had he known about Paul's relentless spying, he would have been more careful about skinny dipping and making love on the pier, like learning to be careful about where he jerked off. Those were mistakes.

He thought of Tom and hugged his pillow, surprised and a little disgusted that he had been crying. He laughed to himself, feeling ridiculous. If nothing else, Tom had made unbelievable changes. *I just pushed and pushed until I got what I wanted*, he thought. He didn't even blame Paul Romaine, that little shithead, who tattled like a rat and made it impossible for Tom to deny the truth, or hide it.

It would have happened eventually. Even Kenneth was not to blame. *People in general hate us for what we are. I knew that. I knew it and I just kept right on pushing...*

In the dark, he sat up on the edge of the bed next to the open window. The night air was cool. The moon was out, waning now, but casting an eerie whiteness over the grass. Kitty Cat was curled on the edge of the windowsill outside. She looked at him, a shadow cat. "Meow-ow," he said. "Come on, Kitty." He opened the screen. She jumped down and ran across the lawn, switching her tail. "Don't like queers, either?" He shut the screen. As usual, he was naked. The moonlight slanted across his body. His face was in shadow. His stomach shined in the light. His pubic patch was dark but, lying in the middle of the cluster of hair like an Easter egg, his cock showed clearly. He stared at it, fascinated by its ability to control his emotions or cloud his mind with its demands.

He lay back, suddenly depressed, wondering if Tom was able to sleep, wondering, too, if his parents could. They had been given quite a lot to handle just back from their vacation. "Especially Mom," he whispered, feeling guilty. He hated to see her cry, had never wanted to hurt her, and didn't know how long it would take her to look at him like anything but a stranger. He thought of his sisters, married and having children of their own. How would they feel toward him? He would eventually tell them, too. Once his parents knew, what would be the point of hiding it from the rest of the family, the rest of the world?

He drifted slowly into sleep, and the next sound he heard was a light tapping on his door. It was still dark, and he thought it was only a few minutes later. He lay there and watched the door opening slowly. His mother came in.

"Joel, honey?"

He pulled the sheet up to his chest. "Mom? What are you doing up?"

She sat on the edge of the bed. "It's time to get up. We have to get ready for church." Her voice was gravely, sleepy sounding. She brushed the hair on his forehead.

Her hand was warm. "I'm sorry, Mom, for hurting you last night."

She sighed. "Your father and I talked. I don't understand, Joel. But you're my son, and no matter what, I love you. You've never given me any cause to think you don't respect me."

He tried to hug her, but she stood up. "We'll talk about this, but right now we've got to get going. So please shower and get dressed. We'll all eat a good breakfast. We'll all feel better."

* * * *

Paul woke up, discovering that in the night he had soiled his shorts again with the sticky sperm. It had been happening more and more lately. He tore at them, hating himself, but blaming it on Tom and Joel. He pulled the shorts off and hid them under the sink in his bathroom. He would wash them out later, as he always did, let them dry and then toss them in the dirty clothes hamper. He showered and scrubbed his genitals, hating their ugliness. Soon, though, soon he would be safe from Joel's continual influence. He was glad now that Joel had ignored him in high school. His naked, sexual influence on Tom would also be destroyed finally. He hated Tom's sin, knew he had to act without hesitation, to force Tom to break Joel's hold on him.

After showering and dressing, he felt better, cleaner, pure again in his new jacket. He thought of them at the pond yesterday. Boy did they put on a great show for the camera! He laughed silently, easily now. Everything had gone just fine; the film would be coming back from the Rexall Drug by Monday, and even though they may think he didn't have proof, he did. Up to now he thought he had played the part perfectly. And soon, how much better it would be! Tom would really be repentant, truly the prodigal returned to the holy fold. And at least, Paul thought, *I can save him from Joel, like I saved myself.* He would be able to offer Tom consolation; Tom would crave it. But he would withhold it for a while, letting the blackness of his activity make him feel utterly abandoned. Then, like an angel of mercy, he would succor Tom, and slowly, very slowly, allow them to become friends.

He could hardly wait! At breakfast he was happy but had to restrain it. As they always did before church, the Romaines prayed. Paul added his own voice to that of his father: "And we especially pray for Tom Allen, Father. Please guide him mercifully back to us, through Your precious son, Jesus, we pray. Amen." He looked up at his parents, who were looking at him strangely.

Paul sat in the back seat of the car with his leather-bound, much-used Bible. He hugged it to him, feeling its rich texture in his hands, smelling its succulent leather, its holiness, and he felt completely satisfied.

At the church, the people milled around outside, moving as usual to the Sunday School classes. There was a chill in the air as he got out of the car. He parted from his parents and looked around for Tom. He didn't see him at first but then—there! Yes! With Joel and his parents. How quaint. The heathen family. He managed to greet them all warmly, so warmly. Only Joel managed to ruin his exit, spitting on the sidewalk when he proffered his hand.

Paul sat with the other guys in the Fellowship group. He felt a kinship with them now, their leader. They would become a circle unbroken again for Tom, in his need.

Rarely had Joel sat next to his parents in church. The last time was when even the girls weren't married and his oldest sister, Kathleen, sang in the choir. She was not a regular church member, but had been invited to sing a solo, "Ave Maria." She had won all-state soloist that year. The family was delighted at her performance in the choir and just as proud to attend the Presbyterian Church for the special services in memory of President Kennedy. His parents cried shamelessly at Kathleen's wonderful, clear voice as it soared sweetly out over the audience that day. She had, in fact, brought the entire audience to tears. Joel sat in awe, loving his sister dearly at that moment. His other sister, Patricia, also sang with the choir. He saw her rise with the rest of the choir and felt the tremendous pulsing of sound that followed the solo. Never had he seen his sisters more beautiful.

Today, he felt the same tremendous anticipation as he sat with his parents, but for more serious reasons. Last night, after Joel's father had talked to him and Tom in the living room, Tom called Pete and they met him at the truck stop near the west end of town.

Pete told them Paul was getting all the guys ready.

"What guys? Joel had asked.

"The...the disciples," Pete said. He turned to Tom. "Tell him."

They were eating hamburgers, sitting in a red vinyl booth by the plate glass window. It was so dark out that their reflection showed clearly in the fluorescent light.

"They call themselves the disciples," Tom explained. "Actually, I mean we…Pete, me, Paul and a few other guys."

"Why?" Joel asked. "Are there twelve of you?" He thought the whole idea a bit silly, the same old weirdness again.

Pete said, "There are thirteen, if you count me, but I'm not really one of them."

"Anyway," Tom said, "the big deal about us being disciples is just a joke. Sort of, except Paul takes it seriously. Our only problem is, we don't have a Christ figure." He laughed and Pete giggled. But Joel couldn't see much humor in it.

"These are the guys Paul's telling? Man, are they going to be a nice, tight, little group," Joel said.

Pete looked more helpless than Tom, more frightened. He was looking up at Tom expectantly. *He adores Tom*, Joel thought, but felt not the least resentment.

Tom smiled across the table at Joel. Then he looked down at Pete's expectant face, treating him much like a kid brother. "It's true what Paul says, Pete. Maybe not all the things he's said, because I never got kicked out of that dance. But the rest is true. Joel and I are homosexuals."

Pete's adoring expression didn't change, except to register determination. "I thought so, but I was afraid to ask the other day…or tell you that you're not alone, Tom." He wrinkled his nose and ducked his head. He looked over at Joel, his blue eyes shining and eager. "You guys! I always hoped it was true. It's what I wanted with Kevin. When I told you what Paul told Kevin about me being queer, I was serious. And the thing is, it's true. It was about the biggest chance I ever took, to see how Tom would act. I knew then, but I just couldn't ask."

Tom took a breath and sighed, relieved. He grinned. "I'm glad we're all able to talk about this." Then he looked sad. "But, Pete, I'm going to be in trouble. Everybody at church will know, and like Joel told me once, if we hang around together, people will think you're like us."

Pete shrugged. "I'm not going to stay in this town forever. You bet I'm leaving, man. I can hitch a ride west with one of these truckers. I've seen guys do it. They just come in here with a bag and hang around until a friendly trucker comes along. That's my way out, man. So let 'em talk." He sat up and looked grim. "But right now, you're in for it at church. Paul's been very busy since seeing you and Joel yesterday. I got wind of it from Kevin."

"What do you mean?" Tom asked.

Pete's eyes darted over at Joel, then came to rest on Tom. "He's going to get you, man. He says he saw you two having sex out in the open."

"We know he did," Joel said. "That little sneak. So?"

"Well, he's telling everybody how disgusting it was. And he also says he can prove it. He says your father will believe him this time."

"One good thing, though," Tom said. "He's not going to catch me by surprise again." Then he laughed. "It gives me a little time to plan what I'm going to do."

"But are you willing to leave the church for Joel, if it comes down to that?"

"Of course I am, Pete."

Pete looked relieved. "That's good, because Paul

is depending on you not being willing to. He's all set to have the disciples minister to you."

"And what kind of stink is he planning at the church?" Joel asked.

"I don't know. He said he's waiting for something he sent away for."

Tom sighed. "Thanks a lot, Pete. I just wish he'd get it over with." He picked up his hamburger, looked at it, and dropped it onto the plate. "I can't stand waiting."

* * * *

Joel realized he'd been in a daze. He looked around the church, full to capacity. The crowd was quieting. An occasional cough cracked the dull, milling sound. He squinted at the title of the sermon: THE CAPACITY TO FORGIVE. Right, he thought. Odd how the preacher manages to direct things so dead center.

His father's face, the profile, revealed his inner calm. Joel noticed his eyes, coolly appraising the crowd, the church, probably studying the physical structure of the building as much as anything else. His mother was more nervous, not about being there, Joel thought, but, like him, she was full of anticipation. He was sitting beside her, smelled the clean smell of her perfume, very faintly, the soap she used. He leaned over and whispered, "You okay?"

She patted his knee. "Considering, yes."

On his left, Tom sat quietly, but occasionally Joel felt his knee add the slightest pressure against his. Everything between them felt fine, and even with Paul sitting ahead only a couple of pews, Tom didn't seem nervous at all. He had even managed to greet Paul as if nothing was afoot. And even more surprising, Paul had conquered his own habitual sneer. *A real snake*, Joel thought. Knowing he was about to ruin Tom's reputation, thinking he had the advantage of surprise, he was as outwardly friendly as the other people who greeted Tom. And how many of them were silently nursing the secret, the vicious rumors?

"The Capacity to Forgive!" boomed the preacher, finally.

His mother sat up. His father put his arm around her. Joel listened intently. The sermon and the other rigmarole passed quickly. When church was over the preacher made a point of thanking the Reeces for attending. His father talked quietly, praised Tom's work for the last week, and shook hands with those farmers he knew.

Strange as it seemed, Joel had to leave Tom. They had decided to act as normally as they could. If they had freaked out, they decided, they might get pushed to do something stupid. They managed to spend a free minute at the car before Joel left.

"You'll be all right?" Joel asked.

"I'll be absolutely fine, Joel. I'll call you, I bet, as soon as you get home, and we'll plan to get together later. Right now, I've got to prepare for everything. Pete's going to hang around with the disciples until our dinner at the Sundowner and see what else Paul is planning."

"Okay," Joel said. "I still don't like that idea, though, confessing to all those guys. Man, that's asking for it."

The Reeces' car was parked across the street from the church in the shade of an elm tree. Tom looked around casually at the crowd. Joel's parents were still at the church and, for the briefest moment, he and Tom were by themselves. Tom leaned into the car window and kissed him softly on the mouth. Their hands touched, and Joel held

Tom's warm fingers. Tom squeezed back. "I love you."

Joel watched him go. He pounded softly on the arm rest in the back seat with a clenched fist, waiting. Waiting.

* * * *

Edna prayed alone, unable to attend church. She prayed for Kenneth. She prayed for her husband, as she always did. She clutched her poor, tattered Bible, and she prayed especially for little Eddie, especially for him.

Kenneth's anger had only increased when she tried to talk sense to him. He was plumb crazy with hatred for Joel. She had given up talking to him after he had hit her again. "You shut up, Ma!" He backhanded her across the mouth. Henry had hit Kenneth for it, but Kenneth only laughed and slammed out of the house.

She touched her upper lip with trembling fingers. It was swollen now, tight with blood straining to burst as she spoke her prayer. She didn't pray for herself, feeling too unworthy.

When she finished, she fixed a meager breakfast of biscuits and flour gravy for the children. After breakfast, when they were playing and Henry was starting in on his whisky in the living room, she slipped out the kitchen door. Her steps were weary, but her heart kept her moving one step at a time. She would not beg for help, but would instead ask Douglas and Eva to press charges for what Kenneth had done to their house. She could at least do that. It would keep Henry away from Kenneth and keep Kenneth from causing more trouble for everyone. If Henry also beat her she would take it, knowing that he would be powerless, at least, against the police.

* * * *

Joel felt awkward leaving Tom at church and, as they were driving away, he turned around in the back seat to look until the church disappeared. His father laughed but there was no amusement in his voice. "He'll be okay, Son. I think he's levelheaded." His mother touched him lightly on the knee from the front seat. He appreciated her touch but couldn't shake the sluggish weight of dread that settled somewhere in his guts.

"Dad? What d'you think his father's going to do when he finds out?"

"Don't worry too much about what he'll do right now. Just keep it in mind that Tom and his father first need to work things out—at least, try to. Don't you agree?"

"No!" Joel said. "I mean, of course, but I don't think it will do any good. What if he grounds Tom again, like he did last time? They don't talk like we do, Dad. They don't."

"But Joel, Tom hasn't been exactly honest with his parents. Let him have that chance. If we rush in and fight his battle for him, he won't get a chance to try standing up for himself. And you know he's got to have a chance to face his father. I can see where Tom is forcing things myself, Joel. If it's as you say, and you two have been…having relations, Tom does have to face his church—maybe not up there in front, but inside himself. And if you don't stand back a little, let him have a chance to win his fight, I wouldn't give much for the kind of person you might see in Tom after that."

"Joel…." His mother looked weary. Her hand left his knee and clutched the back of the car seat. "What you boys did is serious." She frowned at her husband. "I don't think your father has got that in mind. He won't say it's wrong, what you're getting into with your friend. But the preacher has a right to tell his son it is. And he also has the right to try and cure him."

"It's not cancer, Mom," Joel said softly. She looked at him sadly. Her eyes didn't settle on his face. She didn't smile, and when she turned in the seat and began gazing out at the passing fields, Joel settled back and crossed his arms. *Maybe we will just take off*, he thought. His parents were oddly quiet, now that his mother had spoken her mind. It was rare for her to disagree with her husband, rarer still that she would call him down. It bothered her badly, Joel realized, and again he felt sorry for her, sorry that they would probably fight about it later. But there wasn't much he could do about that. *I'm not going to lose him*, he thought stubbornly. He spoke to his parents' backs. "I'm sorry it hurts, but we're gonna be together no matter what."

"And you'll suffer for it, Joel, for the rest of your life," his father said. "In just a year, you'll be out of school, and you'll be your own man. What you do then will be your business. But right now, it's also mine and your mother's. Tom belongs to his father."

"You make it sound like we're property or something."

"In a way you are," his mother said. "If we wanted, Joel, we could have you committed to a mental hospital…just on the basis of what you've told us."

"Jeez! That's not right!"

Douglas chuckled. "I'm sorry. It's not funny. But Eva's right. We could. Those are the facts, like it or not."

Joel's breath felt squeezed, as if he were being choked.

They were nearing the turnoff to their road.

His father slowed the car and turned onto it. "I understand how you feel. But think! If it's like you say, a year from now, if you still feel the same way, I'll be more inclined to believe you. Give us a chance. Right now, I think you should just calm down."

Joel felt a little relief seeing that his parents, shook as they were, weren't freaking out as he had imagined. But from what he'd seen and heard in that church, and considering how even Tom had gone weird at first, he doubted that Tom would have an easy time of it.

"I just want you to see what you're up against," Douglas added. "What I've been tryin' to say. I want you to know what you face. Whether I agree with what you say you feel is my choice. But you've got a long life ahead of you. I can only go so far. Then you're on your own."

Joel wanted to cry, but he wouldn't, not now, not in front of them.

When they got home, the telephone was ringing. Joel raced to it, picked it up. "Tom?"

* * * *

There was work to do, and quickly. There was no decision, however, which in itself saved Tom valuable time. After saying good-bye to Joel at the church, Tom walked quickly home. His parents would still be at the church and would very likely be there for another half-hour. Later, in the afternoon, the disciples, officially known as the Gospel Fellowship, were scheduled to have their monthly dinner at the Sundowner Motel over on Main Street. By the time it started, Tom planned to be ready to do what Joel still seemed to think he would be incapable of, and that was to stand up to his father. Joel was wrong.

He couldn't explain it to Joel. Why he felt confident now. But he understood why Joel was nervous. *I did freak out the first time we had sex,* he thought. But this dinner, where the disciples—Mike, Kevin, Paul, and others—were going to meet was the last responsibility Tom planned to fulfill at his church. More than anything else, he knew Joel was scared by his idea to beat Paul at his own snide little game. As he made his way home, he realized that the affairs of the church, the goings on, the fellowship, the retreats, the banquets, were no longer of concern to him—at least not now. He felt confident that he could survive his father's reaction when the truth was finally told. He was determined, as he'd never been, to prove to Joel that he wasn't going to cave in, or, as Joel said, "knuckle under again," to his father. He passed through the house, taking no notice of it. He hadn't set foot inside for six days, and its familiarity was gone, an ephemeral coziness that had dissipated in comparison to the warm home that Joel and his parents shared; it was one that Tom ached to be part of. There, he could be human; there, he was respected for himself and not reprimanded because he was only human and failed to attain some unattainable perfection; and there, was Joel. In just six days, Tom felt as though he had been recreated, with a mind of his own, with the chance to succeed or fail on his own merits. And he was determined not to fail.

He went directly to his room and started at the closet. No time for sentimental browsing. He cleared the shelf above the clothes. To one side, he tossed only the most valuable of his possessions—jewelry (easily hocked for cash), his high-school diploma, a savings account passbook (which had been built up over many years and never

touched, the principal, gifts from his grandparents), papers that proved who he was, and other
useful documents. He even had a copy of his birth
certificate he'd used for entrance requirements at
the various colleges he had applied to. In another
pile, he discarded everything he could see no sur-
vival value in. These, he put back on the shelf.

He emptied a sturdy box in which he placed
the items he intended to keep. Next, he rummaged
through his clothes, pulling out Levi's, sturdy
shirts, socks and underwear. He grabbed a Levi-
jacket Joel had given him, an overcoat and a cor-
duroy coat with a fur collar. He stuffed the clothes
into a suitcase. He considered books from his large
collection, but couldn't think of anything to take,
amazed that no book however wonderful or moving, seemed important when beginning a whole
new existence. He took his picture of Joel, then
scoured the room for what little money he had lying around and stuffed it into his pockets.

He left his room and retrieved his extra tooth-
brush; everything else he needed he'd forgot to
bring home from Joel's house.

When he was finished, he could scarcely tell
that anything from his room had been taken. He
carried the box and suitcase out the back door.
He looked around to avoid being seen, then went
through the gate to the alley. He left his belongings behind the garbage cans and covered them
with trash.

He didn't know how many precious minutes
had gone by, so he hurried back into the house to
use the telephone. He hoped the Reeces would be
back from church by now. On the first ring, he
heard Joel's voice.

He told him about the clothes and things in
the alley and arranged to call him later in the

evening. "But if I don't call you by eight o'clock tonight, you'll know that I've run into trouble. I'll be walking out to your house by that time. I'll walk by the high school and cut across the park heading south, then down 8th Street all the way to Highway 490, Okay? If I call you before eight...well, you'll know everything is fine. Wish me luck at the dinner, Joel—

"No. I'm doing it, Joel, because Paul and the other disciples will be there. It's a good chance to get them alone. I have to go now. I love you. Bye."

Tom dropped the receiver into the cradle. He had finished everything, and it didn't matter now if his parents came back. The house was silent. Only the ticking of the grandfather clock in the living room sounded. He stepped lightly on the plush, gray carpet of the hallway and returned to his room. There was plenty of time now before the dinner, and while he waited for Pete and Kevin, he wanted to write a letter. He owed his mother that. But it was difficult; she was so brittle somehow, how could he chance breaking such a fragile being? He heard her quiet voice, her prim manner, acquired over a lifetime; outwardly, at least, she made his father a perfect wife. His mother's inner person rarely had been exposed, but Tom was aware of it, at least, even if his father never seemed to wonder. He could only estimate the loss she would feel as she read his letter by the loss he felt in having to write it. And no matter what happiness she found later, he doubted it would be as complete as it could have been had he somehow found a way to stay here. But he would not. He shrugged off his guilt. Joel had told his parents, and the world had not ended. So let Paul do his worst. And when his father found out everything? Never had he disputed a single argument, and because he would not give in on this, he knew that his father's rage would be boundless, just as his capacity to beat an argument to death was boundless. He was incapable of allowing anyone to get the last word.

Finally, he wrote the letter that would change everything for his mother:

> Dear Mother,
>
> I love you. I am sorry that things are like they are. By the time you read this, you'll know what I mean. Just please understand, I couldn't give in to him on this.
>
> As for my going away, I hope you will remember that in the fall, I would have been in college anyway. And even Baylor University would have been Father's choice, not mine. I never had a choice in anything. Father has dictated to me (and you) in everything. If I had stayed, and if it hadn't changed my mind about myself, Father would have kicked me out anyway. I'm sure of this. So if you feel a loss, just think that I have moved out only a few months sooner. So please don't feel bad.
>
> I hope that in your heart, you still consider me your son. You don't have to let Father make that decision for you, do you? I will always hold you dear. You won't be far from me in my thoughts. And, of course, neither will Father, because even though he may not realize it or care, I love him. I just can't be what he wants me to be.
>
> I know I have hurt you. But I should tell you that this is not a new thing for

*me. Since I was 15 years old, I knew I
was a homosexual. I've fought against it
and prayed for help ever since then. But
it hasn't done any good. Father will say I
have chosen this. But I haven't. Nobody
with any sense would choose to be de-
spised. Please understand that. Please
find a little room in your heart to continue
to love me, as I do you.*

*I will call you in a few days to see
how you are doing. I will be fine. I'm glad
you still have the church. I guess I don't.
Maybe one of these days I'll find a way,
a church.*

Please don't show Father this letter.
I love you.
Tom

He folded the letter and placed it in his pocket,
wondering when he would have to give it to his
mother. He looked around. Everything in his room
and everything he stopped to touch whispered the
finality of his leaving. The silk brocade couch,
where he had sat many evenings during family
study of the Bible, was the only thing his mother
had been allowed to pick out especially for herself. In the furnishings, as in everything, his father did the buying. The mahogany desk behind
it, the shelf above it stuffed with religious tracts,
the matching credenza, the choice of pictures, even
the pale-blue color of the walls, were his father's
choice. So Tom sat on the couch, already feeling
like a stranger in this immaculate setting.

He thought of Joel's messy room, the simple
furnishing of the Reeces' home, compared to this
overdressed house. Having no choice now but to
leave, he was ready. Then he saw the picture of

his parents on the mantle above the fireplace. He got up and walked over to it. His mother was wearing her usual blue colors that his father preferred. His father was wearing a black suit. He studied their faces. His mother's smile was timid and her eyes betrayed unease. His father's face was stern. His father had never liked the picture, the photographer having caught too much of their inner tension. But Tom took it off the shelf lovingly. He laid the frame on the mantle and slid the picture out. He slipped it under his shirt.

He went outside, preferring to wait for Pete and Kevin in the bright sunlight.

Chapter 14

Eva washed the dishes that she had left before church. At this hour, the sun was already above the kitchen window and quickly turning into noon. The warmth felt good on her face, but could not quite penetrate into her central feeling of cold. She felt numb. Since the night before, an Arctic numbing had chilled her, hearing the strange words that had come out of Joel's young mouth, seeing his beautiful, youthful face, so strong and healthy, so clean and innocent, admit such awful things. *He is so confused*, she thought. If the boys would just forget everything, wouldn't that be better? Couldn't they just start over? Surely there was a way for Tom's troubles with his father to be avoided—or even if there wasn't, couldn't they be solved?

Joel wouldn't forget it, though. Hadn't he said he loved his little friend? Loved him? Him? Another boy? The kind of love he meant is what frightened her, left her cold. He had run out not more than ten minutes after getting home. Said he was going for a drive. Well, who could blame him?

Douglas had gone out to inspect the place and had come back beaming. "They did real well, Eva. I couldn't have done it better myself. Tools where they belong. All the dirt and mud cleaned off the

tractor. Cotton cultivated real nice. Irrigation finished clear across the field. And your garden's just
fine."

"I knew it would be," she'd said.

Douglas was at the kitchen table now, drinking coffee. She felt him behind her, but she couldn't
think of much to say to him. His reaction to Tom
and Joel's confession was one she should have
predicted, not that he condoned it, but his damned,
reasonable approach to this problem somehow
cheated her of even trying to get Joel to change.
She sighed, looking out the window, then she heard
knocking at the front door. She wiped her hands
on a dish towel and went to answer it.

Edna Stroud stood there, smoothing her hair.
Her face was black and blue, her lips swollen, her
eyes red. Eva forgot everything and hugged her
instantly. "Edna! What is it, honey? You look awful!"

"Eva, I'm sorry to bother you, but I don't have
a soul to turn to."

She showed Edna to the kitchen and poured
her a cup of coffee. Douglas said hello to her but,
after pulling out a chair for her, just nodded, allowing Eva to continue talking to her.

Poor, rundown woman, Eva thought. Her long,
skinny arms reached for the cup; she took it with
her cracked and bleeding fingers, more clawlike
than Eva had ever seen. She had to look away from
the sight. "Joel told us everything. You don't need
to worry about the window, you know."

Edna sipped on the coffee and set the cup down
gently with both hands. "I want you and Douglas," she nodded toward him, "ta press charges.
Henry, he's crazy over this. He and Kenny've been
fightin' bad. They'll kill each other if they don't
stop. Seems like me and the younguns don't mat-

ter. If Kenny goes to jail, least he won't be able to do nothin' worse, 'n I kin bring Henry round to some sense."

Eva patted her hands. "Douglas?

He couldn't stomach the idea of putting a kid in jail if there was any way to turn the situation around. "Tell you what. You send your twins over. I'll pay 'em each a dollar an hour to help me out with the farm work. And I'll deal with Henry about making Kenneth work to pay back the money for the window."

"But Henry won't allow that," Edna protested. She looked stricken. "He don't want nothin' to do with y'all. Pardon me for sayin' it out like that. He'd as soon take it out of Ken's hide."

"He'll stand for it, Edna, because he won't have no choice. I'll see to that."

"I don't know. Henry's proud, in his way. Thinks he kin handle Kenny. Then there's the other children. I gotta think about them. We got no food in the house ta speak of. He drinks up his disability pension—now the truck...."

Douglas got up and patted her bony shoulders. "Don't you worry, Edna. We'll settle everything. Eva, what say we take Edna home? I'll have a talk with Henry." He looked at his wife over Edna's head. Their eyes met. And for all their differences concerning Joel, neither of them registered that problem in the look that passed between them. Here was a problem that both of them were committed to working out together. In this, they were in full agreement.

* * * *

The monthly dinner was paid for by the church and, at first, was well attended; now, as in some other activities, only the small core of those guys who called themselves the disciples were regulars. Other activities better served the real Fellowship group, like the cookouts, the retreats, and bus trips to churches in other small towns. And maybe, after attending church services all morning, most of the other members of the Fellowship had little stomach for the dinner because, from the beginning, it was restricted solely to conversation revolving around religious thought. Its formalities were as set as church services, with an opening and closing prayer, with discussion laced with biblical paraphrasing. The teens who attended did so with the understanding that it was the one time of the month that they would conduct themselves "...as though breaking bread with the church elders," as the dinner was presented to the people of the congregation who were asked to pay for it. In some cases, these dinners had been attended by the elders.

For this reason, the core group in the Fellowship, the disciples, considered themselves elite, the most devout of the devout. Tom had never thought much about the exclusivity. But it was the formality, the attitude of its serious purpose, that had quickly thinned their number to thirteen at these dinners. Pete Thompson, Tom realized, now, was not devout, now that he had gotten to know the kid, but was brazenly trying to keep up his relationship with Kevin, and was apparently willing to suffer through such a dinner to spend another hour with him. Tom had told him privately, this afternoon, that he had always secretly hated them. "But watch out today, Pete. I'm gonna do it!"

Pete had merely smiled stiffly, ducking his head. "Boy, you are serious aren't you?"

Tom was. In fact, he discovered that he now looked forward to it.

They gathered quietly about two o'clock at the Sundowner Motel in a small but well-furnished room isolated from the rest of the motel by a breezeway. By now, the seating arrangement was set. Tom always occupied the head of the table as the preacher's son. Paul occupied the end. Between them on both sides sat the others. Pete and Kevin were to Tom's right at his end of the table; the rest sat along the sides, based more on their personalities and which conversation they were likely to join most often. Today, Tom noticed definite strains in the seating arrangement, which he imagined had something to do with the way each guy felt about him, or about Paul.

The night before, Pete had said, "Paul definitely told Kevin and Mike St. Germaine about you, but, by now, the others have probably gotten wind of it." And as Tom watched, following the opening prayer, he saw eye contact being made across the table; some eyes avoided his. Kevin was unusually quiet and kept grinning, glancing down the table to Paul's end. Kevin had been quiet in the car on the way over, avoiding Tom's eyes. He and Pete had exchanged looks about Kevin's behavior in the car; Tom decided now that Kevin definitely sided with Paul. As at other dinners, Tom let Paul open the conversation. He could always depend on him to jump right into some detailed discussion. Early on, at these dinners, Tom had realized the importance they held for Paul and had casually, thankfully, let him have his way with the other guys.

He picked up a silver fork and poked around in the limp salad. No comparison to the lively, rich greens and tomatoes from Mrs. Reece's garden, Tom thought. Paul munched on a tomato dripping with Thousand Island dressing. "Brother Allen made a good point this morning on forgiveness," Paul began. Crunch. Crunch. "'One must prepare himself for forgiveness as well as he prepares for communion,' as your father says, Brother Thomas."

Pete rolled his eyes at Tom as if to say, *Oh, brother!*

Tom glanced his way, wanted to smile, but decided to play serious for a while.

"What does that mean, Paul?" Mike St. Germaine asked. Then, without waiting for an answer, he said, "That to be forgiven you must be of clean spirit?" Mike was sitting about midway between Tom and Paul on Tom's left. The guys all looked at Mike, then divided their attention between Paul and Tom.

"Exactly," Paul said. He paused, as if thinking. He speared another tomato wedge, then, with it on the tip of the fork, he pointed vaguely toward Tom. Tom saw a familiar blaze in Paul's eyes that said, *Watch this trick.* Paul said, "You can't be forgiven for sins of the flesh just because you ask, Brothers." He looked around, nodded at a couple of the guys, then stuffed the tomato into his mouth. His tiny, rodent's teeth sank into the meat of the tomato and his thin lips closed over the carnage. "Let's say you make quite a show of asking forgiveness..." he paused again, and Tom thought it was well done. He bet every guy at the table remembered his own repentance in front of the church last Sunday, making quite a show.... Paul sneered, "but then you continue in the same old way you always have. Of course, you shouldn't expect Jesus to intercede, should you, Brother Thomas?"

"No!" Kevin said, suddenly, and seeing attention turn his way, he sat up proudly, grinning.

Tom didn't answer, and in the silence that followed, Paul pounced again. "So, isn't that right, no matter how much you pray, unless you fully intend at the time of repentance to…to cleanse your thoughts…that lead to your foulness, you can forget about salvation?"

Pete leaned over to Tom and whispered, "Sounds rehearsed, huh?"

Tom nodded. *Rehearsed as hell*, he thought. Paul sounded like a puppet, suddenly animated of its own volition, sitting in its chair with the puppet master absent, the wooden mind stuck and going through its nightclub act. His knees had begun to quiver under the table. Paul was very good, but completely obsessed with his purpose. *What better way to dig at me*, he thought, *than to think up little, pointed remarks beforehand?*

"Did Mary Magdalene have a clean sprit?" someone else asked. "She was a fallen woman. She made her living that way, yet Christ forgave her."

Tom saw the frown on the questioner's face and the searing look Paul shot him. Tom's answer would have been Jesus' admonition to go and sin no more, but he wanted to see how Paul would handle it.

"Yeah, was her spirit clean?" someone across the table agreed. "She was a hooker, man."

"The Bible clearly says 'be of pure spirit…'" Paul blundered, and Tom felt the smallest smile creep up on his face. He cleared his throat and quickly stuffed a bite of salad into his mouth to cover it.

"And Christ said, 'Let him among you who has not sinned cast the first stone!'" Pete said, almost shouting. He was visibly angry and, Tom thought, too caught up in Paul's game.

Kevin looked at Pete with a smirk. "Whoa, there, pal! This is just a friendly discussion."

"No, it isn't!" Pete said, loudly. "And I'm kind of sick of this whole fake—" Tom kicked him under the table. Their eyes caught briefly and Tom shook his head very slightly. Pete frowned back and began eating.

Tom saw, from the silent casting about of eyes, who believed Paul, who nodded firmly at Pete's challenge. A few of the guys looked at Tom, asking for help, but he went on eating, trying to calm his own nervousness. *I'm going to do it*, he decided finally.

For a moment, the conversation seemed to die. Most of the guys seemed to be embarrassed and began cutting into their steaks. Only Paul and one or two others seemed cool. *These are the ones on Paul's side*, Tom thought.

Tom began to relax, like getting over stage fright when the play is underway. He was glad for the chance to tell these guys his side. At one time or another, they had liked him. They were, after all, the members of the church who, over the past year, Tom had seen most often. Paul had said just last week that they were sometimes in awe of him. He ate quietly, deliberately staying out of the argument. He bet that Paul was itching for him to start quoting scripture. But Tom didn't cooperate. He was tired of Bible thumping, weary of Paul's particularly snotty brand of it. That's what it was, this whole concern of Paul's. Who can be the most religious? Too bad Paul wasn't the Christian he so much wanted to be. He was a caricature of one. Tom laughed to himself at the picture of Paul Romaine, elder's son of a dinky church, in a dinky town, in the middle of nowhere, lurking around ponds, peeking in windows, spreading rumors, and trying to stop Tom's evil sex before it destroyed who knew what?

He had to keep in mind exactly what it was he was doing there. It was like the last day of class before summer vacation, and he felt like just getting up and shrugging off the whole afternoon. But he'd be damned if he didn't take at least one good swing at Paul for trying to force things between him and his father, for getting the disciples involved. They were good guys, most of them, and the church didn't need to be dragged into the mud, either.

Tom still hadn't spoken, but as the dinner was nearing dessert, he put down his fork. He rested his elbows on the table and his chin on his hands. He looked directly into Paul's face and stared until Paul became quiet. Paul stared back, unable to look away. The others soon noticed and sat still. Not a breath sounded at the table.

When he did speak, Tom kept his voice quiet, and Paul had to lean forward from his end of the table to hear. "I know what you're up to, Paul. And because of you, I'm going to leave this church. What you're trying to do, whether you'll admit it or not, is to ruin my life. It doesn't have anything to do with me being a sinner, does it, man? You're working your little heart out, you have been all afternoon, to set me up for a big crash."

Paul looked surprised. "Me?"

"Yes, you."

"No!" Paul said with conviction.

"Really? Aren't you planning to tell my father that I'm having sex with my friend, Joel?"

Everyone had stopped eating, and even the waitress, who had been hovering nearby fiddling with water glasses and dessert plates, stopped to listen. Tom caught a glimpse of her shocked face and knew she'd heard. It made his own face flush a little, but, like Paul, he was now too caught up

in his purpose to stop, regardless of the consequences.

"You're going to upset the whole church, man.
Why have you been making up stuff, spying on
us? Did you know Joel saw you at the pond?" He
watched, satisfied that Paul hadn't. "Just tell these
guys…" Tom looked around, "what it is you want.
Tell me, too, Paul, because I sure can't figure it
out."

"Brother! I swear to you as your true friend,
I'm not trying to hurt the church. Why should I do
that? I love the church. I love you, Tom. I just want
to bring you back to Jesus! You're lost, Tom, and
you don't even know it."

Tom gazed slowly, deliberately, over the group,
then let his eyes rest on Pete's upturned face. Pete
was grinning widely.

"Look, guys. I'm out. Not because I particularly want to be. You've got to understand that. I
think I am a Christian. I think most of you are.
But what Paul is doing is just plain wrong. If it
was one of you guys…you know, who were homosexual, I wouldn't go spreading it around behind
your back. If I thought it was wrong, I'd talk to
you about it to your face. But look what Paul's
doing, how he's doing it. He's spying on me and
lying about facts he couldn't possibly have, and
he's using you guys—not because he particularly
cares how his lies will affect you, but how they
will affect me. He's never once said anything directly to me about what he thinks. Look, when I'm
gone, the rest of you can think what you want.
Snicker about me, use me as a bad example to
scare yourselves with. In fact, what Paul says about
me is true. You don't have to depend on his exag-
gerated reports that he saw me doing one thing or
another. He's just causing a lot of unnecessary

trouble and pain. I didn't ask to be a preacher's son. I didn't ask to be brought up in this particular church, and like a new, good friend pointed out to me a few days ago, the world is made up of hundreds of religions. I'm not sure anymore if being what I am is wrong. I didn't ask to be...what I am, either. It just so happened that I fell in love with another guy. And you never saw a guy as shook up about that as I was. You think it's easy, feeling like you're crazy, feeling like your emotions are evil, trying to not feel what you feel?" Tom looked around and saw that on the surface, at least, they appeared to be listening. Paul had a sickened look, a doubtful expression about his eyes. He didn't intend to say anything more, but Paul was moving his lips, as though he were about to talk. Tom had intended to get up and leave them all speechless, but he cleared his throat.

"When I'm gone," he began, "would you pray for me sometimes? Who's to say that my sin, if it is one, is more—or less—damning than your own? If you believe in Original Sin, like our church teaches, then you also have to believe that you are all sinners. And listen, try doing like Jesus says. Get rid of the junk in your own life before you start hassling someone else about his. If you believe you are already saved because you've judged yourselves and found yourselves to be without sin, you're seriously deluded. And speaking of today's sermon, I think it's a good idea to remember the basis of it. I don't mean to sound so dramatic, but when you pray, pray hard, and pray in this manner:

Our Father which art in heaven, Hallowed be thy name.

Thy kingdom come.

Thy will be done

on Earth, as it is in heaven…

"If you can't find forgiveness, unless some condition or other has been met, Brothers, you are in the wrong business, because the business of Christianity is not to go around finding fault but to find forgiveness in your heart, no matter how wronged you feel."

Whether or not he had reached any of them, Tom felt better, but he had to put Paul in his place for the others' sake. He wanted them to see through Paul, too. He stared at Paul again. This time he smiled at him sadly and his voice was low. "By tomorrow night, Paul, you'll have what you want, but you'll probably be disappointed, because getting what you want may not be what you bargained for. By Tuesday, I'll be gone. You did you're duty last week. My father showed up at the Reeces'; we talked, and now it's none of your damned business what I do. And Paul? There's not a thing you can do to stop me."

He stood up to leave, but Paul sputtered, "You can't! You'll be lost! We'll be denied a chance to save—"

"Oh, shove it!" Tom shouted and walked out.

He called Joel from a pay telephone in the lobby. "It's over, Joel. I'm going to spend one more night with my parents."

* * * *

The box and clothing were exactly where Tom said they would be. Joel looked down at them, feeling funny. He'd been in Tom's room a couple of times and had always been impressed. It was tidy and full of possessions that showed clearly how much more Tom was informed about things. So smart. So many books. He was so much more equipped to go out and make a living anywhere he wanted. He'd often thought, coming away from Tom's house, *All I've got is a chance to make a good living if I stay right where I am.* He wasn't sure if it was right to make Tom give up everything for him. He picked up the small box. It was light and inside he could hear the loose shuffling of a few papers. He had expected it to be stuffed with books or something. The suitcase was small, too. He shuddered, feeling like a thief, feeling inadequate to the trust Tom was placing in him.

But there wasn't much to be done about it now. He couldn't just say to everybody, "Hold on. We were just kidding. Go back to the way things were."

Not now.

He felt the same kind of panic that used to seize him before a boxing match. The tension of waiting was almost unbearable. The solution, when it came, was to explode. To slug and slug and slug until the tension was gone.

He drove home by way of the high school, down 8th Street and south, out of town. This was probably the direction Tom had walked last Sunday in the sandstorm, Joel thought. It was sunny and hot now, much like it had been on the day after the dance. And it was strange that today, so much different than a couple of weeks ago, that Tom was planning to tell the disciples that he was queer. He smiled, feeling strange that he'd won, wondering uneasily what he'd done to Tom. Tom was telling them by now, telling those guys from his church about them—him and Tom. *He's more honest. I didn't tell Nicky. I didn't tell Bill. I let it slide. But Tom was coming right out and saying "Joel and I have sex."* He didn't think Tom would buckle under after all—not to a shithead like Paul. Pete would be there. That would help. At least Tom was throwing the first punch, bringing Paul out into the open.

That would help, too. Tom was right about that.
Joel was certain that Paul would "spill his spiteful
little guts," anyway. So, why not land a punch when
Paul was probably expecting Tom to break down
and beg for his help?

When he got home, Joel left Tom's belongings
in the back of the pickup. He threw a canvas tar-
paulin over them and went inside. His mother had
left him a note saying that they were over at the
Strouds' to straighten things out with them. So he
waited alone, feeling he was going crazy. Tom called
a few minutes later and said it was over. The sound
of his confident voice made all Joel's doubts melt.
He agreed reluctantly when Tom told him he was
going to spend the night with his mother and father. "Well, okay, Tom. But listen, if anything happens, get out of there fast, please. They're your
parents, I know, and I guess it's hard to know
you're gonna leave home. Sleep well tonight." He
hung up, sorry that Tom didn't just run away now,
but like his father said, Tom probably did need to
see it through. Twenty minutes later, the telephone
rang again, making Joel jump. He picked up the
receiver, expecting the worst. But it was Coach.

"We've been wondering about you, Joel. And
we've got someone here who'd very much like to
meet you. Can you bring Tom?"

Joel dialed Tom's number and waited. Hearing the ring on Tom's end reminded him of the
last time he'd called the Allens. But Tom answered
and agreed to go to the coach's house. "Why not?
My parents still aren't home, and I can tell you
about the dinner. You should have seen Paul's
face!"

* * * *

When Tom and Joel arrived, Bill Hoffins led

them through the house to the patio. He introduced the man who stood up from a nylon webbed
chair and shook their hands. "The Reverend
Suskine," Bill said.

"Nice to meet you," Joel said to him. It was
unusual, meeting a preacher who was wearing an
old faded pair of Levi's and a blue work shirt. He
was barely as old as Coach. Way over six feet tall,
he towered over Joel. His grip was firm and his
large hand swallowed Joel's

"Bill tells me you boys..." he nodded toward
Tom, who was standing beside Joel, "are having a
little trouble."

"Well, yessir. We were," Joel said, and smiled
at Coach. "We got over that."

Bill's face seemed confused. "I mean," Joel continued, "Me and Tom are doing fine for ourselves,
now, between us."

JoAnna opened the patio door and motioned
Bill to help with the chairs she laid against the
wall. She disappeared and came out with a tray of
lemonade. Tom took the chairs that Bill handed
him and unfolded them. He put his and Joel's side
by side, opposite from Rev. Suskine's. He tapped
Joel on the shoulder and they sat down.

"Bill told me everything, Joel. You two can trust
me, I promise," Rev. Suskine said.

Joel looked at Tom. "Is it okay with you?"

"Sure, Joel. Maybe I should explain." Tom accepted a glass of lemonade from JoAnna. When
she left, he told in his own words a version of things
that allowed Joel to see that all his doubts had
been groundless. He told about himself most of
all, explaining to both Bill and the minister how
he and Joel had met. Hearing Tom explain how he
had waited in the hallways for Joel to appear, how
he had learned of Joel's class schedule and hung

around outside those classrooms hoping to get a glimpse of him, and what he called discovering how much they loved each other—all this in Tom's words—made Joel secretly happy. "The trouble started when I told Joel it was a sin, you know, as it says in Leviticus, Romans, Corinthians, Timothy...."

Completely out of his league with this turn in the discussion, Joel could only listen. His heart pounded and he felt extremely uncomfortable. He drained his glass and helped himself to another one. Throughout Tom's explanation he had watched the kind face of the minister, who kept nodding at Tom, and saying, "Exactly. Um-hmm. I see."

"But it was no use," Tom said. "I couldn't get over it, and I guess I didn't really want to. Otherwise, I wouldn't have tried so hard to meet Joel."

"And so, in the end, you and Joel consummated your feelings, regardless of the fact that it is considered a sin by our Judeo-Christian heritage?"

"Yes."

"I see."

"And now, we think Tom will probably have to leave home, one way or the other," Joel said.

"That does seem to be logical," the minister said. "And you're not afraid of that, Tom?"

Tom smiled and looked at Joel and Bill Hoffins. "No."

"And what about you, Joel?" The minister turned to him. "Don't you think you two are a little young to be...ah...living together...as a couple?"

Joel felt a surge of anger. "That's right, living together," he said proudly. "Kinda like being married. We can take care of ourselves, sir. My sisters got married right out of high school, and—"

"But they have husbands to take care of them. Isn't that right?"

"Yessir. But—"

"And you two boys think that because you love each other...you, Tom, even though it goes against your beliefs, and you, Joel, even though you haven't even got a diploma...you think you can survive? You think your love can stand the test of all this?"

Joel felt himself growing more angry. But everyone was smiling and being so polite, as if they were having a friendly disagreement about a movie, that he tried to relax. "We don't have any choice now, sir, if you will excuse me. Tom doesn't have anybody but me."

"That's true, Reverend Suskine," Tom said. "I'm not going back to the way I was. I told you I couldn't get over the feelings. I tried, and it just makes me out to be a liar."

The Reverend Suskine put his hands together, touching the tips of his fingers, forming an inverted "V", and touched them to his lips. He studied first Joel, who felt himself sweating, then Tom. "I hope you boys don't think too badly of me, taking you both to task about all this. You see, Tom, you are absolutely right. Your particular brand of religion is very harsh. It comes straight from Martin Luther, and was later influenced strongly by Puritans in this country. In fact, it sounds like your father's particular doctrine is what we refer to as *literalist*."

"Yessir."

"But I think there may be more hope here than I've let on. I only wanted to rough you up a little, because...well...I would be remiss in letting you think you have to give up your beliefs because you are homosexual. We often lose sight of our human side, particularly when the Bible is translated so strictly. Freedom of belief is a characteristic of our

Unitarian Community. That's important, boys. We don't necessarily think the injunctions against homosexuality in the scripture you have referred to are so clear cut."

Tom sat up as if he were about to jump out of his chair. "You don't?"

Joel watched the minister's face, amazed that a preacher could act so calm about sex. He felt himself relax a little. He was more inclined to listen if that were true.

"It does bother me that you two are so young. It bothers me that Joel apparently has not been conscious of being homosexual until you came along, Tom. And I predict that his father has probably expressed the notion that he is just going through a phase. That particularly bothers me, Joel, because Bill has told me that you are a virgin. Are you sure that you aren't just feeling attached to Tom because he has provided sexual release for you?"

"That's a fair question," Coach said. "Joel?"

Joel thought hard about that. He felt like he was under a microscope, peering out from under a glass, being blinded by a light so bright under the calm gaze of the preacher and the coach that he felt tears burning his eyes. Without being conscious that he was doing it, he took Tom's hand, but only became aware of it when Tom squeezed it. He took a deep breath. "It's just so hard to describe what Tom does for me. Sure, we have sex. We love each other, sir. But jacking…masturbating is a release when I'm horny." He felt himself turning red. "But guys have always made me feel neat. I just didn't know you could feel so great having sex with a guy. I did it once with another guy, a long time ago. I mean, he did it to me. And it's true I never did it with a girl. But it was so nothing when I used to date. I've kissed a few, and I swear it was like kissing my sisters on the cheeks or something. But with Tom it was different. Kissing, I mean." There was no way not to focus on the minister and he stopped finally, waiting for this man to respond.

The minister smiled at him, a warm smile, and nodded. "Crudely put, Joel, but I believe you."

"Thanks."

"Don't thank me, Joel," he said, smiling a little less. "Your troubles are just beginning. I only hope that in a few years, all the men and women like you and Tom can come to grips with this problem. As I'm sure you're both aware, you wouldn't be any worse off if you had leprosy. But you two do have something. That's quite obvious. I think I'm a fair judge of character, and I say that you both are admirable young men. Every time a young couple comes to me wanting to get married, I always grill the hell out of them. I don't see, in these times, why you young people are so damned eager to get married. I've seen early marriages fall apart as soon as unromantic things like income and work enter in. There's no way to avoid responsibility once the bills start piling up. And the great love that brings couples together soon dies a horrible death. But in your case, nobody cares. Society has no place for you. There is no rejoicing when two people of the same sex decide to live together as a so-called married couple. And it's far easier to break up. In large cities, you can get sexual release without the least emotional commitment to your sexual partners."

A gust of hot wind blew through the patio. The umbrella over the table caught it and shook everything. The pitcher of lemonade rattled on the tray and almost fell over. Bill reached out and held it until the wind passed. He laughed. "Boys, excuse me. I think I'll take this indoors. JoAnna's always accusing me of being a bull in a china shop. I wouldn't want her to think I broke this."

When he was gone, the minister took charge again. "The important thing is, when it comes to homosexuality, you have no reason to be committed to each other, because there is no binding commitment—legal or spiritual—in the eyes of the law and the church. That was going to be my main point. The injunctions against homosexuality in the Bible are just that. That there is no commitment, no binding."

"You mean," Tom said, "that the scriptural references to lust, giving up natural affection and all that are sins because it produces nothing, other than sexual release?"

"Exactly." He smiled. "If you two could be loving and faithful to each other, why would you think it's a sin? Wouldn't it be far worse, in your mind, Tom, to marry a woman and yet not be loving and faithful? I'm glad that Bill has left us alone. Never tell anyone that he has stuck his neck out for you. Luckily, he's brought us together. As a minister, my major concern is that your relationship with Joel enhance you as a human being. Sorry, Joel. Bill tells me you are staunchly unreligious. That's okay. If you would allow Tom his needs in this area, I would consider it a privilege to remain a friend to both of you."

"Well, sure," Joel said. "I was always sorry that Tom was losing so much to be with me. I'd be glad to go to church at your place if it would help him. Would you like to do that, Tom?"

The minister spoke up quickly. "Before you consider that, Joel, Tom will have to do some reading about my church. It's not the same as his." He turned to Tom. "You're welcome, of course, to visit. Whether you will feel satisfied is of concern. I have some literature I often give out to visitors, concerning Jesus' deity, for example. We are noncreedal about Jesus' mission and the Trinity question. You may be bothered by that."

Tom was still holding onto Joel's hand. He squeezed it. "I think it helps, Mr. Suskine, knowing I have a place to go sometimes if I need it, especially after meeting you."

* * * *

Before they left Coach's house, Joel made a point of thanking JoAnna and Coach. They were sitting at the little kitchen table when he came in through the back door. He had left Tom with the Reverend Suskine, who had continued to talk religion with Tom. And although Joel was glad for Tom, he didn't want to sit through it. JoAnna made him sit down. Coach offered him a beer, but Joel declined. "That guy is neat, Coach. He's the preacher at your church?"

Bill laughed. "Yes. Sometimes. Common is too small to support a full-time minister. He travels a lot in this area. We were lucky to have him today." He waved his hand. "We hope he helped a little, even though you say you and Tom are friends again."

"Friends," Joel said. "And thanks, you guys. I just wish I could do something to return your favor."

Bill winked at him. "Come back to the team. We need you, Joel."

"Well, gee, Coach, I'll think about that! I really will."

—Part Three—

Man is born with his hands clenched;
he dies with his hands wide open.
Entering life he desires to grasp everything;
leaving the world, all that he possessed has
slipped away.

The Talmud

Chapter 15

Monday, June 14

Edna Stroud wet her finger and tapped the stove top. It sizzled. Hot enough. She took a coffee can from the greasy shelf above the stove, dipped out a spoonful of lard, and pushed it around on the hot surface until a sheen of oil covered it. Before it could begin smoking and burning, she stirred the batter in the bowl once more and poured six pancakes on the oil. Since there was no way to regulate the heat, she worked quickly, flipping the pancakes once, then scooping them off onto a plate. She did this until the bowl was empty. That done, she opened the door below the stove top and pushed the burning wood around. On the same surface she cooked eggs and sausage. Occasionally, she checked the coffee to make sure it wouldn't boil over.

She was almost happy enough to sing, but she didn't. When she removed the last of the food from the stove, she walked quickly to the bedroom and shook Henry. "Get up, Henry. I got a good breakfast, nice and hot."

Henry rolled over and pulled the covers over his head. "God damn it, Edna—"

She jerked the covers off. "Up, Henry! You lazy bum!"

She pounded on the boys' door. "Boys! Up! Breakfast!"

In the kitchen again, she washed off the oil-cloth on the table and set it. She set a can of Log Cabin syrup on the hot stove to melt its sugary consistency, and just before it boiled she removed it and set it on the table.

Eddie was the first one who came in. "Gosh, Ma. That smells good."

She smiled at him. "Thought you could use it."

Henry stumbled through the door, scratching his head. He sat down at the table and reached for the food. He piled his plate, stealing glances at his wife. "You shore outdid yourself, Edna."

She smiled at him. "T'weren't much. Thanks to Mrs. Reece. She give us eggs and milk and some sausage." Then she held the hot pot of coffee over Henry, daring him to badmouth the Reeces. "You got anything ta say to that?"

He eyed the steam rising from the old, battered pot and grunted. "What for? Reece. He's a strange one, awright. Wants to hire my children ta work, I ain't agin' that. If he does what he say he'll do, I'll do my part. I'm a decent man."

The rest of the children wandered in wide-eyed, as if it were Thanksgiving. The twins had bathed and dressed for work. Edna stood between their chairs and piled their plates. "Don't turn down your lunch at the Reeces', boys, and be polite." Sally and little Henry sat next to their mother, and Eddie sat next to Kenneth's empty chair. Edna looked around at her brood, feeling like laughing and crying at the same time. Only Kenneth's refusal to eat food the Reeces had given them hurt her. He'd be hungry, too! She wanted to cry for him as she listened to the sounds the other children were making over the breakfast.

When their bellies were full, little Henry, Sally Ann and Eddie went off to play. The twins sat with her and their father a few more minutes, feeling important; then they left because they had to walk the two miles or so to the Reeces' place.

When Edna had told them about their jobs, they couldn't believe it: "A dollar every hour! Mama! We gonna be rich!" She smiled at their childish wonder, not wanting to tell them the pay wasn't much. But she felt rich as well. Even Henry, she saw with some satisfaction, had lost his belliger- ence, and even though he tried to cover it over with meanness, he had worked all afternoon the day before on the pickup. He'd even thanked Doug- las Reece before they left. Even snuffled a little when Douglas had returned later with a radiator and some tools. It was late in the evening when he finished. Patrick and Detrick came in for supper, joking and laughing. "We did it, Ma. Got it fixed for ya! Pa says it'll run as good as ever!"

Like all things in their household, though, her pleasure was short lived. Kenneth came in from a deep sleep brought on by the rotgut he drank. He looked around the kitchen at the scraps of their big breakfast. "Had me a steak th'other day and you kin bet I didn't suck the Reeces for it!"

She moved out of his way as he stepped closer. She gathered up the dishes and watched him pour a cup of coffee. She wasn't going to argue and just stared, waiting for him to move away from the stove.

"You like that, Ma? Suckin' up to people?"

She didn't answer.

"You like havin' your church friends come into

this rat trap? You like them laughin' at you? I know 'em, Ma!" He set the coffee pot back on the stove and took a sip as he leaned against the sink. He ran his hands over the edge of the cup, then launched himself away from the sink and came up to her.

She felt herself flinch, but refused to be cowed. "Eva give us that coffee, too. You like the way it tastes?"

He looked down at the mug and shrugged. His bloodshot eyes narrowed to slits. "Big shit, Ma," he said, his voice taking on a dangerous edge. "They give us shit for the truck but I ain't th'one stuck his nose up old man Reece's ass for it!" Tears welled in his eyes.

In an instant she was next to him, wanting to touch his cheek. "Kenny, honey... Let it go. What're you fightin' so hard for all the time?"

She reached up, but he backed away. "Don't! Goddamn you!"

"They's only tryin' to help us. That's all. They's—"

"Shut up! Jes plug your fuckin' mouth!" He threw the mug of coffee into the sink where it clattered, shattering the plates, and went through the door into the living room.

She heard Henry and Kenneth begin arguing and squeezed her hands over her ears. Hot tears burned her face. She felt faint and reached out to break her fall. They were yelling now, then the front door slammed, followed by the sound of the pickup starting up.

"Goddamn it!" Henry screamed, and the front door slammed again as he roared after Kenneth. He came back in, breathing hard and cussing. He began drinking then, cussing and waiting. "I'll show that bastard who's the goddamn boss of this place, goddamn if I won't!"

Edna didn't try to stop him from drinking, thinking maybe he would pass out, but as the morning wore on she became more nervous. She tried to work, feeling dread that Kenneth had stayed away so long. What if he wrecked the pickup again? Several times she had tried to talk with Henry to get his mind off Kenneth, but he was too far gone to be reasoned with. He just sat in the living room waiting, drinking, getting madder, his mood getting blacker and blacker. She checked on the children several times, seeing that they weren't getting into mischief, and went on working, a little on edge, unable to shake the bad feeling that nothing Douglas Reece could do would bring Kenneth around. She still thought jail would cool him off.

Around ten-thirty, Kenneth came squealing into the yard as drunk and hateful as Edna had feared he would be. She was hanging out wash when he drove up. He was spoiling for a fight now and even yanked some of the clothes off the line; he rubbed his dirty Levi's against her church dress, leaving a black scar on it. He laughed. "Who gives a shit, Ma? We ain't nothin' but trash. You think that fuckin' church gives a flying black shit about you?" He stumbled toward the house and fell against the pickup. Right there in front of her he pissed on the ground. She felt dirty passing by him. She hid her eyes, but could feel his drunken gaze fixed on her and it made her shiver.

She hurried indoors, fighting back the urge to cry out. She would get the children and they would leave right now, before things crashed down around them all. Intending to do just that, she found the rest of her children playing; she tried to herd them together into the kitchen, but her excitement scared them and she only managed to make them scatter. In the front yard, Kenneth and Henry began fighting in earnest. She looked at them from the living room. They were tugging drunkenly on the door of the driver's side of the pickup. Henry was outside and Kenneth was sitting in the seat. Henry screamed, his voice a blood rage: "I said you ain't goin'!"

Kenneth pushed roughly on the door and sent Henry sprawling, but he crawled back, managing to get half in before Kenneth kicked him out again. Henry ran into the house, grabbing up the shotgun, which was still leaning against the wall by the front door.

"I'll teach that bastard!" He tore open a box of shells and pushed two into the chamber.

"No! Henry!" Edna ran after him, but she was too late. He stormed out into the yard, waving the shotgun wildly, weaving on his heels, aiming for the tires.

Kenneth jumped out and made a grab for the barrel.

From somewhere, Eddie appeared next to Kenneth. "Kenny?" he called. Edna ran out, leaving Sally Ann and Henry Jr. on the couch. They looked out the window in horror, and Henry Jr. jerked at the sound of a loud blast. Seconds later, another blast.

Henry Jr. grabbed Sally Ann, pulled her into the kitchen and ran with her out the kitchen door. "Keep quiet!" he whispered. She was twisting against his arm, trying with her small hands to pull his hands off her mouth. He pulled her into the bushes near the road under the tarp that Eddie had played under. He listened for the sound of Kenneth coming to get them. His heart was pounding and he had peed in his pants, but he didn't move. Indoors, he heard things crashing to the floor. Beneath him, Sally was crying. Her tears slicked his hand and he pulled it away. "Please, Sally, keep quiet!"

She looked at him, quieted down. "I want Mommy!" she whispered.

"Okay, Sally." He hugged her. He was crying softly. "Jes wait a min—"

He heard another blast from the shotgun inside the house. Then everything became quiet. After waiting a long time, he peeked out from under the tarp. The yelling had stopped, the crashing noises in the house had stopped, and when he thought it was safe, he crawled out from under the tarp and pulled Sally out with him. He stood on the edge of the road, holding Sally's hand.

She was tugging on it. "Mama! Go see Mama!"

But he was afraid to go back to the front of the house. He had never seen so much blood. He'd seen Eddie's face cave in from a cracking blow when Kenneth had grabbed the shotgun from Pa and, pulling back, had rammed the wooden stock into Eddie's face; it had become a bright-red mask of blood. He had seen his mother's dress tear in the back, with the sound of a loud explosion, then turn suddenly black with blood as she clawed at Kenneth, trying to get to Eddie. His father had been blown off the ground by the second blast and fell against the wall; a splash of blood burst into the air like a fountain. And, what scared him most, he had seen Kenneth's weird expression, his teeth glistening with a grin as he fired the shotgun. It had frightened him, and he knew that they had to get away before he came for them.

He looked up and down the road and listened. It was quiet. No sound at all came from the other side of the house. He strained to hear Kenneth inside the house, but a dead silence hung over everything. He began walking, pulling Sally with him. "We gonna find Paddy and Dete over at the Reeces'." They left the road and began walking through the mesquite bushes. He had never been to the Reeces' but he knew which road they lived on. They walked southeast. The sun was climbing higher. He didn't know what time it was. He didn't know exactly how far it was, but he would keep walking until they came to the road. He didn't know what their house looked like, but he would stop at every one they came to until he found them.

* * * *

Eva and Douglas ate breakfast alone in the kitchen at the breakfast table. Eva was still in her housecoat and Douglas commented on it. "You feeling under the weather, hon?"

She shrugged, sipping on a cup of coffee that had already gone cold. "A little, maybe. It's nothing turning back the clock about a week wouldn't solve."

He studied her for a moment, then registered understanding at her subtlety. "Now, Eva...give it time." He set his cup down. "When the twins get over, send 'em out to the cowshed." He got up abruptly and left.

She gathered up the dishes and took them to the sink. She looked toward the field. In the pink glow of sunrise, she could see Joel's pickup already near the alfalfa patch. She could see him walking along the ditch alone. She watched his tiny figure as she had so many mornings. Douglas was right. He was a good worker. And a good son.

She thought about the night before. As they lay in bed, talking as usual, she had finally admitted how she felt about Joel and Tom. "I just don't see how you could go along with it," she'd said. "It's unnatural. They're only boys."

But Douglas had protested. "I didn't go along with anything, Eva. I listened. When Joel told us he was that way...I thought of my old war buddy. I know you don't think I should have told them about that, but don't you see, I understand him, Eva. I don't necessarily think he is that way. But I understand him, just a little better because of what I did. People are complex." He drew her close. He had just bathed and shaved and smelled of Old Spice. On him it had a warm, cozy aroma. She buried her face in his chest and listened to his voice resonate through it. "Sometimes things are not black and white," he was saying, "especially where emotions and love are involved. Please try to understand that, even if you can't accept it."

"It will take time, Douglas, a lot of time." But it was more than that.

She turned away from the window and went to get dressed, feeling the emptiness of the house as more than just the absence of Douglas. She felt a dread that she had never felt in all the years of her marriage. She knew it had hurt Douglas to remember that man from so many years ago. She had wanted to apologize this morning, seeing the hurt and shame in his face, but she had been unable to. He was right to tell them because they would listen to him, feeling he wasn't just talking through his hat. When he said it was a phase he went through, why shouldn't they be able to realize that time itself might bring similar healing? Obviously, Douglas was not a homosexual. The thought had never crossed her mind. Secure in that knowledge, she thought about Joel. But nothing in her limited experience about such men showed how Joel could be, either. Weren't they wispy, sad creatures who really wanted to be women? Yet Joel had said he and Tom loved each other. Apparently he believed that. Tom even seemed willing to give up his home, he felt so strongly about Joel. What could make the loss of his home worth it, if it was not a deep feeling of something like love? Eva understood that, although she could not shake the feeling that somehow it was wrong. Time. All right, she would give them time to prove that they did love each other, but couldn't she also hope that time would prove them wrong? Yes, it would take time. That's what Douglas had been trying to say.

At eight o'clock, she heard boys laughing and talking in the driveway. She watched from the kitchen as the twins, Patrick and Detrick, walked up to the house. Bless their hearts, they'd walked and still got here early! They wouldn't come indoors, so she sent them to find Douglas at the cowshed. She watched their retreating figures, feeling pity, each wearing baggy pants, obviously hand-me-downs, patched so many times the patches had patches. She decided that, this afternoon, she would go through some of Joel's old clothes and insist that they take them home.

* * * *

Sally tugged on Henry Jr.'s hand. "Henwee I tiahd. Wanna doe home!" She was crying.

Henry Jr. stopped and looked down at her tiny face, dirty with tears. Her dress was torn. She had sat down and her underpants showed. They were dirty. He squatted next to her. The walk had dried his pants where he had wet them, but now his legs felt chapped. He put his hands on his hips. "Sally Ann! Come o-on! It ain't far! I promise."

But Sally wanted none of it. "No!"

He threw up his hands. "I'm leavin', Sally." He started to walk away, but changed his mind. He turned around and bent down. "Git on!"

She climbed up and held him tight around the neck. He stumbled forward and walked as fast as he could. Ten minutes later, he stopped and let her off. He began to cry, but one look at Sally made him stop. As well as he could, he tried to comfort her, patting her head. "We'll be there soon." He took her hand and they continued walking until they came to a road. He looked up and down. There were no cars, so he helped her climb the barbed-wire fence, and they began walking south.

"I tole ya, Sally Ann!"

They hurried now, for Henry saw some buildings. They crossed the road and walked into the Reeces' front yard. "C'mon, Sally Ann. We'll ask these people."

* * * *

They knocked on the front door.

When he heard the knock, Douglas also heard Eva going out through the back door, probably out to the garden. He got up from his lunch. "Sounds like company, boys." Paddy and Dete nodded from the table; their mouths were puffed out like squirrels with the most delicious ham sandwiches they had ever tasted. "Y'all eat. There's plenty more." He chuckled at their faces. "I'll be right back."

When he opened the door, Henry Jr. recognized him and began to cry. It was several minutes before Douglas understood what Henry was saying. But as Henry's tale became clearer through his crying and stuttering, Douglas' horror grew. The twins had stopped eating and had been listening at the door. He looked around at them from where he was kneeling in front of Henry. Sally Ann was

hanging on Douglas' neck, crying, "I want Mommy."
He took the two children into the dining room and
sat them down. He made them eat and, when they
had begun to quiet down, he took Patrick and
Detrick aside. "Did you understand what they were
saying?"

They nodded, speechless, and he studied them
carefully. Being older, their understanding of the
carnage would be more serious, their real knowledge of loss would have more impact. And for right
now he was more worried about them. He spoke
to the two boys directly, making each of them answer. "Are you all right, Paddy? Can I leave you
with the children?"

"Yessir," Patrick said.

"Dete?"

"Yessir."

"What, Dete? Are you feeling okay?"

He blinked. "Yessir."

Douglas left them in the dining room. He was
reluctant to do it, but he had to get moving.

He called the police station and talked a few
minutes. "Yes, that's right. No. I don't know where
he is. There just might be a chance that he'll come
here. He knows where his two brothers are. Yes.
And please hurry."

He went back to the dining room and took the
twins aside. "You boys have to stay with the children now. Okay?"

The boys nodded again. Their calm frightened
him, and he realized that they were probably close
to being in shock. Little Henry was lucky, he
thought, able to cry to release his emotions. Sally
didn't appear to realize what had happened.

Before he left the house, he looked at his watch;
Joel would be coming in soon. He went to the garden to look for Eva. She was bending over a patch
of okra in the middle of the garden. "Eva!" he called,

and motioned her over. She looked up, smiled brightly and waved. He called again and waved his arm again. She dusted her hands. She picked her way down a row of beans as quickly as she could.

"My God! Douglas, you look terrible! What is it!"

He told her what he knew. They walked quickly back to the house and on the way he said, "Keep all the kids with you. I think the twins might be near shock. I called the police. Deputy Gray said he'd be coming as soon as possible. But the children don't know where Kenneth is. Apparently, Henry and Sally were hiding."

"The children don't know where Kenneth is?"

Douglas shook his head. "Henry Jr. thought he stayed in the house, but I don't know."

Eva looked toward the field. Joel was driving up the road.

"Just in case, Eva, get my rifle and keep it ready. Joel and I will wait by the highway for the police."

* * * *

Paul found there was very little pleasure in winning. At the drugstore, he paid for the package without touching it. The package lay on the glass counter between him and the bewildered clerk. "Aren't you going to examine the prints, Son?" The clerk wanted to know. He eyed Paul over his glasses. Paul looked into the frank stare of the man leaning against the counter with the heels of both hands, an accusing gesture that said, *Here's what you wanted; aren't you even going to count it?*

"No. Naw. I trust you, Mister," Paul said nervously. He licked his lips and grimaced, though he thought he was smiling.

"Kids," the clerk muttered, and punched the cash register. "Now don't you come back complainin'. You had your chance."

On the sidewalk, Paul tore open the envelope and looked around before slipping a photograph part of the way out. He stopped when he saw and shut his eyes. His heart banged rapidly. "That's it!" he whispered. He looked again, this time a longer, wide-eyed stare. His pupils dilated, taking in every detail. Again, he shoved the picture back inside the envelope and looked around furtively.

At first, he felt a rush of satisfaction. *I've got you now!* But the victory was hollow, because Tom had said he was leaving the church anyway.

Paul persisted. He couldn't accept that. By the time he got to the Courthouse park where he was to meet a few of the other disciples, he was feeling better. No, the very horror of this disgusting picture in the preacher's hand would shock Tom into submission.

He passed copies of the picture around. "See!" he said, triumphantly.

But the others shoved the pictures back, all except Pete. "That's disgusting," they all said.

Kevin looked at Pete. "Man, give your copy back!" But Pete had already tucked his away. Kevin was stunned. "You going along with this? You?"

Pete answered back, "You're the one thought it'd be neat."

But Kevin shrugged. "Not now, man. Count me out. I'm washing my hands of this whole mess."

Paul watched them all go, including Pete. He felt drained, deflated. "But we have a duty!" he called to the retreating figures.

It was lonely being the only one willing to perform an unpleasant task. Tom had become too sure of himself, haughty at the Fellowship dinner, as if he had an inside track on virtue. All his talk of leaving the church. Pure bluster!

So there was no beating thrum of victory, no praise from the others. He walked home through the park. Under the trees it was cool and could have been pleasant; the grass was freshly cut and its aromatic perfume filled the air. He passed by the gazebo near the street, feeling the springy grass beneath his feet. Light glittered through the over-hanging branches of the wide-spreading trees. It would have been a pleasant afternoon in this park, the town's pride, but the refusal of the disciples to go along with him had hurt. He walked quickly, blindly past the well-tended trees, along the edge of the park, thick with hedges, and soon he stepped onto the sidewalk.

He felt like posting the pictures on the bulletin board next to community announcements posted there by the Lions Club, the Knife and Fork Club, the Knights of Columbus...*and don't forget the Common Sodomites*, Paul thought, derisively. He kept on walking, determined that his purpose was not spiteful as Tom had said, but noble and, yes, right. It would be cleansing to finish this, even if it wasn't pleasurable any more.

* * * *

His father's reaction was an uncontrollable shaking that spread from his head to his hands. He went pale as a corpse and let the pictures fall. He looked at Paul as though he were a murderer. "Did you take these pictures?"

Paul felt helpless. "I—"

"Answer me!" Leon Romaine said in a low voice. "You did, didn't you!"

"Yes! But don't you see what they're doing?"

His father shook his head. "Paul, I can see the

damned picture." He picked up one, glanced at it, then another, then.... With one in each hand he stared at Paul, then glanced at both pictures. "My God!" He looked at the right hand, then the left hand. He dropped these and picked up several more. "My God!".

Paul felt triumphant. "See?"

His father stood up and, without warning, slapped him. "You made copies!"

"I know. I—"

"You made copies! What in God's name were you going to do with these? Answer me!" He slapped him again, and Paul backed away holding his face.

"You were hiding somewhere and watching! How could you?"

Something had gone very wrong.

"But you'll give one of these to Tom's father, won't you?"

His father looked at him strangely, as if he were seeing some crawly thing. "Why? What would be the point?"

"Would Brother Allen believe you otherwise?"

"We will just have to trust that he and his son can work this out between them, won't we? Remember, Paul," his father said wearily, "your mother and I have already reported to Mr. Allen. I see no point in continuing to hound the poor man."

"But Tom lied to him! He denied everything! And now, now it's true! We've got proof! Daddy, he just has to have proof!"

Leon Romaine was not a vindictive man. And he believed that each father should raise his children in a loving and religious environment, that, in some measure, the sins of the children reflected on the parents. Showing this disgusting photograph to the Allens would be the most unkind thing he could do. But it was true, what Paul had said.

Tom himself was in grave, grave danger. Looking
at Paul, he felt nauseated. There was more behind
Paul's desire to show these pictures than to save
Tom. That was evident and damning; it was, in its
way, a measure of the way he had reared Paul—
again a reflection on the parent.

He sank back to the couch and began gathering up the prints. He looked at Paul. "Get out of
my sight. You make me sick!" The very sight of his
son, waiting anxiously, his eyes glittering with vin-
dictiveness, hatred, appalled him.

Wearily, Elder Romaine did call Mr. Allen. He
told him of the photographs; he also told him of
his disappointment in Paul, that he would counsel him to determine the depth of his son's own
sickness. For surely that's what it was. In only a
matter of minutes, the two men came to an understanding, and each would handle his son on
his own terms. Elder Romaine apologized sadly
for again being the bearer of such heartbreaking
news. And yes, he would burn the photographs,
save one. He would put it in an envelope and put
it away. He would deliver it later, after the minister had tested his son's honesty; for both men decided that in truthfulness there was hope, but if
Tom chose to lie a second time....

* * * *

The Stroud's house had always been an eyesore on Highway 490. It was a long, narrow structure with a flat, tin roof. It's outside walls were
covered with a thin coat of unpainted plaster. Seen
from the highway, it looked like a storage shed or
a railroad car that had somehow been dropped
into a raw, barren patch of land along the road.
The front faced away from the road and was entered at either end from the highway by driving

through gaps in the rusting, tangled, barbed-wire fence. Between the house and the highway, Edna Stroud had managed to grow a few trees and a lush patch of uncut Bermuda grass. As they neared the place, it looked to Joel as though she had been trying to hide the house.

It was a little after noon before the police car had appeared at the intersection of their road and Highway 490. By then, Joel was sweating and hungry. His nervousness had long since given way to a slight nausea. His father was also sweating as they sat in the pickup on the side of the road, listening for the siren. There was no breeze at all, and the hot sun magnified the brilliance of the bushes and the hot, dry sand, making Joel's eyes water.

When Deputy Gray arrived, Douglas got in with him to give directions and Joel followed behind them in the pickup. They turned into the Stroud place from the east. The old, red pickup was parked in front of the house at an angle. Heat waves rose off it and the tin roof. The bare ground in front of the house was dry and hot. Joel followed the police car into the yard and parked beside the Strouds' pickup. The driver's door was open, blocking Joel's view.

Deputy Gray got out and walked around the front of his car with his handgun drawn. He stopped and stared at the ground between the car and the front door. Joel could see his father sitting in the front seat, looking at the same thing. Joel got out of the pickup but stood beside it. Nobody spoke, and in the dead stillness, only the sound of Deputy Gray's boots crunching slowly on the gravel could be heard. Then a slight, very hot breeze moved over Joel like bad breath. It stank of feces and had a metallic bite that made his nos-

trils hurt. An incessant humming came over everything like a beehive. His father opened his door
and got out when the deputy motioned for him to.
He turned to face Joel. His face was a death mask
as white as a sun-bleached skull. He moved toward Joel up against the police car, as though one
backward step would send him falling over a cliff.
He was walking unsteadily, as if he were drunk or
feeble. He held onto the top of the car and continued to sidle along it toward Joel.

"You okay, Dad?" Joel asked seeing the
stunned look in his eyes.

His father got to the back of the police car and
waved Joel off with one hand. "It's the flies...so
damn many." His voice was a hoarse whisper. Joel
looked over his father's head and saw the deputy
cautiously enter the house. Still, Joel hadn't
moved. But Douglas looked as if he was about to
faint. He was beginning to keel over when Joel
managed to move. He rushed between the pickup
and the police car and caught his father before he
slumped to the ground.

In that instant of rushing over, Joel saw the
bodies.

* * * *

If Joel had been there, the waiting would have
been bearable. Old feelings of dread and fear stirred
in Tom. Pete was trying to help but didn't seem to
know quite what to say. He was sitting in the
straight-back chair at Tom's desk. Tom was lying
on the bed propped up on one elbow. Pete had
just handed him a photograph.

Two naked figures were entwined on the
wooden pier at Joel's pond. The water in the pond
was a stark, shiny emerald, and the beauty of the
surroundings, including the sharp focus of the two

figures, was breathtaking. Seeing himself as the figure on top, with Joel's face clearly visible below him with a sensuous smile of pleasure infusing it, Tom felt a stirring of wonder. But the very sharpness, the clarity of the setting, the vividness of the water, the central emphasis on the two male figures in the throes of sexual intimacy also made it clear that Paul had all the proof he needed.

"Paul sure has a neat sense of drama," Pete commented as Tom held the picture up.

Tom had to grin. "So do you. How did you get this?"

"Paul had copies made. Boy, he ain't messing around." Pete shifted uneasily. He tapped the picture. "He tried to hand these out to some of the disciples, but they wouldn't take them!"

Tom looked at Pete blankly, as if what he said didn't register. "Can I keep it?"

Pete looked bewildered. "Well, sure, but why?"

"Thanks," Tom said. "I think it's beautiful."

"But it puts you in an ugly light," Pete said sensibly.

"No," Tom said. "Paul's the ugly one. Just think how devious it makes him look, to have watched us, no telling how long to take the picture!"

"It proves he was right about you two," Pete said. "If he shows this to his parents and yours...."

"I guess I'm burning my bridges. Joel and I are going to live together somehow, and I'm ready." He looked at the picture. "How long do you think he hid? By this time," he shook the picture, "we were pretty far along, you know, excited. This picture just shows Paul is a peeping Tom!" He slid the photograph into his back pocket. "Now, if Paul would only—"

The door to his room suddenly banged open, hitting the wall. His father bore down on him in a blind rage.

Chapter 16

"You say the two youngest children witnessed this?" Deputy Gray was leaning against the pickup, talking into the window.

"'Bout all I could understand from the little ones," Douglas said.

His face had gained some color, kind of gray now instead of white, but his voice shook, and Joel got a quick impression of what his father would look like as an old man. He patted his father's shoulder and helped him sit up. "Maybe we should go, Dad," Joel said quietly, but Douglas sat up straight, took a deep breath and shook his head.

"Little Henry and Sally Ann found our place," Douglas explained. "Henry was blubberin' and shakin', Jim, but I don't doubt he saw everything. Sally maybe didn't, but everything looks about like Henry told it. Said Kenneth was comin' to get them, so they ran out the back door. Henry seemed sure Kenneth stayed inside the house. Thought he was going to kill everybody, poor mites."

James Gray shook his head. "You see everything in this business, Douglas. But a slaughter like this just don't make sense. Makes me feel sick." He stopped and studied Douglas' face. "I'm sorry for goin' on. You look pretty sick yourself."

Douglas smiled weakly. "I feel okay. You need anything else, Jim?"

The deputy straightened up and let his eyes slide once more around the yard. "Nope. The sheriff will be here. I'll just wait in the car. Since the oldest son killed himself inside, there's not much else to cover. You two go on home now and, Douglas, you lay down for a spell." He patted the top of their pickup. "More'n likely the state'll take care of funeral arrangements."

Joel's hands shook as he turned the key in the ignition. He backed up toward the clothesline and outhouse to turn around, wanting to avoid passing by the police car and getting another glimpse of the bodies. Even the simplest movements of maneuvering the pickup were jerky, and he saw detail he wouldn't ordinarily see. Edna had been hanging clothes. A few ragged shirts hung on the line, a basket had been overturned, and a few clothes lay scattered on the ground. He noticed that one of the dresses hanging on the line was smeared with grease—odd against the clean, sun bleached brilliance of the other clothes. It was that pitiful dress, more than the shack or the ugly sight of the bodies, that made his eyes fill with tears. She was a kind woman, she had faded into poverty over the years but had never hurt a soul, and now she was dead, leaving four homeless children and a scene as gruesome as the shack, their only legacy.

They rode in silence on the quick trip back. His father offered no explanations that would make sense of what had happened. To hear him tell it yesterday, Henry and Edna seemed happy with what little help he and his mother had offered, and he had said, "Guess they'll get along same as always. Except maybe with the twins workin' for us and your mom loading them down with food, and such, they'll fatten up a little." And then he'd said with an eye on Joel and one on Eva, "We imagined that we'd have a big family, Joel. Too bad, somehow, the misarrangement of kids in this world."

Joel helped his father out of the pickup. He was looking much better, but his legs buckled on the porch, and Joel took his weight on his shoulders. His mother took one look and hurried out to him. She was shaking, but Douglas smiled at her, and she put both hands on her chest, visibly relieved. "Oh, you gave me an awful fright!"

She made Douglas lie down on the couch and opened his shirt. She looked up at Joel. "Stay with the children. As soon as I've got your father resting, I'll take over." She looked at him with something in her eyes that went from pity to a kind of sadness. "Tom called, Joel. He says he's over at Pete's. He says he's fine and to call him later. I told him what happened and where you were. The number is by the phone. But please watch after the children for a few minutes until I can get back to them." She lowered her voice. "Paddy and Dete seem pretty lost. See if you can't help them."

Joel nodded. He looked at the telephone, torn between it and the Stroud children. He went into the kitchen and splashed water on his face quickly and took a hand towel over to the kitchen table, dabbing his face. Patrick and Detrick each held a child. They stared at him, their young, clear eyes regarding him silently, full of questions, as quiet as the two children asleep in their laps. "Which of you is which?" Joel smiled.

One of the twins patted Sally Ann and looked down at her small body against his chest. "I'm Patrick," he said. "She cried herself to sleep. She thinks Mama'll be here when she wakes up. But she won't, will she?"

His question sounded almost casual, but Joel heard the fear in it. He shook his head. "No, Patrick, she won't." Henry Jr., who was also asleep, was sprawled across Detrick. Detrick was holding his brother tightly, staring off at nothing. Joel couldn't find words with which to comfort them, so he settled for action. "Let's go put these kids in my room," he said. He gathered up Henry's arms and legs and lifted him from Detrick's lap.

"Ah think he peed on hisself," Detrick said. "You kin smell it."

You could, Joel noticed, as he carried Henry through the house. His face was tear-stained and dirty; he clung to Joel's neck in his sleep and breathed through his open mouth against Joel's chest, leaving a wet patch of spittle on Joel's shirt. Under all that dirt, little Henry was a cute kid, probably seven or eight. In his sleep he looked rested, and Joel couldn't imagine that he had seen such a brutal killing only a few hours before, so brutal, in fact, that Joel hadn't been able to look directly at the bodies. The dark blood splashed on the plastered wall of the house was enough to make his guts crawl. He squeezed Henry close, more to comfort himself with Henry's live warmth than to comfort Henry, he realized. He laid the boy on the bed and motioned for Patrick to lay Sally Ann down, too. He unbuttoned Henry's baggy pants and slid them over his bare, crusty feet. His underwear was stained a deep yellow and his skinny legs were chapped around the inner thighs. Gently, he pulled Henry's shorts off and tossed them on top of his pants. Over his shoulder he said, "Patrick, look in that top dresser drawer for a pair of my shorts, the smallest ones you can find."

Patrick did as he was told, gingerly opening the drawer. He took out a pair and handed them to Joel. His eyes were wide open in disbelief. "All those belong to you?"

Joel didn't understand at first. He glanced at the drawer where his mother usually stacked his underwear and T-shirts and smiled at Patrick's surprised face. "Oh. Yeah. A lot of 'em don't fit any more." He made a point to remember to sort through them later. "I'll bet there're dozens that'll fit you and Detrick."

Detrick had followed their conversation and silently looked at the drawer stuffed with under-wear. Joel regarded them now, remembering the ragged clothes on the line. They were fairly tall for their age, which he guessed was thirteen or four-teen. He looked at them closely, trying to gauge their sizes. "Why don't you guys take a quick shower and I'll get you both some clean clothes?"

"We'll git dirty agin workin'," Patrick said. "Don't wanna ruin no nice clothes. We's s'posed to be rakin' manure this afternoon."

The absurdity of Patrick's comment startled Joel. Something clicked in him. *Yeah. What do you do on a day like this?* Things were suddenly very complicated. There was nothing he could do. It was up to his parents for now, wasn't it? Without direction, the two older boys just stood by the bed, speechless. He blinked, trying to think. "We're not going to finish today, guys. You'll feel better after a nice, hot shower. Then we'll see, okay?"

He unfolded a light blanket and laid it gently over the two sleeping children, and showed the twins the bathroom. He waited for them to un-dress, put their clothes with Henry's and, while they were showering, went through his closet and found practically brand new Levi's he hadn't worn for years. They smelled a little musty and he shook them out. He got some shorts and T-shirts and socks and took them into the bathroom. Both boys were in the shower and the room was steamy, but he could see their pink outlines through the glass, neither of them speaking. The silence was eerie. He shivered as if cold, feeling their loss just a little more. He laid the clothes on the sink cabinet and pulled the door shut behind him. There was one thing he could do, something he wanted to do, and he intended to suggest it to his parents.

The afternoon looked like it was going to be a long one.

*   *   *   *

Dressed in T-shirts and Levi's, Patrick and Detrick looked even more alike, but in the few minutes Joel had spent with them, he had discovered that Patrick was more talkative. He was also slightly taller. Joel was struck by the dominant family resemblance to Edna, especially in their long jawlines and thin frames. Kenneth had taken after Henry, square at the shoulders and compact. The twins' eyes were a pale blue-green. They had dark-blond, sandy hair, but Patrick's was lighter and more streaked. The T-shirts were a little large in the shoulders and a little short in the waist, but the Levi's fit well on their straight hips and they carried themselves proudly when Joel brought them into the living room. Patrick was actually smiling slightly, and he seemed to be protecting Detrick silently, but communicating it in his closeness.

"My, you two certainly look handsome," Eva crooned. She took control of them and walked them into the kitchen, her hands on their shoulders.

Douglas was sitting up on the couch, looking

fine now. Joel watched the boys for moment. He sat down on the edge of the couch and leaned back, facing his father. "What are we going to do, Dad?"

Douglas leaned forward, elbows on his knees, and clasped his hands. "Looks like we'll have our hands full for a while. I can't see packing these kids off somewhere until we find out about kinfolks, can you?"

Joel shook his head, relieved. "We could take care of them, Dad."

"We're taking them to the hospital this afternoon," his father said, "just in case they're in shock—the twins, I mean. I think the little'uns just need to sleep and eat, and we'll keep them distracted, I guess."

"That's good." There wasn't much you could do, Joel realized, except pick up where you left off, which reminded him suddenly of Tom.

It was nearing two o'clock and he hadn't eaten since dawn. He took a sandwich and sat down in the easy chair by the telephone. His father went into dining room, and he could hear the timbre of his voice rise against the silence. He could almost see the smile on his father's face. Joel dialed the number written on the pad.

* * * *

Late in the afternoon, Tom and Joel returned to the farm. Joel got out of the pickup and took the box and suitcase he'd found behind the garbage cans in the alley. He studied Tom's face as he came around to the other side. The left eye was swollen and turning a little darker now, and from the corner of the eye, fresh tears ran out. His own eyes watered in the glinting sun off the pickup's windshield. Tom's other eye was okay, bloodshot from crying, and he squinted as he looked around bewildered. Joel felt sorry for him. This afternoon, when he'd stopped at Pete's house, Tom had come outside with Pete, his face looking much like it had at the church that day, and Joel had felt the old dread return, thinking Tom had lost in the confrontation with his father. But Tom had quickly said, "No! No! Joel, I'm fine."

They were parked by the cowshed. "You okay?" Joel said now, patting Tom gently on the shoulder.

"Well, I'm a little sad, but I'm ready for anything," Tom said. "I stood up to Father just fi— Joel, where are you taking me?"

Joel laughed. "You'll see." They walked down the road that ran along the east side of the cowshed. It forked east toward the field and north into the undergrowth, little more than a trail through the mesquite bushes, yucca plants and sparse grass and sand. Joel led the way north. Tom followed and caught up to him. When he drew up alongside, Joel grinned at Tom's curiosity, but he didn't want to spoil the surprise. "Well, what happened, Tom?"

In answer, Tom grinned and pulled the picture out of his back pocket. He held it against his chest and watched Joel's curious expression. "If you tell me where we're going, I'll show you this!"

Joel made a grab for it, but Tom snatched it away and laughed. It sounded good to hear him laugh, just the thing they both needed to take their minds off everything. "Okay. I'm taking you home."

"Oh, I get it!" Tom said. "I always suspected you wanted to live in the desert!"

"You guessed it. You wanna live under a mesquite bush or a yucca? Now show me the picture."

Tom handed it to him. Joel felt Tom watching

him. He thought the picture was kind of nice; he held it this way and that. "You have a cute butt," he teased. "I look kind of funny, though, with that goony smile on my face."

"You do not!" Tom protested. "I think you're really beautiful. It gives me chills to think I can make you look so dreamy-eyed."

Joel handed it back. "Paul, right?"

Tom tucked the picture back into his pocket. "Who else? You know he made a lot of copies of the picture? Pete said he tried to give them to the disciples."

"And they wouldn't take them?"

Tom nodded.

"Well," Joel said. "So they're not so bad, I guess."

"But Pete kept his and gave it to me. And it was lucky because not more than a minute later, Father came into my room and jerked me off the bed. He sent Pete home." Tom frowned and sighed.

When they were north of the cowshed, Joel pointed to the rapidly fading path. "Just watch your step along here. Don't let the mesquite bushes scratch your face." He moved ahead, picking his way, holding up the branches of the mesquites while Tom followed. "So what happened?" he asked over his shoulder.

"Wasn't much different than I expected." Tom's voice had lost its playfulness. As they walked along, Joel turned occasionally to listen. "But his tactic was more subtle once he got over his temper tantrum."

"What d'ya mean?"

"He repeated the same accusations again. He said other people saw us kissing at the dance. I think he was just guessing that it really happened, because he knew about the picture."

"But it's true."

"Yeah. Anyway, once he calmed down he was real quiet about everything. I could see that deep down it hurt him to go through with it. But he did, Joel, down to the last detail. He wanted to know what was true and what wasn't. So I told him everything from the beginning. I told him about all the years I've been fighting against it. I think he really felt sorry for hitting me, or maybe he felt sorry for me and that made the whole thing a lot harder. But it felt good to get if off my chest, to be honest with him. If he'd been his old stern self, I probably wouldn't have felt so sorry for him. But at that moment he was just a man, not a preacher. I saw that old veneer of his crack for the first time in my life. And I felt closer to him than I ever have." His voice caught on a sob. Joel tried to hug him, but Tom pushed him away.

"I need to finish this. Just keep walking."

Joel turned back around and continued clearing a path for them.

"Anyway, Father listened—for once—without interrupting. I guess he was sort of shocked or something. So, I told him everything about me, right down to the day the picture was taken. He said that despite everything, I had some character, after all."

"That was a mean damn thing for him to say!"

"Not for him, Joel."

"Why? He made it sound like he thought you're a wimp or something."

"Around him, man, I was. All these years. Believe me, that was one of the nicest things he's ever said to me."

The pond was ahead and to the left, and the ground began to rise on a low hill. The undergrowth became sparser as they began walking uphill toward the west. Joel was carrying the suitcase on his shoulder and he shifted it. Tom followed, carrying the box. Joel stopped and Tom ran into him. Joel laughed. "Sorry, Tom. But turn around and look!" Tom turned around, facing east.

"This is kind of a nice view of our land." Above the undergrowth, the land lay before them, shimmering in the golden yellow of the afternoon. It was laid out in squares, divided by dirt roads and the concrete ditches. The squares were various shades of green and, this early in the summer, the row beds gave the green patches a textured look. Beyond the crops, the Mulligan pecan orchard divided their line of sight from the sudden purple of the Florida Mountains and the pale blue of the sky above them. "You like it?"

Tom nodded, speechless for a moment. "This would be a beautiful spot for a house!"

"Yeah? Then wait till you see when we reach the top. C'mon." He led the way again.

They walked on in silence a few yards, then Tom said, "Father told me that Elder Romaine had a copy of the photograph. He said he didn't need to see it. Then, after that, we got down to fighting it out."

"You mean hitting?"

Tom laughed. "Quoting scripture. I guess that's the way we fight best. He was on autopilot. Reverend Suskine, though, gave me a kind of new light on things, and I think I flabbergasted Father with it. You know, Father is a proud man. A couple of things gave me an edge and, as much as it hurt to see him sort of break down, it was the first time in my life I think I won one of those arguments. First, he was thrown off by hitting me. Maybe his concentration was down. And second, for every interpretation he put on something, I came back with one that sounded at least as reasonable. You wouldn't be interested, and I won't bore you with it. We quoted a lot of scripture. He gave up a lot faster than I thought he would, and he finally said he was sending me away. He wanted me to go to Georgia to some retreat for the rest of the summer, and guess what?"

"What?" Joel said quietly.

"Paul is being sent there! Don't you think that's ironic? It's sort of a retreat for confused young Christians. Anyway, I told him I wasn't sick, I didn't need help. And then, well, he exploded again, which was a relief. A week ago, I was so afraid of his anger I didn't think I could live through it. But I did! I told him I didn't think love between us was a sin. He didn't argue. He couldn't win this time, and he said if I felt like that, he wasn't going to stand in my way. So he said he's disowning me. I told you there's no in-between with him."

Joel stopped again. "I'm sorry, Tom. I just can't imagine how you felt. But didn't your mother have something to say about that? Surely...."

Tom shrugged. "I don't know. I couldn't even talk to her. He's never allowed her any control over me. About that he's a tyrant through and through. But I left her a note, said I'd call her later. I think she'll be okay." He laughed. "After all, she's lived with him all these years—she's used to being hurt. Have you talked to your parents?"

"Not yet, with all that happened. But we can do it today. I don't know about them knowing where you are, though."

"Oh, that'll be okay. Father won't care if I sleep with every boy in town now."

Joel heard the bitterness in his voice, and it angered him. "Well, I do! And Dad cares. You'll see."

Tom moved closer to Joel as they walked, and threw his free arm over his shoulder. "What kind of hole are you planning on hiding me in?" Joel felt a strange exhilaration rush through him.

"Remember I told you we used to have Braceros working for us? We never tore down their house. It isn't much, but we can fix it up. There's no indoor plumbing, but we can get water from the pump."

The house was almost hidden by the high weeds against its wall. But like everything the Reeces built, the house itself was sturdy, plastered, and tight against the weather. The door was jammed, and drifting sand had filled the doorway. Joel scraped it away with the side of his boot. He put his shoulder against the door and pushed. It groaned and gave inward. The interior was dark.

"There's shutters on the outside to protect the glass. I'll go open one to let a little light in."

The burst of light revealed an empty space, except for a wood-burning stove beneath the open window and a bunkbed in a corner. The mattresses were covered with heavy plastic, but the mice had nibbled one corner, and a pile of yellow filling had spilled onto the linoleum. Cobwebs were thick, and the odor was musty. An open doorway led to another room.

"What's in there?" Tom asked, indicating the other room.

"The other bedroom. It's not much, huh?"

Tom stood in the middle of the room, looking around. It's our home, Joel. I love it!"

"Oh, I forgot. C'mon."

They went into the next room. "We stored some junk in here." Joel pulled the lid off a large, wooden crate. He rummaged around and pulled out a kerosene lamp. "And...." He placed some other objects on the floor and pulled a gasoline can out. "Some kerosene!"

Tom took the lamp and blew a cloud of dust off. He took it into the front room and set it on the stove. Joel followed, carrying the can. He took off the globe and opened the bottom. He poured some kerosene in and set the wick down into it. "By tonight, the kerosene will've soaked up to the top and we can light it."

Tom looked around and sighed. "We'll fix this place up, won't we, Joel? I hate to take you out of your house."

Joel hugged him. "I'm happy as long as we're together. You're the one giving up a lot. But I'll make it worth it, okay? Let's go tell Mom and Dad. You hungry?"

Tom pulled away. "You go, and bring back a broom and something to clean this place with. Talk to your parents."

"I'll be back as soon as I can, then." He grinned. "If you have to go to the bathroom, use a bush and not that old outhouse back of here. Snakes've probably infested it. I'll bring some food."

Joel picked his way back down the path to the cowshed, then drove the pickup back to the house. He got out and looked around, expecting to see his father outside somewhere. He ran his fingers through his hair to get rid of the cobwebs and dust, and he went in. But his parents were still gone. It was almost supper time, and he wondered if something had gone wrong at the hospital. How long did it take to check a person for shock? He decided to get their bedding together and was pulling out blankets and sheets when he heard the car drive up outside. He quickly piled the blankets and sheets together and put them in his bedroom. When he came into the kitchen, his mother was there.

"Hi, Joel." She set a box down on the counter,

dusted her hands, smoothed down her dress. She was sweating.

"Where've y'all been?"

She looked tired. "In town and at the Strouds, getting a few things of the kids'."

The memory of it made Joel shudder. "Was it, you know, clean?"

She nodded. "The police took care of all that. I guess they took a bunch of the Strouds' things, too, to see if they could find relatives or something, because I couldn't find much at all to take for the children. It was so sad, Joel. That place. Those poor people."

"But you didn't take the kids back there, did you?" Joel was appalled at the idea.

"Of course not! While I was at the Strouds', Douglas took them to the hospital. The doctor said they were all fine but to expect them to become depressed over the next few days, at least until after the funeral. Then Douglas and I took the children shopping." She laughed. "I think he's happy with all the children around. We've always wanted a big family. Thank goodness we can afford it." She shuddered. "It was eerie being at that old shack. I don't see how people could live there. Thank goodness Deputy Gray stayed with me."

Joel said, "I don't think I'll ever forget that mess."

The door opened and his father herded the children in ahead of him. He was carrying a big load of bags from the department store and each of the children had packages. Patrick and Detrick were carrying as many as his father was. Patrick was the most lively and followed the rest of them in acting as Douglas Reece's second in command. Joel felt sorry for them. The twins looked confused and lost, and he understood how it felt to be a stranger. They looked uneasy and wide-eyed at the same time. But if there were miracles, his parents would work them.

His father grinned. He told Patrick to take the children into the living room and go through the packages. He laid his down on the table. "Looks like we'll be keeping the kids until some relatives can be found." He put his arms around Eva's shoulders. She held his hands and nodded. Then Douglas looked around. "Where's Tom? You've got him hidden somewhere, don't you?"

Joel shrugged. "Yeah. His parents kicked him out. I had to."

"You better go get him," Eva said. She pulled away from Douglas. "He must be hungry. Where're you keeping him?"

"I took him to the Bracero house. We're going to live there."

"But you can't!" she said. "Douglas, do something. Joel, that place is a rat trap!"

"Eva, please. We'll work it out. We're not going to have room to change our minds in this house."

"We'll make room! Joel, you're not going to be sleeping out there! Douglas, tell him!" Joel was surprised at her excitement. He watched her, dismayed. She took the other packages from the table. "I'll be in the living room. I don't want any nonsense! We're going to have a big dinner tonight." She looked helplessly at the brood waiting patiently. She shrugged and left the room, shaking her head.

Joel looked at his father. "Can we have the Bracero house?"

Douglas rubbed his chin. It was an unnatural gesture for him. "It'll take fixin' up. You haven't even got running water, you know. No bathroom. No electricity. Wouldn't you rather let Tom sleep

on the couch? We could get bunkbeds for the boys,
keep all the kids in the guest room."

"Dad," Joel said, "you know why we can't do
that."

Douglas waved Joel off irritably. "You're upsetting your mother, you know. And after all that's
happened, I'd think you'd drop it for awhile."

Joel shook his head. "We can't. You know I don't
mean to hurt you or Mom. We'll be out of your
way, and we'll both work. Okay?

"You'd leave if I said 'no'. I can see that. Or join
the army. You're stupid enough to do that. But
you're crowding me, Joel, and I don't like it. So
you can do as you please but not with me paying
your bills." He paused and saw that he had Joel's
attention. "We made a business deal once, didn't
we?

Joel nodded. "Yes. If you want to go back on
that, it's okay. I understand. But we could work
for you, couldn't we?"

His father looked at him gravely. "I'll make you
an amended deal. I think it'll let me off the hook
with your mother." He chuckled, but his eyes were
humorless. "I will treat you two like hired hands.
Everything I give you, you pay for. Including food
from your mothers' garden. You work for $1.50 an
hour, since you're experienced. Tom works for
$1.00, just like anyone else. Your rent'll be $75 a
month, and for that tidy little sum for that old
house, I'll put in plumbing and electricity. During
school, I'll spot you food, as a gesture of goodwill,
since you won't be worth a shit as a hired hand.
You can borrow the pickup from now on. It's not
yours anymore unless you take over my payments
and pay me my equity. Then, when you finish high
school, you'll become a partner, just like we agreed.
I don't go back on deals, Son; we'll still split the

profits." He paused and looked toward the living room. "Tell you what, though..." he said, lowering his voice. "We're hoping to adopt those kids."

"That's great! Dad, that's great! So you want to take a larger share of the profits? That's fine with me."

His father held a finger to his lips. "I said we're hoping to. Anyway, let's give this thing with you and Tom till next summer in that old house." He stopped suddenly and walked away from Joel, deliberately putting a distance between them and making Joel feel awkward. Then he turned around. He just happened to be standing by the marred china cabinet. The broken dishes were gone and he ran one hand along its gleaming surface. There were ugly pock marks in the hard wood. The frosted panes of glass flowers in the doors were jagged and broken, as though they had frozen in the dead of winter and shattered.

His father was working something out in his mind, evidenced only by the small working of his lips. There was humor in parts of his face, around the eyes, especially, as he studied Joel, who had sat down in one of the dining room chairs. This was a moment Joel would never forget, he realized. He had wondered once how his parents would react if they knew. This was it. His mother didn't like it a bit, but she couldn't stop the flow of her love any more than she could keep herself from spreading her wings and inviting the Stroud children to come under them. His father wasn't upset by the facts as Joel had laid them out. But his limits had been reached now, Joel saw. He didn't want Joel to live with Tom. Tom could, like one of the Stroud children, live with the Reeces, as long as it was to seek shelter, but it stopped there. In a way, Joel saw that he was also being kicked out.

But for him, it was just a logical step into man-hood. It would let him off the hook with his mother. It would put the right distance between him and his parents so people couldn't say they condoned it. And Joel realized that was wise. And now he waited for his father to say it.

"You have a lot to prove, Son."

Joel looked frankly into his father's face. It was easy to smile. "Just tell me what you want. Give me a chance though to prove that what's between me and Tom is something you can respect."

"That's fair. That's what I respect in you, Joel. I've tried to raise you to be just like you are. If you can make it on your own, and fight the problems you're going to have if you and Tom stay here, and finish high school, and if, after all that, you still feel the same way about yourself, I'll support you. I wouldn't be much of a man if I didn't allow you that."

"Do we get overtime pay?"

Douglas laughed loudly. "No. Is it a deal?"

"Deal. Thanks." Joel looked serious. "Dad, I love you and Mom, but I also love Tom, and I don't mean to lose him."

His father's smile faded. "I'm sorry for you, Joel. But I don't see any other way out, leastwise with Tom out of a home. Your mother ain't gonna like it. But I think you need to learn the hard way. Living with someone is no picnic. You'll see. Now you go get him out of that Bracero house. I bet he's hungry. Supper is on me tonight."

Joel left for his room to gather up the bedding. The living room was a mess with papers and boxes, and in the midst of it, Patrick and Detrick were silently looking at their new clothes as if stunned. Eva had turned on the television and the two lit-tlest ones were sitting side by side on the floor, watching with fascination. He stopped by the twins and knelt down by them on the floor. He smiled, wanting to tell them they might soon be his brothers, but it was too soon, too pointless to add to their confusion. "Y'all okay?" he said, instead. Detrick just nodded, but Patrick managed a little smile, then nodded. Joel patted Detrick on the shoulder and stood up. "See ya later."

He passed his mother in the hallway. "Dad said it was all right for us to stay at the Bracero house."

She looked a little shocked and frowned. "Oh, for heaven's sake!"

"Mom, Tom needs to live somewhere. Dad will explain it, okay? I gotta go."

* * * *

She was heartsick at Joel's excitement, especially seeing the sheets and pillows, which brought the reality home of what he'd told them. Even though Douglas had said it was only a phase, she doubted it. And the finality of it had already settled over her like the coming of winter to her garden. But she also felt an overwhelming sympathy for Tom, whose stern, unyielding father reminded her of her own. And she had to give Tom the same understanding for that. But it was too bad that his mother, like hers, was an innocent party. She only hoped that Tom would realize the loss a mother feels.

She cleaned the guest room to make space for Henry Jr. and Sally Ann, then moved to Joel's, deciding to make room there for the twins. As usual, it was messy with dirty clothes, his desk piled with nature books, farming journals, and souvenirs from high school. She placed the books back on the shelf above the desk next to his high-school yearbooks. She looked around her, saw the

Golden Gloves boxing trophy he'd won two years before and stared at it. It flew in the face of all she'd ever heard about people like he now said he was. Nowhere she looked could she find any evidence to the contrary. She was confused. For now, she would do her best to remember that whatever he was, Joel was the same boy he was yesterday and the day before. As for herself, she decided that she would follow Douglas's wishes. She hoped that he knew what he was doing.

* * * *

Joel hugged the bedding close as he picked his way through the bushes. He had also taken a broom and some cleaning supplies with him. At the well, he filled a bucket with water. He readjusted the bedding and cleaning supplies and struggled back to the shack. The sun was falling quickly toward the horizon; toward the west in the barren desert, dust rose and began to cloud the sky, and as the sun sank it turned a bloody color. When he got to the house, he knocked on the door. "Open up in the name of the law!"

Tom opened the door, laughing, and took the things Joel shoved at him. What took you so long?"

"I talked to Mom and Dad."

"Everything went okay?"

"Yeah. They want us to go back and eat supper tonight."

"First," Tom said, "take a look!" He waved his hand around the room.

The dreary, darkened look was gone. He had cleaned out the stove and opened more windows. The cobwebs were gone. "I used some of that salt cedar bush to sweep," he said, smiling proudly. He had moved the bunk bed into the other room, taken it apart, and now a double bed sat below an open window with the afternoon sunlight slanting in on the bare mattresses. Beside it he had placed the wooden crate. On top of that he had placed some colorful flowers, his picture of Joel washing the pickup, and his picture of them at the pond.

Joel looked around, impressed.

"Welcome home!" Tom said.

They made their bed and Joel told him of the deal his father had made. Tom listened, then said, "Hope we can make it. If anything goes wrong, you know we'll really be in trouble."

"Yeah. This isn't play house," Joel agreed. But in the back of his mind he couldn't worry too much about their problems. Nor could he know that Tom was depressed, feeling the loss of his parents as if they had suddenly died and he was not allowed to go to their funeral.

They walked back through the bushes, holding hands in the waning daylight. Joel's grip was tight and, as always, it overwhelmed Tom. He felt the lump in his throat squeezing, but he forced back the sobs for the loss of his family. "We'll make it, won't we, Joel?" He said it lightly, but it almost made him cry.

Joel stopped him and put his arms around his shoulders. "Damn right! Because it's you and me. You've got to understand that. No matter what. And we've got to be just like we are now, no matter how much people hate it."

Tom felt his sadness recede a little, joining the tide of turmoil he felt awash in his stomach.

till you see the house. We worked all day cleaning it and clearing the yard."

They passed the cowshed and walked along the east side of the irrigation pond. "We cleared out the old path the Braceros used. You shoulda' seen how overgrown it was. We're going to terrace it so it looks nice."

Eva followed, listening to Tom's excited voice. She couldn't help but feel strange, listening to him talk about fixing up the old house. Time, she reminded herself, feeling dismayed.

When they reached the house, Tom's T-shirt was soaked with sweat. His muscles showed clearly, and she knew that they would grow larger and firmer if he continued to live here. When she'd first met him, he was just a skinny kid in contrast to Joel; she had thought of him as a child, even though he was older. But that was a mistake. He had proved to be strong, being put out of his home one day and apparently bouncing right back, willing to live in a shack.

He turned around, smiling, his brown hair falling over his forehead and his dark eyes gleaming at her. The bruise on the left side of his face was a dark blotch now, and with the swelling still evident, the sight of it still hurt her heart. "We hauled away all the old brush that was here," he continued, "and we're going to plant grass from here to the path. Joel wants to build a fence around it. That'll help the house look more homey, don't you think? Right now, it looks so abandoned."

She took the box and waited for him to push the door open. The interior looked dismal, but Tom showed it to her proudly. "You should have seen how dirty this place was. We hauled about fifty gallons of water before we could get the floor clean. It's got a real pretty surface once it's clean."

"Real nice," she said, feeling depressed for them. She looked around at its emptiness and set the box down on the bare floor next to the wood-burning stove. "You'll need some shelves—you don't even have a table."

"Oh, that's okay. This morning we used a wooden crate to eat breakfast on. We keep it in our...in there." He indicated the bedroom and laughed. "We ate hot-dogs."

"For breakfast?"

He smiled. "Yeah, we haven't had a chance to buy groceries. Right now we have to get stuff we can keep in the ice chest."

"I remember when Douglas and I were first married...." She stopped, realizing how that sounded.

Tom looked at her. "What?"

Eva saw that he had caught her slip. "I guess it is like that."

He lowered his eyes and looked at the floor. "Yes. I know it sounds strange. But it is."

"Well, anyway, see what I brought you."

Tom looked through the box, carefully removing the dishes and making appreciative comments. Eva watched him bent over the old castoff dishes, admiring them as if they were the finest china. His movements were gentle, although not effeminate. His beauty was gentler than Joel's, too, and she thought that Joel probably appreciated that difference between them. Yet she admitted that someone as surprisingly strong as Joel would want his mate to also be strong. And in Tom he had found one. Maybe in contrast to Joel, a girl, a feminine being, would be too gentle. But the solution didn't make her feel any better. She was surprised she did not feel quite the dread that had first seized her when Joel had told them about having sex in the pickup. But she shut her mind to any further thought about it.

"When Douglas puts in plumbing, I think the shelves should be above the sink, over that window."

Tom looked where she indicated. "Yeah, we were thinking that would be a good place. And over here, we're going to put a refrigerator as soon as we can afford one." He smiled at her, but a look of dismay crossed his face.

"What's the matter, Tom?"

He walked to the door. "Are you ready to go work in the garden?"

She followed him, puzzled.

"Is anything wrong?" As they walked back down the path, Tom walked beside her. "I know this is hard for you. I was just thinking how my parents, you know, said they feel. I don't want to make you uneasy, talking about our house. I told Joel last night that maybe we should just go away."

Eva felt tears stinging her eyes. "No, honey, please. You can stay here. It will be all right. You've had enough uprooting."

He looked squarely at her. His young face was naked; hurt showed in his eyes. "Thank you, Mrs. Reece. I like it here. You and Mr. Reece are so...kind. But how do you feel?"

They stopped at the tool shed in the garden, and Eva handed him a bag of fertilizer. "I'll be honest, honey. I don't know how I feel right now. I hope you understand. We do love you, just as we love Joel, without reservation. You are like a son to us and have been since you and Joel first became friends. And when you had to leave your home, it was unthinkable for us not to take you in. But there is this...closeness, and I am having difficulty with it, but I was just thinking about my own father. He sounds a lot like yours. Douglas and I eloped. We had to because my father didn't approve of my marrying him so young. But, like Joel and you, I felt I loved him, and I wanted to be with him more than I wanted to follow my father's wishes. I know I caused a lot of hurt, but I am glad I married Douglas. We've had a wonderful marriage. We have beautiful, kind, decent children. So I have no regrets."

"And your mother?"

"Oh, Tommy, like yours, I'm sure she was hurt, but I called her often to tell her we were doing fine, even when we weren't."

Eva showed Tom how to sprinkle the fertilizer in the furrows instead of on the plants, so it wouldn't burn them. "You'll be surprised, in a week, after we water the garden again, how fast everything grows." They started the water on the squash against the fence. "These plants and the watermelons take a lot of water to grow real big and juicy."

Tom squinted at her in the sunlight. He was kneeling by the squash. He stood up and stretched. "There sure is a lot to learn."

Eva laughed. "I know."

Tom stepped over a few more beds and sprinkled more fertilizer. "Mrs. Reece? I've been thinking about when I should call Mother. I wrote her a letter but I would like to know how she's doing. Only I'm afraid."

"Would you like for me to talk to her?"

Tom looked appreciative. "That would be great. And tell her I'm doing okay, will you?"

"Tell you what! If you'll finish up here, put the tools away and make sure the water doesn't run into the road, I'll call her for you right now."

"Thanks, Mrs. Reece! Joel will be home early.

He said there wasn't much to do yet in the field. As soon as he gets in, I'll come help you with supper. It must be a big job now, with all the children."

She got up, dusted her hands and hurried off, a little happier with the way she felt.

* * * *

But after hanging up the telephone, she felt drained. The woman's attitude was amazing. Although she had tried to convey Tom's pain, Mrs. Allen had persisted in a sweet, civilized tone. "He has chosen the death of his spirit because of his lust."

"But didn't you read his letter? What do you want me to tell him? He's going to ask."

The woman sighed. "Tell him I follow my husband in all things. Tell him that he should have gone to the retreat."

Eva made one last try. She was close to slamming down the receiver. "What about your son, Mrs. Allen? Isn't there anything you want to tell him for his sake, to let him know you love him? He's hurting, you know."

The woman's tone softened. "Tell him..." she said wearily, "the son I loved was obedient and loving to his parents, and I'm afraid, until he is willing to give up this lustful, sinful life, I consider him dead."

She went to her bedroom to be alone. She cried for Tom and for her own dead children. She cried for Edna Stroud, whose love for her children had been boundless and, in the face of such hardship, more noble and enduring than the Allen woman's high-minded duty to her husband. Had the preacher's wife ever lost anything of value if she was willing to let Tom be as good as dead, preferring his obedience over his happiness? Surely not. She was glad that Tom had been spared this. She thought of him now, anxious to know that his mother was not deeply hurt. It would have been better, she thought, if she could have told him she had died of a broken heart.

Later, she got up and washed her face. The afternoon sun reflected through a window and struck the mirror on the dresser, blinding her with gold. Another day was dying, and she realized she was marking time from yesterday. Nothing yet from the police. She smoothed her clothes and walked through the house. It was quiet. She walked out on the porch. In the yard, Henry Jr. and Sally Ann were playing. They were laughing, chasing the cat, and seemed to have bounced back. It was amazing that for them, at least, one day of sleep and warmth, good food and new surroundings could have such a soothing effect. Maybe it was the blessing of childhood, when such a change seems like an adventure. Sally had cried herself to sleep and Henry had awakened screaming, but in the daylight, in the new surroundings, they seemed to lose their anxiety.

She stopped at the cowshed where the twins and Douglas were working. They, too, seemed to be doing better, but then Douglas was always so kind, he managed to make them feel special. "Douglas. I've just been talking to Tom's mother." She told him what she had said. "You know I don't hate a living soul, but it would be a blessing if those two monsters would get an early train to hell!"

He saw her tears and put his arm around her. "You're going to talk with Tom?"

"I have to, but I don't know what to tell him."

They walked to the path leading to the boys'

house. "I think you'll do okay. Just let him know you care."

* * * *

She knocked on the door.

Tom was smiling. "I thought you were Joel. Come in, Mrs. Reece."

She followed him indoors. "Would you do me a favor, Tom?"

"Sure, Mrs. Reece!"

"I'm not used to being so formal, and considering that you're living..." she waved, "here, would you mind calling me Mom or Eva?" Then she followed him inside and shut the door.

* * * *

Later that evening, the four Stroud children were asleep. Tom and Joel sat with Douglas and Eva. There was little talk now about the Strouds' deaths, and the four of them had been discussing what to do with the children.

"I don't think the police are going to find any kinfolks," Eva said. "They never had many visitors as far as I know, and when Edna and I used to see each other all the time, she never mentioned any sisters or cousins."

"I seem to recall one time," Douglas said, "Henry said his parents were both dead. He had a sister or something, though."

"You mean Irene Stroud."

"That's her. Whatever happened to her?"

"She was committed to the state hospital as a mental incompetent years ago."

Joel and Tom were sitting next to each other. Every so often, Joel looked over at Tom. He seemed to be doing okay, and the changes in the house had seemed to take his mind off what his mother had said. Joel had his arm around the back of Tom's chair and, every so often, he rubbed Tom's back with his thumb. Tom would glance at him and smile slightly, then return his attention to the conversation.

"So, the question now is what to do with the children," Eva said. "I would sure hate to see them get carted off to an orphanage and get split up, after what they've been through."

Tom said, "I think if you and Mr. Reece really do want to try, you know, to keep them, the church would probably support you in court."

Eva brightened. "That might be a good idea. But I'm not sure the church would think we'd be fit, because of Joel...and, well...."

"Us," Tom finished for her. "The Romaines aren't going to make an issue out of that. He's the senior elder, and since his son, Paul, caused all the trouble to begin with, he might be less inclined to cause any more. Besides, I've been dealt with as far as the church is concerned. And you and Mr. Reece are the most capable of taking on four children. You've got a healthy environment, and work, and certainly the ability to give them advantages."

Eva frowned. "You think the Romaines would help?"

Tom looked at Joel, then turned to her. "Paul's parents are very nice people. They visited the Strouds all the time. They know what a rotten life those kids had, and besides, I bet nobody else has expressed much interest in taking in the whole bunch."

Eva got up and got the coffee pot. "You want anything, Son?"

Joel looked up, but saw that she was talking

to Tom. He smiled, grateful to her. Tom had not looked up, but Joel nudged him.

Tom looked at her. "No thanks, Mrs....I mean, Mom." His face turned red.

Eva bent down and kissed him on the cheek. "Every time you call me 'Mrs. Reece', I look around to see who you're talking to. We'll get used to it." She looked at Douglas over Tom's head. "Won't we?"

Douglas smiled at her. "It just takes time to get used to things, Tommy." He waved away the pot of coffee. "No more for me, Eva." He slapped his knees. "I'm going to bed."

She set the coffee pot back on the stove. She kissed Joel and Tom. "I guess I'll turn in, too. Turn out the lights when you two are finished. I'll see you in the morning."

They walked to their little house. The moon was full and, in the clear, night air, it was almost as light as dawn. When they got inside, Joel lit the lamp and carried it into their bedroom. He set it on the wooden crate, and sat on the edge of the bed, pulling his boots off. "How do you feel, Tom?"

Tom managed to pull off his shirt before he began to break. He opened his arms in front of him in a helpless gesture, then put them around Joel. "Mother actually wants me dead!"

Joel held him, tightly, rocking him gently. Tom squeezed him harder. "Cry it out, Tom. Go ahead. Get rid of it." Joel was angry, feeling the tears soak his shirt. Tears like these should only come at death. *Bury them, then*, he thought. *Disown them like they have you.* He had been shocked when his mother had told him. Considering all that had happened to him, Tom had done very well. Unable to find words of comfort, Joel pulled Tom down on the bed. They lay together until Tom had quit crying. In the dim, yellow light, Joel sat up and looked down at him. He wiped Tom's sweaty hair from his forehead. He bent down and kissed his eyes, tasting the salt of his tears. "Just don't hate them, Tom."

"I don't. I can't. But I would probably feel better if I did."

"No, no," he soothed. "It's their loss."

They kissed deeply. Joel felt the warmth of Tom's arms on his back. "I'm just glad that you didn't go away."

"And I'm glad your parents helped us. Joel, if they'd acted the same way as my parents, we'd really be in trouble."

"I know. I don't think I'd be able to handle it."

"Really?"

"Yeah. I've acted so damned smug these last few weeks. I haven't lost a thing, but you've been through shit, just to be with me."

Tom smiled. "Are you worth it?"

"What? Me? Only if you married me for my looks, buddy."

"I did, Joel." Tom looked serious. "That and to have a place with you."

Joel grinned and kissed him again. "You know how close we came to breaking up. If we ever fight again—"

"Which we probably will," Tom added.

"Okay, when we do, let's remember why we're together."

Tom sat up on the bed. "I feel better now."

"I feel lucky," Joel said, and blew out the lamp.

Chapter 18

To every thing there is a season,
and a time to every purpose under the
heaven:
A time to be born,
and a time to die;
A time to plant,
and a time to pluck up that which is
planted;
A time to kill, and a time to heal....
Ecclesiastes 3:1—3

Wednesday, June 16

Funerals had never affected Tom in quite the same way as this one. In Wheeler's Mortuary one block off Main Street, two blocks away from Common's downtown area, a small gathering attended the Strouds' funeral. Perhaps fifty people signed the registry that would be given to Edna's children. Neither Eva nor Douglas had the heart to make the twins attend the registry, nor did they want to greet mourners. So as he passed by, Tom was greeted by a woman from the church behind the table. She handed him a pen to sign his name, but she could hardly look him in the eye. She had

no doubt heard rumors. Tom could hardly recall
her name. He wrote his signature self-consciously:
Thomas Mathew Allen. Why not Mr. Mathew Reece-
Allen? A new name to face a new life, but he settled for his old name—for now.

The woman at the registry could and did look
at the twins. She hurried from around the table
and made sure to press a Christian hand on the
cheeks of Patrick and Detrick behind Tom; she
whispered quietly, filling the air around them with
soft hisses, saying she was so sorry, so sad. Her
sympathy was well meant, he supposed. But he
was affected by the total emptiness of the senti-
ments—or maybe by feeling that no words could
allay the confusion and sorrow the Stroud children had shown as this day approached.

He'd attended many funerals as a member of
the Allen family, attendance being mandatory as
part of his father's ministry. But he had never felt
so affected by a funeral. Before now, the dead person lying in the coffin at the front of the funeral
parlor had always been "deceased," and the person's "passing" had meant little to him; it was easy
to believe that what remained was only flesh and
not the person at all. The real person was a soul
winging its way to Heaven, literally entering a place
where it would dwell forever. That is, if the person
had been saved through Jesus Christ. But at this
funeral, he felt a greater loss. A loss not his own,
but he felt strongly the loss of the Stroud children.

Edna Stroud was dead. Henry Stroud was
dead. Kenneth Stroud was dead. Eddie Stroud was
dead. And now he didn't confuse the abstraction
of death with the real thing. Beneath all four coffin lids lay the bodies of the Strouds. Dead, gone if
there was no soul. And he didn't really know any

more if there was a soul, as he was reminded, once again, of Joel's statement: "If you bust my lip, my soul will bleed down my chin." Because of that, the loss was greater to the Stroud children left alive, alone. Edna's spirit, if there was one—what love she had managed to infuse in her children—lived only in the flesh of her flesh. But if there was no eternal life for her, neither was there eternal torment. Then how much more precious the energy of her love, living in the flesh through her children?

But what about Kenneth? If you were a believer, you would say that, yes, there really is a hell. But did he ever have a chance to be saved? What a cruel punishment, if there was literally a hell, that he should burn forever in a pit of damnation for snuffing out four lives, one of those his own, with no chance of redemption because he had committed an unforgivable sin by killing himself. Tom couldn't imagine even Kenneth's brutal murder of his family as justification for hell. Kenneth had killed in a rage, then killed himself. Why? Because he wanted to? Or because he drew a bad hand at birth? Or because, somewhere along the way, he made a selfish choice and decided to be an evil person? Wasn't it punishment enough to now be dead, to also be gone? It would be easier to justify eternal damnation in hell if you had eternity to screw things up, but Kenneth was only nineteen. And for a few thousand days of life, if you took the teachings of his old religion to heart, Kenneth would be condemned to hell for billions of days and then after that, billions more. But days without number? Unendurable, everlasting torment? What would be the point?

Until now he hadn't realized how much his religion asked of its followers. A person faced cosmic punishment for finite, infinitesimal life on Earth and the mistakes he made there. Of course, if a person was truly repentant, by the Grace of God, he might be saved. But the true believers would have to live in utter fear on this Earth, being accountable for sins forever, like Kenneth, for moments of despair.

He thought of Joel sitting on the other side of the twins, watched him waiting for the eulogy to begin. What did he think? Surely he believed that when a person died there was nothing more, because Joel really was a creature of the flesh, totally happy with life in general, and even in their roughest days, he had only given his love—first to me, he thought, and now also to the Stroud children. Joel's left arm rested lightly on Detrick's shoulders. And although Joel was just staring blankly ahead, Tom new that his attention was on Detrick and the other children. But Joel had talked in terms of God as simple being, and maybe then, the Strouds had just been...being. To a human, such a complete, literal loss of life would be more complete if, when he died, he simply ceased to be. So one's life on this speck of cosmic dust was that person's only time to be alive, and then would come the time to die and be no more.

Organ music played continuously, sad music, low, appropriate, Tom thought. Most of the people were members of his old church. The Strouds had very few friends, it seemed. A couple of guys Kenneth's age showed up looking uncomfortable, and Tom guessed that for a while Kenneth would live on, too, through what friendship he had sparked in someone else's life. Maybe he had even loved his family.

Eva and Douglas sat in the front row on either side of Sally Ann and Henry Jr. These two children at least seemed to have cried themselves out. Maybe, like the shortness of their attention spans, their grief would be blessedly short. But even though Henry Jr. seemed merely curious now, earlier today he had asked, "You mean Eddie's not sick anymore?" showing that he dwelled on the mystery of death a little while longer—in Eddie's case, allowing him to rest from his sickliness. The hurt, the tears, though, had passed. Sally Ann had cried off and on for her mother until the afternoon before, and Eva had to win her over by degrees, had to win her trust, and now Sally sat with Eva as if by right. Tom thought that Eva had also become Sally's mother by the same right.

But Patrick and Detrick had only begun today to break down. Earlier, Douglas, he, and Joel had taken just the two of them to pay final visits to their family. The twins had cried over Kenneth and Henry, but passed quickly to their mother, whose face looked even more bony and stark lying in the casket. She was wearing probably the finest dress she had worn in many years. They had held up well passing by her. Not until they stood next to Eddie's casket did they break. Detrick fell to his knees, his face twisted in pain; he wailed, "That ain't his face! Paddy, he never looked like that!" He had clung to Patrick, crying. Patrick, too, racked with sobs, had sunk to the floor, and they cried, holding onto each other until Douglas and Joel helped them out onto the sidewalk.

Tom felt Patrick beside him now; from the corner of his eye, he saw that the tears just wouldn't stop rolling. But he was silent. And Detrick drew ragged breaths and kept swallowing, staring straight ahead.

Across the aisle, the elders and deacons of the church sat staunchly dignified, heads bowed. Decent men, all of them, Tom thought. Elder Romaine had even come over—made a point of it—and pressed his hand into Tom's shoulder. "You're to be respected for coming here, Tom, considering many members of the church...." Tom knew what he meant. The elder struggled with the right words. "I'm sorry for your loss, as well. If you ever need help or any counseling I can provide, you are welcome in my home."

Tom's eyes had burned with quick tears, but he had managed to smile. "Thank you, Mr. Romaine. I probably will need to talk, one of these days."

He watched his own father now—no longer his father—go quietly to the lectern behind the four gray caskets. They were arranged like spokes on a wheel. A few flowers had been donated, but the central focus was the four caskets. It was the gruesomeness of their deaths that was hardest to forget during his father's eulogy. He talked of carrying on the family name, the Stroud children in turn bearing children. Generations hence, he said, there would be Strouds. Beginning with the three surviving sons of Henry and Edna Stroud, there was hope that one day they would be three strong fathers to carry on the Stroud name. "In that there is hope," he intoned. "Where today we can only see loss and grief over such tragic deaths, tomorrow Patrick and Detrick, and Henry Jr. will have families." Once, during his talk, his father caught his eye. "Tomorrow is hope, my friends. For today is Jesus, God's only begotten son, in whose name, by whose Grace, by whose own death on Calvary Cross, by whose resurrection, we know God's Love and mercy, so that we can hope for the morrow."

There were tears in the gathering, real tears, tears of emotion, tears squeezed out in some cases, stingily, misplaced tears recalling other loved ones. But it was the dead Strouds that Tom cried for. He felt a quickening within him, a way to view death, face it, know that the most important contribution he could make toward God's being was to contribute affection and love and work to the living, to the Stroud children, to teach them that the world Joel loved so much, the physical knowing part, was itself sacred, that the very transitoriness of flesh and bone, blood and brain, the stuff of what made a human, was to be cherished, now, today, while breath and thought animated them. And the passing of his love to them all, to these boys, to the two little children, to Joel, to Eva and Douglas, made him a part of the Reece family, also.

As they left the funeral home out the side doors that led to the hearse and family limousine, Eva sat in the back of the limousine with Sally Ann asleep on her lap. Patrick and Detrick sat beside her. When they were in the car, with the door closed, Douglas pulled Tom aside. "When we leave the cemetery, Son, you and Joel take the twins out on the town this afternoon. Have a hamburger, drag Main. Ride 'em around. Show them it's good to laugh, and show 'em they have to start fresh." He patted Tom on the shoulder. "When you finish, pick us up at the Romaines. We're going to have that talk with them about adopting the children."

Tom and Douglas smiled at each other. "Good, Sir," Tom said. "I know they'll help you."

* * * *

What struck Joel so strongly about the funeral was how quickly it dissolved as they came out of the chapel into the bright, noon sunshine. The streets were busy with lunch-time traffic as they got into their car and followed the hearse out onto the street. Sunlight and wind flickered in and out of the car window as they picked up speed on Main Street, as they headed for the cemetery on the east end of town. Most of the gathering did not follow the motorcade. When they parked along the fence under the evergreen trees, maybe five cars pulled up behind them. He stayed close to the twins through the short ceremony and, as gently as he could, pulled them away from the sight of the raw earth that lay open to receive their parents and their brothers.

"What kind of music you guys like?" He said now as they drove away. All four of them, Patrick and Detrick, Joel and Tom, were sitting in the front seat of the Reece's Cadillac.

Patrick grinned. "I dunno, Joel. We din't have a radio. You choose."

He tuned in a station with an endlessly rocking rhythm. He and Tom moved in time to the music on either side of the twins.

Detrick patted out the rhythm on his knee, and Patrick tried to hear the words. "That's neat," he said.

Joel laughed and nudged Patrick. "We know lots of neat things, huh, Tom?" He screwed his eyes and mouth into a clown's face, looking at Tom. Joel felt happy seeing Tom grin back, but more, seeing that Tom was able to comfort Patrick and Detrick at the funeral even when the preacher and his wife were there.

"You and Dete are lucky to be in our family," Tom said, then, and Joel thought again of their connectedness.

"You ever been camping, Dete?" Joel asked.

Detrick said proudly that he had. "Out at Red Mountain. You could see all the way to town from there!" He sat up then, excited. "Could we go campin'?"

"You bet, guys," Joel said. "We've got some cousins in the mountains above Alamogordo. Just the four of us could go up there some weekend before school starts."

Joel and Tom had not been out together since the night Kenneth had wrecked his truck, but the streets were quiet at this time of the day. The west end of town, usually crawling with cars at the Triangle drive-in, was almost empty. In the early afternoon under the canopy of the drive-in, they ate hamburgers and drank Cokes, and Joel got to know his new brothers and, he hoped, they got to know him and Tom. "We're fourteen, goin' on fifteen in September," Patrick told him. The twins ate hungrily. "These are great!" Paddy said, his mouth full. He drained his Coke between bites.

It was hard for Joel to realize how much Paddy and Dete had missed out on. They told him school was the only place they usually went, hardly ever into Common, never anywhere else. "You haven't ever been anywhere else, ever?"

"Naw," Dete said. "Kenny—did. All the way to Texas! He 'as allus goin' somewhere."

"Well, we will, too," Joel said. "Me and Tom are going to take you everywhere we can think of. Mom and Dad like to take trips every summer. They usually take me along, but it's your turn now. Yours and Paddy's"

"You just name it," Tom said.

But Detrick got quiet again, his mouth full of hamburger, his cheeks bulging. He gave Tom a quick smile, then swallowed hard to get the mouthful down his throat. "Thanks. I jes' can't think of nothin' better'n right now!"

They spent the rest of the afternoon in town with their parents. Suddenly the Reeces had become a large family, and Joel walked along proudly with them all. Douglas took the twins into Lindyer's Boot & Saddlery and got them new boots. Eva outfitted Sally Ann with Oxford loafers and some girlish little dresses and some boyish little play clothes. Henry Jr. chose tennis shoes over boots, and in the toy department in White's Auto, Douglas bought him a football and a hand pump.

They ate dinner in town as the sun was setting on the long, June afternoon. They took up eight chairs and the waitress had to put two tables together. Douglas sat at one end of the table and Eva at the other, and between them on either side Tom and Joel regarded each other with goofy, teasing smiles. Sally Ann had scooted her chair as close to Eva as she could get. She was busy picking through her food and showing Eva various parts of her salad. Joel laughed to himself at Sally's fascination. Douglas was equally beset with Henry's adoration. Henry babbled at Douglas ninety miles and hour. "I kin' run real fast in these shoes! I kin' climb up real high now. Can I play with my stuff when we git home? And you know what?"

Douglas nodded between bites. "What, Henry Jr.?"

Paddy and Dete, Joel regarded together like one glass of water in two containers—one half empty and the other half full, or like two sides of an argument. Each was unique and had his own personality, but so many of their gestures and reactions were interchangeable. Detrick seemed to be the least happy most of the time, the quietest. But he didn't miss out on anything Patrick said or anything said to him. They laughed the same way, but Dete had a way of pulling in his shoulders after laughing and ducking his head, as if someone might steal the feeling from him. Patrick was most likely to be embarrassed, but in a way that made a person feel it was all right. If he turned red, he didn't try to hide his embarrassment. When he laughed, he looked around, sharing his laughter. And tonight, Joel saw that when Patrick was happy and laughing, he was a very handsome young man. He was most like his mother in that way; before Kenneth got kicked out of school, there had been times when Edna was happy, and when Joel had seen her laugh. He had thought she was a beautiful lady.

The waitress flirted playfully with the twins, but hovered over Patrick when she stopped at the table. "You promise to come see me in about four years, hon?" she had said to Patrick finally, as the Reeces were getting up to leave. "And bring that cute twin brother with you!" Patrick and Detrick had enjoyed the attention. And at the cash register, when she made them show her their muscles, Patrick got embarrassed and laughed hard. He and Detrick ran outside together.

On the way out of the cafe, Henry Jr. took Douglas's hand. "Will you always be my dad?" he asked shyly. Douglas hugged Henry Jr. to him. Henry's head came up to his stomach, and he patted it. "I reckon."

Sally Ann frowned at her brother. "A'corse, Henwee! I be ya' sista too, and Tommy be my bwudda! Mommie said."

On the way home, the twins giggled like boys again and Tom slipped his hand into Joel's in the darkness. Eva sang Sally Ann to sleep. Douglas drove with the window down, his elbow hanging out of it. "Welp," he said to no one in particular, "I got me one pack of helpers now."

Joel smiled at Tom in the darkness. Then he leaned forward and tapped his father on the shoulder. "Does that mean I can get out of my chores now?"

Douglas chuckled but didn't say anything for a moment. His head swayed back and forth with the rhythm of his driving. Looking around in the darkness, he said, "Think maybe we can double our livestock, Joel, plant some fruit trees, build ourselves a real barn now."

"I got you, Dad."

A time to break down, and a time to build up...Tom thought happily.

Sunday, July 4, 1965

Douglas and Eva sat in the living room enjoying the rare opportunity to relax alone. As usual, the television was on, more to provide faint light than anything. Douglas's arm rested lightly on his wife's shoulders. He was listening to her. In profile he saw remnants of her beauty, now settled into the faint beginning of middle age. She was talking softly.

"I guess I've got to rejoin the PTA at Mimbres now, with Henry starting second grade." She laughed silently and laid her head on his shoulder. "Then Sally in kindergarten next year. It's just like starting over. Douglas, it seems like yesterday that I registered Joel in school, and I thought, my last one! Now he's turned eighteen...." She sighed. "The Fourth has always been such a big day for Joel. Wasn't Sally awed with his birthday cake tonight? With the lights off, she looked so cute sitting on Tom's lap, so bright-eyed you could see the candles glowing in them. I think the twins enjoyed the fireworks though, more than the children."

He patted her. "They're more like grandkids,

the way they've taken up with Joel and Tom. Tom especially. I'm sure proud to have him with us. You know he makes Paddy and Dete study now, trying to get them ready for high school? He took it on himself to get them interested. He even corrects their speech. And they just love it. They're really trying."

"They must have been pretty far behind in their learning," she agreed. "But you're right. If anyone can teach them and help them with their schoolwork, it'll be Tom." She sighed again. "You really don't think we're too old to have children again?"

"We're young yet, honey. And I'll have so much help with the farm work now, I'll just supervise. I'll get fat."

"Sure you will, Douglas. You've been working harder than ever, helping the boys on their house."

"Have you seen it?"

"Of course! I went over this afternoon. Tom just had to show me the new refrigerator." She sat up and pushed him playfully. "You're an old softy, Douglas. I seem to recall they were hired hands. That was the deal wasn't it?"

"It was a birthday present. And besides, I'm their landlord. They're paying me rent, so I didn't mind plumbing the place. They needed electricity."

"And a bathroom, and a gas stove." Her voice seemed sad and Douglas studied her face and listened carefully for the reason. "Douglas, Tom is a beautiful young man, and it hurts me every time I think about his parents disowning him. At the funeral, he tried to say hello to his mother, and she just turned on her holy heels and walked off." She wiped her eyes with her hand. "But you know I'm having a lot of trouble…with things, the way they've turned out."

"I know you are." He squeezed her. "And I'm proud of you for trying. But don't you think—"

"Time? Douglas, you keep saying that. I don't think your year is going to make a bit of difference." She laughed suddenly. "Even I can't decide who's more in love with the other—" Her voice caught on a sob. "But it still hurts."

"Yes, ma'am," he said. "I imagine it does."

"And I'll be the first to admit it isn't easy on them, either. I got put on the spot yesterday when I went grocery shopping at the Farmer's Association. You know the Lynn girl, the checker?"

"The blonde? Jeannie?"

"Yes! She made a big fuss about getting me in her line. She started going on about what a tragedy it must have been. I thought she meant the Strouds. Then she said, 'At least you have the courage to show your face, when everyone knows your son is a queer.' I felt like slapping the smirk off her face! And she was talking so loud and pretending to be sorry for me."

Douglas laughed in spite of himself. "So what did you do, Eva?"

Eva laughed bitterly. "I told her it took more strength than courage to show my face, considering all the gossips I had to push out of the way just to get my shopping done! I couldn't deny it. And I thought, if I feel embarrassed, Joel and Tom will, if people do things like that to them."

"And they will, Eva. They will. I'm not having an easy time of it either, what with the boys down at the Ford outfit, for instance. I guess in Common, small as it is, a thing like this gets around. I bought spindles for the picker the other day. One of the boys says loud and clear how he'd horsewhip his son if he caught him with his hands in another man's pants. But I don't pay it any mind.

They know as well as I do, if I take my business elsewhere, they'd have a hard time of it. And I'm not one to fool around with their joking if they take it too far. Claud Benson, the owner, cleared that fool out pretty damned fast." Douglas chuckled. "I didn't say a thing, but I guess Claud knows I help support his expensive tastes."

From down the hall they heard Sally Ann cry out. Eva got up to check on her, and Douglas switched off the television. He stood for a moment in the darkness. How long people would badger them was hard to say. Eventually, they would get bored with the subject and find something else to whisper about; but he didn't think much would change between Joel and Tom, and, damn it, he wouldn't interfere. Douglas Reece was proud of his son. It took character to make a go of things in a place like Common. He also felt proud of Tom and loved that boy for trying to stand up for himself, and considering that fool of a father had disowned him, he wasn't about to let Tom go fatherless.

* * * *

Sally Ann and Henry shared the big, double bed in the guest room. Eva tiptoed across to the bed and clucked at the two sleeping children. They were a tangle of arms and legs, completely uncovered. Henry's arm was lying on Sally Ann's throat, and she was snoring from the pressure, taking in short, strangled breaths. Her little fists held Henry's pajamas. Eva couldn't untangle them without waking them up so, as best she could, she moved Henry's arm. It was so thin and brittle Eva felt tears burn her eyes. It would take a lot of nourishment to make these young ones healthy. She placed his arm across Sally's nightgown and held his small hand for a moment. "Better days are coming, honey," she whispered. She pulled the covers up over them and went into Joel's old room.

Most of his things were still there. The twins had been staying here for almost a month, and yet not a thing was out of place. So much were they in awe of Joel that they acted as though his room was a temple. Eva couldn't imagine what a thrill it was for them to sleep in his room. Their new clothes were folded neatly and placed on the chest of drawers side-by-side. Their new boots were lined up at the foot of the bed. They had intruded on this space with the greatest reluctance, and even though Joel had said, "Just shove my stuff aside," they hadn't touched it.

She stood quietly over them, her hands clasped. They had taken the death of their parents the best, the death of Eddie the worst. How they felt about Kenneth she was never able to figure out. She lightly touched Detrick's forehead. It was cool to her touch. They both slept on their backs, both pairs of arms outside the covers; they were breathing softly. In the dark, it was hard to tell them apart except for their habitual sleeping arrangement. Eva reached over Detrick to touch Patrick's cheek, a gesture she made with love each night for all the children from the Stroud family.

"I'm awake," Patrick said.

"Oh, honey, you should be sleeping," Eva whispered.

Patrick rolled over on his side and propped himself up on an elbow. I 'as…was just thinking about Eddie, Mrs. Reece. Mama believed in heaven. She told me once that Eddie would go to heaven before any of us. And now she's there, too."

"Yes, honey. I'm sure she is."

"Well, do they see each other?"

Eva wanted to burst into tears. "Oh, Paddy, of course! And you know what?"

"What?"

"I'm sure they're also very happy."

Patrick swallowed. "I was hoping they were. Thanks, Mrs. Reece. I was worried, is all. Me and Dete and the children, we're lucky. I hoped Eddie and Ma and Pa—and Kenny, too—'as better off now."

"Well, don't fret, honey. They are. Good night."

"G'night. Mrs. Reece?"

"Yes, dear?"

"Kenny. What about him?"

"I don't know. But I think he will be taken care of because every person is a miracle. Special."

"He was bad, though."

She sighed. "When you get angry, there are right ways and wrong ways to act."

"I know. But, well, he always said it warn't fair, us bein' poor. He ain't lucky like me."

"Paddy, your brother didn't plan to kill anybody. When he got angry, he just didn't control it. And then, seeing what he did, when he killed himself, I think showed how bad he must have felt. Just please, come to me any time you feel like talking, about anything at all. Anything, you understand? We'll try to figure it out together."

"Okay, Mrs. Reece. Thanks."

"Paddy? I know I can't replace your mama, but I would really love it if you would think about calling me Mom, like Tom and the little ones. Douglas and I are going to keep all of you and raise you just like our own. Okay?" She listened and heard him crying. "Paddy? What's wrong?"

He snuffled. "I was afraid Ma would cry if she heard me call you Mom."

Eva patted his cheek. "I have a feeling she

would think it was just fine; you know, she and I
were good friends when you were born. And I lost
two children when I was a lot younger. I sure would
like to have you kids fill their place."

"All of us?"

"I wouldn't have it any other way."

Patrick sat up and hugged her across his twin.
He kissed her cheek. "Goodnight...Mom."

She closed the door softly and, as was her new
habit, she slipped outside on the back porch and
peered across the yard toward the irrigation pond.
The electric lights Douglas had installed at the
boys' house shone through the darkness. They had
cleared so much brush from their land that the
little house stood out now, like a light in the wilderness.

Very faintly, she heard sounds coming from
inside and outside their house. One or the other
of them had worked constantly on it since they
had moved in. Just this afternoon she had dropped
by to visit with Tom, and the changes astounded
her. The smell of new wood was everywhere. They
had framed in a small front porch and Tom had
served her iced tea there. Now that Tom had settled into the small house and now that he seemed
less depressed about his parents, Eva saw that he
was still nervous around her. That realization made
her feel less unique in her own pain. As Tom went
in and out of the house, she stayed on the porch
and listened to him talk and watched him work,
secretly appraising the miraculous changes in his
features. His eyes radiated his boyish happiness.
His face was sunburned and his dark eyes seemed
confident. He gave her a grand tour. Inside, the
kitchen appeared less dismal than it had on the
first day she had seen it. The refrigerator and the
stove helped bring a brighter gleam to the small

room. Outside, the yard was cleared for trees and shrubs.

"When do you rest, Tom?" she had asked.

"We don't!" he laughed. "We stayed up all night last night drawing plans for the rest of the house."

"Rest of the house?" The idea of such permanency dismayed her.

Tom told her that Joel planned to become his father's partner after high school, as they had always assumed he would.

"But aren't you going to college in the fall?"

He waved his hand as though the idea were frivolous. His face brightened. "In a few years. Right now, I feel too free to get caught up in school. Joel and I, well, the future is so open, I want to enjoy being with him."

Later, when she got up to leave, Tom had stood up next to her, smiling earnestly. "I always feel like explaining everything to you, so you won't feel so badly, and I can't tell if you feel okay or not. I really do want to contribute to this family. Maybe I should go to school, you know? But when I see what I can do best, Joel and I will decide."

"Give them a year," Douglas had said. The year seemed too short to bring Joel back, to make him the way he was. The fact of Joel's sexual life with Tom, who now smiled and talked about their plans, assailed her hope that in a year, Joel would admit that he was wrong. As she gazed out at the light from her back porch, she quietly let go of her old hopes for Joel and only hoped that he could be happy.

Epilogue

May 1966

They held hands, he and Sally Ann, outside the front gates to the Reece home, standing by the side of the road. It was almost four o'clock, and Sally Ann was excited and impatient. Occasionally, she evoked laughter from Tom with her single-minded track. They had been here all of ten minutes, but she thought it was forever. "Ain't they ever gonna come, Tommy?"

He looked down at his little sister. She came up almost above his waist now. Over the past year she had grown at least a foot. She was still thin, but her arms were healthy and suntanned. Her cheeks were dirty as usual, but Eva had cut her hair short and it bobbed and bounced as she squirmed and jerked. Dressed in her pants and a boy's shirt, she looked tough now, a tomboy. "It'll be along in a minute, honey. Remember I told you it was the last day of school and all the kids had to clean out their desks and lockers?"

I 'member, Tommy. But when?" She looked down the road and tugged excitedly, "I see it! I see it!"

Tom felt excitement too, knowing that finally

it was over for Joel. In the distance the bus was still no more than a spot of yellow, but Tom's heart pounded in his ears, his anxiety growing as the bus drew closer. Joel's last year of school had been rough for him. Too many people knew Joel, and too many people spread the old stories. New stories grew continually out of a few facts and a lot of lies, and when school started, Joel was attacked from all directions. On the bus to school the first day of class, when the students like Bill Crawford and Nicky Coleman boarded at Mimbres for the last eight miles to the high school, Joel was the butt of their jokes. They wondered aloud if Joel really was a queer. On that first day, Nicky sat in the seat behind him and whispered gruffly, "You fuckin' the preacher boy?"

"Nicky was pissed because I said it was none of his business," Joel had told Tom. "But I didn't care." Tom had tried to tell Joel that it was reckless not to deny it, but Joel was shocked at Tom's attitude. "Why should we hide it?" And he got into several fights at school, because he challenged every passing remark he heard. "They make it sound dirty!"

"But do you *always* have to make an issue of it when they call you names?" Tom asked.

Joel had simply shrugged. "It's not the names, Tom. I don't mind being called what I am. I just can't see apologizing for it."

When he got beat up once by a gang of ag boys who got him alone in the agriculture classroom, Tom had tried to tell him enough was enough. Joel had laughed through swollen lips, "You think I look bad? You shoulda seen them when they got through with me."

The worst day had come at the beginning of boxing season, though, when Joel tried to rejoin the team. The other members got him in the shower, fully clothed, and beat him until he said he wouldn't join. They turned the water on and left him there. Tom had received a call from Bill Hoffins, who could hardly talk, and without being able to understand much of what he said, Tom knew that something terrible had happened to Joel. At the hospital, the doctor told the Reeces that Joel had two fractured ribs and a broken nose, then added sadly, "Looks like he was also kicked in the groin a few times."

That night, on the way home from the hospital, with Joel lying on the back seat and Tom squeezed in beside him, crouched on the floorboard, Tom had said, "Joel, you've got to quit going to that school. We can move to Las Cruces or something until you finish." Eva and Douglas agreed, and told Joel to listen to Tom.

But Joel had managed to laugh and hug Tom to him. "Not on your life. I've got a right to be there and nobody's going to make me run away."

But Joel consented, reluctantly, to have Tom drive him to school and pick him up in the afternoons after that. And Tom thought, hopefully, that Joel had finally come to his senses, had finally seen the wisdom of laying low. But one night at dinner with Bill and JoAnna, Joel had broken down completely and cried, "They made me give in, Coach. I wanted to be back on the team!" Tom saw that it was a matter of shame for Joel to have been beaten, to have been made to quit, and it was only after a long session with the coach that Joel seemed to recover some of his pride.

To other suggestions Tom made for staying out of trouble, though, Joel would not bend. He insisted that they always go together when they had business in town. "You're crazy, Tom, if you think I'm going to let you go by yourself!"

"But people won't even notice me!" Tom insisted. A few times, Tom had gone with Eva and Sally Ann during the day, but twice in a row, Eva had been embarrassed by some loudmouth, and although she tried to hide it from him, Tom saw how it bothered her and he began refusing her offer, saying that Joel wanted to go later. But together, they attracted even more attention. In the grocery store, as they moved up and down the aisles, filling their basket, people would stop and stare the same way they would have at an interracial couple in their midst.

Tom often thought of what Pete had said one day about the town being violent under its pretty surface. Because Common was a small town, it didn't matter where they went, someone would recognize them, someone who knew the rumor might come up to them and make some pointed remark. Tom had thought the teasing, the fights, would never end. He knew what Joel was trying to do, being so defiant. It was a matter of pride. The example he always used to explain himself was Leo Johnson. "He never fights back. He gets teased and I don't see where crying helps. Look how damned nervous he is, how wrecked he looks!" And on that issue, Tom admitted that Joel's attitude had some basis. Joel was the first in the family to point out the news specials on the television. "That guy…" he said proudly of Martin Luther King, Jr., "has got his whole race on the march! That's pride, man!" Eventually, Tom admitted that Joel was right. The reckless, constant teasing at school almost stopped completely—at least where Joel was concerned. There were students, boys and girls, who secretly passed Joel notes in the hallways, which simply read, "Thank you!" There were telephone calls from nervous people who wouldn't give their names, wanting to talk to Joel. Joel would get off the telephone beaming, "Man! That was a woman who said she was a homosexual!" Or he would shake his head sadly and say, "That was a married guy. He says he's like us, and he wanted me to tell him what to do about it." Leo Johnson had finally come over one night, keeping Joel and Tom up into the wee hours of the morning spilling his life story, crying, then going away, they hoped, knowing he did have friends who shared something in common. And Joel and Tom would go to bed, holding each other, amazed that even in Common they were not unique.

At home, the Reeces were a happy, busy family, and the trouble they had on the outside from the community only bound them closer. Patrick and Detrick admired their new older brothers, and when Douglas and Eva had tried to explain the special friendship between Tom and Joel, the twins had only shrugged. No one knew if the twins understood what they'd been told, but their adoration of Tom and Joel didn't diminish; their constant willingness to do what their older brothers wanted only increased as the summer ended and school began. When the fights had begun, Patrick and Detrick quickly made it clear, when they jumped in to help Joel, that if you messed with him, you answered to them, too. Henry Jr. and Sally Ann were too young to understand. But the four adults decided that Tom and Joel should act naturally around them, which meant only that they would sit together on the couch on those evenings that they spent with the rest of the family. Or sometimes, one of the little ones might see them kissing if they burst into their house without knocking. Eva and Douglas admitted that, to outsiders, they might appear lax on the children's behalf in appearing to condone the relationship between their son and Tom. It was true the Stroud children would grow up far different from the mold that had been cast for them, but it had been broken by the death of the rest of their family, and no one could deny that their new life with the Reeces was far richer and healthier.

Today, especially, Tom's heart leaped to his throat when the bus stopped. Joel had decided with his old defiance to ride the school bus on his last day. Tom was afraid that Joel would be hassled since it was the last day and the last time guys like Nicky would get a chance to tease him. But as he watched Henry Jr. and the twins bound happily off ahead of Joel, he began to relax. The crowded bus was noisy, and Tom heard a few half-hearted catcalls, but none of the Reece boys paid attention. He craned his head around the twins, who had scooped up Sally Ann as they came off the bus, and saw that Joel was talking to the bus driver. Joel shook hands with him and came lightly down the steps. He was smiling strangely as he walked up to Tom. He put his hands on Tom's waist, then turned back to look at the students on the bus, peering through the windows. Many of them began yelling and hooting. Joel turned back to Tom, his face goofy and grinning and, without warning, kissed Tom on the mouth in front of them. The screaming ended abruptly and a shocked silence settled over that one moment in the afternoon, broken quickly by the sound of the bus gears grinding as it moved off down the road.

Patrick and Detrick laughed a little nervously but considered it good fun. "You're crazy, Joel!" Patrick said. "You could've caused an accident!" Then he laughed and pushed Joel's shoulder.

Joel laughed and said good-naturedly, "Hope I

didn't ruin your chances with Donna." But Tom could feel that he was trembling slightly.

"Naw," Patrick said, grinning sheepishly. "She doesn't like me anyway."

The twins, Sally Ann, and Henry Jr. went into the big house, and Tom and Joel continued walking toward their home. Joel sighed and held Tom close. He was sweaty against Tom. Tom noticed he had lost too much weight during the school year and the strain of the last year showed in his face. Above his left eye, the scar from a broken bottle thrown at him from a passing car once in town would never go away. It had cut his left eyebrow in half and gave Joel's face a perpetually curious expression, but Tom thought his beauty had only increased now, tempered as it was by the maturity in his features. "Thank goodness that's over," Joel said.

"School?"

"Yeah. You notice I don't have any books? You wanna know why?" And without waiting for an answer, he said, "You should've seen my locker. It was trashed. Someone smeared it with shit. Human shit! And the lock was broken and my things were torn up and pissed on."

Tom hugged him closer. "Well, I figured somebody would do something on the last day. It's over except for graduation ceremonies, but surely people wouldn't—"

Joel pulled a folded-up sheet of paper from his back pocket and slapped it into Tom's hand. "Nope. We don't have to worry about that." He flicked the paper. "I got my diploma early. Whitman said he couldn't have me cause a disruption at the ceremonies."

Tom sighed. "Well, I can believe it. You were too proud to stay out of fights at school. People just wanted to see you give in, then shut up, but you wouldn't."

"I know. I couldn't and still live with myself. But don't you feel better, standing up for yourself?" Joel laughed and squeezed him. "I get tickled thinking of the way you handled the draft board. I wouldn't have thought the way you feel embarrassed sometimes that you'd ask the board if you could take your boyfriend with you!"

"Yeah, they thought I was being smart with them at first, and they sent me to the psychiatrist. There were a few others guys who said they were homosexual. It's interesting to see which guys the psychiatrist believed."

They walked slowly up the walkway. In the last year, much of the undergrowth had been cleared away and Tom had managed to get a lawn started. This afternoon, he had borrowed lawn sprinklers from Eva, and they were sending up fans of spray the colors of the rainbow in the slanting sunlight. "Coming home always gives me a thrill," Joel said. He opened the gate to their yard. "You've got this place looking like heaven!"

"Thanks, Joel." Tom looked around proudly at the yard and the small trees. Sitting up on the side of the hill, their house looked out over the Reeces' farm. Often they had breakfast on the porch, watching the sunrise, and during warm weather they often slept there. As they neared the porch, the gentle perfumes of herbs and flowers greeted them.

Tom made Joel pull off his clothes and relax in the easy chair on the porch. He brought him a light robe to cover with. "I've got a pleasant surprise." He handed Joel a thick envelope. "I haven't opened it yet because it's addressed to both of us...see?"

The address read, "Messrs. Tom and Joel Allen-Reece." Joel squinted at the return. "P.T.? Who's that?"

"It's from San Francisco," Tom said. "Remember Pete?" Joel grinned.

"Well, I'll be!" He tore open the envelope and spread the letter out on his lap. He held up his arm and Tom slid onto the easy chair against him. "Read it to me," Joel said.

Tom took the letter and read Pete's story, which unfolded much as his had. When the preacher had recovered from the shock of having Tom refuse his demands and had kicked him out, he polled the other parents to find out what kind of activity there had been among the other teenagers. Many of the young men of the church were suspected of being infected with the contagion, by which he meant any he found to be in support of Tom. It could only mean one thing. The other "disciples" had managed to clear themselves of the whole matter. They had also denied being part of Paul's plan. Only Pete had confessed to being Tom's friend, but that was enough for the preacher. He counseled Pete's parents to send him to the retreat in Georgia, and when Pete had refused to go, his parents had attempted other means to discipline him. One night, he just disappeared from Common.

Pete's tone was rushed, as though he had too much to say and couldn't write fast enough. When Tom had read about three pages, he stopped and looked at Joel. "Poor kid."

Joel nodded and pinched Tom's leg. "Don't stop reading."

...so I hung out at the truck stop for almost twenty-four hours before a trucker finally agreed to take me. I had to convince him I wasn't a twelve year old (ha! ha!) before he would let me hitch a

ride. But it turns out, well, we made it together in his truck! Guys, I tell you I loved it! It was my first time, and it was as good and as delicious as I always dreamed it would be! He was helpful, too. He set me up with some friends of his in SF and told them to take good care of me. I just finished high school and will be starting in college. I'm still living with this male couple, the friends of the trucker. His name is "Blue," by the way. Anyway, I wondered how things are back there. I hope you both write.

Now for the lecture...

Tom and Joel laughed as they read that. Tom stood up. "If we're going to be lectured, I'd better check the roast." Joel got up, pulled on the robe, and followed Tom into the kitchen. "Anything you want me to do? I don't like being waited on, you know."

Tom turned from the oven. "Supper's all taken care of, but you can do the dishes."

"Good," Joel said. "Can I get us a snack before we eat?"

"You're hungry?" Tom asked and smiled. "That's a good sign. You're feeling better?"

"Sure! Now that I'm free of school, I can get back to work like I'm supposed to."

"And free of all that crap you've had dished out all year. I don't see how you put up with it."

"Because I had you to come home to every day," Joel said simply. He pulled Tom to him and hugged him hard. His body was so familiar that Tom knew just where to put his hands to make Joel melt. He squeezed there and Joel cried out against him. "Don't," he laughed, "you'll make me come!" He pulled away.

Tom felt chills down his back. He shivered with pleasure. "Sorry, you just get to me. I can't help it."

Tom opened the refrigerator and pulled out a

bowl. "Okay, Popeye, you can have a spinach salad." He shoved the bowl into Joel's stomach. Joel laughed and grabbed it. They made a table next to the easy chair on the porch. They climbed back into the chair together and Tom picked up the letter. He shook his head at the bite Joel held under his nose. "You eat, baby. I have a feeling that tonight you'll need your strength." He laughed and smoothed out the letter again.

"Let's see...."

Pete lectured them endlessly, saying Common was a hick town, saying they should leave. He could get them an apartment just down the block from where he lived. He described the neighborhood where all the "gay" men lived. He stressed that word. He said the men came out into the open, sometimes making love right there in the streets. He described the gay bars and told them of the bathhouses open all night where sex was free and open.

Living where you are, guys, you're missing out. Things are happening out here you wouldn't believe. And we have our own name! Don't call yourselves 'homosexual' any more; it's like 'nigger.' We're 'gay.' Say it: 'GAY!'

Tom and Joel looked at each other. "Gay!" they said, and shrugged.

And you know what, guys? My other gay friends here say it's astounding what you did—especially in that place—to come out and live openly. But I bet it's been rough. There are a few areas of SF where gay bashing is popular, but for the most part you can be what you want. I can't even begin to tell you what's happening out here. People are changing all over; you can feel a tingle in the air. People are in the streets day and night. And, oh, the lovemaking!

Tom read slowly to the end, then dropped the letter. Overall, Pete sounded happy and confident to them, though neither envied him his "free" love.

"Gay. I do like that better than homosexual," Joel said.

Tom agreed. "It sounds clean and innocent. But I wonder if it'll ever catch on."

"Who knows?"

Joel's face looked sad, and Tom brushed his forehead. "What's wrong?"

"You could have been a part of all that stuff Pete talks about," Joel said in a flat voice, "if you'd gone on to college. I never cared myself because I like this farm and the work, but you have so much potential. It's a waste for you, living here."

Tom studied Joel's face, feeling nothing but the pounding of love in his chest that had only increased month after month. "Sure, I could move out there, I could also live on the moon if I gave a shit. But without you, there's no place, and nothing happening, any better than what we have right here. I don't ever want to hear another word of regret! I have everything I want. We can go to college someday and maybe visit Pete."

Tom got up and set out the roast and Joel set their table. They sat across from each other, and Tom said, "I think I will get a teaching certificate. I enjoy helping the twins and the children, you know? But first, maybe we should cash in our savings and stay up in the mountains this summer—just us."

Joel relaxed, finally. He had felt disturbed by Pete's letter, feeling his old anxiety, feeling inadequate, thinking maybe Tom would get restless and want to move on. "Yeah, let's do. Maybe rent a cabin up in the Gila Wilderness." He reached for a bowl of potatoes and smiled. "We'll do it for our anniversary each year."

"Okay, Joel," Tom said seriously, then smiled. "As long as we always come back here."

Joel's rural life of high school and farming in Common, New Mexico, is changed forever when Tom comes to town. The son of a preacher, Tom reaches out to Joel in friendship, and their bond to each other becomes as tight as brothers. Joel's openness to his own feelings and acceptance of himself, yet another healthy trait instilled by his loving parents, lets him explore some confused feelings he has for Tom. His confusion clears after a reckless drinking bout ends with a very public kiss from Tom, but Tom's torment of sin and self-incrimination are far from over. *Common Sons* is a moving tale of self-discovery, love, and finding the courage to come out and come to grips with the truth in the face of hatred and adversity.

Common Sons

by
Ronald L. Donaghe
